WINTER TRIALS

Threads of Fate Book Two

MICHAEL HEAD

The Gods

The void between worlds and dimensions was a dark and cold place. The two Guardians—some might call them gods—stood above what could be described as a hole in the floor, looking down on what appeared to be a boy playing with a sword. The boy was more than just a child, and he was doing more than just playing, but to the gods, it made no difference.

"Has he moved on yet?" Pride was—wait for it—a prideful god. It didn't help that he was handsome enough to make women swoon at the sight of him, or that he was the most powerful of the Guardians, if only slightly. He embodied the sin in all aspects, including the way he spoke to Wrath. Which really wasn't the most intelligent way to speak to the god of rage, anger, and vengeance.

"No. He is still waiting for the weather to change. Events will force him into motion soon enough." Wrath was as beautiful as Pride was handsome. The kind of beauty that made sailors drive their ships onto deadly reefs, and incited kings and emperors to send their armies to war, just for an opportunity to win her affection.

"I still think it is foolish that you didn't tell him the rest of the Prophecy." Pride looked up at Wrath, his eyes narrowed in accusation. "After all, a lot hinges on his actions, and he spends his time playing with his toys instead of pushing to get stronger." Wrath met Pride's gaze with indignation.

"You sent him into a place even *we* feared to tread, with no warning, which nearly killed him in the process. All just to fix a mistake you allowed to happen generations ago. And *you* want to lecture *me* on holding back information? Please." She waved her hand as if brushing his words to the side. "Besides, there is only so much pressure a mortal can endure before they break. The weight of billions of lives on his own continent is enough for now. Letting him hear that all of existence might hinge on his actions would be too much." She looked down on the boy. "For now, anyway."

"Very well. I guess it doesn't matter much anyway. He is still a few years from reaching Saint, and we won't be able to talk to him again until then." Pride let out a sigh of frustration. "Just think about it some more. If he *did* know how much his actions and advancement meant for the future, he might take it more seriously."

Wrath looked up at Pride again, this time without her customary glare. "I will think on it, but Jim already faces a foe unlike any he has seen before. A local leader of the *nox* has risen, and arrayed his forces against him already, and he may not have enough foresight to see it." The boy in the picture stomped around in a circle, as if throwing a tantrum. "He knows not what it might cost him."

"At least he has forgotten about chasing after the man who betrayed him, that Ming character. It was such a waste of time." The hole closed up, and the gods parted ways, both moving on to their duties as Guardians.

CHAPTER ONE

Visitors

It was nearing my eleventh birthday, some would say my 651st birthday, and my life had become an evolving shitshow. I stood outside the hidden fortifications of the tiny compound I had built on the outskirts of the deep forest, trying to keep myself from screaming out loud in frustration. The green glass sword in my hands was humming strongly enough that it was hard to hold on to, making my teeth hurt with the vibrations running through it.

"Damn you, Ming! When I find you, I am going to rip you apart with my bare hands!" This was all his fault, after all, and I hadn't forgotten about finding a way to kill him for it.

I had just tried to use the sword to slice through an ingot of a strange metal I had found in the temple that had been destroyed about ten months ago. It didn't work. The sword was supposed to be able to cut through nearly any material, as long as it wasn't actively being strengthened by qi, the energy that cultivators used to empower items and themselves. If someone hadn't already destroyed the temple, I might have been able to go back to it and find more clues about the mystery metal that kept eluding all forms of manipulation.

Okay, maybe *I* had been the one to destroy the temple. While waiting for the reverberations from the sword to die down, I looked through my open gate and out across a perfectly circular lake where the temple used to reside. I had accidentally made the lake while sealing up a potential gateway to another realm at the behest of a god, and I personally saw the body of water as an improvement over what used to be there. The temple had been a dark place, and I wasn't referring to its lack of proper lighting.

The ruins of the village that had surrounded the temple were also destroyed, spreading hundreds of large stones for miles in all directions around the crater lake. That had provided ample building material for the little fort I had been forced to build.

I had been living on my own for nearly a year, working hard to consolidate the gains earned from not only killing my first dark mana demon, or *nox*, but also for stopping a coup within my clan, the Roh. I may have been the reason that the *nox* were here in the first place, but I was on a mission to redeem myself and save my entire world and all that lived in it. If I failed, which was not an option, then I put billions of lives at risk of being destroyed indiscriminately by the gods to stop the *nox* from expanding beyond our plane of existence. To this end, I had gathered a wide array of crafting and alchemy ingredients, as well as a few nice surprises. The time was also necessary to strengthen myself enough to handle the coming journey across the province. You see, at the time of my reincarnation, I had just broken through to the cultivator rank of Emperor, and was quite the cultivator if I do say so myself. Though, I will begrudgingly admit, a bit naïve despite being 650 years old, consequently allowing myself to be betrayed by one who I thought I could trust with my life.

Being essentially thrust back into my ten-year-old body, in an abnormal form of reincarnation, was quite the experience, but the definite drawback was being weak—with my meridians and cores needing to be drastically expanded and strengthened.

In so many ways, I was starting over again on my cultivation, but this time I couldn't afford to make the same mistakes. So, I wouldn't.

The journey I had planned through the swamps to the southern province would be difficult, to say the least, and I needed to be as strong and prepared as I could make myself. Also, I wasn't quite done with the Roh Clan. They owed me for saving them, and I wasn't going anywhere until I had been paid my due.

It was almost time for me to move on, and continue my mission to destroy the dark mana creatures known as *nox*. I was just waiting for my friends to finish putting together an expedition to the capital where I could continue on the path the gods had set before me. The amount of planning that went into a trip that could span multiple years was extensive, and only made harder by the fact that I was still a wanted man in Roh City.

We had also needed to wait for the yearly change in seasons. The coming year was winter, and it was shaping up to be a cold one. The air was already crisp, hinting at the cold year ahead. Unfortunately, I wouldn't be spending it around a warm fire and concentrating on my cultivation like the majority of people. Moving wagons through the swampy expanses of land that covered the south was much easier when the ground was frozen. After three years of warm and wet weather, the depth of mud in some areas made ground travel impossible. We would have to travel across the swamplands when they were frozen, or be forced to travel at a dangerous crawl through regions of land infested with aggressive beasts and conclaves of bandits.

Those problems were still there during winter, but we at least had a chance during the ten months of cold. Some of the larger and more powerful beasts would hibernate the year away, and bandits would be forced to stay closer to their fortifications. Otherwise, they might risk freezing to death in the unforgiving cold of the winter nights. Or storms. Some of the snow storms could be rather punishing, especially in the northern province of the empire.

The sword finally stopped its vibrating and I sheathed it in the homemade scabbard I wore on my back. Since that hadn't worked, it was time to try something else. I moved back into the shaded shelter of my covered front porch before sitting down to think. The cauldron sitting next to me on a makeshift wooden table was still putting off enough heat from my earlier attempts at alchemy that I didn't feel the cold bite of the wind blowing over the low walls of my compound.

I took a minute to look over the small home that I had made here in the woods. There was a small courtyard that held my traveling forge, a wagon pushed up against the wall near the gate, and smooth walls of vine-covered stone that were eight feet high. I had designed the walls to blend in with the forest, making it harder to spot my little fort. The stone hut behind me was a cube broken into four equal rooms, one for bathing and such, one for sleeping, one for cooking, and one for studying and cultivating. The room for studying was another source of frustration for me.

I had pulled out a library's worth of material from the temple that required translation, but even after a year I had made little headway. Without any clues to pin my attempts at converting the material to a language I could recognize, I was stuck with only the most basic understanding. The secrets that could help me master the aspects of light and dark qi contained in the books and notes still largely eluded me. If what I had translated so far was correct, the oily metal I had found was the key I needed to unlock the mastery of the two hidden elements of qi which made it easier to kill all the *nox* I would come across.

The same stupid metal that was *impossible* to shape and mold into any form besides the ingots I had found, and the scepter that still creeped me out every time I touched it. It had been used in a ceremony involving ritual sacrifice—some might even say mass suicide—which made it very uncomfortable for me to use. Especially since I still had no idea what I was doing.

I didn't want to accidentally crack open a doorway into a hostile realm the next time I was trying to use light qi in place of a torch when the sun went down. Considering my track record, it wouldn't even be a surprise if *exactly* that happened.

I stood up to walk over to the forge, willing to try to heat the metal to ridiculous levels one more time, when I felt something break the outer wards I had set along the borders of what I considered to be my territory. I guess I had some company coming.

The wards were far enough out that I had plenty of time to prepare a welcome, be it hospitable or hostile. I used a thread of earth qi to close the heavy stone gate to my complex and moved to the top of the wagon that was pushed against one wall. It was my makeshift tower, allowing me to see over the side and into the trees around me.

I snatched a simple wooden longbow off the wagon seat and nocked an arrow before leaning against the wall to wait. It was only a few minutes later before my inner ring of wards set off a warning inside my head. From the direction the interlopers were coming from, I guessed them to be friends. They knew not to approach directly, following the stream that fed the lake to my compound instead of from the direction of Roh City. There were several traps that way.

Waiting to make sure it was actually them before opening the gate, I set the bow down and moved into my kitchen to warm up some tea. They would appreciate a hot drink after walking several miles down the forest trails in this climate that was getting increasingly colder. Since I was hiding, my kitchen used a warming stone instead of regular fire. I didn't want any smoke giving away my location. It only took a few seconds for the pot to boil and I carried it with me back to the front porch.

I had just finished pouring the tea into eight cups when I heard the voices of my friends and family coming down the trail. The low timbre of my father lecturing one of my friends was unmistakable.

Climbing back up on the wagon once again, I tracked their

progress while sipping my tea. Since they approached from the opposite side of Roh City, they would have to walk from the back of the fort to the front. I waited until they rounded the corner before opening the gate, trying my best to make the rumbling of the heavy stone sound as dramatic and ominous as possible. Hey, I never claimed to be above some simple theatrics.

"Jim?" The voice of my mother called out. "Are you trying to scare us? Because if you are, it isn't working."

Dang. I guess I still needed some work on the ominous part.

"Just go in, dear." My father must have been in the rear of the group, keeping an eye on their trail. "He is probably inside waiting for us."

The seven people that rounded the corner made up the major part of the Roh Clan I actually cared about after the events of the last year. My parents, my cousin Donny, Chu, Jamila, Valerie, and Scout Captain Kory all rounded the gate and strode into my little compound. I couldn't contain the smile that spread across my face.

"I was expecting you two weeks ago," I said as I jumped down, doing my best not to spill my tea, "but I am glad everyone was able to make it this time." I took the few steps necessary to walk up and hug everyone in turn. It required some shuffling about, since my courtyard wasn't very big.

"We would have come sooner," Kory answered as he pulled the gate closed behind him, "but the clan leader was having us followed again." My father grumbled under his breath as Kory continued. "It took time to make sure the scouts that were loyal to me, and not him, were all on the same shift."

"Well, you took your sweet time doing it." My father's grumbles became audible as he looked at Kory. "It was taking long enough that Jim's food stores are probably running low!"

"I'm fine, Father," I cut in before an argument could form. "The forest and lake provide me with more than enough food." I waved my hand towards my front porch. "I made tea. Let's sit and you can fill me in on what's been happening."

There were general murmurs of agreement, so I led the way to my porch. There weren't enough chairs for everyone, but a few judicious strands of earth and wood qi raised up some stone chairs, which I tried to make comfortable by lining with thick moss for padding. Better than nothing, I supposed.

Everyone took their seats as my mother passed me a statue in the shape of a raven. It was a storage device I had found when clearing out the temple I had destroyed last year. I had given it to them to help shuttle supplies to me from the city. I spun a thread of qi into it to see what was inside.

It was filled with food, bales of furs, and warm winter clothes, enough to see me through several months. I transferred everything inside to one of the storage devices on my worn-looking belt. The belt looked beat up and old, but it was the most valuable object I owned in my second life. Really, the most valuable object I had owned in either life.

"Thank you," I said as I handed the statue back to my mother. "I appreciate the warm clothes too. They will surely be worth their weight in gold this winter-year." I pulled out a storage ring from a pouch hanging off my belt. "Take this as well. It doesn't hold as much as the raven figurine, but it is easier to carry." She reached across the table and grabbed it from me.

"Jim, you don't need to give your father and I anything else. The raven is more than we could ever need." She took a moment to look inside the ring. "And you don't need to give us all of this, either." She dumped out a rather substantial pile of gold and gems onto the table in front of her. Everyone looked at the pile wide-eyed, and Jamila reached over to close Chu's mouth before his tongue could fall out. "Your father and I don't need money. What we need is you."

Well. That was one way to tug on a guy's emotions.

"Mom, you know I can't go back." My voice had the tone of someone tired of arguing the same points over and over again. "The clan leader would doom the world with his short-sightedness." She looked down at her cup of tea as I spoke, the truth no easier to hear now than it had been almost every week over the last year. "Locking me away as his secret weapon isn't any better than me heading off to complete my mission. At least this way, you have a chance at seeing me again." Unlike my first life, when I had been exiled due to the clan mistakenly thinking I had no brain core. My parents had no say in that exile and had to go along with it, despite how much they loved me. They had died before I had the chance to reconcile with them. I had already made sure that wouldn't happen this time around. My father leaned over to put a comforting hand on her knee.

"Son, we know how important it is that you leave. Your mother and I staying here is what's bothering us." My mother nodded in agreement with my father's statement. "It would be easy for us to travel alongside you."

"No, it wouldn't," I said with a sigh. "You saw how dangerous the *nox* can be. I can't focus on fighting them when I also have to worry about your safety." I pulled out another storage ring from my pouch to pick up all the treasure laying on top of the table. I didn't want Chu to have an aneurism. "It would put my life at risk, just as much as yours. Besides, you are both vital parts of the plan to keep an eye out for any more *nox* that move into the area." The look of resignation on their faces told me they understood, even if they didn't like it.

"Enough repeating old arguments," Kory interjected. "I think I found a way to get you access to the vault." That caught everyone's attention. If I could finally get into the vault, we could start heading to the capital in less than a week. This would be a great start for the Roh Clan to begin paying me back.

Mixed in with all the treasures and *surprisingly* frilly clothing I had found in Councilman Yisi's storage rings—the guy who tried to take over the clan—there had been six tokens for the Roh Clan vault. Two had been for the first level, two for the second, but the last two had been for a portion of the vault I hadn't seen yet, the third and final level. The way access worked, I would need one token to even enter each level of the vault, leaving me only one token to select an item from each area. That was how it worked for most people, anyway. Lucky for me, I wasn't 'most people.' Finding a way to get into the secret area that the vault entrance was contained in had been the biggest thing holding me back from leaving right away. Well, that and waiting for the ground to freeze.

"How?" Donny was the first to ask, his brain wrapping around the realization of what was to come faster than the rest of us. "If we can get Jim to the vault soon, moving up our time-line just became a lot more important. They will surely double the search for him once they notice some treasures have gone missing."

Kory pulled a rolled sheet of parchment from his vest before answering. "This is the list of who is supposed to be on guard rotation inside the hill where the vault door is hidden." He spread out the parchment on the table, using empty tea cups to hold it down at the corners. Kory pointed to the time slot two weeks from now. "It just so happens your parents were selected to replace the couple that were originally scheduled." Kory looked up at me. "The two who are supposed to work that week suddenly fell ill. Something to do with blockages in their meridians flaring up. Very mysterious." Ah. Several months ago, I had given a few of my alchemy pill failures to Kory. Now I know why he asked for them.

"I will gather the items for the wagon train as soon as we get back," Chu interjected, leaning forward to catch our attention. "If you have any more storage items you can spare, it would help me get everything arranged faster." I nodded at him, handing over the ring I had used to pick up the gold and gems.

"Use what you need to get us the fastest and strongest animals to pull the wagons. And don't forget to pack as many cold weather items as you can get your hands on. The winter-year is looking to already—" I was cut off by the sound of an explosion. One of my traps in the direction of Roh City had just gone off. I looked around at everyone, seeing surprise on their faces. "It looks like you were followed after all. There isn't any more time. You all need to go, before they get here. They can't prove any of you know where I am as long as they don't find you with me." There were some raised voices of disagreement, but I cut them off. "No. We can't risk everything over something stupid like this. Go. I need to prepare."

It only took them a few minutes to gather their things and head back out the gate, running back up the stream behind my fort before they disappeared from view. Now, I supposed, it was time for me to greet my visitors.

CHAPTER TWO

Pop Goes the Leader

The first thing I did was activate the storage runes on my traveling forge. I didn't want to risk it getting broken in a fight. The next thing I did was move the stone chairs I had formed into a makeshift wall that blocked the door to my stone hut. Now it just looked like a solid block of stone with a lean-to, instead of a tiny house with a porch. Good enough.

Then I put all the bits and bobs laying around the tiny courtyard and my porch into my storage belt. Last, but not least, I walked over to the wagon and put it in the largest storage space my belt had, the buckle. Stars, I loved extra dimensional storage. Finally, I used some strands of earth and wood qi to level out the ground and make things look a little overgrown. I left the gate cracked open a bit, making it easy for them to get in one person at a time. Hopefully, they would send in a scout or two who would see it and think the compound was an abandoned camp.

By the time I was finished, it was time to relocate. There was a massive group of people who had just passed through my inner circle of wards. Big enough that I knew it would be a bad idea to take them head-on, but not so big that I couldn't arrange a few 'mishaps.'

I slipped on my flight ring and used its ability to reduce my body weight so I could jump over the rear wall. It was a short sprint to the nearest cluster of trees, where I hid myself by lying flat on the ground in the high ferns. It wouldn't be long until the undergrowth was killed by cold weather, but I was more than happy to use the camouflage while it still hung around.

The past few months had given me a long time to build up my supply of tricks and traps. Since I needed to give my friends and family time to get away, now seemed like a good time to use a few of them.

I pulled out a sack filled with stone disks the size of a copper coin. The faint lines carved into their surface were barely discernible, ensuring it was hard to tell them apart from a simple pebble. They were something I called 'poppers.' When they were thrown, or someone stepped on one, a bubble of compressed air the size of a fist would almost instantaneously form around it. A split second later the bubble would 'pop,' causing a shockwave of air and noise to blast out in a five-foot radius. It wasn't enough to kill anyone, but it was definitely disorienting, causing the person to be stunned for a bit. Well, a popper might be able to kill a squirrel, but those little jerks deserved everything they got.

I poured out a pile of the poppers on the ground and used some strands of invisible air qi to spread them out around the rear of the compound. I took my time, making sure they blended in nicely with the ground. I even made sure to bury a couple a few inches under the topsoil closer to the lake. Even if they knew what to look out for, they wouldn't find all of them.

Then I pulled out a few of my more nefarious designs. The thick copper disks I used for my more complicated traps were a mainstay in my repertoire, as my current lack of a high cultivation level demanded. I selected three of the more nonlethal versions and put the rest back in storage. No need to kill the people invading my space. There was nothing personal in their pursuit of yours truly, they were just following the orders of a narcissist hellbent on destroying the world.

It turned out I was in for a long wait. The group coming towards my fort was taking their time, trying to avoid or disarm the traps I had laid out along the faint trail leading to the lake. There had been plenty of time for me to fine-tune the traps I had hidden, so they were having some real problems.

There was a solid mix of mundane and not-so-mundane surprises, ranging from simple deadfall and pit traps, to potentially lethal qi attacks such as wind blades and fire walls. There was a reason why animals stayed away from my side of the lake.

I was just about ready to give up waiting on them and see if I could just attack the group directly when the first few scouts finally showed up. They were all wearing cloaks that made them blend well with the forest, their hardened leather armor not making a sound as they crept up on the clearing around the lake. It must have been engraved for silence. They were so good at hiding that I might have missed them if I hadn't been specifically looking for them.

It took the scouts almost ten minutes to notice the compound. The first one to slip through the gate had taken the time to send another scout back into the far tree line to inform their patrol leader they had found something. Smart. If I had actually wanted to kill them, I would have started with that one.

The scout came back out after a few minutes and I saw him shake his head. Good. My plan to have them bypass the compound was a success. It only gave them enough of a clue to know I had been in the area at some point, but they would think I had moved on. I just needed to make sure they didn't see me, otherwise they would keep coming back.

A few minutes later, the main group came pouring out of the woods. I stopped counting at thirty people. They were all wearing the thick leather and chainmail uniform of the Roh Army, worn under the traditional gray clothing favored by the clan. This looked to be at least a full platoon of the Roh Army that had come looking for me. They all appeared to have had a rough time, their uniforms dirty and scorched in more than a few places. A handful were moving with some difficulty, proving that my traps at least wounded a few of them.

The platoon leader, discernible by the silver filigree on his shield, went to check the compound for himself while the others waited outside. He was inside for a lot longer than the scout, probably doing a more thorough search of the area. The leader came out with his shield slung on his back.

His relaxed posture told me he wasn't suspicious of the hasty job I had done to disguise my hideout. He walked over to the group, signaling for them to gather close so he could pass out orders. Luckily, his voice was loud enough that it carried enough for me to listen in.

"It looks like he was here less than a week or two ago. Keep an eye out, the density of traps has been increasing." The group looked around with a bit of nervousness as he continued. "We will take a few minutes so everyone can refill their canteens, then I want everyone to spread out and look for anything that might tell us where he could have gone. I don't know about you lot, but I am ready to find this kid and get out of these stars-damned woods." There were general nods of agreements before someone shouted a question from somewhere near the back.

"Sir! How do we know this kid isn't dead somewhere, feeding the worms? I mean, this is just one kid all alone out here! It's hard to believe he could survive on his own for this long." That got even more murmurs of agreement, a few soldiers even going so far as to pat the speaker on the back.

"We don't know if he is still alive, I'll give you that. But our mission is to bring him back to the clan, so we will damn well bring him back, even if he is just a pile of bones!" The platoon leader turned away from the crowd at that point, stomping his way towards the lake to fill his own canteen before the others could question him further. Unfortunately for the platoon leader, he was the first person to find a popper.

His plodding footsteps were enough to set off one that I had buried close to the edge of the lake. The stone was deep enough that instead of throwing him off his feet and making a loud noise, it caused an eruption of mud that smacked against the platoon leader like the full-bodied slap of an especially wet earth elemental. The force of the blow was barely enough to knock him off his feet, but the suddenness of the attack was more devastating than it should have been.

Since most of the platoon had been watching him walk away, almost all of them saw the platoon leader go down as *something* seemed to have attacked him from the edge of the lake. I guess my earlier traps had put them all on edge, which might explain what happened next.

The soldiers all reacted, but they didn't coordinate well. Some threw fireballs at the lake, a few launched ice darts, and some threw up shields of earth or wind. A few others rushed over to assist their fallen leader, contributing to the mass confusion as the myriad of attacks hit the water.

The mix of fire and ice created an interesting reaction, throwing up a hazy fog along the edge of the lake. The wind stirred up by the shields of swirling air made it seem as if something inside the fog was moving, causing the soldiers to double down on their attacks. Since there still wasn't someone coordinating their element of attack, it just created even more fog to spread from the edge of the lake. At this point, I was having some trouble holding in a rather uncharacteristic giggle. These guys were hilarious.

I saw the platoon leader finally get to his feet with the help of the people who had come to assist, but that didn't go well either. One person was trying to assess him for injuries, while another was trying to physically drag him away from the shoreline. To put the icing on the cake, another cultivator decided to use his qi to erect a wall of earth between themselves and the insanity happening a few yards away at the shoreline. This had the happy side effect of triggering three more poppers, which were just strong enough to blast the hastily erected wall of dirt and stone right back at the group surrounding the platoon leader. They all went down in a heap, the stones hidden in the dirt doing far more damage than a simple popper would have managed. I was literally choking now, because the laughter building up inside me was doing its best to force its way out.

The group casting qi attacks at the lake once again saw *something* take down the platoon leader, but they still had no idea what was attacking them. This caused them to give it everything they had, pouring massive quantities of qi into their constructs before launching them into the fog. The shockwaves of the impacts sent columns of water into the air, drenching everyone in the area with a mix of freezing and boiling water. The air shields did a fine job of throwing around the falling water, making sure absolutely everyone was soaked.

Finally, the platoon leader made it to his feet, a line of blood leaking across his left eye from a scalp wound. He had a dazed look on his face, taking a minute to look around at the scene in front of him.

"Stop! Cease fire!" I watched as he formed an air construct commonly used to enhance the sound of your voice. "I said, *cease fire!*" That finally got their attention. It was loud enough that it caused my ears to ring almost two hundred yards away. The guys still on the ground around him might need healing to fix their ear drums.

The attacks finally died off, and the bedraggled platoon regrouped closer to the tree line. They were far enough away that I couldn't hear what they were saying, but I could tell by their reactions that whatever the platoon leader was telling them, they didn't like hearing it. I did manage to hear a few raised shouts about 'invisible monsters,' but that was it.

Eventually they broke apart, one group swinging around the far side of the lake while another spread out around my compound. Three cultivators were detailed to disperse the fog that was still hanging around, their arms waving about as they directed the wind to blow out across the lake. The soldiers seemed to hesitate as they formed a ragged line on either side of my little fort. Someone shouted something, and they finally started to walk across the field toward the tree line behind me.

It took longer than I thought it would for someone else to step on a popper. The already frayed nerves of the platoon couldn't take it. They finally snapped. The soldier who had found the popper the 'fun' way was thrown back off his feet, causing everyone nearby to jump backwards in fear and surprise. This caused another soldier to find a popper, but this one was holding a shield. The small explosion of air caught the circle of wood and metal and yanked it out of his grip. The angle was nearly perfect, forcing the shield to fly as if thrown on purpose toward the next man in line. He wasn't expecting it.

The shield hit him in the chest hard enough to take him off his feet. The look of surprise on his face was one I hope I never forget. I had to bury my face in the ground to muffle the guffaws of laughter that I couldn't hold in anymore. These guys were going to kill me with all this!

The rapid downing of three soldiers in as many seconds caused another storm of qi constructs to be launched. The platoon must have thought there were hidden monsters every-where, because they were indiscriminate with their attacks, tearing up the field all around themselves. This, of course, set off the rest of the poppers.

The rapid-fire explosions were set off so close together that it sounded like one constant roar of sound, loud enough that it shook most of the leaves free from the trees I was hiding under. I lost sight of what was going on through the falling foliage for a minute, but when my line of sight cleared all I saw was the platoon in full retreat, the platoon leader doing his best to keep up with his men. Huh. I guess that worked. I stowed the three copper disks back in my belt, since it looked like I wouldn't need them.

I waited a bit before standing up, taking a look around at the torn-up ground surrounding my compound and the shredded lakeside. It was going to take me *hours* to get this back to rights. Oh well. My latest battle with the Roh Clan was a resounding success. The poppers had been far more effective than I had ever hoped. Who knew something so simple could work so well? I would have to make more of them before we headed out on the trails. After a showing like this one, I would definitely be keeping them close.

CHAPTER THREE

Getting Close

The cleanup and fixing of the ground around my little forest home was finished in less time than I originally thought. Bonus? All the uproar had caused several fish to be knocked ashore. I should send the Roh Army a thank you card. They had provided me with dinner, after all.

I took the time to unload my wagon and put my belongings back the way I liked them after uncovering the door to my hut. It was getting close to the time we would be leaving, so I did my best to organize things in preparation for a sudden exit. If necessary, I could just seal up the hut again and come back for the items inside. Really, the only thing of note I left lying about were the books and documents in the unknown language of the people who had created the dark temple. I had a few choice bits saved in my belt I could still work with in case I had to abandon the rest. The trap plate stuck to the bottom of the bookshelf the rest were stored on would make sure no one ever got their hands on the records and instructions for the nefarious practices that took place in the past. Since I was planning on robbing the Roh Clan of everything valuable inside their vault, I wanted to make sure I had plenty of room.

I sealed the gate and double checked my wards before settling in for the night. Cooking up the fish took less than ten minutes, and I was finished eating and ready for bed shortly after. While I ate, I used half a dozen metal qi threads to carve markings into stone pebbles, mass producing more poppers to replace what I had used earlier. The markings were simple enough I could manage several at once, and I had no lack of small stones to make more.

Instead of going straight to bed, I went back into the study and meditation room. I tried to spend at least two or three hours a day working on increasing my cultivation, but I would call it an early night after the excitement of the day.

I had been working on my level for almost a year now, and the gains were finally starting to show. Considering the fact that I had access to all three cores and every meridian was open, I was technically a Brain cultivator. However, my cultivation system and body had only been strengthened and reinforced by qi enough to hold the energy a Heart cultivator could safely manage. I was nearing the point where I might be *considered* a Meridian level cultivator, which was pretty impressive. The average age around the empire for someone to reach the level of a Meridian cultivator was mid-sixties, so pretty much managing it at the age of eleven was excellent, if I did say so myself.

Another, and more important benefit, was that I would finally be able to move while slowing down my perception of time when using my upper core. Remember when I mentioned that my clan didn't think I had a brain core? Well, it turned out that I did. The problem was that mine was so large, encompassing my whole brain, that they didn't even realize I had one. One of the side benefits turned out to be that I could speed up my perception of time rather than just have increased reaction speeds like a regular cultivator. To me, the world slowed down to a crawl, giving me the chance to do much more in a limited amount of time than anyone else I had met. In either lifetime. At my current level, that of a Heart cultivator, any movement I made at all would tear me to shreds with the rapid acceleration my body would go through if I moved while in that state. After this increase to Meridian, I would be able to make some smooth and controlled motions without injuring myself. Drastic changes in body position would still be a very bad idea, but any movement at all was a massive improvement over my previous restriction of not moving at all.

Increasing in cultivation rank would also help me with two other problems I had run into over the past few months. I had been having some real difficulty when trying to create alchemical pills, or smith new weapons and armor. The inability to maintain the constant flow of refined qi for long periods of time had limited me to only the most basic of pills, weapons, and armor. All the practice over the last year had only led to the creation of decent trade goods. Almost nothing was of a high enough quality that would make it an upgrade over my current equipment.

I took a horse stance, feet spread wide, and slowly moved through the first twelve katas taught to me by my former martial arts instructor from my previous lifetime. They were good exercises, and an even better way for me to focus my internal qi before I sat down to cultivate.

After completing the exercises, I sat in my favored lotus position, my hands hanging loosely in my lap. I took in a deep breath and flexed my willpower, forcing the qi stored in my lower core to slowly spin in a clockwise direction. Then I exhaled, using the contraction of my abdomen to help the qi spin up through my life meridian that connected all three cores together.

The qi that was pushed up into the middle core set the liquid qi inside my heart core spinning. I inhaled again, using the rise in my chest to impart more motion to the qi stored there. I repeated the process, slowly and deliberately spinning the qi up into my upper core and setting it in motion.

Once all three cores were spinning at the same rate, I started to pull on the energy of the world around me. The qi around me reacted quickly, its density higher than normal. Probably from all the qi expended by the platoon that had fought against the 'invisible monsters' around my compound. I absorbed the qi through all thirteen meridians, pulling everything into my lower core before spinning it higher. Most cultivators had twelve, but their meridian walls were thicker and more resilient. My extra meridian meant I just needed to manage the way I used them better, but for something like this, I just made sure the pull of the energy around me was evenly distributed.

The qi was purified in my heart core, then condensed from a fog into liquid once it reached my brain core. I pushed the liquid qi into my body, making sure to equally layer all eight elements into every part. The process was a long and exhausting one, but I was only days away from finally reaching the benchmark of a Low, or Vapor Meridian cultivator. My narrow meridian channels would be forced to stretch and expand to accommodate the increased levels of qi inside my body, and my cores would nearly double their current size. It would also naturally increase the strength of my bones, muscles, skin, and organs.

Of course, the increase in core size would make it that much harder to concentrate the qi inside them from gas into a solid, but that was simply the cost of advancement. If you wanted to grow in power, you had to put in the work. Nothing was ever easy. Well, unless you used poppers. Then, occasionally, things might go easier than you expected.

The chuckle that escaped from that thought caused me to break my concentration, and my cores lost their perfect synchronization. I was almost there. I just needed some form of boost to push me into Meridian. I guess that was the signal to give it a rest and go to sleep.

I stood and stretched before moving into my bedchamber. The simple wooden frame and linen mattress filled with goose feathers looked like my version of heaven on earth, and I tumbled into bed. I barely had time to kick off my thick canvas shoes before I fell asleep.

CHAPTER FOUR

Shadows That Talk

———

I was standing in an office, looking at walls covered in maps. I was dream walking again, which was worrisome. I hadn't dream walked since I had escaped into the forest almost a year ago, meaning the gods wanted to show me something. They did this, since they couldn't talk to me directly until my next true breakthrough in cultivation level, so I would have an idea of what was taking place in the world where it concerned the *nox*. Not that they cared how this affected my sleep.

The maps on the walls were mostly of the Southern Province, with one larger map focused on the forest and fields surrounding Roh City. There were small red pins pushed into the map, marking a rough line from Roh City to the former location of the dark temple. My location. I was about to move closer to study it when the door behind me opened.

A man I hadn't seen in a few hundred years walked into the room. He was incredibly tall, probably close to seven feet, and thin enough that I wondered how he was able to stand up in the heavily decorated robes he was wearing. They were black, with enough thread-of-gold scrollwork sewn into them that they probably equaled his body weight. His features were all narrow, to match his frame. His pointed chin looked sharp enough to cut glass, and a thin mustache drooped down below his stiff collar. Even his ears seemed pointed, their tips rising higher than I had ever seen on another human. His skin was a dusky brown, and his blue eyes were so pale they looked almost white, nearly matching his solid white hair. He exuded an air of intensity, but not the good kind. The creepy, make you take a few steps backwards kind of intensity. Basically, just looking at this guy would make anyone's skin crawl.

It was the Chancellor of the Southern Province. I didn't recall his name, but I remembered the man as a diehard politician, always vying for more control and power. He was second only to the king within the southern capital, and it made him someone that Ming, my former mentor and the emperor in my first life, had been forced to deal with on multiple occasions. Personally, I had never liked the guy. He came off as slimy. The man had died in my first timeline from some form of disagreement with an underling, if I remembered correctly.

A man wearing a green forest cloak walked in behind him. His hood was up, keeping his face in shadow. I was betting on spy, but maybe he was just cold. The Chancellor turned to face him.

"You haven't heard anything else? What might have caused it?" He walked over to the map I had been studying, squinting at the pins. The cloaked man cleared his throat before answering.

"Milord, the report has just arrived. There aren't enough transmission keys for more details. Unless you wish to disrupt the reporting schedule." He pulled a square metal tablet from within the folds of his cloak, holding it up for the Chancellor to see. "This is everything they said, sir." He passed what must have been the device used to communicate over long distances to the taller man. He took a moment to look at it before answering.

"No, it isn't that important. The ravings of a crazy man about 'invisible creatures' isn't enough to risk losing communication. Just make sure the team we bribed to travel that direction is made aware of the development, and look into finding a replacement for the man we currently employ in the region. His lack of detail is disturbing. With any luck, the group we paid will still take care of this little problem for us. It has vexed me for too long." The Chancellor looked back at the map, pushing in another pin near the northern border of the forest before continuing. "It appears as if their trails will shortly intersect. I have no doubt there will be something we can learn when they meet."

"What of the other problem, milord?" He seemed to steel himself, as if he was afraid of what he was about to say. "We won't be able to hide it from him for much longer. Once he hears of it, things could turn out badly for us."

The Chancellor spun back to the spy, his fists clenched in rage. "If you do your *job*, he will learn of what is going on far too late to stop it!" A fair amount of spittle went flying. Enough that I was starting to think the spy had left the cloak on to protect himself from this exact eventuality. I mean, how much spit could one guy produce? "Now get out there, and do what it is I pay you for!" Yep. At least a pint of spit. This guy was a nutcase.

The spy ran out of the room, his hood falling back just far enough that I caught the profile of his face. I didn't recognize him, but I would be sure to keep a look out when I reached the capital. With the way he was being treated, he might be open to working for a new employer. If he could be trusted, of course. My faith in people was still on shaky ground, after the betrayal by Ming.

The Chancellor waved his hand, and a servant I hadn't noticed standing outside closed the door. He moved to a desk sitting in the corner opposite a lit fireplace and sat down, his head cocked to the side. It was like he was trying to hear a faint noise, or listen to someone whispering from across the room. As

I watched, I could have sworn I saw something behind him move. It was as if there was another, darker shadow hiding inside his own.

"I know!" he whispered sharply. "We still have *time*. The emperor isn't scheduled to visit for three more years." The whole room seemed to darken, and he let out a low hiss, as if in pain. "I swear, everything will be in place before he arrives. Chaos will spread, and the unrest will force him right into our trap! Trust me, I—"

The room got even darker, as if the fire in the fireplace was being smothered, and I saw the Chancellor double over in pain.

Then, suddenly, it was gone. The room was once again a comfortably lit space, the fire crackling merrily away. The Chancellor sat up, his face almost as white as his hair. Blood leaked out of his nose into his mustache, staining it red. I took a step closer, to try to figure out what the hell happened, but instead I stepped into a wall of light.

CHAPTER FIVE

Return to Roh City

I woke up to an alarm ward blaring in my mind. It was one I had placed near Roh City as a failsafe for my friends to use in case of emergency. Only they knew where it was hidden, which meant I needed to get back to Roh City in a hurry. Something had happened.

I sat up in bed, trying to stretch myself to fully alert. I had forgotten how little rest I actually received when I dream walked. The first few weeks of my reincarnation had been exhausting since I was pulled into whatever scene the gods wanted me to witness nearly every night. Hopefully, that wouldn't be the case this time around.

I took the time to get all my best gear on for the day. I wanted to be ready in case I needed to fight. Most opponents didn't give you the opportunity to take a break and put your armor on, or position your weapons just how you liked them.

First, I got my self-cleaning clothes on. The tan linen shirt and brown leather pants were beginning to show signs of wear, which was why I had stopped using them every day. I wanted to make sure I could copy the qi matrix that made them work before they finally quit.

Next, I donned a little something I had been working on the past few months. I had been having some trouble finding boots that could stand up to the situations I kept finding myself in, so I had settled for using strips of red leather taken from the armor of my enemies to wrap around my feet. I had given myself a little upgrade. I was still using strips of the red leather, but I had lined them with small blackened steel studs. I had sewn the inner side with linen to make them a bit more comfortable, and even had a set with fur for when the first snows fell. I would have to figure out a way to cover my toes when the time came, but for now I felt like I was decently prepared.

After tying the wraps on my feet and up my calves, I pulled on the leather armor vest that was almost completely covered in throwing knives. Then my belt, and finally my flight ring and spirit wood ring. I left my green glass sword and silver-inlay bow inside the belt. I was still small enough that carrying a serious weapon like that in plain sight might draw too much attention. I would be wearing the thin set of the traditional gray robes most people wore in Roh City over my armor to hide the vest, but the larger weapons were too big to hide.

Finally, I pulled the wagon out of my belt along with all the trade goods I had been making. That just about overloaded the poor wagon but it made room in my belt for anything I might want to *borrow* long term from the Roh Clan. Since I was headed that direction anyway, I made sure I had the tokens for the vault that Yisi had been carrying. I didn't know how long I was going to be in Roh City and didn't want to miss my chance to enact Kory's plan. I covered the wagon and the crates of goods with a tarp and started the long trip towards Roh City just as the sun finally cleared the horizon.

It would normally take the better part of two days to reach the city from my compound, but I didn't have that kind of time. Instead, I used a few strands of qi from the meridian in the small of my back to fling me along the treetops. It required some qi usage, but my reserves had grown enough over the last few months that I felt like I could spare some.

The trip was mostly uneventful, with only a few detours to avoid the occasional predator or beast. Now wasn't the time to get sidetracked, no matter how much I wanted to test myself against them. It was late afternoon before I saw the end of the trees that marked the borders of the farmland surrounding Roh City.

I swung to a stop on the edge of the western fields, sitting on a tree branch to survey the area and have a light snack. My lower back meridian and lower core had a dull ache from their extended use, so I did my best to recover the qi I had used using my other meridian channels.

From my high perch, I didn't see any sign that something was wrong, but I was still too far away to see many details. My qi was already nearing acceptable levels, so I decided it was time to get closer. As I hopped down from the tree, I heard a twig snap from somewhere in the tree line to my right.

I froze. Had my movement been noticed? If it was a patrol, I was in trouble. I wasn't wearing the robe over my armor yet, so pretending to be an adventurous kid lost in the woods was out. I also couldn't just tie them up and leave them hidden in the woods, because their absence would quickly be noticed.

I kept running scenarios through my head, trying to figure out what to do, when a Bristle Wood Hog walked past. It was so focused on finding food, it completely ignored me. I let out the breath I didn't know I had been holding, and pushed back into the woods a few yards so I could put on the robe to help me blend in with the pedestrian traffic inside the city.

My first stop needed to be the site where I had hidden the alarm plate ward my friends had used to summon me. It was located in a culvert pipe that separated a rice field from a sorghum patch, right next to an isolated tool shed. It was the only structure in the area, so spotting it from a distance was easy. It also made it nearly impossible for anyone to set up an ambush around it, which was the reason why I had picked its location.

It took me less than ten minutes to work my way across the

sorghum patch. I took my time, trying to look like I was inspecting the crop. Anyone looking my way wouldn't see anything out of the norm. Hiding in plain sight was the best form of invisibility I knew.

Once I reached the culvert, I ducked down inside it to look for any clues. Unless they didn't have time, whoever summoned me should have left me a note of some kind. That was the plan, anyway, and I had made everyone repeat the plan until they could recite it in their sleep.

It took longer than it should have, but I found the note wrapped around a brick toward the back of the culvert. Instead of an actual letter, it was the guard rotation Kory had shown me. The placement of my mother and father on the list had been moved up to tomorrow. I couldn't help but feel a little uneasy. Had someone figured out our plans? Who could even put together all of the moving pieces to figure out what I was doing? My instincts were telling me someone had, but I couldn't think of a way for them to do it. My friends and parents wouldn't say anything, and I hadn't been back to Roh City since leaving it.

The only thing I could come up with was that someone had connected Chu's upcoming trip to the southern capital to me. That still wouldn't explain how they knew I wanted to break into the vault. This was certainly troublesome, but I would have to see how things turned out. I wasn't going to let this stop me from getting into that vault. The Roh Clan owed me, and I was going to balance the scales one way or another.

I burned the list with a wisp of fire qi before crawling back out of the culvert. No sense in letting someone else get a look at it. I looked around while brushing myself off, trying to see if anyone was paying me any attention. Still in the clear, I started walking toward the road leading into the western gates of the city. Since I was here, I might as well pick up a few things.

I timed my arrival at the road with a group of field workers on their way back to the city. I was pretty much ignored by them, their lively conversation about the upcoming harvest proving a better distraction than anything I could come up with. The guards only waved us through after a cursory and subtle inspection using a qi construct that looked for any prohibited or overly powerful items. I was doubly glad that I had put all my larger weapons in my belt.

The group quickly dissipated as people returned to their homes. I kept walking toward the city center where the traders and shops were located. I kept my head down and my robes closed tightly, trying to make sure that I didn't stand out to anyone else on the street. It took less than ten minutes to reach the crowded market district. I stuck to the edges of the market, looking out of the corner of my eyes to make sure I wasn't being followed.

I went into a large shop selling traveling goods first. I loaded up on rations and other camping supplies, as well as a few creature comforts. A large tent that could easily hold a dozen people with room to spare would give us a place where the entire group could stay when it got extremely cold at night. I also got a high-quality cast iron stove that could run off wood, oil, or qi to help warm the tent and provide a place to cook meals. I also made sure to purchase several wagon-repair kits and tools. The unforgiving frozen ground of the coming winter would be hard on a wagon. The sales clerk's eyes widened when I pulled out a handful of gold coins to pay, but it couldn't be helped. His eyes got even wider when everything disappeared off the counter and into my storage belt.

"Your discretion on my purchases is appreciated," I said as I dropped five more gold coins on the counter. "Just in case you were thinking about how to explain your reduction in inventory."

"Of course, young sir." The coins quickly disappeared as his eyes met mine. "Not everyone has forgotten who freed them when that bastard Yisi tried to kill everyone. You might be surprised at how many people didn't approve of the clan leader's actions towards the boy that saved the city." He waggled his eyebrows. "Not that the young hero has been seen since. But if you happen to see the boy Jim, do let him know that the Merchant's Guild appreciates his actions."

"I will be sure to pass on the message, if I ever do see this Jim." I winked and headed out the door. That was nice. I hadn't really thought about how the people I had saved might view the situation. Although, I did notice the merchant wasn't so thankful that he returned my five gold coins. Best to still be careful and not draw attention to myself.

My next stop was the inscription store. I quickly bought a large supply of blank copper and stone disks, as well as a higher quality carving set. It had more fine-tip chisels that would be useful for more intricate designs, along with an 'eraser' chisel. It was an extremely thin chisel that took off the top layer of a formation plate disk in case you made a mistake, or if you wanted to reuse a plate for something completely different than its original carving. I left the store without bribing the clerk. He showed no reaction when I paid with gold. Apparently, he was more used to seeing large amounts of coin for his goods.

My trip to the blacksmith shop took far longer than it should have. I wanted a few specialty tools to add to my traveling forge, as well as a large selection of iron and steel ingots. Buying anything more exotic, such as mithril, orichalcum, or malachite would draw too much attention. If they even had any to sell. The boy minding the small storefront wasn't prepared for such a large purchase, so I had to wait for the actual blacksmith to finish what he was working on to authorize the sale.

The store was set up with a small display area out front, with the actual workshop and forge in a much larger room behind the counter. I looked over what was being sold in the weapon and armor racks before sitting on a bench near the door to wait.

It was getting close to sunset by the time the man finally came out from his forge. The blacksmith was massive, with arms and shoulders that showed he had been working his job for a long time. His face and head were clean-shaven, probably because the sparks and embers inherent in his job would make them a fire hazard. I was surprised to feel his cultivation level was at the Peak stage of the Saint level. This man was easily one of the strongest members of the Roh Clan. Why didn't he play a bigger role in the fight with Yisi? As he rounded the corner of his counter, I saw the reason. He was missing his left leg from the knee down. A metal rod replaced his missing limb, making it possible for him to walk around.

I was more than a little surprised to see an injury like that on such a high-ranked cultivator. Someone of his means should have been able to afford advanced healing. Any worthy healer above the Brain level could easily replace a lost limb with the help of a few alchemy aids. Either the man liked having a missing leg, or he was having enough money problems that he couldn't cover the cost of the alchemy ingredients. I was about to ask him which one it was, but he beat me to the punch.

"I see you staring at my leg. In case you forgot, the best alchemist the Roh Clan had ran off into the night during that bastard Yisi's coup attempt. I lost the leg in all the fighting." He tapped the metal rod for emphasis. "And now I have to wait until someone can come back from some other village with a Bone Regrowth Pill. That stupid Hu threw in with Yisi, and none of the other alchemists are capable of making one."

I immediately felt bad. It was my own Uncle Hu that he was talking about. And of course, it would be difficult for him to get the pill he needed, especially when the only person who could make the stupid thing had run off with a small fortune in gold the same day the chief elder and I had killed Councilman Yisi. Which reminded me. I still needed to track down my Uncle Hu and cousin Xiao.

"I apologize for staring." I gave him a slight bow, trying to convey my sincerity. "And for bringing up such a sore subject."

He waved my concerns away. "You didn't say anything; it was my own need to explain that brought it up. I should probably just make a sign and post it by the front door, that way I don't need to keep repeating myself every time someone new walks in. Now, what is this about buying up all my iron and steel reserves?" He walked over to his sales counter. "And why in the world would a young kid like yourself need so much?"

"I am making a trip with a wagon train to the Southern Provincial Capital as soon as the swamps freeze over, so the expedition requires a large stock in case we need to make repairs on the road. As I am sure you know, a wagon train can go months without seeing civilization along the way. There might not be another chance to get steel or iron." I pulled out a pouch filled with a handful of uncut gems I had obtained from the dark temple before I blew it up, tossing it onto the counter. "I can pay. I also need any tools you might have for working and shaping chitin, and a spare set of regular blacksmithing equipment. In case something breaks on the road." He dumped the contents of the pouch onto the counter, his eyes widening once he saw what I was offering.

"Quite the riches, for a kid. Okay, you have impressed me. Follow me into the back." He scooped everything back into the pouch before turning around and heading back into the forge.

The workshop area was impressive. There were rows of storage bins along three walls, with the forge and four anvils running along the rear. The entire space was neat and orderly with enough room for several people to work at the same time, almost one hundred feet wide with half again as much depth. The blacksmith walked to the set of bins closest to the forge.

"You can have what is in these four bins." He pulled out the four he was talking about. "While you grab those, I will look for some suitable tools for working on chitin."

I walked over to look inside. The first two bins were almost completely full of iron ingots, probably well over two hundred pounds of the stuff. The third and fourth bins had around half as much steel. Not as much as I had hoped, but it would have to work. I scooped everything into my belt and walked over to where the blacksmith was sorting through tools. He looked over at me as I stood next to him.

"I don't have much in the way of chitin-working equipment, but I do have plenty of tools that can work hardened leather armor. They should get the job done, as long as you are careful." He handed me two tool belts, along with a rolled-up sheet of soft leather. "The stuff for detail work is inside the roll. Be careful with them; you don't want your tools to break somewhere you can't get a replacement." I nodded and put them in the same storage stud on my belt that held all my other blacksmithing equipment.

"Thank you, sir. I noticed that the value of what I paid you is a bit more than the things you have provided." He opened his mouth to argue, but I continued before he could speak. "But I have a way to fix that."

He raised an eyebrow in question. "Well, boy, what do you have in mind?"

I pulled out an ingot of the oily mystery metal I had been trying to manipulate for months. "Can you tell me what this is?"

He took the ingot from me and looked it over. Then, the guy licked the metal. Actually. Licked. It. With his own tongue. This guy was nuts.

The blacksmith stared at the ingot of mystery metal for a bit, then walked to a bin nearest the door. He started digging through a pile of slag and junk metal, finally finding a piece of metal that looked like a broken pickaxe. He turned and held it up to me.

"This is a broken pickaxe." Well, I guess I got that bit correct. "Miners send me their broken tools for repair all the time. Occasionally, I have to throw what they give me in the trash bin. Not because I don't want to fix it, but because of *how* they broke their pick. Come and take a closer look." He held it out to me, so I took it and looked at the lump of metal.

It was completely shattered, like a piece of glass only being held together by its frame. Cracks ran through the whole thing, and I could probably break it into tiny pieces with only a little bit of force. What could shatter thick steel like this? Even a metal cultivator using a qi hammer would only bend steel, not completely destroy something like this.

While I was looking at the pickaxe, the blacksmith had

moved to another bin. He had pulled out several lumps of raw ore that hadn't been melted into ingots yet.

"What broke that pickax was something we call the Miner's Bane. Come look." I walked over and saw tiny lumps of silver oily-looking metal mixed in with the rusty red lumps of iron ore. "When the tip of a miner's pick hits a big piece of this silver-looking stuff, it breaks it. The metal is as hard as diamond, and basically immune to any heat. When I melt this ore down, the silver stuff will just get thrown out with the slag. It's unworkable. The proper name is Adamantine, and everyone thinks it is nothing but garbage. I have never seen it in ingot form before, only tiny raw chunks that people just throw away. Where did you get this?"

"I found it in a bunch of old ruins in the forest. I didn't know what it was, or if it was worth anything."

The blacksmith eyed me a bit before handing it back over. "Maybe the ancients had a way to work it, but no one knows how now. My advice? Throw it away. It will just weigh you down."

I thanked the man and left. No need to let him know I had a ton of the stuff.

The information let me know that I needed to start looking at more options for shaping the metal. If traditional black-smithing was out, I would have to start looking at some more interesting options.

It was fully dark now, and all the shops were closed. I had wanted to buy a few more things before I had to leave the market but now wasn't the time. Instead, I started to walk toward the part of the city where a park was located. Near the center of the park was a small hill that contained the secret entrance to the Roh Clan vault, and tomorrow would be my chance to break in. I needed to find a place nearby to lay low and wait for my chance.

CHAPTER SIX

Second Time in the Vault

I was perched in a tree less than a hundred feet from the door that led into the hillside containing the vault. I had slept until sunrise in the boughs of the trees, hanging from a hammock of canvas I cobbled together using an old tent and some leather cord. Probably should have spent some time cultivating, but I was afraid the fluctuations in qi it would have caused might alert the guards in the area. The park was surrounded by guard posts, and a roving guard patrol passed near the vault door at least a few times during the night. No sense in tipping them off. Not that they noticed me up here in the tree.

As I was waiting for the change in guards to occur, I decided to be as productive as possible. I pulled out a blank stone disk the size of my palm from the formation plate store and started carving a complex series of runes into both sides. The design I was using should form a shield that protected whatever was inside it from physical assault and reflect any qi attacks back at the sender. By the time I was done carving both sides, the sun was well above the horizon. I was about to inject an influx of qi into the stone disk to power the inscriptions when I suddenly heard voices coming from farther down the trail.

"…Don't see how this will work!" It was a male's voice, his tone almost whiny.

"I don't care what you think, just do as you are told." The speaker was female, and she sounded angry. "Put the stupid hat back on! What if the kid is already out here? Do you want him to get a look at who is really going in to guard the vault? You could give the whole plan away!"

"There is no way that brat is here already, and you know it! We would have heard reports of him coming through the gates by now." The whiny male now sounded whiny *and* petulant.

The speakers at last rounded the final corner of the trail leading to the vault entrance, letting me put faces to the names. I was surprised to see the chief elder walking in front of two cultivators that looked remarkably similar to my parents. As I watched, the man who looked very similar to my father put on a straw hat that hid his features. There were three more men dressed as guards following behind the imposters, their eyes locked onto the back of the man leading them. Poor discipline, really. They should have been looking around and acting like the guards they were supposed to be, not focused on the chief elder. He turned and spoke to the others as they reached the end of the path I was hovering over.

"Once you get inside, be sure to leave the door to the vault unlocked. We want to make it easy for him to get in. Don't spring the trap until he walks past the inner door. Then, there will be no way for him to escape." The chief elder took a long look at the people standing in front of him. "This might be our last chance to capture the boy. Whatever you do, don't let him get away. The clan leader will *not* be happy with failure."

His comments stung more than they should have. I had held out hope that the chief elder was secretly on my side, but his comments and actions said otherwise. That led me to an even worse realization. If my parents weren't here, where were they? And where were my friends? I knew that none of them would have revealed any of my plans willingly, but I was beginning to think that torture was well within what the clan leader could accept in order to capture me. The thought of what these people might have done to my family made my blood run cold. Was I being betrayed yet again? Could I not trust anyone?

"What happens if we kill him on accident, Chief Elder? This kid might try to fight back, and who knows what could happen?" The woman pretending to be my mother asked while rolling a throwing knife over the knuckles on each hand.

The chief elder frowned at her before answering. "Killing him would be worse than letting him go." The woman stopped playing with her knives as his stare caused her to shiver in fear. "There is always a chance of recapturing him if he escapes, but if he is dead, our clan gains nothing! Control your attacks, and keep the boy alive." He walked over to the vault entrance and knocked sharply on the door.

As he was waiting for the door to open, my anger at the situation started to rise. I had refrained from actually killing any members of the Roh Clan during my time away and their pursuit of me, but that was all about to change. I had done nothing but help the Roh ever since my reincarnation into my young body. They had repaid my kindness with nothing but contempt and their incessant need to capture me for their own selfish ends. Now, the Roh had decided to up the stakes. That was fine. Two could play that game. I would not be used for others' selfish pursuits again!

It took several minutes for the vault door to open. I could sense defensive qi wards being deactivated before the entryway finally allowed entrance to the people waiting outside. I waited until the group outside the vault bunched up before reaching into the bag that held my poppers. I pulled out a heaping handful and threw them at the group.

The results weren't as spectacular as the first time I had used them, but it was certainly better than nothing. Several poppers impacted around the actual doorway instead of the clan members, throwing up clumps of dirt and debris. The ones that did impact the people went off as they struck the armor of the three guards bringing up the rear. They were forcibly thrown into the two people pretending to be my parents hard enough that I heard bones break. I even heard shouts of pain from whoever was waiting inside the vault, meaning at least a few poppers made it through the doorway to give them a nasty surprise.

The only person not brought low by my poppers was the person I was most worried about. The chief elder was at the Peak level of Saint the last time we met, and it wouldn't be a shock if he had broken through to Sage over the time I had spent in hiding. Someone of that level was far above a cultivator at my current stage of advancement, making any fight against him something that cooled the hot anger I was experiencing. He was standing in the vault entrance, a thin blue shield of qi protecting him from the shockwaves and dirt thrown up by the poppers. Since surprise didn't work, I figured I should probably try to talk first, maybe deescalate the situation a bit.

"What have you done with my family? Where are they, and where are my friends? Have you stooped so low that you even imprisoned your own granddaughter?!" Okay. Maybe I was still mad. It wasn't easy feeling betrayed.

The dust thrown up by my poppers was finally starting to die down, so I jumped off the tree I was hiding in and landed in front of the vault entrance. I spun out four threads of metal qi from the meridian on the small of my back and used them to pull out three spears and a round shield from my storage belt. I readied the spears to throw, and positioned the shield to my left. I was already planning on how to attack once he made his move. Throw two spears to make him dodge to my left, then slam the shield into him while using the third spear to hold him against the hillside. After pinning him, I could wrap the two free qi threads around his ankles to slow him down, and grab—

"Jim, thank the gods you came in time!" The chief elder did a great job of interrupting my train of thought. "Kory said you would come, but I was afraid it would be too late." Now I was really confused. What in the stars was going on? "I know you have questions, but we need to hurry. The next group of guards will be here any minute." Before I could even say anything, the chief elder had bent over and started to drag the injured and unconscious clan members deeper into the vault. "Hurry up! We need to get this door closed and the wards back up!"

I stepped forwards slowly, still expecting a trap. "Why should I trust you? I heard you planning to capture me. Once you get me inside, it will make it even harder to defeat you." I stood with my arms crossed and the spears still hovering over my shoulders, in position to attack. The shield was now held down low in front of me, protecting my legs, and *other* things.

"Jim, I know this looks bad, but I need you to trust me right now. I was only putting on an act in front of the others. We needed a way to stop the clan leader from making his own plans, so we set up a fake ambush." I raised my eyebrow, pointedly looking around at the people I had knocked out. "Okay, a real ambush, but one you could easily defeat. All of this was Kory's idea, and for it to work, you need to stay undiscovered for a little longer." He dropped the woman who looked like my mother to the side before grabbing the feet of one of the guards to drag his head clear of the doorway. "Now hurry up and get in here, before anyone comes!"

I finally relented and lowered the spears. Then I used the shield to basically scoop the unconscious people into the room, dumping them in a pile next to a desk near the door. I made sure not to turn my back on the chief elder as he walked past me and closed the vault entrance before reactivating the wards. He walked over to a chair sitting near the back wall and sat down with a sigh.

"Jim, I know it has been awhile since we last saw each other, but—"

"The last time we saw each other, I had just saved your life. And the leader of the Roh Clan. Oh, and the majority of the entire city. In fact, right after the last time I saw you, I was run out of town like some criminal! Now, I sneak into the city to find you leading a group of people planning on capturing me?! Explain to me why I shouldn't kill you, and everyone else in this room, *right now!*" I was breathing heavily, trying to control my rage.

The elder was leaning backwards a bit, a mixture of shock, fear, and shame on his face. It took me a moment to realize I had raised the spears to point them towards him, while simultaneously spinning out enough metal qi threads from my various meridians that I could easily kill the injured people laid out on the ground with nothing but a flex of my willpower.

The chief elder let out a shuddering breath before answering. "I know the way you have been treated by your own clan is abhorrent, but you have to know that not everyone wants to lock you in a cell. There are people all across Roh City who do what they can to disrupt the plans of the clan leader. Didn't you ever wonder why none of the more capable members of the Roh Clan ever went searching for you in the woods? Why only the greenest units were sent your direction, while the more experienced teams were left to guard the city streets?"

I actually had been wondering about that. Kory had told me during our infrequent meetings that the military and guard rotations for extended patrols were outside his purview, so he had no way of influencing the teams sent to search for me. I had just thought luck was finally on my side, but apparently it had been more than just luck that had kept me hidden from the Roh over the past year.

"Let's say I believe you." I slowly pulled the dozens of metal qi threads back into my body and lowered the spears again. "You still haven't told me where my family is, or what has happened to my friends." I put the spears and shield back in my belt before pulling out a large steel formation plate the size of a serving platter I had prepared over my long year of solitude. I activated it before tossing it on the floor next to the group of injured people.

The qi in their bodies was instantly sucked out of them, pooling as a silvery liquid at a small depression in the center of the plate. It would keep them from healing quickly and waking up while the chief elder and I talked. The formation I used wasn't strong enough to affect the qi inside a person who was awake, but it worked perfectly for something like this. The chief elder waited for me to finish what I was doing before speaking.

"Your parents are being held in my family compound, along with Kory and your friends." He held up his hands as I tensed up again. "No harm has come to them. As we speak, a team of my people is preparing the wagons and supplies your friend Chu has set aside for your journey to the capital. As soon as we are done here, you can join them. I wasn't sure about letting you go before, but after all of this, I am more than convinced that you have been touched by the gods. It would be foolish to stand in your way."

I took a step back and sat on the edge of the desk behind me. "What do you mean? What finally convinced you? Was it my help in defeating that bastard Yisi? Or my ability to wipe out half an army single-handed? Oh, or maybe it was me freeing most of our clan from prison? Tell me, *Chief* Elder, what actions have I performed that finally convinced you to let me go?" I was breathing hard again, my anger at the entire year of being forced to hide trying to break free again, along with all the feelings of so many betrayals. Being stuck back in the hormone-riddled body of a pre-teen boy was really straining my self-control.

"It was more than that, Jim. It was how you ambushed the second strongest member of the clan and took down his security team while they were actively expecting you, all without expending a bit of your qi." He waved his hands toward the people lying unconscious on the floor. "It was how you casually pulled out one of the most advanced formation plates I have ever seen and just tossed it on the ground, instantly ensuring you weren't disturbed by enemies you could have easily killed instead. And finally, it is how you can sit across from someone monumentally more powerful than you and threaten them without a hint of fear in your eyes." I felt a fluctuation of qi come from the old man, his aura pushing up against my own to gauge my power levels. "I don't know how you managed it, but

I actually felt a moment of fear when you let your temper get the best of you."

I looked the chief elder in the eye before I replied. "You should trust your instincts, old man. It might not be easy, but I most certainly could kill you." I let that sink in for a bit before continuing. "After hearing what you have to say, I don't think it is in either of our best interests to fight. I need to use my tokens in the vault, and then we can get moving."

"I know you want to go into the vault to reach your prizes, Jim, but we are running out of time. The shift change at the western gates is in less than two hours, and the people I positioned to let you out of the city will be replaced with people I cannot vouch for. Please, let us go now and make sure you escape." He stood up and walked towards the door, holding out his hand for me to follow.

"No." My refusal caused him to spin in place. "I did not come all this way to just give up. I will take my due from the Roh vaults, and then we can go."

The chief elder frowned in thought before replying. "Fine. But we certainly don't have time for you to sort through multiple rooms of tempting items." He pulled out a thick gold coin. "Trade me your tokens for the first two levels of the vault, and I will give you an extra token for the final room. There are only a few items in there, which should make your time spent in the room even shorter." I took a few seconds to think it over, but that was an easy choice to make. There was a golden cauldron on the second level of the vault that I had planned on taking, but a chance to get something even better was something I couldn't turn down. Even if I had planned to take most everything.

"Fine. I promise to make it fast." I pulled out the first and second level tokens and went to hand one of each to him. Instead, he pulled back his hand and shook his head.

"No, give me all of them. You won't need the others." I raised my eyebrow in surprise and handed over all four of the tokens I was holding, even if it felt like I was being cheated somehow. Instead of handing me the golden token, he walked to the wall behind the desk. "Here. I will use mine to open the door. You use your two to choose your items." This mollified me a bit since I wouldn't have to use one of my tokens to gain entrance now. He placed the coin on a seemingly blank spot of the wall. As he pushed forward, a portion of the wall just big enough for the token to fit slid back. "The highest-level treasures are held in a separate room. Hiding in plain sight, just like the vault itself. Good luck, and choose wisely."

I walked to his side as the coin fell into its slot, and a thin door slid into the floor. I stepped into the room and the door closed silently behind me.

CHAPTER SEVEN

Treasure

The room was almost pitch black, the only lighting coming from a single glow stone placed above the room's only door. For a moment I couldn't help but think this would be the perfect way for the Roh Clan to capture me, but as I took a step forward my fears dissipated. As I moved farther into the room the light grew brighter, and I realized why only one stone was needed.

The third level of the Roh Clan vault, containing the greatest treasures the clan had ever found, was a glorified closet. The room was tiny. I could reach the back wall in only three steps, and it was only slightly wider. The back wall held only seven alcoves, two of which were empty. As I got closer, I could see why. Each cutout had a small bronze plaque describing what was supposed to be inside, and I instantly knew the location of the two missing items.

The first empty space was perfectly sized for a spear, and the plaque indicated that was exactly what it used to hold. *Spear of the Defender: Amplifies the owner's qi attacks.* Now I knew where Councilman Yisi had gotten the spear that he used during his coup attempt. Too bad it had been destroyed in the fight.

The second empty alcove was much smaller. *Phoenix Lotus Pill: Completely cures any cultivator of any illness or injury. Rise from the ashes of defeat.* That would explain how the clan leader had recovered from his fight with Yisi so quickly the night of the battle. I had briefly wondered how the clan leader was able to order my capture so soon after returning to Roh City. Now I knew the selfish man had used a treasure that could have saved any number of sick or injured people to instantly heal himself, instead of going through a lengthy recovery period.

His injuries had already been stabilized. There was no need for the clan leader to use something so precious on himself besides his own vanity. For a moment, the urge to hunt down the clan leader and choke him to death with his own entrails was almost unbearable. I took a minute to calm down and went back to look at what treasures were still left.

The five remaining items were all much smaller than the spear Yisi had used, but that didn't mean they were any less impressive. The first item I looked at was a hand mirror you might find in any store, except this one didn't show my reflection when I looked into it. I read the description. *Mirror of Far Sight: Allows the owner to view whatever they are searching for. Requires Sky-Level Beast Core to function.*

Wow. With something like this, a general could see enemy troop movements without risking his scouts. Stars, a general could literally watch the leaders of an enemy army as they made battle plans! With something like this, I could track down Ming and kill him with little effort. Or hunt for the *nox* plaguing the land without leaving Roh City! The possibilities were nearly endless. Of course, the catch was finding enough Sky-quality cores to actually do all of that. I would have to hunt down powerful monsters for their cores, and finding them while in the southern regions of the empire would be next to impossible. The only place to reliably find beasts that strong was the northern mountain ranges, or maybe the desert sands of the eastern province. Not something I could feasibly do right now.

The next item was almost underwhelming compared to the

mirror. It was a rather plain-looking steel dagger with a blade that was about ten inches long and a simple wooden handle. *Dagger of Strength: Absorbs and stores qi attacks. Unleashes stored qi upon demand.* I had actually owned a sabre that could store qi in my past life. Future life. You get the idea. It had been a useful tool for many years, but it became obsolete after I reached the Duke-level of cultivation. Being able to release a blast of qi into an armored foe had won me more than one fight. This one was worth my time.

The alcove I inspected next held a thin chain necklace of mithril, with a pendant of red metal. It took a second, but I recognized it as orichalcum. It was a type of metal that was anathema to qi, normally used as an outer layer on armor, and I was surprised to see it on something that could directly touch a cultivator's skin when worn. That was, of course, until I read the description. *Necklace of Nullification: When worn, keeps a culti- vator from using qi. Mithril chain makes it impossible to remove once the clasp is sealed.* This was a slave necklace. Fancy, yes, but I knew its true purpose.

Slavery was illegal in the empire, but that didn't stop people from trying. In my first life, I had spent many years tracking down illegal slaver rings stretching from the western forest prov- ince to the eastern desert regions. Ship captains, especially, liked to capture young cultivators for use as rowers. War galleys had fallen out of common use, but pirates still liked to use them to ambush slow-moving merchant ships out of sight of the major port cities along the coasts. There was a small peninsula known as 'The Claw' on the southern coastline where I had finally captured a ringleader of pirate slavers a few centuries ago. Actually, a few centuries from now. Maybe they were operating out of the region right now? I shook my head and looked back at the fancy slave collar.

This necklace looked like it was meant for a woman to wear, and the implications of what it could be used for made me mad enough that I almost bought the necklace in order to destroy it immediately. The fact that it still sat in this vault, and not in the pocket of some nefarious cultivator, was the only thing that stayed my hand. I knew that the emperor also used orichalcum necklaces to restrain powerful cultivators that had committed crimes against the empire. If a Sage-level cultivator did something bad enough to warrant extreme punishment, but not execution, something like this might be used to keep them from escaping. I left it in place and moved to the next alcove.

The last two items were a paired set of items. The first alcove held a pair of sturdy black boots, while the second had a dark gray hooded cloak. I read about the boots first, since my current footwear situation was a bit problematic. *Boots of the Night: Internal qi matrix makes the wearer virtually silent and leaves no trail. Self-cleaning and waterproof. Can be repaired using qi.* Now we were getting somewhere. These boots were exactly what I needed.

Next was the cloak. *Blanket of Night: Internal qi matrix allows the wearer to hide their face in shadow, no matter the level of brightness. Reduces aura of the wearer to half its normal size. Self-cleaning and waterproof. Can be repaired using qi.* Not as impressive as the boots in my opinion, but I could see a thief thinking this cloak was the find of their life. You could commit virtually any crime, and no matter the number of witnesses, there would be no description for the guards to use. Even their exact cultivation level would be hidden. Very tricky.

I looked at all of the items and realized that I wanted all of them. Just two items would barely make up for the betrayal of the Roh Clan after I saved them from certain destruction. It wouldn't make up for the last year of isolation I had to endure, nor the ridiculous amount of strain it had put on my mission from the gods to find and destroy the *nox*. I wasn't leaving until the scales of karma were balanced.

I pulled out my two tokens and inspected them closely. The subtle qi matrix embedded in their structure was incredibly complex, and would require a cultivator with an absolutely insane amount of qi control to create. Lucky for me, I was exactly that kind of insane.

I spun up the qi in my upper core, drastically slowing my perception of time. Then, I used the meridians in my hands to create three exact copies of the vault tokens using metal qi. Layering in the qi matrix took over an hour for each one from my perspective, which meant it had only been two or three minutes in reality.

The strain of slowing my time perception was on the verge of giving me a terrible headache, but I couldn't leave any of these items to the Roh Clan. They had already proven themselves to be unreliable, and I didn't trust the clan leader not to abuse these items for his own personal gain. He had already done so with the Phoenix Lotus Pill. I had no doubt he would use the mirror to track me down, the dagger to help defeat me, and the collar to capture me. No thanks, Roh Clan. I would rather pull your claws now. I did not intend to become another puppet to dance at the whims of a vain and worthless leader again.

I quickly released my hold on time, and dropped the qi construct tokens and actual tokens into the slots at the base of the alcoves. I snatched everything up and placed the slave collar, mirror, and dagger into a dark qi storage stud. Now no one but another dark qi user could get to them, and I was the only person who could use dark and light qi in the entire city. Maybe the entire empire.

Then I quickly took off the foot wrappings, along with my simple clan robes, putting on the boots and cloak. I made sure to form a blood bond with the items so no one could simply steal them from me. The qi matrix they contained was easily ten times more complex than the tokens I had just spent hours copying. To recreate something like this would take months of careful study. Something to worry about after I figured out the mystery metal. And the secret language of the dark temple. And got my friends some proper gear. After we escaped the Roh Clan.

My to-do list just kept getting bigger.

After donning my new gear, I released the qi constructs,

allowing the protective barriers to spring back in place. The barriers over the boot and cloak alcoves stayed off, since I had used my real tokens to unlock them. Finally, I turned around and pulled the lever that opened the glorified closet door, stepping out into the vault reception area.

The chief elder had been busy while I was inside, laying out the injured guards and imposters in more comfortable positions. He was currently bent over my qi containment formation plate, trying to decipher the carvings along the edges. It was difficult, considering the pool of qi in the center had grown. It nearly covered the entire plate, and it would take less than an hour for the liquid qi to escape the design and return back to the environment.

I walked up and pulled out a clear glass vial that had faint runes inscribed on the sides and glass stopper. I unceremoniously picked up the plate and dumped the qi into the empty vial, filling it until the liquid qi was overflowing and spilled over the sides. The liquid qi that spilled evaporated before it even hit the ground, but everything inside the vial stayed. I popped the stopper in place before putting the plate in my belt and qi vial in my coin pouch. To me, the liquid qi was easily replaceable, but to someone without my knowledge, that vial was worth at least ten gold coins. Maybe more, considering the look on the chief elder's face.

"You have to tell me how you did that. I know it is a secret the gods must have shown you when you touched the testing stone, but surely that is something you can share with the rest of the world. To be able to contain qi, and condense it like that, would save cultivators *years* of hard work!" Ah, that explained the look he was giving me.

"Chief Elder, what I just did is no secret in the empire. Crafters in the Imperial City use liquid qi like you just saw to empower formations and help create high quality goods, but it is useless to cultivators. We can only absorb qi naturally, or from a core. The liquid has to be released back into the environment before we can use it in our bodies. Enough liquid qi released in an enclosed space might increase the level of ambient qi in an area, but no better than a qi gathering formation would."

He seemed to slump a bit with my revelation, but he perked up a bit when I pulled out a smaller stone version of the same formation plate I had used. "You can have this one to study. It works slower, but it will eventually form the liquid qi you saw earlier. Experiment as much as you like, but don't let the plate overflow with qi. It can burn out the formations, making the plate useless." I handed it to him and watched as it disappeared into a storage ring he was wearing. I hoped I wasn't making a mistake by giving up the item so easily. Were they being made in the Imperial City by this point in time, or was it much later in what would become my life? Stars, this whole reincarnation thing could get tricky.

"I can't thank you enough, Jim. The possibilities that liquid qi could give our own crafters are a boon I won't soon forget. Now, we need to go. You spent longer than I expected to make your choices, and there is little time left for you to make your escape." With that, he deactivated the wards and pulled the vault door open.

He waved me forward and closed the vault doors behind us as we made our exit. There was no one awake inside to reactivate the wards, but we couldn't do anything to change that. I stopped as we reached the deeper shadows cast by the trees surrounding the hill.

"Wait. How are you going to explain all of this to the clan leader? He will quickly notice your betrayal, and I don't imagine that will turn out well for you."

The chief elder turned to me and smiled. "Whatever do you mean? As soon as we were attacked, I sent out a distress call from my alarm ward to the city guard. If the guard captain, a stooge of our illustrious clan leader, is too hungover from a night of raucous drinking to notice the alert, that is no fault of my own. After no response from the guard, I will be forced to leave the vault and search for the attacker myself."

His grin stretched nearly from ear to ear, and I couldn't help but snort in laughter. I would have to remember that he was a tricky one, in case we ever found ourselves on opposite sides.

"I should have known better than to question you. Still, it would be best for you to watch yourself after this. After we leave, don't wait long before sounding the alarm."

He nodded in reply before turning and continuing towards the boundary of the park. "Don't worry, Jim, everything has been arranged. Just be sure you look after my granddaughter. While I know your cousin and Kory will be there to protect her, I would sleep better at night if you vow to ensure her safety."

"You have my word that I will do everything within my power to protect her. To protect all of them. One day they will return to this clan, in better condition than they left it, if I have anything to say about it." I looked him in the eye as I made my promise. While we both knew I couldn't swear an oath to her safety, I would certainly do my best to bring her back in one piece. He seemed satisfied with what I could offer, if not exactly happy about it.

We hurried along the park trail leading toward the city center where the chief elder's compound was located. I pulled up the hood of my new cloak and activated its ability to hide my features as we stepped out onto a city street. While I didn't exactly blend in with the crowd, I was far from the only person wearing a hooded cloak. The weather was cold enough now that you could see your breath, but not quite cold enough to freeze. Just the right temperature for a hooded fellow to walk about the city without drawing attention.

As we approached the gate to the chief elder's complex, I saw a group of three guards positioned across the square. They seemed to be focused exclusively on the whitewashed walls of his compound, and set my senses tingling.

I pulled the chief elder into an alleyway before he could cross the street to his home. He was about to say something to me, but I held up my hand to stop him.

"Look. They are waiting for you. Is there some other way to get in your compound? Some way they won't notice?" I was surprised to hear the cloak had also changed the sound of my voice to sound deeper than it actually was. Nice.

"No." He shook his head as he looked around the area a bit more carefully. "But I have a way to get *out* of the compound without them noticing." He pulled off a bracelet and snapped one of three wooden beads it held in half. "Hold on." He held the broken piece up to his mouth and quietly whispered into it for nearly five full minutes. Finally, he snapped a second wooden bead. "It should only take a minute for them to reply. I only have the one communication bracelet with me, so we only have one chance to get this right."

The final wooden bead cracked on its own, which must have been the signal. A regal-looking gentleman wearing some of the most ornate silver robes I had ever seen walked out of the chief elder's compound and walked directly toward the clan leader's palace. Two of the guards broke off to follow the man, while the third stayed to watch the compound.

"Damn," cursed the chief elder. "I should have expected that. Now I have no idea how to get the gates open without them noticing."

I took a moment to think before turning to look at him. "I have an idea. Tell me, can you see my face at all in this cloak?"

He turned and looked me over for a bit before shaking his head. "No. You don't even sound like yourself. The only thing that might give you away is your vest. The cloak doesn't close all the way, and I can see it. No one else has a vest like that in this city." I nodded, and took a moment to take it off and store it in my belt. He looked me over again and smiled. "Now you could be anyone. Nothing to make you stand out."

"Good. I am going to make a scene, and you are going to get everyone else out. Tell them to go on without me; they know where to meet. Make sure Chu doesn't forget to purchase spare horses for the wagons. We have a long road ahead of us."

I turned toward the lone guard keeping my friends and family from escaping safely.

"I will find my own way out of the city."

CHAPTER EIGHT

Havoc

The guard was hunkered under a thick woolen cloak, trying to stay warm in his hardened leather armor. People walked quickly past him, not trying to draw attention to themselves. Even the more influential clan members that frequented this part of the city wanted nothing to do with him, which spoke volumes about how the clan leader had restructured the city guard after Yisi's rebellion. The clan leader had cracked down on anything resembling insubordination, which only meant those thinking of overthrowing him would just do a better job of hiding their intentions.

The entire situation was a stark reminder that the empire was in drastic need of a fundamental shift in the way things worked. For as long as the empire had existed, the Rule of Might reigned supreme. Whoever was strongest determined the sole requirement for leadership. Actual qualities that denoted proper leadership were cast aside in favor of those who could simply rule with an iron fist.

This meant that the people in charge of a clan or sect were strong enough to defend it, but it didn't always mean they were smart enough to run it. Usually there were enough people in positions of power that understood the basics of running a large organization to keep things going, but not always. Many clans and sects over the years had fallen apart at the seams when the wrong person came into power, and I was afraid the Roh Clan was getting close to that point. If it wasn't for the savvy leadership skills of the chief elder and his supporters, the Roh would have faded into obscurity long ago. I shook my head and focused back on the problem at hand.

The guard was so focused on the compound across the square that he hadn't noticed me walking up behind him. My new boots made my footsteps silent, and my already low cultivation level meant that my aura was almost nonexistent thanks to my cloak. He literally didn't notice my presence until I reached both hands around him and simultaneously stole both his coin purse and yanked his sword out of its scabbard. The look of sheer incredulity on his face sincerely made my day. Apparently, in his mind, the thought of someone stealing from him was simply beyond anything he could imagine.

I turned and sprinted for the nearest alley, jumping over waste bins and dodging between stacks of crates stored next to side entrances to the buildings on either side. I made sure to scream like a madman and wave the sword and coin purse over my head as ridiculously as possible as I ran, drawing the attention of everyone in the square. The peals of laughter meant my antics were working better than I could have hoped, and the angry shouts of the guard following me only made everyone laugh even harder.

As I reached the end of the alleyway, I ducked to my left, hiding behind a decorative outcropping of stone sticking out from the corner of the building. I quickly stashed the coin purse and sword in my belt before crouching low. The guard rounded the corner and looked both directions before running right past me, his breath steaming up in billowing miniature clouds behind him.

I stood up and walked back towards the square, making sure to keep my pace steady as I reentered the flow of foot traffic. A few people pointed in my direction, but they quickly lost sight of me as I continued towards the market district. I saw the gates of the chief elder's compound swinging open as I passed by, but my shorter stature made it impossible to see what was going on with all the people in the way.

It was a short walk to the city markets, so I stopped along the way to grab breakfast from a cart vendor. I enjoyed the fare, so I bought two full baskets of steaming dumplings stuffed with some kind of spicy pork. My shadowy face meant the old lady selling the food gave me a few odd looks, but she didn't seem to pay much attention after I paid. It would be a nice surprise for my family and friends when I caught up with them. Storing them in my belt would make sure they came out just as warm and fresh as when I put them inside. I resumed my casual stroll towards the marketplace after looking around to make sure I was still unnoticed.

I wanted to take my time to give the city guards plenty of time to respond to the reports of a cloaked and crazy child stealing swords and coins from guardsmen. I had no doubt there would quickly be an increased presence towards the center of the city, which meant fewer guards near the gates. Exactly what I needed to happen. That should give enough time for everyone to make their escape. Once I bought a few things I failed to pick up yesterday, I would make another scene to make sure. Hopefully in as spectacular a fashion as possible. One event would cause an alert, but two close together would send them all running straight to me.

The first shop I entered was a feed store. I made sure to put my hood down before entering. If we were to feed horses over the ten-month winter-year, we would need a *lot* of food for them. The woman standing behind the counter was close to my mother in age, but she was nearly the same size as the black-smith. Her cultivation level wasn't much lower, either. I guess handling animals required an inordinate amount of strength. I pulled out the last storage ring I had in my pouch as I walked up to the counter.

"I need as much feed as this ring can hold, please." I handed over the simple silver band when the clerk held her hand out. The woman's eyes widened in surprise when she inspected it with her qi.

"This ring can hold a lot of feed, child. Are you sure you can pay for all of that?" Her mouth dropped open when I laid a single ruby the size of my thumb on the counter.

"Will that be enough?"

It took her a minute to pull herself together, but she finally answered me. "It is enough to buy most of my inventory! Your ring can't hold nearly that much, though. And I can't make change for something like this, not without taking out a loan." I went to pick the ruby back up, but she held out her hand to stop me. "How about this? I have six bags of holding here in the store, each big enough to hold fifty times their regular size. The ring shouldn't have any problem holding its containment. Why don't I include those in your purchase, to balance the cost?" I thought about it for a second. I was still getting ripped off, but it was almost a fair deal. She saw me hesitating and pointed towards the back corner of her store. "I can even throw in that old saddle and tack set to sweeten the pot."

I turned to look, and saw what she was talking about.

It was definitely an old saddle, but it had clearly been meant for someone rich or important at some point. There was tarnished silver filigree worked into the saddle horn, and matching silver inlay on the rest of the tack. With a little bit of work, it could really be a nice setup.

I turned back to the woman. "You throw in a sack of apples, and you have yourself a deal." She snatched the ruby off the counter faster than I could blink and got to work. In less than ten minutes she had everything sorted and stored securely in the ring. I picked it up off the counter and inspected the contents before slipping it on. Everything was sorted and in its place, with enough feed for six horses to eat for at least six or seven months. It was completely filled to the brim, so it would have to do.

I waved my thanks as I walked out the door, but the woman behind the counter didn't even look up from the ruby. I guess she liked shiny things. I put my hood up and blended back into the crowd.

My last stop was a store I had never been in during my first life here in Roh City, but I had been in many like it over the years. It was a corner store on the outskirts of the market district, and the only one with a guard standing outside the entrance. There was no sign out front, but I knew what was inside. You could feel the qi fluctuations from across the street, and I couldn't stop myself from shivering as I approached the door.

There was a branch of this organization in every city across the empire, with its headquarters located in the Imperial City. It was simply known as 'The Auction House,' but the plain name did little to describe the massive entity behind it. If the business organization was a sect, it would easily be considered one of the top three in the empire. Since it *wasn't* a sect, it avoided all of the political maneuvering the most powerful entities had to deal with. It made their auction houses a great neutral place for meetings between enemies or rivals, and the rare goods they sold made them a friend to the rich and influential.

One of the more underutilized functions they offered was that of a bank. Considering their wide reach, it was easy to drop off your money or valuable items and receive their equal in coin or similar items of worth all across the vast empire. Since I still had a *lot* of valuables I had found in the dark temple, I decided it was important to store a good portion of them in a place I had easy access. Gods forbid, but if my belt was lost or destroyed, I needed a way to make sure I didn't have to start from the bottom once again. This was the best way to do it. As I walked up to the door, the guard held up a hand to stop me.

"Do you have a pass, kid? If not, I'm going to need you to come back with your parents before I let you in." He was good at his job. Not condescending or mean, just matter of fact with the information. He was short and stocky, almost as wide as he was tall. The thick robes he was wearing almost hid the sharply defined muscles hiding underneath, but I could still tell he was not a man to be trifled with. His cultivation was at the Medium, or Fog stage, of the Saint level. He was strong in body and mind. I liked him.

"I don't have a pass, but you are going to want to let me in." I pulled out the vial of liquid qi from my coin pouch, holding it up for him to see. It wasn't anything special to a person from the Imperial City, but out here on the edges of civilization something like this was rare enough to catch his attention.

"Okay, kid, I'll let you in." He held up his index finger. "On one condition. You drop the hood, and promise me not to cause any mischief when you get inside." His faint grin let me know he was only a little serious.

I dropped my hood before returning his smile. I liked this guy. "I promise not to cause too much mischief, but none at all seems like an unrealistic request."

He laughed as he stepped out of the way, holding open the door for me as I passed by.

Walking into the office was like passing into an invisible soap bubble. As soon as I cleared the doorway, all sounds from outside ceased. The warding on the building included a privacy protection screen. No eavesdropping inside The Auction House.

I didn't see anyone waiting when I walked in, so I walked around the room to inspect the items on sale. Each item had an extensive description written on a sheet of thin parchment with a date of the auction it would be sold, along with a price that would be acceptable for immediate purchase for those who couldn't wait. It was a common practice, but you could usually buy the item for much cheaper if you simply waited until auction.

Most of the items for sale here in the Roh Clan branch were things hard to find in the region, like high-level beast cores and the occasional weapon or suit of armor. I made a full lap around the room but I didn't see anything better than what I already had. I was about to walk out to speak with the guard about the possible location of the auction manager, but as I spun to head out the door, I nearly collided with a very tall and extremely beautiful woman.

"Interesting." She was standing very close, but I couldn't sense any aura from her. Either she couldn't cultivate, or she had some device similar to my cloak that could disguise her level of strength. Her eyes roamed over me, inspecting me as if I was an intriguing insect. Her hair was a deep brown, which matched her eyes. Her skin was incredibly pale, which made a sharp contrast to her dark blue robes.

"Hello. I was hoping to arrange for an account with your organization."

Instead of answering, she walked in a circle around me. "A child with the eyes of a man, who disdains treasures he couldn't possibly have seen before, and walks with the quiet grace of a hunting cat." She stopped her circling when she returned to stand directly in front of me again. "What are you? A lost soul? No. A *found* soul. Touched by the gods. But not in a nice way. They were rough on you, weren't they?" Okay. That one hit a little too close to home.

"I just need to open an account, with access to the funds from any of your locations around the empire." I needed to get out of here. I had no idea how this woman was reading me, but it was definitely sending up warning signals. "Please. I don't have much time, and I know the process for opening a new account is a long one." She closed her eyes, and I finally sensed a tiny fluctuation of qi from her.

"Time is a rule you have already broken, but I will help you nonetheless." She held out her right hand. "Give me your hand, and I will take you to the accountant." I tentatively reached out with my left, and she walked me down a narrow hallway that led to a row of tiny cubicles like a mother leading her child. I was ready to bolt at the slightest sign of ill intent. I wasn't going to get caught up in something with these people. I had to avoid Ming's people as it was, I really didn't want to add another powerful organization to that list. We walked to the desk at the end, where a man with thinning hair and brown robes waited behind a simple desk covered in loose papers and small statues. Probably storage totems. "This is the man you seek."

"Thank you, ma'am. I appreciate your help." I went to pull my hand free, but her grip tightened like a vise. She must have noticed how reluctant I had been when walking with her.

"Change follows you. Not bad, but not good. Just… change." Her eyes seemed to flash in the light, and her hand started to warm. "We need to hasten your progress. I will mark you as a friend to the organization. This will help you to seek our assistance in times of need." Her warm hand quickly grew hot enough to burn, but I still couldn't pull free. I activated the spirit wood ring on my right hand, choosing the dagger-like stake so I could fight back in the tight confines of the cubicle. Before I could bring it to bear, she let go and I stumbled back.

"No need to fight me, lost soul who is found. I will not hinder your path." She stepped backward and seemed to fade into the shadows of the hallway. I rushed forwards to confront the insane cultivator, but she was gone. When I turned back to the man waiting behind his desk, I noticed he had been affected as well.

"Did you see that?!" I stomped up to him as I shouted. "What was that all about? Who was she, and why did she burn my hand?" I held up my left hand, expecting to see it charred to the bone.

Instead, there was a faint symbol on my palm that had an exact copy on the back of my hand. It was like three needles had pierced my hand long ago, leaving a faint scar on either side. They were shaped like an obtuse triangle, with the base running parallel to my knuckles and the point in the center. I tried to inspect the damage with my qi, but my senses told me that there was nothing physically wrong. Had she burned my soul?

"I must apologize, young man." His voice was shaky, and there was sweat on his brow. "That was the branch manager's daughter. She seldom leaves her rooms above the show floor. Many people find her to be strange, and the manager likes to ensure she doesn't disrupt the flow of business." The tone of his voice let me know he was genuinely sorry for her actions. Whatever the hell those actions actually were.

"What is wrong with her? And what are these markings on my hand?" I held them closer so he could inspect them.

His eyes widened in surprise, and he instantly bowed to me. "Sir! I didn't realize! How rude of me to not offer refreshments!" He jumped out of his chair, and moved to leave. I grabbed the hem of his robes before he could get away, pulling him back into the cubicle.

"Hold on, sit back down." I pointed back at his seat. "You literally just saw everything that happened. I have no idea what these markings mean, and now you want to run off without answering my questions?" He took a deep breath and sat. I gave him a second to collect himself. "Now, how about you start with what is wrong with her, and finish with why these markings made you so nervous. After that, we are going to set up an account with your banking system. And do it fast. I am in a hurry."

He nodded in reply before answering. "The young woman is an untraditional cultivator. She was born without any meridians. This affliction strikes many members of the founding family of The Auction House. Somehow, instead of just aging and dying like a regular mortal, the founding family discovered a way to access qi without using traditional forms of cultivation." He leaned forward conspiratorially. "Some people call them witches," he whispered, "but they don't cast spells. It's more like they force things to just follow their will. No one knows how they do it." He leaned back in his chair, seemingly exhausted by just revealing the secrets.

"Are you okay? That seemed to have drained you somehow."

He shook his head and grabbed a glass of water from a shelf behind his desk, taking a few shaking gulps before answering. "When we become an employee of the business, we swear a life oath not to reveal the secrets of the organization." He waved a hand towards my new markings. "Your status as a Friend to the House barely qualifies you to know the things I am telling you, so there is some discomfort."

I looked down at the faint markings. "So, this signifies a ranking of some kind with the organization?" I was more than a bit surprised. In my past life, I had been one of the most powerful individuals in the empire, yet I had not received nor heard of anything like this.

The accountant nodded. "Basically, yes. You will receive the same benefits as a visiting branch manager at any of our locations. Each member of the founding family can only mark a few people, so the fact that a young boy who simply walked in the building this morning ended up a recipient of such a gift is more than a little surprising." Maybe I needed to open up a bit.

It seemed like she was actually trying to help me. He took another drink of water. "I could explain more about the perks of the mark if you wish, but you did say you were in a hurry..."

I nodded quickly and pulled out three heavy storage bags from my belt.

"You're right, I am in a hurry. I need the value of this put in an account under my name, Jim Roh. Please make sure I can withdraw funds from any location across the empire." The sacks were filled with the strange coinage from the temple, the older denominations I had found hidden in my storage belt, and a few silver and gold ingots, along with the majority of the gemstones I had left. I only left myself with a few small gemstones and about fifty gold worth of coins in various denominations, but I didn't really need much more than that. The average city guard might only make one gold a month, so the amount I still carried was somewhat excessive.

By my estimate, I probably had enough wealth to buy a small palace in the Imperial City and simply retire. Or, I had just enough in those bags to purchase the alchemy pills I would need to reach the Duke-level of cultivation within the next decade or two. Pushing cultivation levels was ridiculously expensive. I would need even more funds to advance to King, and probably double everything I currently had of worth to reach Emperor. There was more than one reason why less than one in a billion people even had the opportunity to reach the highest known level of cultivation.

The accountant was shocked at the wealth I casually displayed, but he dutifully sorted everything by type and value before placing everything in the storage totems on his desk. Then he recorded everything on some ledger sheets and handed me a copy. I noticed a column to the side that had a bunch of question marks.

"What is all of this? Is there a problem?" I pointed to the discrepancy.

"Some of your items require a higher approval for their value than I currently hold. There are several denominations of older currency that are worth more than the gold they are printed on to certain collectors. Since you have a high standing in the House, we will have them appraised with no additional fee, and the amount will be added to your account." He wiped the sweat off his forehead. "Is that acceptable, young sir?"

"It's fine. Do I need to present this to make a withdrawal at a different branch?" I held up the ledger. He shook his head.

"No, the mark on your hand has been recorded. They cannot be faked, and no two marks are the same. Just show any member of The Auction House your symbol and they will be happy to help." He looked down at his copy of the account ledger. "*Very* happy to, um, help…"

I think I might have broken the poor fellow.

With that done, I shook his hand and quickly left the building, pulling the hood to hide my face back in place.

It was time to wreak some havoc.

CHAPTER NINE

Escape

It was nearly midday by the time I had finished, everything having taken a bit longer than I originally planned. Which meant I needed to hurry and cause a distraction to reduce the guard numbers at the gates so I could make my exit. And, if my friends were having problems getting out still, it would clear the way for them as well. I pushed through the crowds towards the center of the square, pulling out the shield formation plate I had carved earlier in the day.

I went to activate it with my internal qi, but I changed my mind. Instead, I pulled out the vial of liquid qi and hefted the sack of poppers I had left. I would need every bit of internal qi I could keep to make a getaway, so using an external source just made good sense. And since I didn't want to actually kill anyone, the poppers were my best bet. I said a silent apology to Healer Hai for all the work I was about to give him, and got started.

I dropped the shield plate on the ground and poured the liquid qi on its surface. The silvery substance quickly filled in the carvings, activating the shield. It was a thin yellow film of energy, stacked on top of a slightly smaller blue film. The yellow layer would stop physical attacks, while the blue layer protected me from outside qi constructs. I would just stay here until the qi ran out. Seemed like a reasonable timer. The shield snapping in place drew a bit of attention, drawing a roving patrol of a trio of guards closer to where I stood.

Next, I set the sack of poppers on the ground next to me before pulling out a handful with my still aching left hand. I hefted a single small stone with my right, taking the time to line up my shot before throwing it. The results continued to impress.

I managed to hit the shield of the guard standing in the middle, the tiny explosion slamming the man into the guard to his right. They both went down in a heap, while the guard who had been standing next to the shield arm fell to his knees, screaming as he clutched at his bleeding ears. Probably burst his ear drums.

That little scene caused quite the uproar, sending the crowds of people scrambling for cover. The guards stationed around the square tried to calm everyone down while searching for the source of the disturbance, but I made it easy for them to find me.

I knelt down on one knee and started skipping stones in a circle all around me, the explosions throwing shattered cobblestones outward in a quickly growing ring of destruction. The bag of poppers in front of me slowly diminished as I threw handful after handful. I made sure to angle the poppers so they threw the rocky shrapnel toward empty walls and the occasional guard, doing my best to limit civilian casualties.

It took less than five minutes for a ring of guards to finally surround the area, most of them hiding behind corners, overturned tables, and the occasional heavy tower shield. I was down to only a handful of poppers, so I put them back in the pouch and hung it on my belt. Better to keep some on hand, just in case I wanted a nonlethal option.

After securing the pouch, I looked up to see the ring of guards closing in on me. They had finally gathered enough people to form a shield wall, and were closing the distance. As soon as I stood up, a steady stream of arrows started impacting the shield around me. Several rooftops now had archers emptying their quivers as quickly as possible, trying to run the shield out of energy. Unfortunately, it was working. The liquid qi on the shield plate was starting to run low due to stopping all of the impacts. I estimated I had somewhere around five minutes left, and then the wall of energy protecting me would run out.

The guards were all shouting at me to surrender, mixed in with the occasional death threats and a few guard sergeants barking orders to close ranks and push closer. Since I had stopped doing anything, they were able to get close enough to the shield that the archers on the rooftops were forced to stop firing, otherwise they risked hitting their comrades. This had the happy effect of extending the life of the shield.

Eventually, a guard with a plume on his helmet approached the shield. He took a few minutes to look me over before deciding to speak.

"What is this all about?" After I didn't answer, he smacked the shield with a cudgel. "Turn this thing off, drop the hood, and hold your hands out to your sides! I'm not playing with you!"

I activated my spirit wood ring, ordering the internal qi matrix to form its programmed walking stick shape. The spear would be easier to fight with, but I was the instigator in this fight. No need to kill some guards just for doing their job. The guard took a step back after the walking stick took shape, eyeing me with no small amount of trepidation. I think my lack of reaction and hidden face were starting to intimidate him. Looking around at the square filled with guards, I was pretty sure my distraction had gone on long enough for my folks to escape if they had needed to. Seeing how packed the side streets and alleyways were, maybe my distraction had worked *too* well.

As soon as he opened his mouth to shout another order, I moved. I spun up my cores, strengthening my body with qi. Raising the walking stick above the shield plate, I slammed it down with all the power my enhanced musculature could impart. The shield reacted violently, blasting outwards in a circle around me. The guards in the first three rows surrounding me were thrown backwards into the people waiting behind them. I took off running toward the guards on my right, using the downed shield bearers as a ramp to help me jump over the heads of the men standing behind them.

My move was just in time, a few archers using the opportunity to take a few shots at me. Several of the guards around me went down screaming, their over-eager comrades hitting them with the arrows intended for me. I started dumping qi into my flight ring as I kept running at top speed toward the northern gates. The ring wasn't very good at making me actually fly, but it did a great job of reducing my body weight. Reducing my weight meant I could move fast enough that I was practically a blur, zipping past the still-stunned guards as I tried to make my escape.

Unfortunately, the blast wave from the shield exploding didn't reach the guards farther back. They had activated their own cores, several of them holding glowing qi constructs in their hands as they watched me speed towards them. I held up my staff with my right hand while my left dipped toward my storage belt. It was time to use one of my newly acquired treasures.

The Dagger of Strength, which was a ridiculous and pretentious name I absolutely hated, could absorb qi attacks. I was sure it had an upper limit to how much energy it could store, but since I had gotten it from the highest level of the Roh Clan vault, it probably had a pretty good storage capacity. I hadn't had the time to really inspect it yet, nevertheless I would have to make it work.

The first few blasts of qi were easily dodged, but as I got closer, they were too numerous to avoid. I held the dagger along the flat of my forearm and ran with my left arm leading my charge. My right hand still held the spirit wood walking stick, its length trailing behind me as I sprinted.

It had only been a second or two since the shield plate had exploded, but I was already more than halfway across the square. The mass of offensive qi constructs in front of me were sucked into the dagger as soon as they came within two feet of my arm, barely giving me enough room to keep running straight at the line of guards blocking my exit. I swung my right arm forward and down, slamming my walking stick into the cobblestones directly in front of the guards.

I used a trick I had seen once at a fitness competition held in the Western Province, imitating something called a pole-vault and throwing my body high over the heads of the people in front of me. My flying ring was still active, meaning I was able to leap high enough to reach the roof of a two-story building and scare the crap out of the three archers standing there.

One was brave enough to try to fight, but the other two took off running. As the guard fumbled between dropping his bow, trying to pull out a short sword from his scabbard, and forming some kind of wind attack with his off hand, I simply bopped him on the head with my walking stick. Not hard enough to crack his skull, but definitely hard enough that he lost all interest in fighting. I ran past his crumpled form, jumping across the gap to a roof deeper into the city.

My goal was to escape from the northern gates in order to leave a false trail. We would actually have to travel west for a few months before intercepting the nearest major road that headed north towards the capital. I could hear the shouts of the many guards following close behind, the archers on the other rooftops around the square guiding them toward my location. I could have gone faster if I had used some qi threads to help me along, but it would be a dead giveaway as to who was hiding under the hood.

I ran from rooftop to rooftop for well over fifteen minutes before I finally saw the gate to leave the city. There was still a large group of people following me, and I occasionally had to dodge an arrow or qi construct as they tried to bring me down. A few concerned citizens had joined the guards on the ground, chasing the person who had demolished their marketplace. There was one in particular that seemed exceptionally angry, his shouts to just kill me echoing across the rooftops.

By now, my pursuers knew where I was headed and they had communicated it to the guards at the gate. They had closed the gatehouse and stationed the better part of an entire platoon around it. So much for diverting more guards away from the gates. Lucky for me, Roh City didn't have traditional walls, and I wasn't a wagon forced to use the road. I simply shifted a bit to the east and picked up the pace. For some reason this caught them completely off guard, giving me a chance to pull ahead. I was only one outer compound away from a clean escape when I sensed a flare of energy spike directly in front of me.

I was loath to do it, but I was forced to spin out four qi threads to avoid running into the wall of blue fire that had just been thrown up from the gap between the buildings. I was moving too fast to do anything else, and I wasn't keen on getting my face burned off. I just hoped I was far enough away from anyone that no one could see what method I had used to save myself.

Unfortunately, I was out of luck. Whoever it was that had used the massive wall of flames immediately followed me into the fields abutting the city, screaming in anger.

"You! I knew it was you all along!" His voice was familiar, but I was having trouble figuring out where I had heard it before. They were certainly powerful, probably near the Middle stage of the Saint level. I kept running deeper into the waist high grass that divided two fields of rice, but the voice was getting closer. "I knew that if I waited, I would get my chance! You ruined *everything*! Years of planning *wasted*, just so a petty tyrant could continue to rule the Roh Clan! Thousands of gold sacrificed, my place as the treasurer usurped, my son ran away in disgrace, and my whole life *destroyed!*"

I finally placed the voice. I remembered a time while dream walking when I followed the guard captain working with Yisi to a compound near the center of the city. I hadn't been able to see the speaker at the time, but I had overheard them planning to kill the chief elder and clan leader.

I skidded to a halt. Time for the gloves to come off. I knew I had missed a few of the traitors inside the Roh Clan, but I had sworn to myself to kill any that I found after discovering what their plans were. They had carefully allocated nearly every young woman inside the Roh Clan to Yisi's supporters as wives or concubines as an incentive to get them to join his cause. I was not pleased with their thought process in the matter. While I might hate the clan leader after the way he had treated me personally, at least he wasn't forcing women into relationships with evil men. It was time to show this walking pile of filth why being a bad person was not a good idea. Also, now that I knew he was the treasurer for the Roh Clan, I had some news I needed to share with him about his son.

Since this was a powerful enemy, I would have to fight intelligently. I needed him to get angry enough that he forgot any form of tactics. I knew I could beat him eventually, but I didn't have time for a long, drawn-out battle. There were a lot of people who would be right behind this guy.

I only had a few seconds until he reached me so I quickly pulled out four stone formation plates I had made weeks ago. I put three in a line right in front of me and immediately hurled the fourth directly at the man following me. He held up a thin rapier vertically in front of his face, flicking it to the side in order to deflect the device I had thrown at him.

Just as his sword impacted the plate, I flexed my will and activated it. Instead of shattering the disk, his sword was yanked out of his hand and he slammed into the ground face first. Pretty impressive skid mark, if I do say so myself. He jumped up to his feet, spitting out dirt and grass. His eyes were practically glowing with anger, but I could tell that little surprise had hurt him more than he was letting on. The arm that had been holding the rapier hung at his side, and I would bet twenty gold it was either broken or dislocated at the elbow.

It was actually a very costly device I had just used. The qi I had been required to layer into the design had taken over a month to accumulate, but I had made it to fight someone just like this guy. It was an earth qi formation intended to increase the gravity in an exercise area to help fighters grow stronger. If used normally, the force would be spread out over several yards and only slightly increase the training intensity inside a fighting ring. Instead, I had compressed and layered the design into a space that only covered an area that was six inches from the edge of the disk. Definitely a nasty way to adjust a simple training formation, but I was devious like that.

The man walked closer to me, this time taking his time. He ignored his sword laying on the ground. I didn't blame him. If a simple rock thrown by a child had just ripped my sword out of my grip hard enough to dislocate my elbow, I wouldn't want to risk trying to pick it up either. I could see the flow of qi building up around his arm, trying to heal the damage before directly engaging me in a fight. We couldn't have that now, could we?

"Hey, skid mark! Can I call you skid mark?" He quickened his pace. I guess he didn't like my nickname. "So, skid mark, I have news about your son!" He froze mid-step, the rage in his eyes being replaced by confusion.

"What do you know of my son? Where is he?! Why hasn't he been answering his speaking medallion?" He was really wound up now. Time to push him over the edge.

"He was one of the people I saved before the temple exploded. After I nearly died during the fight to save his life, he returned the favor by assaulting me and trying to rob me." Skid mark started to smile, apparently proud of his son's behavior. "So, I cut his head off and buried him in an unmarked grave out in the woods."

That wiped the smile off his face.

"*I will destroy yooooouuuu!*" He amassed a huge amount of qi, dumping the power stored in his cores into his hands. It was ridiculously fast, but a cultivator at his level would easily have the ability to do so. But, as they say, just because you can, doesn't mean you should. He wouldn't have any qi left to protect himself after this. The fireball he was forming was easily the size of a wagon wheel, but even I was shocked at how dense the energy was. This guy was a master of the fire element. In almost no time at all, the flames went from blue to white. I could feel the heat from almost ten yards away start burning my skin. With zero windup, the fireball was launched directly at me.

I immediately spun qi into my brain core, slowing down the world as I saw it. The fireball was still moving fast enough that I was starting to get concerned my plan wouldn't work in time. Ignoring the certain death tearing through the air towards me, I stressed my willpower and activated the formation plates I had placed in front of me. In a painfully slow motion, three inter-locking sheets of blue qi started to form. It was a darker shade of blue than the qi shield I had used in the square, but it was missing the layer of yellow energy intended to protect me from physical attacks. This set of plates was a different color because it was made to perform a slightly different function.

The set of shields was intended to block the qi attack, true, but it was then supposed to reflect the attack back in the exact same direction it came from. The design for such a shield was incredibly complex, and had taken even more time to create than the gravity plate. That was also why it took three separate disks to work instead of just one. Thankfully, the shield popped into place a few moments before it was too late.

His fireball impacted the shield right where my chest would have been, nearly dead center of the three interlocking shields. That gave the system plenty of room to stretch in my direction, nearly brushing against me before losing forward momentum. It held in place for a heartbeat before being catapulted right back at Mr. Skid Mark.

The slow transformation from a look of satisfaction to shock on his face was a moment that would do a great job of keeping me warm over the long and cold winter to come. Having made sure I memorized the image of his face, I relaxed the qi in my brain core and allowed my perspective on time to resume as normal.

I was glad I did, because seeing what happened to him in slow motion would not have been pretty. I guess that when his rage pushed him over the top, he really went over the top.

His body pretty much disintegrated, or maybe it was just flash-fried out of existence. There was nothing left but a light red mist sprinkling down and coating the ground in a semicircle from where he had been standing. I was genuinely surprised that the fireball didn't pass directly through him and keep going until it hit something much farther away. I guess he had formed it somehow for maximum damage with little to no piercing ability. I would have to try doing that some time.

I bent down to pick up the formation plates that had made the shield, but the heat had been so intense that their surface had melted and ruined the runes carved into the stone. It was a little humbling to realize just how close I had come to total annihilation. If they had stopped working only a split second earlier, I would have been the one watering the grass instead of Skid Mark. I did manage to recover the gravity disk and his rapier, so that was a small bonus.

Some shouting in the distance let me know that our kerfuffle had drawn the guards back to my trail, so I stopped looking for any additional loot and took off towards the stretch of trees far to the north. I still had a long way to go before I made a clean escape.

CHAPTER TEN

Preparing to Leave

It was well after dark by the time I made it back to my compound. I had lost my pursuers right after reaching the woods, but I wanted to make sure the trail I left took them towards the northeast. The clan might eventually figure out where we were headed and I wanted to be far enough away that they would think twice about trying to chase us down. Especially after I laid a few traps for anyone following us.

My friends and family weren't waiting for me when I arrived. I was mildly worried, but it was still well within expectations for them to be working their way towards me. After all, a single person could travel much faster than a wagon train, even if it was only a train of two. Getting over the two rivers would take them some time as well, since they would have to cross at a low point so they didn't risk losing a wagon.

Since I was alone, I decided to arrange everything for the upcoming trip. The overloaded wagon wasn't ready to travel, so I moved stuff around. The only things I wanted in the back were the lower-quality weapons and armor I had made while trying to figure out how to be a blacksmith in my much smaller and weaker body. If some bandits waylaid us and we had to abandon the wagons, I wouldn't be losing out on much. Conversely, they were of a high enough quality to pass off as trade goods to any guards that might want to inspect the wagons when we visited the smaller towns and villages on our way to the capital. I might even be able to make some money on this trip, depending on how accomplished the local smiths were.

After situating things in the wagon, I took some time to rearrange the items in my belt. My prized possession had twelve copper studs running along its length, two of which were actually qi batteries that held as much energy as a cultivator at the Low stage of Saint. Each. The other ten studs were smaller storage spaces, along with a much larger space that the plain-looking buckle could hold. Of those ten studs, only three could be accessed using normal qi. The other seven, and the buckle, could only be accessed using dark qi, making them some of the most secure storage items I had ever seen. If someone couldn't use dark qi, they wouldn't even be able to sense that there was a qi matrix in place, basically making them invisible to anyone inspecting the belt.

I put most of the camping gear, medical supplies, food, and wagon-repair kits in the studs other people could inspect. Some places required an inspection of all storage items before entrance, and I didn't want them to see most of my other equipment.

I split my higher-quality weapons and armor into two studs near where each hand would pass while walking, just in case I needed to pull something out quickly. There were several weapons I had collected that were nice enough to tempt a thief, and I had even made multiple sets of weapons and armor that were almost as good as an advanced Journeyman could produce, after I had practiced my skills. Altogether, I had dozens of sets of weapons and gear ready to use.

I moved all the coins and gems I still carried into a stud all by themselves, right next to the coin purse that hung from the belt. That way, I could pull out more than just coppers without it appearing as if by magic. Depositing most of my wealth with the Auction House meant I had more room for anything we might find on the trail as well.

The buckle, I decided, would hold all of my blacksmithing supplies and magical weapons, like the green glass sword, silver bow, and Dagger of Strength. Ugh, still hated that name. I also put most of my random acquisitions, such as the hundreds of glow stones I had found in the dark temple and all my formation plates in the buckle. The traveling forge, stacks of various metal ingots, all the mystery metal, and the books and notes on the unknown language only filled up about half of the space, so I still had some room to work with if I came across something I wanted to grab.

Finally, I put all of my crafting supplies for alchemy in the remaining studs, splitting them by type and purpose. I had a large supply of several different medicinal herbs, a few cores, and other like items, so there wasn't much room for anything else. I needed to increase my strength before trying more alchemy concoctions. Everything I had tried so far had failed except for low-level healing and meridian cleansing pills. At the last minute, I decided to put a simple stiletto knife I had grown partial to recently in the stud that rested below the small of my back. You never knew when you might need to stab someone standing directly behind you. Especially those weirdos that stand too close to you when you are waiting in line to buy something. Jerks. Next one that tried that crap on me was getting a surprise.

By this point, it was getting late into the night, but I was still filled with nervous energy about finally getting to leave. I cleaned up the living area of my hut one more time and decided to go ahead and store the rest of my 'library' in my buckle with everything else. It didn't take up much room when I stored everything neatly, and I didn't want it destroyed before I translated its contents.

I finally felt like I was as ready as I was going to be. My parents would probably have to stay here for a few weeks while things calmed down in the city, but I didn't think it would be too much of a hardship for them. They spent most of their time in the forest anyway, so they might even decide to stay here.

Just as I was about to lay down, I remembered that I now had tools to work on the chitin armor I wanted to make for my friends and I. The chitin from the giant scorpion I had killed was qi-resistant, and would make excellent armor as protection against qi attacks. It wouldn't take long to shape it into something usable now that I had the equipment to do it, so I got out of bed and set up the traveling forge in my courtyard again.

I had begun to realize that even if I was powerful on my own, I needed my team to be the best they could possibly be. True leaders used their abilities to strengthen their supporters just as much as themselves, which was what I had done in my first life. Great leaders strengthened their people even *more* than they did themselves, and I was aiming to do better in this life. So, my people were going to have the absolute best I could provide.

The process was difficult at first, but I was eventually able to heat the chitin until it was malleable enough to gently shape into the forms I wanted it to take. Ironically, the best leather armor I had available to attach the chitin to was the red leather armor Councilman Yisi's people had worn. Most of it was cheap junk that I had cut into strips for foot wrappings, but there was enough high-quality armor that his senior people had worn for my purposes. There were a few gaps between the pieces of chitin that showed the red armor underneath, but I managed to cover all of the most vital areas with the thick material.

The sun was peeking over the horizon by the time I finished, but after looking over the seven sets of armor, I decided it was time well spent. No two sets of armor were identical, but the matching color and material would make it look as if my friends were part of some kind of mercenary band with a standard uniform. The two sets I had made for my parents only had smaller bits of the chitin instead of whole sheets, but they weren't traveling with us into territory frequented by rogue cultivators and bandits looking to steal from merchants. The chitin-studded leather would still break up qi attacks, just not provide as much defense against more mundane attacks.

For myself, I had shaped the chitin to go with the strips of leather I had used as foot wrappings. Since I now had boots I could wear, I decided to use the same strips of red leather to wrap my calves and forearms instead. I would be able to block attacks with my arms and legs, but my back and torso would still be vulnerable to qi attacks. The compromise was worth it, in my opinion. I still had access to the throwing knives lining the front and back of my leather vest, and they gave me almost as much protection as the chitin provided anyway. The only downside was that it made me look more vulnerable than my friends would appear, making me the easy choice for anyone ambushing us to target immediately. Or, given my size, the person to ignore as I would seem like less of a threat. Either way, after we were in this armor, I felt bad for whoever tried to take us on.

I made everyone, even myself, a thick chitin helmet lined with fur. It would provide warmth through the coming cold season, and protection from any qi attacks from above. I didn't make any boots or gloves that included the chitin since we wouldn't want it interfering with our own qi attacks. It would take some adjustments by everyone, but I knew it would be worth it in the end.

Since I was at it, I decided to finalize the weapons I had been working on for everyone. I had thought long and hard about how everyone fought and I thought I had come up with improvements to help them complement one another as a team. Each person needed something they could fight with at short, medium, and long range, depending on how a situation unfolded.

I laid out my choices for Kory first. He was the strongest person on our team, with decades of fighting experience. That meant I had probably only seen a tiny portion of his abilities, but the weapons I had made were something I knew he could use. The bow I had designed was something I had copied from my time in the Eastern Province. There, the people traveled across the deserts on the backs of tame lizards the size of a horse. This required them to use short recurve bows made of hard materials such as bone or spring-leaf metal instead of the normal longbows found elsewhere in the empire.

I had made Kory's with a steel handle that was attached to two pieces of curved chitin I screwed in place using the new tools. The black material was similar to bone, and he would be able to smack away any qi attacks sent his way with it. The other three items were simple but efficient. I had made them months ago, but now I finished up the last-minute details to make them perfect. He would have a stout boar spear with a cross guard at the base of the extra-thick steel blade, a steel broadsword, and a round wooden shield with a steel cap in the center and matching steel rim for added strength.

The shield could be used with either the spear or sword, but it was heavy enough to use as a weapon in its own right. The thing that set these weapons apart from their normal counterparts were the engravings I finished up on each of them. While it only looked decorative, the swirling designs included runes that infused qi into their structure. I had several metal runes that increased their durability, as well as a few air runes that made them lighter. He would be able to swing and carry these around for a lot longer than normal weapons.

Next up was Donny. He was more partial to chopping, brutal attacks that took advantage of his height. I had decided to give him a war axe, with a heavy crescent head on one side and a lethally sharp spike opposite the regular blade. It would allow him to punch through plate or lamellar armor with ease, making him a danger to any opponent. I included a dagger almost long enough to be considered a short sword for his off hand, in case he was fighting multiple opponents at the same time. I knew he wasn't great with a bow, so I had included a heavy crossbow that would be easy to use. He got the same sets of runes, along with an extra one that could give his axe blade a fire attack. It could be easily activated in battle, provided he refilled its qi reserves between uses. Since he was primarily a water and air cultivator, it would give him a third element to fight with.

For Valerie, I envisioned her in a support role. She already had a necklace that could provide healing, and her natural talent with the air element would make her the perfect archer. Providing Valerie with a four-foot longbow made of yew with the ends capped in sharpened bits of chitin would make her a great distance fighter. She would probably do most of the hunting for us during the journey, so I made sure to include a cleaver-like short sword and long skinning knife to assist her with butchering animals. They were versatile enough weapons that I knew she could use them while fighting if her bow wasn't an option, making her a deadly member of the group.

Jamila was primarily a fire cultivator, and after giving it some thought I realized we had been underutilizing her during our fights last year. She was capable of inflicting far more damage to our enemies than she currently was providing, so I adapted her role to fit with something the sects in the Imperial City liked to do. Or at least used to. Will do. Ugh. You know what I mean.

I had created two matching single-edged swords called katanas that included metal and fire runes in their design. It would make her a dual-wielding nightmare to fight, since her natural affinity with fire would only enhance the scrollwork designs. She already had a bracer that could launch wind blade attacks, so I included a few dozen shuriken that fit along her sword belt. They would turn her qi-only wind blade attacks into a physical assault as well. I finished up with a thin wire garrote. It was a gruesome weapon that I wasn't sure she would use. I only included it because it complemented the fighting style most of the sects utilized. I would have to teach it to her, but we had plenty of time on the road ahead of us with nothing better to do than train.

Last, but not least, was Chu. He was the hardest person to account for because the chitin armor disrupted his normal fighting style. Chu was a wood and metal cultivator, meaning he was incredibly durable during a fight. He could cover his skin in metal, while healing any injuries with his wood qi. Now he would only be able to cover the portions of his body not covered in the chitin-enhanced armor, but it was an improvement nonetheless. He wouldn't drain himself nearly as fast, and the extra layer of protection meant he would have a chance against a more powerful cultivator. Since he was an in-your-face kind of fighter, I decided to go with a brutal two-handed solid steel mace I formed from a war maul I had picked up during my fight with the *nox* inside the temple.

The mace head was in a bladed style, with six thick ridges of steel surrounding a short cylinder of metal. The handle was almost three feet long, meaning it would do some serious damage when it connected. I used earth symbols to make the weapon even heavier, and balanced it out with a qi collection design hidden under the leather-wrapped grip. It would allow Chu to refill his energy as he used the mace, hopefully allowing him to stay in a protracted fight. For long range, I went with a more unique idea. I gave him a bronze blowgun. The darts could be coated in any number of poisons, and I made sure to use a bit of chitin where the needle connected to the base. He would be able to easily penetrate a qi shield if he blew hard enough. Chu was pretty full of hot air, so I had faith he could manage.

After completing all my projects, I sat down in the chair on my front porch to rest. I propped my feet up on the small table that normally held my cauldron and leaned back a bit. The sun was high in the sky, meaning I hadn't slept in quite a while. My body was screaming for some rest. I needed to pack everything I had pulled out back into my belt and get some sleep. All I had to do was stand up, walk over to the forge, and put it away. That's all. Just get out of this suddenly very comfortable chair and finish what I was doing…

"I can't believe we snuck up on him for once!"

I jolted awake, looking around me to figure out what in the stars was going on. I had apparently fallen asleep sitting in my chair and somehow, my friends and family had approached without triggering any of my alarms. I would need to fix that. Everyone was lined up on the porch while my parents were unhooking some horses from two wagons they had parked outside the open gate.

"Good, you're awake." Kory was sitting on the ground next to me, sipping from a steaming cup of hot tea in his hands. "I think everyone is curious as to which set of gear is intended for each person." He nodded his head, indicating the piles of equipment sitting in front of them. "But you are going to need to explain how all this stuff works."

"Right after we hear what happened! We could hear the explosions all the way from the gate!" My mother cut into the conversation as my parents walked up. The horses were finally free to wander around just outside the courtyard, so they left them to graze. "What in the stars above were you doing? Are you okay?"

I nodded and used some earth qi to reform some chairs for everyone to sit in. "This is going to take a few minutes to explain, so let me clean up a bit and we can eat something while I talk." They nodded in agreement. I went inside and used the facilities while Chu and my mother puttered about in the kitchen. I made them wait while I took a short bath, as I wanted to get one in before everyone else realized there was only one bathroom and eight people.

When I finally walked back outside, everyone was eating skewers of meat and vegetables and chatting about the new gear. They all looked up at me as I walked to my chair and sat down. My father handed me a skewer of food and a cup of tea before pointing at the gear.

"You better talk fast, son. This lot is about to fight over who gets what if you don't explain what all this is for, soon." There were a few nods of agreement, so I quickly recounted the story of what had happened after I got to Roh City. Kory threw in a few comments about how the chief elder and he had come up with the plan to get me into the vault, and everyone was suitably impressed with the way I caused a distraction. It certainly helped the wagons escape unnoticed as they left the city. I left out the part about killing the old treasurer since none of them knew about me killing his son when he attacked me last year. Not that I was ashamed by my actions, I just didn't want to rehash past events. I also had to show off a popper, and I promised to show everyone how to make their own later.

Finally, I got to hand out the new armor and weapons. Everyone was suitably impressed. I made everyone try on the armor to make sure it fit properly, and test the weapons so they could familiarize themselves with their functions. The only real hiccup was Chu.

"What is this supposed to be?" He held up the metal tube in question, looking at me with a fair amount of genuine curiosity on his face. "Did the gods show you how to make some form of super weapon?" The look of hope in his eyes almost made me wish it was. Almost.

"Nope. Chu, you know how you like to talk?" He raised an eyebrow, refusing to answer me. "Well, I found a way to weaponize it. What you're holding is a blow gun. You can shoot darts straight through any form of qi shield using the darts I made. All you have to do is put all that hot air inside you to good use!" Chu blushed as everyone laughed, so I went over and slapped him on the back good-naturedly. "Seriously though, this will let you take down anyone thinking themselves invincible behind a qi shield." I held up one of the darts. "If you look closely, you can see the needle on the end is hollow. There are all kinds of *interesting* things you could use to bring down an enemy." He smiled as he grabbed the dart from me.

"Alright, I can see the appeal. It's a good thing this mace is so nice though, otherwise you might be in trouble!" Chu hefted the heavy item, rolling it in his grip. "We are going to look pretty intimidating when we are all in our new gear." I agreed. We certainly would.

I spent the next few hours making minor adjustments to all the armor, ensuring there were no spots that limited movement or chafed the wearer. I was surprised at just how much of a good feeling I got knowing that I was helping to protect my team. That it was more than just me facing what, at times, felt like an insurmountable task. I had more than just people willing to risk their lives for me. I ended up forging more than armor and weapons. Somehow, I had forged a family. As I worked at the anvil, the sky steadily darkened. A storm was moving in, driving the temperature down as the sun went lower towards the horizon. My parents were last up for getting fitted, everyone else having gone inside to get out of the cold.

"Son, you have been given many gifts by the gods. Your ability to craft such fine things is mind boggling to me." My father put his hand on my shoulder. "I know you don't want your mother and I to go with you, but I am glad there is such a strong complement of friends to help keep you safe in the months ahead."

My mother put her hand on my other shoulder. "Jim, we know you will be gone for a long time. Stars, it will take at least two years to make it to the capital!" She shook her head, and we all took a moment to think about the vast distances I would have to travel. She looked back up at me, fighting back the tears in her eyes. "Promise me. Promise you will come back to us as soon as you can." She wasn't the only one fighting back tears now.

I blinked away the moisture blurring my vision before answering her. "Don't worry. I'll be back before you know it." I had lost them to a massive wave of beast attacks in my first life. I wasn't going to take them for granted a second time. "And you two can stay here for as long as you need. Let the ruckus in Roh City die down a bit before you go back. Just make sure you push some qi into the protection wards every few days and everything should be fine." I started to pack up the traveling forge as my parents turned back to head into the stone hut. My father put his arm around my mother as they walked.

"We still have some time before they go. Let's get something warm in our bellies and get some sleep. Jim will need our help getting the horses prepared in the morning."

The first snowflakes of the year started to fall as I watched them disappear inside.

CHAPTER ELEVEN

Roadside Inn

Kory and I were in the lead wagon, the cold wind making the canvas covering the supplies in the back snap hard against the wooden hoops supporting it. I looked behind us, Chu driving the wagon following in our trail with Jamila bundled in furs by his side. I couldn't see Donny and Valerie bringing up the rear in the final wagon, but I knew they were back there. Otherwise, Jamila would have activated the alarm plate wedged into the back of their bench seat.

We hadn't seen anyone else since leaving, and the weather was most likely the chief culprit. The snow was blowing in hard from the north, practically blasting us in the face as Kory tried to keep us on the trail. It had been two weeks since we had left my parents in the compound I had made, and the storm had only grown stronger the farther we traveled. Such a long-lasting storm wasn't unheard of during winter-year, but to have one this intense early in the season didn't bode well for the empire. It was almost as if the natural order was slowly being subverted by some kind of outside force, or the balance of the elements had been thrown out of alignment. This was nothing like the winter I remembered from my first life, meaning the harsh winter certainly had something to do with the *nox* making their way into our world. How could they already be affecting so much? The shiver that went down my back had nothing to do with the cold.

Kory pulled out a sheet of waxed parchment, trying to spread it out on his lap while holding the reins. It was a map he had dug out of the clan archives that was supposed to lead us to a little-known side road that ran north to south the length of the province. Taking the main roads meant dealing with tax collectors, stronger bandit gangs, and more chances of running into problems. This older road should have less traffic on it, meaning fewer opportunities for things to go wrong.

The issue was finding it. With all the snow, we could roll right over it and not even notice. I had gotten into the habit of sending out a few strands of earth qi to search for buried paving stones under the snow every few minutes, but so far, I hadn't found anything. According to the map, we should have reached it hours ago. But it was an old map, and we didn't know how accurate it really was.

"We should stop there and figure out where we are!" Kory was pointing to a faint light off in the distance. I had been checking on the wagons behind us, so I had missed the building looming through the blowing snow off on the side of the trail. It looked like a roadside inn. We had to be getting close to a major intersection if we were seeing buildings. I exaggerated a nodding motion through my furs to show Kory I agreed with him. He turned the pair of horses towards a gap in the trees leading to the inn.

I looked behind me to make sure everyone was following the change in direction, and an eddy in the wind showed me they were closing the gap at the sight of shelter. Personally, I was ready for a warm bath. We had been setting up one large tent to sleep in at night to better take advantage of the single stove I had bought. While the tent I purchased was certainly big enough to fit all of us inside, it definitely wasn't big enough to fit a bath tub. It was an oversight I had grown to regret. Especially after having to smell Donny's feet every night. I mean, honestly, the guy could kill a goat with one whiff of those things!

It was a struggle for the horses to haul the wagon up the small hill where the inn rested like a waiting beast in the swirling snow. The two lanterns hung on either side of a stout metal-banded wooden door made it look like glowing eyes were watching us as we crested the hilltop. The location on a hill meant that the area surrounding the inn was most likely marshy swampland when the weather was warm. Why would anyone set up a place of business in a location like this?

As we topped the hill, I could have sworn I saw something scuttle back across the roofline so we couldn't see it. I raised up a formation plate designed to act like a torch in my hand, raising it for some light. Had I seen glowing red eyes? Or was it just the firelight reflecting off the snow? I think the darkness was just getting to me.

There was no one waiting for us when we made it up the hill, so we parked our wagons around back and untied our horses ourselves. The barn behind the inn had a large cross-beam holding its two doors closed, but it was no match for Chu's strength. He lifted it clear off the brackets and leaned it against the side of the barn before leading the way into the dark entrance.

The barn smelled of moldy hay and dust, leading me to believe there weren't normally many visitors to the inn. I was surprised to see three pure white stallions already in the barn, the tack hung next to them fairly dripping with silver and gold filigree, shining in the dim light cast from a single glow stone placed high in the rafters. Whoever was already here fancied themselves as important. We would need to be careful not to draw attention to ourselves. There was a fourth animal that looked like a giant pigeon in another stall. It was probably a bonded creature of some kind, but I hadn't seen anything quite like it before. It watched us quietly as we led our own horses into the adjacent stalls. Before leaving, I made sure to pull out plenty of feed for our overworked animals from the storage ring on my finger.

We closed the barn back up and silently trudged back around the building to the main door. Kory trailed behind, making sure the covered wagons were sealed up against the snow. Donny led the way, stomping into the main room of the inn to knock the snow off of his boots.

"Close the door! Gods, you lot trying to freeze us to death in here!" A poorly timed gust of wind brought in a wave of flurries with us. My vision adjusted to the room, and I saw three large men wearing black lamellar armor sitting next to a sputtering fire in a large common room. The largest of them was looking at us with an angry look on his face, marking him as the one who shouted. A fourth older man wearing a dark green cloak sat hunched over at a long counter running the width of the room. As we walked in, a painfully thin woman in threadbare clothes came out from behind a drop cloth separating what was most likely the kitchen from the main room. I had no idea how she hadn't frozen to death.

Kory slammed the door closed as he finally made it into the building. I stood off to the side, trying to hide as best as I could from the men near the fire. I knew exactly who they were, and the presence of the horses and gaudy tack in the barn confirmed it. It was a team from the Emperor's Recruiters.

"Take your furs off, good sirs! You can hang them on the pegs near the door to dry. Sit where you like, and I will be by to take your order when you get comfortable." The thin woman waved her hand, indicating the room was free. "Try to warm yourselves as best you can. This weather doesn't look like it is going to let up any time soon."

"Thank you, ma'am. I'm sure we will be happy with whatever you are serving that can help take the chill from our bones. We have been traveling in this storm for days." Kory's voice was muffled by the furs wrapped around his face, but he was loud enough the woman understood. We all did as we were told, unwrapping the layers of furs we had worn for the past two weeks. To put it mildly, we didn't exactly smell fantastic once our bottom layers of clothing were revealed. The common room was barely above freezing, but after days out in the blowing storm it was almost balmy.

We hadn't been wearing our armor since the heavy storm negated the risk of an ambush by bandits, so we weren't exactly an intimidating group that shuffled deeper into the room to find a table. No one had said anything yet, but all eyes in the room tracked us as we sat in the farthest corner from the bar. The group of recruiters was far enough away they wouldn't be able to easily hear us talk, as long as they didn't use some type of qi enhancement to listen in. Before we could fully settle in, the woman was standing next to us.

"Welcome!" We all jumped as she spoke much louder than necessary. I hadn't felt her approach, which was more than a little unnerving. "We have a boar stew with day-old bread for one copper if you don't want to wait, or blackened fish with rice for two coppers if you can hold off long enough for the cook to finish up. Meals come with one ale included, and a copper per pitcher after. Will you be wanting a room?" Her nose wrinkled a bit. "Baths are only another copper if you rent a room for the night."

We all looked at one another for a moment before Kory answered. "Three rooms, if you have them, and we would all like a bath." There were vigorous nods all around. "And I imagine we would all like the fish. We have been eating stew for several days now." The nods were even more energetic with that decision. Kory wasn't wrong, we were all pretty tired of stew, no matter how good of a cook Chu was starting to become. For some reason, the woman winced before answering.

"We'll call it four silvers for everything, and I'll have the bathing room prepared by the time you finish your food." It was Kory's turn to wince as he pulled out five silver coins and handed them over. I understood why he winced. Five silvers should have been enough for us to stay for at least three nights, meals included, not just one. Especially in a place as dark and dreary as this one. "The extra silver is for my thanks."

Her smile turned a bit more genuine. "Thank you, I'll bring your ales right out." She looked at me for a moment. "I'll water his down a bit for you." Kory smiled at her as I sighed. I was eleven now, but my more advanced stage of cultivation made me appear closer to thirteen. Still not old enough looking to warrant a regular drink in an inn, apparently.

We waited for her to bring out our drinks before leaning forward to talk. The watered-down ale was as awful as I suspected it would be. Jamila was the first one to speak as the serving woman walked away.

"I don't like it here," she whispered, looking around. "It feels wrong in this place. We need to be careful."

I heartily agreed with her, but Donny cut in before I could say anything. "Did anyone else notice how she just snuck up on us? There is something about her that I don't trust." Everyone nodded, looking around to make sure she wasn't sneaking up on us again. Good. I was glad I wasn't the only one who noticed, and the group's instincts were spot on in my opinion. There was definitely something wrong here.

"The group by the fire is a concern." I pointed subtly to the men in black lamellar armor. "That is a team of the Emperor's Recruiters." Everyone looked over as I talked, but thankfully the three men were too busy arguing amongst themselves to notice. One of them kept jabbing his finger into a scroll rolled out on their table, but the larger man kept shaking his head and talking over him.

"What is that?" Valerie was fingering her skinning knife as she asked. The little bit of training we had been able to do inside the tent had shown her to be lethally quick with a short blade, and her inclination was to reach for one. "A recruiter, I mean. What do they do that we should be worried about?" Kory took a drink of his ale before answering.

"From what I have heard, it is their job to seek out the most naturally talented cultivators throughout the empire. Once they find one, they bring them to the emperor's personal academy in the Imperial City for advanced training."

Chu looked confused. "What is so bad about that? I mean, to be selected to join the emperor's private school is a high honor. Any of us would be lucky to get recruited."

Everyone was quiet for a bit to sip on their ale, so I cut in. "There are several reasons why we don't want that to happen." I looked at Kory. "Have you ever heard of someone selected by the recruiters ever returning home after their training?"

He gave it a few seconds of thought before shaking his head no. "Now that you mention it, I haven't. In fact, I don't think anyone ever hears of what happens to them once they leave."

I nodded, looking everyone over as I did. "Exactly. Because once you get there, you aren't *allowed* to leave. You have to complete the fifty years of training—in full—before ever stepping foot outside the academy again. If you survive the process." There were some wide eyes at the table after that. Most sects had academies for the people chosen to join them, but the longest and most arduous only lasted a decade.

Chu was the first to break the silence. "Still, after the fifty years, wouldn't you be able to return home afterwards? I mean, fifty years is a long time, but it is just a drop in the bucket for a cultivator that advances far enough to live past five centuries."

I shook my head. "You're not wrong, but only someone who advances to the level of Duke can live that long, and only one in ten thousand cultivators ever reach those heights." Chu grimaced at my comment. "Not only that, but fifty years is more than long enough for you to forget about your family and focus only on the needs of the empire. Where do you think the Elemental Guard comes from? And the Emperor's Enforcers? Even the recruiters themselves are most likely people who just failed out of the academy. But they were still there long enough to get brainwashed into serving the emperor." We all looked over at the men by the fire again, this time a hint of pity mixed with the caution of earlier.

I fought off memories of my own time at the academy. It

was probably the hardest time of my life, but it had forged me into one of the strongest men in the empire. It was where I had gained the realization of just how powerful my oversized brain core could be. That a few tiny strands of qi could accomplish what a construct the size of a mountain couldn't. If it hadn't been for all the brainwashing, I might even recommend it as a place for everyone to train.

"Well, Jim's mission from the gods is too urgent for any of us to spend fifty years locked away." Jamila finally spoke again, breaking me out of my thoughts. "We risk the end of the world if we fail, so no mistakes from anyone. We need to keep our eyes and ears open while we are here." Everyone lifted their mugs in agreement. I literally couldn't have said it better myself. Deciding to include these five with me on my mission was a compromise I was happy I had made. It was also nice that they didn't constantly question me on just *how* I knew so much. Eventually, I would most likely need to come clean with them about the whole reincarnation thing, but now wasn't the time.

During my involuntary exile from Roh City, I had spent plenty of time explaining the situation I faced to everyone seated at the table when they could visit me. None had balked at the difficulty in what lay ahead, and each had reaffirmed their decision to stand beside me on multiple occasions. Was it the gods that saw me so blessed this time? Or just dumb luck?

I was brought out of my thoughts when our food finally arrived. This time the serving woman was joined by a portly fellow wearing a stained white apron. He made absolutely no noise as he approached the table, and I felt an incredible sense of danger from him. If the woman was setting off warning bells, he was an entire orchestra of alarms. The part I couldn't reconcile was both of their cultivation levels. Neither of them were past the level of a Heart cultivator, though I felt more threatened by them than anyone else in the room. Including the three extremely powerful recruiters.

"Here you go, folks! I hope you enjoy. As soon as you are done eating, you can head through the door past the bar for your baths. You six have the rooms at the end of the hall." The smile on the cook's face was eerie, like it was wider than it should have been possible for him to grin. And it showed too many teeth. "The first door on the right is the bathing chamber for the men, the one to the left is for the ladies." His grin lingered on the girls a bit longer than it should have, but he silently moved away before we could say anything. And I do mean *silently*.

"Want some refills on your ales?" The woman had moved to stand next to Kory. I noticed she had put her hand on his shoulder. Was there an extra joint on her fingers?

"Please. And thank you." Kory handed her another copper and she topped off everyone's mugs. I waved her off when she came to refill mine. I had barely touched the swill.

I shook off my misgivings and ate my food. We were already on alert, and I had faith in our ability to fight enemies far more powerful than the cook and server. Thankfully, the food was good. The fish was flaky and the rice wasn't overcooked. It might have just been the change in diet, but we all finished off our plates quickly.

"I'll stay out here with Jim, while you four take your baths first." Kory pointed to the others. "We will take ours after you finish." Everyone agreed, and they shuffled off to get clean.

Before they left, I reached out and stopped Donny. "Tell the others to keep their weapons and armor handy. And no one goes anywhere alone."

He nodded, and hurried to catch up to the others.

Kory and I sat in companionable silence, neither one of us willing to interrupt the quiet. Well, relative quiet. The three men by the fire were still arguing. I couldn't quite make out what they were saying, but the leader kept pointing to something on the paper in front of them. Whatever it was, the other two weren't taking it well. Finally, he got up and stormed off, shouting something about thick-skulled idiots being as useful as a pair of crocheted pants.

I was still chuckling about the idea of crocheted pants

when the guy at the bar stumbled over to our table and plopped down in the seat across from Kory. He was clearly very drunk, but I wasn't getting any malicious vibes from him. The man leaned over the table, ignoring me and focusing on Kory.

"Yous needs to gets outta here. It ain't right, you stayin' here." He was slurring his speech, and I suspected he had been drinking for most of the day. "It ain't right. You bringin' all these kids in this place. You tryin' ta kill 'em off young, is ya?" He pointed back towards the entrance. "My bird and I smelled this place. We know what's lurkin' under this here roof. It use ta be a nice place, bu' tha's all changed. Yous best be leavin' now, hear me?"

He stuck his finger in Kory's face, but I cut him off. "Is that your giant pigeon in the barn?" I had been wondering about it. I mean, who rides a giant pigeon?

"That ain't no pigeon, boy! It be a mighty hunter! Him and I been through it, we 'ave. We'll be leaving this place, no matter the cold. Just as soon as I finish me ale, we be movin' on." He took another swig, spilling some down his chin in the process. "Best ye listen now, boy. Get outta here afore the dark sets in. It ain't safe here after dark." With that, the man moved back to his stool at the bar.

"That was… interesting." Kory took a drink of his own ale after speaking, as if to wash the taste of the experience out of his mouth. "What do you think, Jim? Should we take our baths and move on? I can't say I disagree with the drunk about the vibe this place is giving me. And I know you noticed how dangerous that cook was." He paused, looking me in the eyes. "I'm not sure why, but he scared me." Kory looked into his mug, as if searching for the answer to his fear in its depths. I reached over and put my hand on his arm.

"You are experienced enough to know that fear is nothing to be ashamed of, as long as you don't allow it to control you." He looked back up and nodded, straightening his shoulders. "As for leaving, I am beginning to think it is a good idea. There is too much going on in this place for me to think staying is a good idea."

Kory nodded in agreement. "I'll go let the others know. You stay here and keep an eye on the cook." He pointed to where the man wearing an apron was standing. The curtain had been pulled aside, letting us catch glimpses of him as he puttered about in the kitchen.

"Sounds good. Don't take too long, I want to get my bath in sometime soon." Kory smiled and headed toward the door, leaving me alone. I didn't mind. It was the first time I had been by myself in a little over two weeks. I had gotten used to solitude over the past year of living alone in the woods. Being around everyone constantly had worn my patience thin at times.

I sat by myself for a good bit of time, the old man at the bar eventually stumbling out the front door as the temperature outside had dropped to even lower extremes. The snowfall didn't make any sense. It was far too cold for any form of precipitation, but the storm didn't seem to care. It kept on dumping snow outside and the drifts were piled up almost to the rafters.

Eventually, the two recruiters got up and headed back toward the rooms. I was entirely alone, except for the cook working in the kitchen. Wait. Where was the cook? I got up to peek behind the curtain, but I didn't see anyone. How long ago had he disappeared? I stopped and listened, but I didn't hear anything. From anywhere.

It was as silent as a grave.

CHAPTER TWELVE

Don't Eat the Stew

I expanded my senses, trying to see if I could detect anything. Normally, if I was actively looking for it, I could feel the aura put off by a powerful cultivator from several yards away. I should have been able to detect Kory and all three of the recruiters as they were certainly strong enough to qualify, but I felt nothing. This was bad. They were either completely drained of qi, or somehow, they had been killed without making a sound. I wasn't sure which was more terrifying, but I really hoped my group was okay.

Walking over to the door that led to the rooms and bathing chambers, I made sure that my weight didn't cause any of the floorboards to creak. I held my ear against the door, trying to listen for any movement. Still not hearing anything, I cracked the door open. It led into a long hallway with doors on either side all the way to the end. There was light coming out from under each of the doors, giving me just enough illumination to see there wasn't anyone waiting for me down the hall. As I closed the door to the hall silently, I thought I might have seen a shadow pass behind the door at the end. If there had been, it was too fast for me to see clearly.

I pulled out a generic spear from my belt, wedging it into the doorframe behind me. Since the door opened inwards, I knew it wouldn't stop someone from opening the door leading back into the common room, but it would at least hopefully make some noise if they did. Anyone trying to come *in* from the common room would have to break the shaft of the spear to get the door open. I could have used some kind of formation plate trap, but I didn't want to hurt my friends if they somehow came back this direction. Besides, I didn't *actually* know if something bad was going on. All I had were the warnings of a drunk man and my own instincts telling me I was in danger. Not exactly enough information to allow me to rip this place apart. Yet.

The first door I checked was the one that was supposed to lead into the bathing chamber for men. As soon as I opened it, I heard a thump from inside a room somewhere further down the hall. Damn, this place was creepy. The bathing room looked empty, but I went inside to make sure. One wall was lined with wooden cabinets, and a large barrel-like tub sat in the middle of the room. It was full of steaming water, obscuring it enough that I would need to get closer to ensure there was nothing floating in it. Just as I stepped up to look into the water, the door behind me slammed closed.

I spun around, activating the shield function on my spirit wood ring. Nothing was there. Just a closed door, and the faint sound of light footsteps running down the hall. I took a deep breath and let it out slowly. This place could go straight to hell.

I quickly inspected the room, making sure there wasn't anything hiding in the cabinets. As for the tub, it was extremely odd. When I went to look at the bottom, it wasn't there. It seemed to just go on forever. Maybe it was just a trick of the light. I put my hand in the water, but it felt normal. It was surprisingly warm, considering how cold it was inside the inn. Hot spring, maybe? Oh well, time to check everything else.

I opened the door leading back into the hall, this time with the spirit wood shield up and ready and a long dagger I had made that I pulled from my belt ready in the other hand. The hallway was still empty, but this time all the lights were out. There wasn't even light coming from under the door leading back into the common room. What in the stars was going on?

A faint giggle came from one of the rooms farther down the hall. Now I knew someone, or some*thing,* was certainly messing with me. Okay. They wanted to play games? I could play games. I *loved* playing games. Whoever this was, I couldn't wait to show them how good I was at playing games.

I pulled out a handful of glow stones, throwing them farther down the hall. I was expecting to see something waiting for me, but it was still empty. I then kicked the door across from me open, finding it a mirror version of the male bathing chamber. I tossed in some glow stones to be sure, but it was as empty as the first room. I didn't bother going in to check the cabinets, since none of them were big enough to fit my friends inside.

The next door down the hallway was a room meant for guests to sleep in. The door was locked, so I knocked it open using a qi-enhanced kick. I tossed in a glow stone, its green light casting eerie shadows into the room. It had two beds, both barely big enough to fit two people. Against the wall across from the beds was a small table that held an oil lamp with two chairs turned upside down on top, and a wardrobe pushed into the corner. It looked like no one had been in the room for a long time. There was a faint covering of dust over everything except for some smudged footprints leading from the door to the table.

Pushing farther down the hall, I kicked every door open and repeated the process. Throw in some glow stones, check for people, move on to the next. There was nothing, and no sign of whoever or whatever was messing with me. The only room left to check was the one at the end of the hallway, opposite the doorway to the common room.

Since I was pretty sure this was where the source of the giggling had to be hiding, I swapped out my ring's shield form for a mundane spear. I used a regular one with an actual blade, since the spirit wood ring spear only had a sharpened point. The narrow hallway meant that I would be able to easily hold them at a distance with the bladed end for enough time to disable or kill them with qi attacks. Before opening the door, I went back to every room along the hall and broke off a chair leg I used to wedge the doors shut. It should make it easier to keep anything in the last room isolated in the hallway. I finished my preparations by taking a few moments to slip on my armor. I was still smelly and disgusting under my always-clean clothes, but I wanted as much protection as possible.

Finally, I was ready. I spun up my cores, slowing down my perception of time just enough to give me an edge in combat. Then, I used the meridian on my right foot to spin out a thread of metal qi. I balled up the end of the thread into a hammer I used to smash the door open. On the other side, there was a scene straight out of the realm of nightmares.

I had found the larder. From what I could tell, there had been at least three different groups of people that had come to stay at the inn. I knew this, because their dead bodies were hanging from the rafters like sides of beef. As I stood in the doorway, the smell of blood washed over me.

They were hanging by their ankles, what was left of them anyway. From the scraps of clothes still on their remains, it looked to me like they were most likely groups of farmers trying to get their excess crops out to the major roads for sale to the traveling merchant trains that were responsible for bringing food to the larger cities in the province. Just like my friends and I, they were probably caught out in the storm and stumbled across this place for shelter. It was cold enough in here, especially in this back room, that they were frozen. I was really, *really* glad we didn't get the 'boar' stew for supper.

I pushed into the room, moving aside what was left of the swinging bodies. As I neared the back of the room, I came across a fresh kill. The last person in this row still had a bucket under their head, blood slowly dripping into it. My heart was practically in my throat. Was it from one of my friends? The body was naked, and turned away from me, so I couldn't tell. I used my spear to spin the corpse, and almost felt guilty when I let out a sigh of relief. It was one of the recruiters, the big man who left the common room first.

I had seen enough death through the years to know that from the condition of the body, he had to have been killed mere moments after leaving the common room. Whoever was responsible for this hadn't had the time to 'process' the 'meat,' so his body was still relatively in one piece.

Looking around the room, I didn't see any sign of my friends or any equipment. The recruiter had been wearing a set of heavy lamellar armor and there was no sign of it here, meaning he had been disabled and undressed somewhere else before being brought into this room and slaughtered like a farm animal. I took a closer look at the other bodies hanging from the rafters, and noticed there was more than one that was small enough to be from children no larger than my current frame. Probably the older kids of the farmers, trying to learn the ropes of the business from their parents. And these monsters had killed them. I could feel my heartbeat pick up its pace from the anger I was feeling. These bastards were going to *pay*.

Just as I was about to leave the room, I saw a bit of dust drift down from the rafters above me. Stars, I forgot about the ceiling! I dove forward, barely dodging the gleaming scythe that swept through the space where my unarmored neck had been. Instead, it glanced off the chitin helmet on my head, throwing up sparks from the impact. That reaction meant the weapon had been reinforced with qi somehow. The fact that I hadn't felt whatever was hiding among the rafters using their cores meant this was something new. Something I hadn't faced before.

All those thoughts raced through my head as I turned my forward dive into a rolling motion, using it to get me out of the room and back into the hallway. Unfortunately, the unexpected attack made me drop my spear to complete the escape. On the positive side, I had managed to drop it so the door couldn't be closed. It was pure luck how the bladed end pierced the floor in such a way that the handle blocked the door from moving. I knew from long experience that sometimes luck on the battlefield was better than pure skill, but having both was even better. As I spun around back on my feet, hissing laughter followed me.

"You are not a normal child, are you, little one? Heehee-hee…" The voice echoed from the rafters above and in front of me. It was only now that I realized all the rooms were lacking a complete ceiling; they were only made from walls going up about twelve feet. All of them were completely open to the rafters for the final three feet or so, giving someone who wanted to come in from above more than enough space to move around. "I'm glad you aren't like the others. I like to play with my food sometimessss…" The rasping voice almost sounded like dry leaves scraping across the ground.

"This time, monster, you might have tried to bite off more than you can chew!" I punctuated my shout by throwing up a handful of glow stones into the rafters. If I was going to get a look at my attacker, I would need to get more light into the darkened hallway. The glow stones only showed me a glimpse of my attacker, but it was enough to make my blood run colder than the temperature outside.

I had fought something like this before, but last time it wasn't bonded with a human. I was dealing with a *nox*. The serving woman was hanging from the rafters using six hardened limbs of darkness that originated from her back in an imitation of a spider. The hands I thought might have an extra joint now ended in sharp claws that gleamed in the green lighting. Her face had morphed into a facsimile of a spider as well, with two mandibles coming out of her mouth that rubbed together and imitated the sounds of speech.

"Bite off more than I can chew? Not likely, little boy." The creature looked over her scythe, noting a chip missing from the blade. She dropped it on the ground as she skittered closer to me, hanging from the ceiling almost directly over my head. "In fact, I think you will be deliciousss…" The hissing sound was from the mandibles trembling in excitement. I wasn't sure if it was drool or venom that was dripping from them onto the ground, but I sure as stars didn't care to find out. We stared at each other for a few seconds, frozen in position by some unspoken agreement. Studying each other.

The moment was broken as something slammed into one of the doors behind me, making me jump forward in surprise. I still wasn't sensing any qi fluctuations around me, which I was very concerned about. I suspected there was at least the cook to deal with besides the serving woman, and I had no forewarning from my senses about where he might be. Or if there were more of them besides these two.

As soon as I jumped forward and then glanced behind me, the *nox* woman-spider hybrid sprang at me. I had just enough time to look back in her direction and activate the spear function of my spirit wood ring before she impacted with me. The dagger in my other hand was knocked free by one of her spider appendages, but the ring morphing into a spear at the last second had caught her completely off guard. The butt of the spear had caught on the edge of a floorboard behind me, providing the stability required for the sharpened end to puncture her straight through her abdomen. She opened her malformed mouth in a surprised 'O' shape, the fact that I hurt her at all shocking her into inaction. If she had kept her head about her, she would have been able to easily injure me with her sharpened appendages. Instead, I took the advantage.

The spear had pierced her low, just above her right hip. The spirit wood didn't go all the way through, so I pumped some qi into it, allowing the shaft of wood to extend far enough that she was pushed back into the wall next to the door leading to the larder room. The impact with the wall seemed to jolt the woman back to her senses, and she struck downward at the spear in an attempt to break it. All she managed to do was tear the hole in her abdomen wider, the spirit wood far too strong and flexible to break from such a relatively feeble attack.

Her scream of pain and rage shook my head inside my helmet. It also roused the fury of whatever was behind one of the doors back down the hall. I looked back just in time to see the door to the woman's bathing room bow outwards in its frame. The door held, but it let out an ominous crack as the pressure from the other side went away. By the time I had looked back at the woman *nox* pinned to the wall, she was almost back up in the rafters. She had literally *ripped* herself free of the spear and was scuttling up the wall, dripping viscera and blood.

"Oh no you don't! You don't get to run away now!" It was time to take the gloves off. I knew how hard *nox* were to kill from my first fight with one, and I couldn't hold back if I was going to survive. Especially if I wanted my friends to have a chance at survival as well.

I spun up the qi in my cores *hard,* not having time to do it gently. Being so close to the next level of cultivation meant I was risking damaging my cores and meridian walls, but I didn't have any choice. My perception of time slowed the world to a stop, forcing me to hold my body still so I didn't rip it apart with incredibly fast movements. I could still move when time was slowed a little, but not when it was nearly stopped. Shockingly, the woman infected with a *nox* was still moving up the wall. She should have been practically frozen, but the powers she must have received from the dark mana demon attached to her seemed to have given her super speed. After just a few seconds from my perspective, so basically no time at all in real time, I had gauged her speed and direction enough to know what to do.

I spun out twelve strands of fire qi from each hand and pulled all twenty-four throwing knives from my vest. Using all of them would reduce the effectiveness of my armor, but right now I needed offense, not defense. I lined up my shot and whipped all of the thick hunks of sharpened steel straight at her head. The spirit wood spear not penetrating all the way through her body let me know she was tough, but I didn't think her skull could stand up to *that* many impacts. As soon as the knives were released, I let time return to normal.

As it turned out, I was wrong. Her skull had no problem taking that many impacts. What *couldn't* stand up to my assault were her eyes and open mouth, which is where seven of the blades struck. Her body collapsed, falling face first back onto the floor, driving the throwing knives in even deeper. Not one to take chances, I used the strands of fire qi I already had out like lengths of the finest wire and wrapped them around her before tightening them. You couldn't deny the laws of physics, and the large amount of force applied over such a small surface area meant she was sliced apart like a stack of disgusting and bloody pancakes. I was totally not cleaning that up.

CHAPTER THIRTEEN

Finally Get a Bath

After killing the woman *nox*, I spun to confront whatever was behind the door to the bathing chamber. Instead of facing a monster, I was greeted with silence and an empty hallway. Interesting. I had killed the first one too fast to give the second one a warning. Were they linked somehow? And just what was I dealing with? I was almost positive it was the cook on the other side of that door, but I certainly didn't know for sure.

The other thing that was really bothering me, besides my missing friends, was how easy this kill had been. My first battle with a *nox* had been much harder. It had required the destruction of miles of forest and an ancient temple to kill the first one. Comparatively, this one was easy. Was that due to the original strength of the host body? The Spotted Snow Leopard had already been an extremely powerful beast, making the addition of the dark mana demon a terrifying opponent even more difficult to fight. I felt the cultivation level of the serving woman during the fight, and she was much weaker than the giant cat had been pre-possession by a demon. Or, had the *nox* been attached to the woman for a shorter period of time? No, that didn't make sense. The cat had only been attached to the *nox* for a short time when I had fought it. There had to be some kind of connection to the strength of the host. Either way, it was time to go after the cook and find my friends.

I formed the spirit wood spear back into a shield and plucked my knives free of the mess that used to be a freaky spider lady before I started back down the hallway. I didn't actually put the knives back into their sheaths on my vest. They were too icky. I just held them out to my sides with the qi strands I hadn't released yet. The other doors were still wedged shut, so I didn't bother checking them again as I walked back towards the bathing room. As I got close, I could see the door was barely standing. A determined squirrel could take it down now.

This just confirmed my earlier thought. Somehow, the two creatures were connected. Were all the *nox* connected? Ultimately, it didn't matter. I needed to kill all the *nox*, and I was more than happy to do it after seeing what these monsters had done to their guests. My only question was if the *nox* had made them eat their customers, or if it just made them better at it? Ugh, other people's kids, I swear.

I kicked the door in with little effort, my knives poised to give the cook a bad day. Once again, all I found was an empty room. I stormed in, flinging around the knife-tipped qi threads in case this jerk was somehow invisible.

I even made sure to check the rafters this time. I needed to stop neglecting the basics I had learned long ago. Basics like, 'hey Jim, look up sometimes, you blathering idiot!' Despite the current situation, I chuckled a little bit. My old instructors in the Elemental Guard had been pretty good at getting their point across. And those lessons were important. I needed to use them or I might become complacent.

Not finding anything, I dunked my knives in the bath water to clean them off. Oddly enough, the water was still warm. Wait. How could the bath still be this warm? It was cold enough to freeze water in here and it had taken me time to get this far. I walked up to the edge to look in, trying to see what was going on. Once again, I couldn't see the bottom of the wooden tub. How was this possible?

I put all my knives back in the vest before holding my hand over the edge of the tub. I needed to figure out just how deep this was. I activated the spirit wood ring again, this time extending its spear form straight down. I pumped qi inside it to extend it, expecting it to bottom out after just a few seconds. Instead, the spear kept going. It hit the limits of the spear extension before touching the bottom, meaning this was at least fifteen feet deep.

Suddenly the weird position of the inn made sense. Of course, it was built over the top of a hot spring! Somehow, they had set up these tubs right over two of the spring's openings to the surface. It wouldn't be such an exciting place during the warmer years, but a location like this would be a favorite destination for travelers that passed anywhere near the area during winter-year. The inn might even be a prosperous business, if the proprietors didn't have a bad habit of eating their guests. The comments from the old man with the giant pigeon made more sense now. In the past, this must have been an important place to stop along the road to the capital. Now, it was a slaughterhouse.

Just as I retracted the spear back into its ring form, the door leading to the male bathing room exploded. I barely had a chance to look back at a massive form barreling down on me before I took a nose dive straight into the tub in front of me. The weight of my armor was dragging me deeper as the monster followed after me, its shadow blocking out the light coming down from above. The creature was barely able to fit in the opening but, true to form, it had tentacles. The rubbery bands of muscle wrapped around me to crush my much smaller form. The thin fire qi threads I hadn't released from my hand meridians yet were the only thing that saved me.

They were bubbling away in the water, reducing the already limited visibility to almost nothing. The draw of qi from my cores increased drastically to keep them from dissipating in the water, but I was happy to pay the price in energy to save my life. The tentacles didn't like getting burned, so I wove a net of fire around me and swam deeper. I didn't know where this tunnel led, but I didn't have much choice. Wherever it went, I just hoped I would be able to get a breath sometime soon. I hadn't had a chance to take a deep one before having to take this somewhat involuntary bath.

I pushed water qi out of the meridians on my feet, trying to propel myself deeper. The pressure on my eyes and ears was building quickly. I was always surprised at how dangerous going underwater was, and going in unprepared made it even worse. It had only been a few seconds since I had submerged, but the edges of my vision were already starting to darken. I needed air, and I needed it fast.

The *nox* was right on my tail, its size and my fire qi net the only things keeping it from quickly catching up and killing me. Water was clearly its natural environment. A massive blow from behind set me spinning just as the tunnel widened into an underwater cave. I couldn't be sure, but I thought I saw three more tunnels branching off from the cave when I was knocked into the cavern wall. There was some form of illumination from a blue-glowing lichen-like growth along the bottom where the water was warmest, but it was barely enough to see by. The monster above me shifted position to make sure I couldn't go back through the tunnel we had just come from, or try to escape through another tunnel next to it that probably led up to the other bathing room. That left me with going for one of the two openings I thought I had seen towards the bottom. My vision was mostly swirling stars and darkness due to lack of air at this point, but I finally got a look at what was chasing me.

It was definitely the cook, and his lower half had turned into a bulbous mass of tentacles in imitation of a giant octopus or squid. His face was elongated like some form of predator fish, kind of a blend between a barracuda and a shark. He grinned at me, showing off his rows of pointed teeth. Nasty. I had to fight off a spasm from my body trying to force me to take a breath. Time to focus, Jim. Get air, kill bad guy, stop messing around.

Not having a choice, I used the water qi from my feet to shoot toward the nearest dark spot along the bottom edge of the cave that I really hoped was a tunnel entrance. The cook tried to follow, but I burned through even more of my qi stores as I cast my net of fire qi right at his tentacles, wrapping him up and doing my best to slow him down. He made a sound that made my brain vibrate in my skull and shook my poor lungs in my chest. The distraction gave me just enough time to reach the indentation in the cave wall, and I pulled myself inside. Above me, there was a dark silver shimmer I really hoped indicated there was a pocket of air. I pushed out almost all the qi I had left in a burst to shoot me up the narrow tunnel.

It was air! I breached the surface like an arrow shot out of a bow, smashing my head on the low ceiling above me hard enough that it nearly knocked me unconscious, despite me wearing a helmet. I didn't care. I could breathe again. It was moist, muggy, and tinged with a smell like rotten eggs, but none of that mattered. I didn't realize how close to death I had been until I felt the small wooden focusing disk hidden in my waistband start to funnel a sizable amount of wood qi into my body to help heal me.

I wanted to just float there for a few minutes, but my armor was already starting to pull me back down. I struggled to stay on the surface as I looked around. The blue glow from a patch of lichen near the waterline was the only source of light, but my vision had long since adjusted to the dimness. There was a long ledge running the length of the small cavern a dozen or so feet higher on the wall, but no clear way to reach it from my position. I was just about to try to use the last vestiges of qi in my cores to pull myself up when I saw a familiar pair of eyes peek over the edge.

"Jim!" Valerie called down to me, her pale face and white hair looking ghostly in the blue light. "Thank the gods it's you! I finally got everyone up here, but I don't know when they will be back." She dropped down a knotted rope, its end splashing me in the face when it hit the water. "Hurry up and climb!" I grabbed the rope and pulled myself out of the water, struggling a little from the weight of my armor and waterlogged clothes. She must have been helping to pull the rope higher because in no time at all I was able to roll onto the ledge, still gasping for air. While I caught my breath, I looked around at our situation.

All five of my friends were here, along with the two remaining recruiters. The only person awake, however, was Valerie. She was huddled against the back wall, trying to give me some room to sit up. The others seemed to be okay, they were just unconscious. The ledge was much smaller than it had looked from the surface of the water. It was narrow enough that two people would have a hard time passing one another without falling off, and it was barely long enough to hold all the people currently laid out. I finally felt like I had caught my breath.

"I think we are safe for a little bit. There is no way that creature can fit through such a narrow tunnel. Okay Val, tell me what happened. How did you get down here, and why is everyone knocked out?" She took in a shuddering breath, and I finally realized how scared she must be. My stupid ass just popped up out of nowhere and the first thing I did was start interrogating her. Damn. I was better than this. Before she could say anything, I scooted closer and wrapped an arm around her. My current body was actually smaller than hers, but she was curled in on herself so much it made me seem bigger than I actually was. She put her head on my shoulder and let loose a few sobs. I didn't blame her in the least. This had been a really bad day.

"Thanks Jim, I needed that." She pulled herself together quickly, wiping at her eyes and sitting back up to her full height. "We don't have time for me to cry about how scary and hard this has been. I'm still alive, and I can fight. We need to make a plan." Valerie was no weakling. Her actions were proving that to me once again. There was a reason I had brought these people with me on my mission, and it was far more than just the fact that I liked their personalities. They were all powerful in their own right. "Why don't I go first, and then you let me know how you got down here?"

I nodded my head in agreement. "Sounds good to me. Now, how did you go from trying to take a bath, to ending up in this underwater cave?"

She held up her necklace, waving it around. "Do you remember how I got this pendant? I told you this before, but it holds three healing charges." I nodded, showing that I knew what she was talking about. It had been her prize for placing in the top five of the competition held last year. "Well, this little thing saved my life. As soon as Jamila and I closed the door to the bathing chamber, that serving wench dropped down from the ceiling and bit us in the neck! She had these creepy-looking spider fangs coming out of her mouth, and some black spider legs that came from her back. We were so surprised we didn't even get a chance to put up a fight! The venom she got us with knocks you out, but right before I fell unconscious, I activated my necklace. It takes a minute or two to work, so all it did was keep me awake while she threw us into the bathtub. Then, some kind of monster pulled us under and dragged our bodies into this massive underground chamber." She pointed down and to the right, in the direction where I had seen the other place I thought might be a tunnel. "There were all kinds of things in there, along with a bunch of skeletons. I pretended to stay asleep and the tentacles just threw us on top of the piles of bones." She shuddered before continuing. "It was only a few seconds later when Donny and Chu were tossed on top of us." This must have been happening while the drunk man was talking to Kory and I. Had he distracted us on purpose, or was it just an accident? She continued. "I tried to wake everyone else up, but nothing worked. I was about to use my healing necklace on Chu, since he could heal everyone else, when the tentacles came back and threw Kory at us. I waited until they left and tried to follow through the water. Instead, I got turned around and found this place. I went back to try to get everyone over here, but then the two people that work for the emperor were thrown at me just as I was about to heal Kory since he was the strongest. The other two hit me so hard that it broke my arm, so I used the necklace to heal me again instead." She looked up at me, a guilty look on her face. "I wanted to heal Kory with the last charge, but I forgot I used it on one of the horses yesterday. It looked like it wasn't feeling well, so I tried to make it feel better. Now, I might have doomed us all!"

I shook my head. "No, Valerie, you didn't do anything wrong. How could taking care of an animal entrusted to your care make you a bad person? Besides, did you forget? I can heal everyone with no problem after I recharge my cores a bit." She took another shuddering breath and let it out before nodding. "Now, how did you manage to get everyone over here by yourself?"

"Oh, that part was easy. I just tied everyone together using some rope I found in all that junk they had stored in the cave, and formed a giant air bubble around everyone before dragging them through the tunnel." I stared at her, a dumbfounded look on my face. "Air cultivator, remember?"

"But how did you keep the air bubble from collapsing from all the pressure this deep underwater?" She smiled.

"Easy. I just made the bubble really big at first, and let the pressure out on the side of the bubble opposite the direction I wanted to go. It was like steering a raft going downstream. I just guided it and the water did all the work for me."

Wow. Like I said, each of my friends was powerful in their own right.

"That's incredible, Val. I wish I had thought of it. Not that I had a chance to create an air bubble around my head before I had to dive into the water. I would have just created an airless space around my head."

She nodded in agreement. "Now, your turn. How did you end up down here? Did the spider lady bite you too?"

It took a few minutes, but I told her everything that had happened to me. She was very happy to hear that I had already taken care of the spider lady, but not exactly happy to hear that our opponents were *nox*. Also, hearing about their choice of cuisine didn't do her stomach any favors, if the greenish tint to her skin was any indicator. It hadn't done mine any, either.

Eventually, after getting all caught up, we were finally ready to make a plan for getting out of here. I had just enough room to stand up and shuffle over to start healing everyone. We were going to make this monster pay for what it had done.

CHAPTER FOURTEEN

Sushi

It took some time, but I managed to refill my cores with qi enough to heal everyone. After everyone was back on their feet, I decided to wait on waking up the recruiters. None of us were sure how they might react, and I wouldn't be able to fight in front of them anyway. If they saw me go full out, it would certainly make them want to snatch me up for the emperor's academy. I couldn't take that risk.

I let Valerie tell the story to everyone else about what had happened so far. While she did that, I went to go check on the *nox*, this time forming an air bubble around my head before diving back underwater. I also took off most of my armor, not wanting to deal with the extra weight. I still wasn't back to full strength, and using qi to keep me moving was far too wasteful. I still had the two qi batteries in my belt I could use, but those were my weapons of last resort.

I swam quickly back to the tunnel entrance, carefully peeking my head around the opening to try to see if I could find the creature. It was waiting for me. One of its tentacles flashed out of the darkness fast enough that I had no time to react. For some reason, it decided to smash me down into the floor instead of wrapping around me. I made sure it regretted that mistake.

While I had been swimming down the narrow tunnel, I had pulled out the Dagger of Strength. Screw it. Not the stars-be-damned Dagger of Strength, I was calling it the Dagger of Boom after what it did to that massive tentacle. Still a ridiculous name for an oversized knife with delusions of grandeur, but at least it made sense now.

I had never discharged the qi attacks it had absorbed during my escape from Roh City, meaning it was holding in several powerful attacks just waiting for the perfect moment for me to use. That cannibalistic *nox* asshole attacking me *was* the perfect moment.

The Dagger of Boom had barely creased the rubbery skin of the monster when I activated it, meaning there was only a tiny surface area where all that energy could be released from. It worked gloriously. The shockwave blasted me halfway back up the tunnel, along with a huge chunk of tentacle. At first, I thought I had killed it due to the incredible amounts of black-looking blood polluting the water, but I was wrong. The under-water scream the *nox* had let loose during our first exchange was nothing compared to this. I was genuinely concerned it was going to cause a cave-in, or maybe liquefy my brain from the underwater vibrations it caused. Luckily, it did neither.

It did pop the air bubble I had formed around my head, forcing me to swim back up to my friends. When I surfaced, I noticed the air was noticeably thinner. Whatever it was we were going to do, we needed to make it fast.

"Jim, get up here!" Kory called down to me, his voice echoing around the small chamber. I swam over to the rope they dropped over the side once again, this time only having to grab on before being lifted out of the water. "We heard what had to have been you fighting with that creature. What happened? Did you kill it?" Kory barely let my feet touch the ledge before he started questioning me.

"I hurt it, but I don't know how bad. I know it is down by at least one tentacle, but this *nox* is a whole lot tougher than the one I killed earlier. It has more body mass, too, meaning it can take more damage and keep on fighting."

Kory nodded, then looked over at Chu. "Chu has an idea I don't think you are going to like, but hear him out. There are a lot of plans we made while you were swimming and everyone agrees his is the best one."

I didn't realize I had been underwater long enough for them to make a bunch of plans, but I was willing to hear them out. After all, I was out of energy in the Dagger of Boom. Gah, I still needed a better name!

Chu started speaking when I looked his way. "Okay, I know you don't want to wake up the emperor's men, but hear me out." I had already opened my mouth to protest, but Chu held up his hand to keep me from saying anything. "None of us are really in fighting shape except for you and *possibly* Kory. Those two are both really strong, and we could really use their help right now."

I still didn't like the idea, and my refusal must have been apparent on my face. Chu waved his hand, indicating everyone sitting around us. "Just take a look at us, Jim. Really *look*." Everyone appeared to be a whole lot better compared to earlier, but we were all far from being in the best of conditions. That spider venom had been hard to heal, and I knew they might not be fully recovered. Maybe Chu was right.

"I say we wake them up, and let them fight it out. They are both at the Saint level, so they clearly know how to fight. Either way, we win. If they die, at least they can weaken the monster. If they win, we just have to swim back up to the surface."

"Okay. I get it. I don't necessarily like it, but I get it." I sat down. "If this is how we want it to work, I have an idea to make it so they don't try to take any of us back to the academy. We all need to put on an act. Especially you, Kory."

I laid out my idea, and everyone took their places. Chu knelt next to the two men, pumping wood qi to heal them while Kory stood near the end of the ledge. Donny, Jamila, and Valerie all huddled back against the wall like the teenagers they were, just pretending to be the scared teenagers they weren't. I sat huddled in the farthest corner, peeking over the edge down at the water. I was in position to take them down quickly if things didn't go well. It took a few minutes for them to wake up, but when they did, it didn't take long for them to orient on Kory as the strongest cultivator present.

"You! What is going on, and what have you done with our friend! Answer quickly, as if your life depended on it. Because it does!"

Kory kept a cool head and explained what had happened in the version of events we planned to describe. Basically, Kory told a story about how we were all attacked by the spider lady and woke up in this cavern. The missing member of their party had saved us all by fighting off a tentacled creature, and had gone off to fight the underwater monster alone while Kory guarded the rest of us. Their friend hadn't returned, and we were just waiting for the venom to work its way through them so we could all make a plan. Predictably, their plan was to attack. I couldn't judge them too harshly. I was the same way after graduating from the academy. It had taken almost a decade for me to grow half a brain, and *another* decade for me to start actually using it.

"You six stay here while the two of us take it down. We will come back for you when both monsters are dead." The older-looking of the two loudly conferred with his compatriot. "I haven't heard of any creatures like this, have you?"

"No, but if Cair didn't come back, we need to take this fight seriously." The younger recruiter accentuated his words by pulling out a massive halberd nearly twice his size. "This should help cut them down to size!" The older man nodded in agreement, pulling out his own gigantic weapon, an oversized sword that barely fit on the ledge. He nearly skewered me, not paying attention when he pulled it out of his storage ring.

"You're right! Let's go make us some sushi out of that dung heap!" The younger man seemed confused about the connection between a pile of feces and food, but jumped in after the old man.

We all sat silently for a few minutes, staring into the rippling water below.

Chu was the first one to speak up. "Well, sorry guys, that was a terrible plan." We all nodded.

Donny had to chime in next. "Yeah, those two are probably already dead. How do you think they even fit those weapons into the narrow tunnel?"

I just shook my head, disbelief at their stupidity clearly shown on my face.

"Maybe they could at least hurt the *nox*, after Jim took off one of its tentacles." Jamila tried to look on the bright side, but Valerie shot her down.

"No, they were entirely too stupid to hurt it. The best shot we have is that now the monster won't be as hungry after eating them." We all looked at Valerie before bursting into laughter. Well, at least the mood had lightened up some. Now that we had used Chu's plan, it was time to go with mine.

"Okay guys, time to end this. Kory, your job is to shield everyone. Valerie, you make sure we all have air to breathe. Donny, you provide the propulsion to the group. Jamila and Chu, make sure we all stick together. I will be our offense." I pointed to each person as I told them their mission, each of them nodding in agreement. "First goal is the tunnels leading up and out. If we can't make those, go for the cavern where they are storing stuff that Valerie told us about. The entrance tunnel must be wide enough for the *nox* to enter, but that's fine. We want to fight this thing with solid ground under our feet. Any questions?" There weren't any, so we jumped in the water.

I led the way down, Kory right behind. Valerie had formed a narrow air bubble that wrapped around everyone's head using her air qi that connected each of us, but the already thin air was quickly getting worse. I hated being rushed, but with the air quality there was no way around it.

As soon as we reached the end of the tunnel, I was shocked to see one of the two recruiters still fighting with the *nox*. Fighting was a strong word, of course, since it looked like the tentacle wrapped around his torso was almost finished crushing him to death. Donny saw what was happening and used his water qi to boost us toward the lower chamber, not wanting to waste the distraction. I went to break from the group and signal them ahead.

"Jim, don't bother. He is already dead. Come with us and set up the fight with this thing in a place where we aren't fighting in its element." Kory had his hand out, urging me to take it.

"I can't. How can I sleep at night knowing I left an innocent man to die?" I looked back at the weakly struggling form. "Stop wasting air and get in there. I might be coming in with that thing right behind me." Since we were still connected through the air bubble tube, I could hear Kory sigh before turning back towards the entrance to the other cavern. The rest just waved at me as they shot past, disappearing into the darkness.

I took control of my air bubble as soon as they passed out of range, but it was getting pretty foul by this point. Looking up at the fight above me, I saw that I was nearly out of time.

I wasn't wearing any of my armor, so I could use all thirteen of my meridians. That was exactly what I did. I spun out ten threads from each, making all of them metal qi this time. Each was thin by itself, but I braided them together to make twelve extremely flexible whips. I used the meridian between my eyes to form a cage of metal threads around my body. It wasn't enough to stop a blow from the *nox*, but if it tried to wrap me up like it had the recruiters, I was going to slice through that thing like a hot knife through a stick of butter.

I swam upwards toward the center of the main cave, the motion drawing the attention of the cook-turned-monster. He dropped the recruiter, focusing all of his attention on me. As the man drifted down, I saw the two halves of the other recruiter lying on the cave bottom. I tried to position two of my whips to catch the falling man, and another wrapped around the corpse of his friend. I would bring them both out of this pit if at all possible. While they were surely idiots, they at least deserved a proper burial.

The *nox* struck, his seven remaining tentacles striking out at me from what felt like every direction. I met his limbs with my whips, their braided forms easily slicing into the rubbery flesh. The monster retreated, and I pulled both the living and dead recruiter closer to me. As soon as they were within what I considered to be a safe enough distance to my body, I started swimming for the cavern that my friends had gone towards.

Instead of following me like I had expected, the wounded monster above me swam for one of the exits to the surface. Damn. If my friends were still out here, we could have just swum for the other exit and gotten back to the surface. Oh well, no time to get them now. The surviving recruiter was choking on the water, his own air bubble long since dissipated.

It took less than a minute to swim the larger tunnel into the other chamber. As I surfaced, my nose was assaulted by the smell of rotting flesh and spoiled produce. Not a fun smell, believe me. Donny was there in an instant, grabbing a hold of me and dragging me back onto a solid stone floor. I was glad for the assist. My meridians were aching from all of the fine detail work manipulating all those qi threads, and my cores weren't much better. Emptying them twice in a short period of time was taxing on a guy.

Chu had grabbed the surviving recruiter and was already healing his limp form, while Jamila and Valerie each took the gruesome duty of grabbing the halves of the other recruiter. Kory stayed on guard, his spear out and ready in case the *nox* had followed me through the tunnel.

The whole fight had lasted less than five minutes, but I was exhausted. Fortunately, while this cavern might stink, the air wasn't thin. I took deep breaths, trying to get myself ready to fight as quickly as possible, all the while ignoring the stench as best I could. I reabsorbed the metal qi threads, and made sure to try to pull in as much qi as I could while I rested.

Looking around the cavern, I saw signs that the owners of the inn had been killing their customers for a long time. Far longer than the *nox* had been let loose in this world, meaning the cook and serving woman had already been monsters before the dark mana demons had bonded with them. That was how the *nox* worked. They could only bond with someone who already had a dark soul. This pair was clearly an easy choice for them to form a connection with.

There were piles of bones spread out, each seemingly based on time of death. The oldest bones were towards the back, while the newest were almost at the water line. Beside each pile of bones there was a smaller mound of goods, armor, weapons, and equipment. I would have to take a look at it all after I knew we were safe.

Chu fell back from the sole surviving recruiter, his face pale and covered with sweat. I could tell he had emptied his qi reserves trying to heal the man, so I got up and walked over to see how it had gone.

"I think he is going to pull through, but he won't be ready to fight for a long time, Jim. His organs were pulped, and the bones were almost ground into powder. I don't know how he stayed alive long enough for you to get him here." I put my hand on Chu's shoulder, helping him sit up. "I feel bad now, since we were just laughing about them rushing to their deaths a few minutes ago. Then you rushed in to save them. I had to do my best."

"You did a great job, my friend. Better than many professional healers could ever perform. You seem to have a real talent for it. Make sure you cultivate and try to restore as much qi as possible. As for laughing at them, it doesn't make us bad people. It just means we all have a dark sense of humor, brought on by the circumstances. It would have been evil if we hadn't tried to save them." He nodded and closed his eyes to meditate.

I walked over to the man he had been working to heal, just now realizing it was the younger of the two.

"You... saved... me." He held up his hand, so I grasped it, willing to lend him whatever intangible strength the action might impart. "Should... know... looking... for... you." I moved closer, his struggling words hard to discern.

"Did you say someone is looking for me?" He nodded his head, the action clearly causing him pain. "Who is looking for me? And how do they even know about me?" The lone survivor took a deep breath before hissing in pain.

"Don't... know." He pointed in the direction of the older man's corpse. "Leader... paid... by... someone... at... capital." Pointing at a ring on his own hand first, he nodded towards the body again. "Look... in... ring... sent... to... take... you... to... him." That pretty much exhausted the poor man, so I let him rest. Kory waved me over to him, so I went to see what he needed.

"This cavern is much bigger than the first one, but we will eventually run out of air. I don't think that monster is going to come to us, so we will need to go to him. Otherwise, all it has to do is wait and it wins by default."

I looked around, trying to gauge how everyone was doing. "You're right. I think it is hurt enough that it won't risk fighting us without holding the advantage somehow. We have enough air to rest for a few hours at least, so let's recharge as best we can. Let me set up a trap that will warn us if it tries to ambush us while we rest." I hadn't used any of my formation plates so far, since the underwater environment might make them malfunction. A simple earth spike trap set up by the waterline should be okay to use though.

While I placed the trap wards, Kory went to check on everyone. Donny, Jamila, and Valerie had started sorting through the piles of random stuff after laying out the body of the older recruiter as respectfully as possible. Chu was still cultivating, and occasionally moving to help the injured man.

After setting up the trap, I went to see if the body of the

recruiter was still wearing a storage ring. It felt a bit macabre to dig through the corpse of a pseudo-ally instead of the usual loot search of an enemy, but I needed to know what was going on.

I eventually found the ring on a cord around his neck, probably because of his oddly fat fingers making it a tight fit. It held a decent amount of space, around one hundred and fifty cubic feet of storage room. There were three matching swords like the one he had used earlier, their ridiculously huge size making them almost useless for someone who fought with skill instead of pure strength. At least I could melt them down and turn them into something useful. Or use them to make metal walls for a fort. I mean, it was honestly hard to describe how stupid *big* these swords really were.

Besides the absurdly large weapons, there were a few sets of replacement parts for his armor, a few bags of grain for the horses, and a chest filled with two hundred gold coins. Last, but not least, was a steel tablet that looked a whole lot like the one I had seen in a dream not long ago. It was a communication device used to report over long distances, and this one was most likely connected to the Chancellor of the Southern Province. The team of recruiters must have been the 'group' he had sent towards Roh City, but the timeline didn't add up for me. It was still several months of travel to the capital. Was there more than one group out there? Or was this team just incredibly fast? Either way, I was keeping the gold and the tablet, along with the swords. I put the items in their respective slots in my belt, and left everything else for the surviving recruiter. I placed the dead body still in its armor inside the ring before tying the necklace around the injured man's neck. I spoke to him, seeing his eyes open as I touched his neck.

"Thank you for the warning about what awaits us in the capital. I put your compatriot's body inside this ring, and I left you with the feed for the horses. Tell me, how did you come from the capital so fast?"

His eyes widened in surprise before answering. "How did you know we moved quickly?" His ability to speak had already improved greatly. I guessed his own ability to heal had kicked in. I just stared at him instead of answering, waiting for his reply. He sighed in defeat, not willing to force the issue in his condition. "The horses. They have horseshoes that are engraved with air qi runes. It means they can travel incredibly fast for as long as the cultivator is able to supply the qi needed to empower them." I nodded, thinking back to my own time in the Elemental Guard. There were very few units with horses that had enchanted gear while I had served, but that was in the future during Ming's time as emperor. Maybe his father, Emperor Li, used more of his treasury to better equip his sworn men, instead of spending it on himself.

"We will be taking two of those horses when we go as payment for your errors. Make sure, when you return to the Imperial City, you report them as killed along with their riders. Your other friend's body is hanging in their 'larder,' the room at the end of the hall where you were attacked. I will let you decide how to describe their deaths, but I would leave out the part about taking a bribe from a provincial official." He hung his head, knowing there was nothing he could do to refute what I had said. "The thing you need to remember to tell your superiors about are the monsters. They are called *nox*, and they are demons that can attach themselves to humans and animals with a dark soul. Anyone evil enough to draw their attention is already a menace to society, and they should be hunted without mercy. Make sure you impart just how dangerous they are to those in charge."

The recruiter just stared at me, wide-eyed in disbelief. "How do you know all of this? You're just some kid! How am I supposed to take you at your word? No one has ever heard of these demons before." The urge to slap this idiot was pretty extreme, but I held myself back. I was really trying to be a better person, but this guy was pushing the limits of my patience.

"You don't have to take my word for it, you saw these monsters with your own eyes. Just be honest about how two creatures with almost no cultivation base were able to easily kill two of you, and almost end your own life with little struggle. If that isn't enough to convince you that *nox* exist, I don't know what will." With that, I turned around and left him to finish his painful healing.

I walked over to see how my friends were doing, and to finally make a plan to kill that damned *nox*.

CHAPTER FIFTEEN

Learning New Tricks

The piles of goods my friends were picking over had already been separated into piles of usefulness. Most of it was junk, but some of the stacks of goods had items worth taking. I let everyone else load up their storage items with what they liked before picking through what was left. Anything made of wood got thrown in my belt for fires, along with unspoiled food items and any feed for the horses. We would have two more to take care of now, so it was important to stock up. Everything left over was pretty much junk, so we left it.

"Should we bury all these bones?" Jamila was looking at the stacks of human remains, her eyes bright with unshed tears. I looked over the group, seeing a similar sentiment on all their faces.

"We should, but not now. This is solid rock, so we would have to use qi to make a grave, and I have a feeling we will need all the qi we can hold to take down that monster waiting for us." I motioned for Chu to stand next to her, but he was already on his way. I had no doubt those two would be getting married as soon as they were old enough.

"Jim is right. We can come back down here and take care of

it after we kill the monster responsible for all of this." Chu wrapped his arm around Jamila's shoulders. It took a minute, but she nodded in agreement.

"Okay. As long as we come back. We can't leave them like this. There are the bones of children down here." The air grew tense at her words, all of us feeling the rage build at what these people had been through.

Donny was the next to speak up. "Some of these bones are old. Like, decades old. They must have been poisoning their customers for years, until the *nox* bonded with them and they could kill them in other ways. What kind of people could do such a thing?"

Now it was Valerie's turn to comfort her future spouse. She leaned against him before answering. "The soon to be dead kind, that's who. Now, what do you say we all go out there, and rip that freak a new blowhole?" That got an enthusiastic cheer from everyone.

"Okay guys, here's the plan. We split into two groups, one attacks from the side while the other attacks from the bottom. We don't stop until that thing is dead. Make sure you don't accidentally miss and hit each other with an attack by mistake. Everyone got it?" Nods all around. "Donny and Chu, you are with Kory attacking from below. Donny is responsible for your air bubble. Valerie and Jamila, you are with me attacking from the side. Valerie, you have our air bubble. Try to focus your attacks on the head if you can. Everybody good?" And with that, we turned and headed back into the water.

The tunnel leading into this cavern was wide enough that it allowed us to leave side by side instead of single file. We swam into the main chamber as one, ready to deliver some long-awaited vengeance on the bastard who was waiting for us. Instead, the cave was empty.

We swam quickly for the surface, our two teams breaking off into each of the tunnels leading toward the surface. I pulled myself out of the tub inside the female bathing room just as Kory climbed out of the one in the male's room. It looked as if squid man decided a hasty exit through the men's room door was the order of the day, as it was barely hanging from its hinges. An even smaller squirrel could take this one down now, as well. Both of us took up defensive positions, ready to fight the creature in the narrow hallway as soon as it showed itself. Nothing.

After everyone was out of the water, we stayed as a single group. First, we inspected all the rooms down the hallway. The spider and woman amalgamation was still on the floor in pieces, and the larder was untouched in all its horror. Chu threw up when he saw it, but no one blamed him.

We formed up back at the end of the hall, ready to take on the monster in the common room. It took a few extra minutes, but all of us put on our armor. Now that we were out of the water, it might give us the edge we needed to win this fight. Donny blasted the door off its hinges with his axe, and Kory was the first man through the door. Once again, the only thing waiting for us was an empty room. We spread out, checking everywhere. Besides some more horrifying revelations in the kitchen, we didn't find anything. Finally, Chu let out a shout and we all came running. He was standing by the entrance, the door cracked open wide enough to let snow come tumbling through the door.

"Look, the storm has finally ended!" As we got closer, he held up one of my glow stones. "And there is a fresh trail leading back to the barn." We rushed out the door, trying to see where the fresh footprints led. Mixed in with the boot prints was a trail of blood, its color not quite red enough to be called strictly human. It was the *nox*, and it was still injured.

The trail led to the barn, but the doors were still closed. It looked like the cook had tried to lift the bar holding the door closed. From the blood smeared along its length, the monster's injuries had kept it from managing to lift the massive hunk of heavy wood. Another trail led from the door of the barn into the woods. The son of a goat lover was running. Okay, that wasn't fair. Maybe his parents were nice people. The goat lover was running like the spineless coward he was. That's better.

I rushed forward along the trail, making sure to stay a few feet to the side so I didn't mess up the signs he left behind. Everyone else formed up behind me in pairs, Kory automatically taking up the rear.

We had been trudging through the snow for almost two hours in subzero temperatures tracking the *nox*, but not one person raised a single word of complaint. They each knew that this was more important than a couple hours of discomfort. Every time we fought an enemy together, I was reminded of why it was such a good decision to include them on my mission. They were far from the strongest group of people I could have assembled, but I couldn't imagine a team more reliable or honorable.

Finally, I saw the trail up ahead end at a frozen pond. The *nox* was laying on its side, a pool of blood forming around it. It had returned to its human form, its left hand missing from the elbow down. By now, the sun was starting to peek over the horizon, our long night of hell finally over. We spread ourselves out in an arc, surrounding the dark mana demon on three sides. I knew that the most danger an animal presented was when cornered and near death. None of us wanted to make the mistake of thinking this would be easy.

We stood silently for a minute, all of us waiting for the monster to make its first move. The wind was brutally cold, blowing in from the north and making me fight to hold my shivers at bay. After waiting for it to act, I pulled my silver bow out of my belt and nocked an arrow. I didn't even bother to infuse it with qi, just pulled it back and nailed its remaining hand to the ice. It sat up and howled, more monster than man at this point. I thought it apt that its true nature should show itself at the end.

"We know about *you*, seal-breaker!" its voice echoed, as if there were more than one creature speaking through the monster at once. "We are waiting for you, and now we know your friends." It looked at everyone, and I was pretty sure its eyes were glowing red. Stupid demons. I lifted my bow again, this time infusing it with enough earth qi that the arrow felt like it weighed at least ten pounds. "How long do you think you can keep them alive, *destroyer*? We will be waiting for you to reach the city, and when yo—"

It cut off abruptly when my arrow impacted its knee, the heavy arrow managing to blow the limb off in an impressive display of gore.

"You don't get to talk anymore, *demon*. You are an infestation, pure filth, worse than scum, and I will eradicate you all like the vermin you are. Tell your friends who sent you when you get back to *hell*!" My friends, none of them missing such a perfect moment, all unleashed their attacks simultaneously. The *nox* started to transform back into its monstrous form, somewhat diluting the attacks across its greater surface area. It still screamed in agony, only managing to prolong its suffering.

I didn't mind. I was *mad*. This *thing* had threatened my friends. Its sheer existence threatened my world, and everything I fought for. It represented the destruction of all things good and right in the universe, and I *wasn't* going to allow it to continue to live. My body moved by instinct. I raised my hands, and my rage manifested itself as two solid white bars of heat the size of my thumb that burned straight through the monster's head. It dropped to the frozen pond, a few more attacks from the others blasting into its dead body.

Whatever I had just done had drained me, my anger quickly turning into exhaustion. I dropped to one knee, looking at my hands. There were no visible signs of injury, but it had burned the meridians that went from my lower core all the way to my palms. I couldn't be sure how bad the internal damage was, but that ray of light was hot enough that all the snow was melted in a straight line as far as I could see through the dense trees. That was really hot.

Taking a closer look at my cores, I realized I had used up almost all of the light qi stored inside my body. That was light qi? It was far hotter than any fire qi I had ever managed to produce in all my years, and I had been around for a *lot* of years. I immediately started to pull in as much light qi from around me as I could, the imbalance in my cores threatening to damage my entire cultivation system.

I heard shouting going on around me, but I had to turn all my focus inward. I couldn't afford to be distracted. The nearly complete absence of light qi in my system had allowed the dark qi to spring free of its bindings of earth qi, throwing my lower core into turmoil. The early morning sun wasn't providing enough light qi in the environment for me to rebalance. My only recourse was to expel the dark qi in the same way, preferably through the same meridians I had just used. Maybe there was a reason why the gods had warned me to use light and dark qi equally through my meridians. If this didn't work, I might lose the ability to cultivate through my hands entirely.

Regaining control of the dark qi to try to impart an intent was impossible. All I could manage to do was direct it through my burnt meridians, the black energy raging through me like a river trying to crest its banks. Once again, I raised my hands and pointed it at the corpse of the *nox*, my friends instinctively backing away. This time, the qi didn't form neat little bars of energy. It sprayed out of my hand like pressurized water from a broken aqueduct pipe, coating the dead *nox* and much of the surrounding area. Instead of burning it, everything it touched seemed to *boil* away into nothingness.

I collapsed on the ground in agony, my cores and meridians spasming with the rapid changes I had just put them through. This pain was familiar, it just came at an inopportune time. I was leveling up to a Meridian cultivator. The strain on my system, along with the fights over the past few hours, had allowed me to have a breakthrough. Instead of fighting for scraps of qi from the environment, I drained the energy from one of the batteries on my belt. It was already filled with all eight forms of qi, and it held more than enough to sustain my advancement.

The process of stabilizing my new level would take hours. My expanded capacity to hold qi meant I needed to layer reinforcing qi throughout my entire body equally, and strengthen my meridian and core walls with all the elements in perfect balance. I was able to check my hand meridians, looking there first for any lasting damage. Thankfully, the dark qi had repaired the damage done to them by the light qi. I still needed to reinforce them like everywhere else, but using the light and dark qi in equal measure seemed to restore my meridians with no ill effects. After confirming I was still going to be able to channel qi through my hands, I refocused on consolidating my advancement.

If I had been alone, I might have frozen to death in the frigid cold. Instead, I had five friends to look after me. I felt them pick me up and carry me back to the inn. There were several hours of intense activity around me that ended with a massive blaze as the light started to fade.

I came out of my cultivation trance near sunset, bundled up in my furs and sitting in front of a fire big enough that I could have stripped to my underclothes and still been comfortable. While I was focused internally, my friends had pulled all the bones out of the underwater cavern and turned the entire roadside inn into their funeral pyre. I couldn't have done it better myself.

CHAPTER SIXTEEN

One Step Forward, Two Steps Back

We spent the night in the barn with the horses, all of us willing to sleep in the hayloft instead of bothering with setting up our tent. The lone surviving recruiter left as soon as he was able to ride, not willing to wait for sunrise. We were off at first light, the two new horses tied up behind the middle wagon. They would come in handy as we traveled, allowing Valerie to hunt far and wide while still keeping pace with the wagons. Having fresh meat for the stew pot would become a necessity through the long months of our journey. Though it would be a while yet before I could get the images of the other stew pot out of my head. I mean, that just wasn't *right.*

The other horse could be used to scout ahead, or check our back trail from time to time. The maps we owned were decades old, and trails through the forest were frequently unreliable. Having a scout to check which route was best would be invaluable, while making sure no one was following us was an absolute necessity. We would all take turns scouting to keep our skills sharp.

Valerie and the horse that chose her got along famously. They spent the next week zipping around the woods, bringing in a plethora of game to supplement our food supplies. When it wasn't tied up, the horse followed her around like a puppy. She spoiled it with apples and carrots, and it was even learning tricks. It was a crazy smart horse. Valerie was spending her days either riding the horse or sitting with Donny. Which was probably the reason why the horse would stare at Donny for hours at a time. Was the horse actually *jealous*?

It was midday around two weeks after the inn incident when we found the road on Kory's map. There were trees growing through the cobblestones buried under the snow in some places, meaning no one had bothered to maintain it in a long time. Perfect.

We turned onto the road, the horses now walking straight into the wind. Instead of it slowing us down, our pace actually picked up some compared to what it had been on the seldom-used dirt trails we had been traveling on for the past month or so. Even though this road wasn't in great shape, it was still a *road*. The poor horses wouldn't have to deal with nearly as many hills, dips, and curves as they pulled the wagons.

The additional two weeks had also given me enough time to settle into my new power. I cast my newly expanded senses around me, testing out the extent of my range now that I was at the relative strength of a Meridian cultivator. The increased amounts of qi in my body had also changed my appearance again. It had aged me, making me look more like the physical age of Chu and Jamila at sixteen instead of my body's true age of eleven. The change wasn't surprising, considering our cultivation system would always try to keep our bodies as close to our strongest form as possible.

Normal cultivators would appear to turn back their physical age as they increased in power, which was why a three-hundred-year-old Sage appeared to be in their late forties or early fifties. Qi could only turn back time so much, so the older you were when you advanced, the less effect it would have. Since I was in a weaker, younger body, my cultivation system was trying to age my body into a stronger form. If I was to venture a guess, I would probably level out at the physical age of my mid-twenties. Since it was qi aging me instead of nature, I should be able to maintain that appearance for a *long* time. I don't know if anyone had ever made it this far on the path of cultivation as young as I currently was, so I couldn't be sure, but my sense of reason told me I was correct. Only time would tell.

While I might technically be a Brain cultivator, my true power levels were that of a weaker-level Meridian cultivator. That was okay. My actual combat capabilities meant I was a match for any Saint level cultivator. If I used my two qi batteries, I had no doubt I could beat a High Sage. Peak Sage cultivators might pose a problem, but they weren't exactly common.

Only one in a thousand people ever made it that far on the path of cultivation. Meaning, out of the one billion people living in the Southern Province, only one million were at the level of Sage. During the winter-year, most would be living the easy life as a sect elder or clan leader, not traveling an old road in the frigid snow.

Speaking of snow, it looked like another storm was moving in from the north. It would probably reach us sometime close to sunset. I wasn't detecting any wildlife around us, making it more difficult to accurately gauge my new range. If all the animals were hiding, this storm was probably going to be a bad one. The weather definitely shouldn't have turned this bad so early in the year. Our progress was going to slow to a crawl if things kept going like this.

One negative about traveling on the road was the snow drifts that could pile up. On the forest trails, there were enough trees close to the paths that they were manageable. The road was wide enough to fit six wagons side-by-side, giving the snow plenty of space to build drifts up higher than the covered wagons.

I pulled out six blank formation plates and started carving. First, we needed some way to move the snow to the side so the horses would be able to see the road even as the snow grew deeper. No sense in zig-zagging back and forth across the road when we could just go straight.

Second, I had to develop some kind of mobile heat source that would keep us all from freezing to death. When we had planned this trip, none of us had expected the air temperature to drop to these extreme lows so soon. It hurt to even breathe, and if it was hurting me, I knew the horses were in even worse pain.

The fix for moving the snow to the side was a relatively simple design that used air qi blades to churn up the snow in a line ten yards in front of the wagons, then spit it out to the sides. It would also shred any small trees in the way, allowing us to move in a straight line. Bigger trees would take more time to chew through, but there shouldn't be many of those in the middle of the roadway. Only the lead wagon would need it to be active, but since the people riding on the wagon would have to supply the qi to keep the formation active, we would need to rotate who was in the lead anyway. It only took a few minutes to install on the front of the wagons and explain how they worked to everyone. Kory and I fell to the rear, letting Jamila and Chu's wagon take the lead to start.

The heat source was where I ran into problems. The best place to mount the plate would be on the pull bar, or whipple-tree, between the horses. That just so happened to be made out of wood. Which burns. Bad for a place to put a formation plate emitting fire qi. A shield similar to the one I had used to make a distraction back in Roh City using fire qi would be too energy-intensive, meaning we would only be able to use them for short periods of time every day. Maybe a *really* weak version? No, it wouldn't be able to hold together against the blowing snow.

I was still trying to figure something out when we stopped and circled our wagons for the evening meal. The snowstorm would hit us soon, the horses needed a break, and everyone needed a chance to recharge their cores anyway. The bigger the snow drifts, the more qi my designs drew from the person powering them. Even though we were rotating the responsibility throughout the afternoon, it was still exhausting. And it made us all need to eat more to keep up our strength. Our food supplies were definitely going to need to be supplemented by whatever game we could scare up as we traveled.

Kory and Chu were scraping a patch of ground clear for a place to set up our large tent, while the rest of us unhitched the horses and rubbed them down. While we worked, the wind was so strong it required us to shout just to be heard. We had circled the wagons as tightly as possible, but the gaps between them were still horse-sized, making it impossible to find a place out of the wind. I was just finishing up tying the horses to a line strung between two of the wagons when I realized how dark it was starting to become. I looked around the edge of the wagon and finally realized just how massive this storm was going to be. We were in trouble.

The clouds were blocking the evening sun, and instead of the normal dark gray of a regular snowstorm, this one was a blanket of black for as far as the eye could see. I could even see lightning in the roiling cloud bank. There was absolutely no way this was natural, especially this far south. Worse, we were out in the open, in a natural wind tunnel formed by the tall trees on either side of the almost arrow-straight roadway. I looked over and saw everyone else just as dumbfounded as I was at the size and intensity of the blizzard coming our way. I ran over to get everyone in motion.

"The tent isn't going to be enough to shelter us from this!" I was shouting so everyone could hear me over the wind. "We need to build something stronger!" I pointed at the horses and wagons. "The horses will freeze to death, and I don't know if the wagons will still be standing by the time this thing blows over!"

Kory nodded, waving his arms for everyone to get behind him. "I can raise a wall, but you will have to manage the roof! No one else has enough qi left in their cores to be of any help!" He put action to his words, doing his best to raise a wall of stone two feet thick that slowly rose in a perfect circle around the wagons. The horses weren't exactly happy about the rumbling of the ground, but Jamila and Valerie ran to calm them before they hurt themselves.

The wall was nearing six feet in height when Kory fell to one knee, his internal energy completely drained. Donny ran over to check on him, while Chu and I climbed up on the nearest wagon to look over the wall. Kory hadn't been able to raise them high enough to cover the tops of the wagons, but it was better than nothing. In the distance, we could see flashes of lightning striking the trees through the blizzard wall moving toward us. It almost looked like the world was being eaten by a wall of white, topped in a crown of angry black clouds.

"We are going to be buried alive as soon as you build that roof ! We'll suffocate before the storm ends!" Chu was right. Stone walls erected by qi were nearly air tight, and the blanket of snow coming our way would turn *nearly* air tight into *perfectly* air tight. "But if you don't build it, we'll die anyway! That is practically an avalanche coming towards us!" From what I could tell, it was pretty much exactly what was about to hit us. An avalanche with an extra helping of lightning on top. What in the stars was going on with the weather?

I hopped down from the wagon and moved to the center of our circle. Since my own cores were nearly drained, I tapped into the battery I hadn't used to help push me to the Meridian level. This was going to take a lot of qi.

First, I raised a thick pillar of stone twenty feet high in the middle of the ring Kory had created. Then, I pushed up the wall he had started another six feet, lifting it to the height of our covered wagons at twelve feet tall. Next, I grew branches of stone in imitation of a tree from the top of the pillar out to the wall. As soon as they were connected, it was easy to build out and thicken the cone-shaped roof. I made sure to create some narrow windows all the way around in imitation of arrow slits on a castle, and put an arched doorway wide enough to fit a single wagon on the same sides as the road traveled. A quick flex of metal qi formed thin double doors that swung inwards, and I made sure to include locking pins at the base that could be dropped in the ground. Now, when we left – and I would make *sure* we all left this place alive – there would be a useful and defensible structure for any travelers that took this route in the future.

My next act was to build a giant qi gathering formation right into the floor. It required me to raise a smooth layer of stone under our feet, which really pissed off the horses. Oh well. They would get over it. After creating the required pattern from memory, I formed another layer of stone right over the top of it. It ensured no one could copy my design, and prolong the life of the formation.

The final addition was something I copied from the mountain people of the Northern Province. Since they had heavy snows and cold weather all the time up in the higher elevations, they imbued the floors of their homes with a simple trick that took almost no qi to function. Instead of trying to warm the air, they put a small fire qi collection inscription inside hollow sections of flooring. The collected fire qi would warm the surrounding stone, keeping their feet nice and warm when they walked around their homes. It was especially useful for them, considering they needed time out of their heavy snow boots to keep from getting infections or fungus on their feet. Not exactly what we needed, but the idea would work.

Instead of the floor, I made small hollow spaces in the roof using concentric rings, and included the fire qi collection inscriptions. It would keep the snow from piling up so high that the weight collapsed the ceiling on us, and hopefully melt enough of it that we wouldn't get buried and suffocate.

After doing all of that, my qi battery was nearly empty. I would need to refill both batteries soon, especially now that I had a giant qi collection formation right under my feet. As I finished up, I was honestly expecting to see my friends looking at me with appreciation or gifting me with kind words. Instead, no one was paying any attention to me at all. They were crowded around the arrow slits, watching the blizzard get closer.

Not gonna lie here, I was a little miffed. I had just built everyone a fortification that wouldn't look out of place in some of the most dangerous regions of the empire, embedded one of the most powerful qi collection formations ever devised, and then figured out a way to keep us all from freezing to death, just for them to look at the weather? Why did I bother?

Instead of making a scene like my young body's hormones were trying to demand—the only thing *worse* than a teenager was actually having to *be* a teenager—I went to see what it looked like outside. I admit, I knew it was bad, but after seeing what was going on, I wasn't mad about them ignoring me anymore.

The storm was less than a mile away from us now, but that wasn't what kept everyone's attention. There was a wave of animals running in front of the wall of snow approaching, and the largest of them were using the roadway to help them run faster. They were trying to outrun the storm. If even the wildlife knew how abnormally dangerous and deadly this blizzard was, I had no doubt this weather was unnatural. I needed to figure out what was going on, and then stop it.

Not all of the animals running from the storm were built for speed, and we all watched as they were slowly overtaken by the vertical wall of white. It was as if they just disappeared, pulled from reality by an invading world that lacked all form of color. There was no way to know if the animals survived, but my gut told me there would be a noticeable drop in the amount of wildlife seen in the region next year.

In what felt like just an eyeblink, the mixed herd of creatures reached us. Even though the arrow slits were extremely narrow, they were still enough of an opening to let in the stink of fear the animals excreted. As the wave of beasts passed us by, some of them slammed into the walls. The obstruction of the building was too big for all of them to skirt around. The impacts of the larger animals made the walls shudder, and I felt my sphincter tighten when I thought about what would have happened to us if we had just set up our tent instead of building this stone shelter.

The bulk of the animals took less than a minute to run past us, with only a few stragglers trickling past. Kory, ever the realist, stuck his arm outside the arrow slit and used his ring to store the nearest corpses of the animals that didn't survive the impact with our wall. Or the trampling afterwards. Just as he pulled his arm back inside, the storm finally reached us.

It was insane. The impact was like getting hit with a meteor. My carefully constructed building of stone was almost cracked open like an egg. The central pillar cracked near the base, blasting out stone like a piece of glass being crushed by a hammer. Corresponding cracks formed all across the ceiling, causing a deluge of dust and bits of stone to rain down.

The only thing that saved us was the thickness of the stone pillar. Even though it had cracked at the base, it was still wide enough to stand and provide support to the roof. I had to pick myself up off the floor. It took me a minute, but I realized I couldn't hear anything. The explosive pressure change had blown out my eardrums. Now I knew what people felt like when I hit them with a popper.

The arrow slits had allowed sheets of snow to shoot into the room like solid vertical streamers. My mind was boggled by the amount of pressure required to do such a thing. Even in the worst winter storms, at the highest elevations of the northern mountain range, there was nothing like this. I had no doubt in my mind now, this was an attack. From whom, or what, I had no idea. But this blizzard *had* to have been manufactured in some way.

Everyone else was already up and walking around. Kory had taken the worst of it, so Valerie was using her healing pendant to get him back on his feet. Chu was healing the horses. It looked like they had gotten hit by a fair amount of stone shrapnel when the central pillar had cracked. Donny was inspecting the wagons, and Jamila was looking over the actual building. She had already started melting the snow that made it inside, her affinity to fire qi making it an easy job for her.

I tried to take a look outside, but when I opened one of the doors, I was faced with a solid wall of snow so dense it was practically ice. So, I guessed we would be staying inside for a bit.

And stay inside we did. For almost two weeks. Which, if you were wondering, was plenty long enough for six people and eight horses cramped in a tiny space to drive each other bonkers. I was pretty sure I saw Valerie's horse orchestrate an elaborate plan involving a bucket, two strategically placed bales of hay, and a strand of rope that culminated in an opportunity for the suspiciously intelligent animal to kick Donny halfway across the room. Not completely sure, but the look in its eye as Donny went airborne basically confirmed it, in my opinion.

There were also a few mistakes in the building design that I had created. It was missing any form of waste disposal, which was a problem considering we were in the same space as eight horses. And they made big poops. It was also missing a chimney, meaning using a fire to cook warm meals turned the whole thing into a smokehouse. Which had an even more detrimental effect to the smells created by all the horse dung. Also, big metal doors that are great for defense are not necessarily great for insulation from the cold. Meaning, the area around the two doors was *freezing* cold. Chu had tried to open a door a few days into our stay, but it had actually burned his hand as if he had stuck it in a fire when he touched it.

I would have fixed all of those issues, but the weight of the snow made it pretty much impossible at first. On top of that, the damage to the structure was so severe in some portions that I would have actually needed to deconstruct those sections before moving around or adding any stone features. With the extreme cold, that wasn't an option. And to make any kind of waste removal system, it would have required me to adjust the qi collection formation. Which wasn't something I was willing to do. So, we lived with the poop smell. I won't even mention how we dealt with the horse urine. Let's just say, 'don't eat the yellow snow' was always good advice.

The reason it took so long for us to leave wasn't because of the snow burying us. If we had stayed buried, we would have died due to lack of fresh air. My trick using pockets of fire qi in the roof had worked well enough to keep that from happening. No, what had kept us inside was the temperature. It was so cold that even Kory, with the constitution of a Saint-level cultivator, would suffer from frostbite after only a few hours outside. That meant the rest of us faced freezing to death in only minutes. On the positive side, the extreme temperatures meant the snow had stopped falling and the skies had cleared not long after the blizzard had swept past the area. It was too cold for the air to hold any kind of moisture, despite whoever or whatever had made this storm.

We all did our best to use the two weeks to our advantage. The qi collection formation I had embedded in the floor gave everyone the opportunity to work on their cultivation level and weapons training, while it gave me the chance to refill my qi batteries. I also set up dozens of the smaller qi-concentrating plates and used them to bottle *gallons* of liquid qi. I was hoping it would be the thing that allowed us to leave sooner rather than later.

Part of the reason why everyone was going crazy was because of me. Okay, most of it was because of me. To create something that allowed us to travel in the unexpectedly extreme cold temperatures, I had to use my traveling forge to smith some items. And in a small enclosed space like the stone hut we were in, that meant driving everyone crazy with the banging of a hammer and anvil. We tried setting up some formation plates that reduced the sounds, but it ended up throwing me off while I was trying to make something new. I hadn't realized it before, but the ringing sound metal makes when you hit it was important for a smith to hear. It can help him determine if there are any weak spots hiding in the design before they create a catastrophic failure. Like, say, shattering into hundreds of metal splinters when Chu was cooking nearby. That soup had been extra crunchy.

I felt bad about the whole thing. Really, we probably would have gotten along just fine if I didn't have to spend several hours a day working steel ingots into something new. But since I *did*, the weapons training had a sharper edge to it the longer we stayed cooped up inside.

"Ha! That will teach you to keep both hands on your weapon!" Jamila was dueling against Chu, and she had just kicked the shaft of his mace hard enough that it bounced off his chest with enough momentum to lay him out. "I told you I was too strong for you to hold it with just one hand, but *noooo*, you're too strong to listen to your girlfriend. More like too stupid!" She was sent flying by a hammer of metal qi that Chu threw with the hand not holding his mace.

"I needed the other hand free so I could form *that*! How do you like my new attack?!" Chu stumbled to his feet as he finished shouting, while Jamila rolled to her feet across from him inside the square of ropes we had demarcated for sparring. "I don't know, I might be too *stupid* to tell you this, but you need to pay attention to your opponent! Especially when you don't know if they are actually down!"

Kory jumped between them, holding out his hands to stop them. "Enough! Both of you, go to your corners. Think about what you did wrong, then cultivate for an hour. You still need to finish solidifying your gains." He dropped his arms as they walked away, neither looking back at one another. They would be boyfriend-girlfriend again by the end of the day, but for now they were too angry with one another to apologize. Kory waited for them to sit down before walking over to where I was working, letting out a sigh as he approached. "Please, tell me you finished that so we can finally get out of here."

"I think we should be ready to go by tomorrow morning. As soon as everyone has cultivated enough to refill their cores, I will go over how to use this and we can pack everything back up." I held up one of the hollow rods of steel I was assembling, the end caps finally screwing into place properly. "It took me a while, but I think this will work." Kory nodded, looking it over as I handed it to him.

"I sure hope so. This stay has been good for our cultivation levels, but awful for our temperaments. Any longer and we might kill each other." Kory was talking about the people, but I knew where the true threat of death was lurking. I looked over at the horses, noticing the shifty one staring at Donny as he and Valerie sat meditating with their eyes closed. I don't know what Donny did to piss that horse off, but it was definitely plotting something.

"You aren't wrong. But now that Donny is almost a Meridian-level cultivator, and the others just broke into the Heart level, we will be much more formidable as a team." The long period of time living in increased levels of qi, along with the guided assistance of Kory and myself, had allowed for explosive growth from the others. Kory had even increased his cultivation base, concentrating the level of his internal qi from vapor into fog. That meant he was now a Medium stage Saint cultivator. Everyone in my group would be considered a cultivation genius now. Their levels were much higher than they should be for their ages, and any sect would fall over themselves for the opportunity to recruit them into their ranks.

The average age for a Heart cultivator was mid-thirties, meaning the four currently meditating could stand up to people twenty years their senior. I was lucky to have them. I looked back at Kory.

"Your own increase in power means we shouldn't have any problems getting bullied when we reach the capital. Medium stage Saint cultivators aren't exactly rare, but you could easily get a job as a Captain of the Guard when we get there." Kory didn't exactly blush, but I could tell he was embarrassed.

"I couldn't let you catch up to me so soon. How am I

supposed to protect you, if you are the stronger cultivator?" His smile let me know he was only mostly kidding.

"Either way, I appreciate your dedication to self-improvement. Getting stronger is never easy." I held out my hand for the rod and he passed it back to me. "Just a few more tweaks and we will be ready to go."

Kory left and went to go work on the evening meal while I finished up. The device I had finally come up with to help us survive the cold was much simpler than what I had initially been trying to make. The more complicated items either weren't viable for long-term use, or too qi intensive for us to power alongside the snow-clearing formation plates. Instead, I went with an adaptation of the system I had installed in the roof. The biggest change was instead of collecting only fire qi from the environment, I went with a system of runes that could turn all of the elements into heat. The liquid qi I had stored would help make sure we always had enough energy to power the formations, which was why they were hollow rods. Just pour in the liquid qi, screw the cap back on, and it was ready to go. It wouldn't put out enough heat to keep us toasty warm, but it would keep us from freezing to death. And I could hang them on the horse's tack without burning anything.

We all sat together and ate as night fell, the cold making us group together to share the warmth of the stove. I explained how the foot-long rods functioned and handed them out to everyone. I made enough for each person to have two, plus four to hang on each horse. There was enough liquid qi to keep them going for several weeks, but I would set up qi collection plates every night to supplement our stores.

I laid out my bed roll between the horses and the stove. It also happened to be between Donny and the white horse that hated him. I wanted to make sure I was ready in case it went after him while we slept. The others might not have noticed it yet, but I had seen it carefully watching Donny the entire time we were eating. Sneaky thing had an evil gleam in its eye, so I needed to separate them.

As I laid down to sleep, all I could do was hope we could finally start making some progress toward the capital tomorrow. Every time we seemed to get moving in the right direction, something out there kept doing things to hinder us.

CHAPTER SEVENTEEN

Stopping the Snow

I was in the corner of a dark room, the only source of light coming from a massive clear crystal tube that was inset into an intricately carved stone table. Great. Another dream walk. I guessed the gods had decided I didn't need sleep tonight. Figured it would be right before we were supposed to leave. Great timing as usual.

Surrounding the table was a ring of cultivators that were meditating with their eyes closed. As I was trying to figure out what was going on, a door opened right next to me. In walked the Chancellor to the Southern King I had seen the last time I had dream walked. This time, his presence carried more weight, as if he had grown in power recently and hadn't had time to manage it yet. He had the hooded spy with him again, and they were both hunched over another of those long-distance communication squares.

"It hasn't moved for two weeks, my lord. They are either dead, or they no longer carry it with them." The spy was holding the device out far enough that I could see a map carved on its surface. There was a divot near the center, and I recognized it as the location of our camp.

"Are you certain?" The Chancellor's voice was deeper than normal as well, an entire octave lower than what I remembered. "They are proving to be more difficult an enemy than initially thought. I don't want to risk them interfering in my plans any longer."

"Yes, my lord. The other communication square hasn't moved since you ordered the storm dropped on their heads. Even now, I have a team focusing on the region." The spy indicated the men circled around the crystal. "Nothing could survive this long out in the open, and they only had wagons. There is nothing nearby to shelter them, and temperatures that cold could kill even the Saint cultivator traveling with them."

The Chancellor nodded. "Very good. Keep an eye on it, and don't let up the weather working. I don't care how exhausting it is to manipulate the crystal. Nothing can get in my way." He turned and walked out the door, leaving the spy in the room. I followed.

The Chancellor continued down a long hallway lined with iron-wrapped doors, his heels clicking on the stone floors. From the looks of things, we were probably in the basement of the castle on one of the levels just above the dungeons. I kept close behind him until he stopped at a door near the end of the hallway.

He unlocked the door and stepped inside, lighting a simple torch held in a sconce on the wall. It was a pretty average torture chamber, complete with tables of sharp metal implements and a brazier of hot coals warming a few choice tools. Pretty unoriginal, in my humble opinion. But I had been tortured by the best. This wasn't even close to the methods used by the Elemental Guards to train their people to withstand the most excruciating of punishments.

Chained to the back wall was the recruiter that had run off after the fight at the inn. He didn't look very good. His face was swollen, and one of his feet was facing the wrong direction.

Whoever had worked him over had started to do quite the thorough job.

"Good news!" The recruiter flinched awake at the loud voice of the Chancellor. "It seems as if your mission wasn't a total failure. It has cost me a fortune in elemental cores to power it, but the weather crystal was able to defeat the child you were too afraid to capture." The relief in the captive's eyes was palpable. He cleared his throat, trying to speak. The Chancellor walked over and tipped a cup of water from a nearby table up to his lips.

After taking a few sips, he finally spoke. "That is excellent news, my lord." His voice was raspy despite the water, and the fear he exuded when speaking to the Chancellor told me exactly who had done the torturing. "Does this mean you will release me, now that the boy is dead?" I watched as the Chancellor took a step back and picked up a sharp metal rod from the table.

"Release you? Of course!" He blurred forward, slamming the hunk of iron through the man's skull. "Now you are released from this life. Enjoy the mercy of not existing on this plane when it is subverted to the dark." The whites of his eyes flashed to black, and the light in the room dimmed. He seemed to twist in on himself, his skin writhing as if there were worms crawling under it. It was disgusting. He straightened back up, and then did something I had never expected. He started to talk to his shadow.

"Yes, once the bond is complete, we can do so much more!" He squinted, looking at the wall where his shadow was. "You promised me more power, and I demand you make good on your word before I do that." The shadow got darker somehow. This time, I could almost swear I heard something whispering from the darkness. "There is no going back from it. Once I set events in motion, there will be no recourse for me. I want to know you stand by your promises before I ostracize myself like that." He doubled over in pain, grabbing at his head. Blood poured out of his nose as if from a bucket.

"Stop! If you kill me, you will lose months of work. I am no fool, demon. I know my worth. Keep your word and all will be as you wish. I have already stopped the boy and staged the pieces of the plan. As soon as I have what I want, you finish getting what you want!" The blood slowed to a trickle, and he stumbled back against the hanging body of the recruiter. His shadow lightened back to normal. This time I was sure I heard something, even though I couldn't quite make it out. "Yes. Exactly. By this time next year, the tournament will bring the strongest fighters straight into your clutches. There will be plenty of hosts eager for power your brethren can bond with. Best of all, the king suspects nothing. After that, all the pieces on the board will be exactly where you desire." The Chancellor's face was pale from blood loss, but his smile was still bright.

It had to be a *nox*. That was the only thing that made sense. This one was different, though. It hadn't changed the man into some kind of deformed monster that I could see, like the man with too many teeth or the woman with extra finger joints. Instead, it was living in his shadow somehow. Or maybe that was just how he interacted with it. Were the *nox* intelligent enough to have a rank structure? If they were, then this one was some kind of leader amongst the dark mana demons. I was beginning to suspect it had manipulated others of its kind into my path in a concerted effort to kill me. Well, it would just have to try harder.

I watched as he walked out of the room and turned to the exit. Instead of following him, I went back to where the spy was working with the other cultivators around the table that held the massive crystal. I had seen devices that could manipulate the weather before, but nothing like what this table could apparently do.

The implications were massive. If the king of a province could control the weather, he could extend growing times, ensure that his favorite clans got the proper amount of rain, and even hurt the clans or sects that stood against him. The fact that the Southern Province had been known as the breadbasket of the empire for several generations now made much more sense. He was using this table to make his province rich.

My first instinct was to find some way to destroy it. If I was willing to sacrifice some of the memories of my first life, I could manipulate the real world while dream walking. This might be worth it. After thinking about it some, I realized that could have a terrible impact for billions of people if I outright destroyed the table. The economy of the entire empire was predicated on the Southern Province providing the majority of the food for everyone living in the large cities. Millions would starve to death if this weather manipulation device was made inoperable.

I took a closer look at the crystal. It was filled with engineered flaws that helped control the power fed to it by the table near the base, and a complex knot of designs too intricate for me to understand at the top. Probably the part that actually controlled the weather. In the middle, there was a set of six metal rings inset into a groove that could spin around the clear tube. That must be what they used to choose what type of weather went where. I crawled under the table to see what it looked like from underneath.

The grooves the rings were in corresponded with a simple set of sharp and precisely carved runes embedded within the actual crystal. It really was a masterful creation. Too bad I was going to have to mess it up. I could only think of a single solution that didn't involve risking the complete destruction of the entire device. Mess up the targeting runes. Or at least what I *hoped* were the targeting runes.

If I made the area of impact larger, it would make it impossible for them to precisely target any specific spot. The energy used to manipulate the weather would have to be spread out more, making it less extreme as well.

It would mean the king could only order broad swaths of his province to be impacted by whatever precipitation he wished to impart or withhold. I had no doubt his supporters were about to get angry that their special treatment wasn't so special anymore. But, in the long run, he would still be able to ensure his province continued to produce the same number of crops as they did before. Maybe even more, since he would have a harder time limiting the land owners he didn't want to support. I counted it a win-win situation.

Since I was already sitting under the table, I just crossed my legs and started meditating. I knew the trick to changing the real world was to manipulate the ambient qi in the area into mana, and then direct it where I wanted. I had only done it once before, and thinking about what memory might be washed away in the process was distracting me a bit. What if I lost something important? What did I even consider to be important? It didn't matter. I had to do this. If they ever got word of our location again, they might actually kill us. Not to mention this would even things out for so many within the province, since the king would no longer be able to harm certain land owners.

After what felt like hours—but was probably only thirty minutes—I finally formed a wisp of mana. Actually directing it inside the crystal to smudge the edges of the targeting runes was incredibly easy, as if the mana already knew my wishes. It only took a minute to finish 'fixing' the crystal, and I made my way out from under the table.

As I moved to take a closer look at just who exactly the spy was, I fell forward into a bright light. Ah, stars! Not *again*.

CHAPTER EIGHTEEN

The Long and Lonely Road

I woke up to Chu nudging me with his foot, a plate of breakfast ready in his hand. I took it from him, grateful for the food.

"Almost time to get out of here. Kory decided to wake you up last, to let you get some more sleep." I looked around, noticing that just about everything was loaded back on the wagons and a bucket of warm water was waiting by the area we had designated as the place to wash.

"Thanks. I did need the sleep. Give me a minute to get ready and wash up, then we can go."

Chu nodded and walked over to pack up the stove and cooking implements.

The first thing I did after eating was try to review my past to see if I had any noticeable blank spots in my memory. Nothing popped out at me right away, so I moved on. I was sure it would come back to bite me in the future. My next step was to pull out the steel plate I had taken off the dead recruiter. I hadn't bothered to inspect it yet, but after my dream I thought it prudent. You know, since the stars-damned thing had let them know exactly where we were.

I didn't see anything with the naked eye, but actually

touching it with my qi might set off an alarm or something. I felt like I might be able to get some insights into the organization trying to kill us if I could tap into the device, but it really wasn't worth the risk. Right now, they weren't even sure if we were alive or not. Alerting them to the fact we were still kicking around didn't seem wise. I spun out a thread of earth qi and made a thin divot in the ground, dropped the plate inside, and covered it back up. They wouldn't be getting that thing back. I hoped it was expensive.

After getting rid of our little spy, I washed up as best I could and helped hitch up the horses to the wagons. Luckily for Donny, Valerie handled her horse that was probably plotting his death even now. Everyone activated the warming rods, we got the doors open, and started on our way.

The days flew by as we traveled, most of them exactly the same. Wake up with the sun, collect the liquid qi that formed in the plates left out overnight, eat, travel until noon, stop to refill the warming rods and rest from powering the snow-clearing formation, eat, travel until the sun went down, set up camp, train, eat, meditate, sleep, and repeat. It wasn't actually as bad as it sounds, but it was pretty boring. Besides the occasional murder attempts by the horse that hated Donny. Some of those were hilarious. We all grew closer as friends, and everyone was progressively growing stronger. Our fighting ability as a group increased as well, which became very apparent around three months into our trip.

It just so happened that the first people we came across on the seldom-used road weren't interested in making friends. In fact, it was the opposite of that. The group of bandits sprung up around us as we were setting up camp one evening, their weapons already aimed in our direction. None of us were surprised, of course, as Valerie had spotted them following us several hours ago while on a scouting run. It had given us time to put on our armor under our furs, and we all made sure to keep our energy levels as close to maximum as possible. The leader of the bandits stepped forward, a spear held carelessly in his hands.

"It would be best for you to just lay down your weapons and keep your hands out to the side. We wouldn't want any of you to get hurt. Your things aren't worth your lives." He looked around at his men, about twenty or so, and pointedly looked back at the six of us. They were ragged-looking, with rusty weapons and dirty uncured furs layered on their bodies in a poor attempt to keep themselves warm. Apparently, business hadn't been good for these guys for quite some time. "You can see that fighting won't do you much good."

Kory stepped forward, his shield and spear appearing in his hands from his storage devices. "You said our things weren't worth our lives. Tell me, do you think our property is worth your own lives?" Kory flexed his Saint-rank aura and spun his spear around his head before slamming it butt-first into the snow in front of him. "As you can see, fighting won't do you much good." There was doubt on their faces now. None of them were higher than Meridian, meaning Kory might be able to handle all of them on his own.

"How about this. You just leave one of the wagons, and we part ways. No muss, no fuss, everybody wins." He stood up straight and spun his own spear in a mildly impressive display of skill. "Otherwise, somebody might get hurt." All of the bandits chuckled, their leader's little show giving them their courage back.

"Sorry, we need all our wagons. And you really don't want to do this." Kory shrugged his shoulders, dropping his furs so they could see his full set of armor. The rest of us pulled out our own weapons and let our furs fall to the ground. The uniform appearance of our matching black-on-red armor was certainly intimidating. There were already a few bandits trying to step back off the road and move toward the cover of the forest, where their small number of archers were standing. The bandit leader saw it too.

"Men! Some fancy armor isn't enough to stop us, it's time to

—*urk!*" The rallying cry was cut off by an arrow from Valerie's bow. It struck the man high in his chest near the base of his throat. The impact caused him to stumble backward and fall to one knee. We used the moment where they were all frozen in surprise to launch our own attacks.

Chu leaped for the wood line, his goal to reach the enemy archers scrambling to nock arrows to their bows. Donny and Jamila sprinted to the sides as they threw out qi attacks, each of them taking position to protect the wagons. I ran to protect the rear, and Valerie stayed in the middle so she could support each of us. With Kory still in the front, we made a diamond shape around the horses and wagons, Valerie in the center and Chu off on his own near the end where Kory was standing.

The bandits rushed us, a surprising amount of them choosing to attack me. I had eight of them in my face just as I reached my position, their weapons stabbing at me in an undisciplined manner that was far more dangerous than a concentrated offense. There was no pattern to their attacks, forcing me to fall back. I was using a plain round shield and a short spear from the stores in my belt, the combination giving me good reach and stout defense.

I didn't have time to see how the others were doing, but from the sounds of things, the fight was more fun for them than dangerous. Chu, especially, seemed to be having a good time. His laughter was echoing around the battle, and the screams of his opponents made the sounds of battle even more chaotic.

I was also enjoying the fight. The mix of spears and swords stabbing at me in an arc was exhilarating, forcing me to use more of my purely physical combat skills than I had utilized in a long time. Some of the bandits attacking me finally started to flank farther behind, meaning I couldn't see all of them at once. I spun out two threads of metal qi from the meridian at the base of my neck and grabbed two of the throwing knives from the back of my vest. Not bothering to slow time to aim, I whipped the knives into the uncovered faces of the two bandits circling to my right. Now there were six.

The sudden death of two of their companions made them pause. Then, the arrow from Valerie's bow thudding into a sword-wielder's thigh broke their concentration. As he fell to the ground screaming, I stabbed out with my spear and used the edge of the leaf-bladed spear point to slice the side of a spear-wielder's neck. The ensuing spray of blood from such an important artery was impressively pressurized, hosing down the two men closest to the spear-wielder. Now there were four.

I took a quick look to see how everyone was doing, and saw that I was the only one who still had multiple opponents. The only bandits still fighting were their version of elites, meaning they had the fullest sets of armor, and weapons with less rust than the others. None of my friends seemed to be struggling in the least, our long months of training making their breathing even and controlled. The bandits were huffing and puffing, their attacks coming in slower and with less frequency.

I turned back just in time to block a sword hacking down at me with my shield. My distraction had allowed the bandits I faced to regroup and better coordinate their attacks. I had to use my spear shaft to deflect another spear headed for my guts, pushing it into the path of the third man swinging for my side. The fourth man had almost made it all the way around me, so I had nothing to block his spear thrust into my back. Except for my two metal qi threads I hadn't reabsorbed yet.

The two threads wrapped around the spear shaft right behind the blade and redirected it right into the chest of the swordsman banging away at my shield. He looked from the spearhead piercing his chest to the man still holding the end of the spear, disbelief on his face as he fell. I snatched the sword out of his suddenly limp hand with the qi threads and used it to stab the man behind me in the groin hard enough to lift him off the ground a few inches. Stars, that must have been *very* uncomfortable. Not that a stab wound was ever really comfortable, come to think of it. Now there were two.

The final pair took several steps back, one of them with a sword and the other with a spear. It looked like the one with a sword was about to talk, but I didn't give him a chance. I threw my spear at him hard enough that his attempt to deflect it just drove his own sword back into his face as it took him off his feet. The last man turned to run, but an arrow appeared between his shoulder blades. And then there were none.

Looking around, there wasn't anyone still fighting. Chu had returned and was walking around crushing the skulls of any bandits still alive. It was brutal, but we couldn't exactly take prisoners on the trail with us.

Not a single person from our side had so much as taken a wound. The victory was absolute. The fact that three of our number were still just Heart cultivators that had defeated a group of mostly Meridian cultivators didn't escape me. Our combat power was much more than it should have been. I couldn't help but feel a sense of pride at the accomplishment.

It took us almost an hour to loot the bodies and bury them in a snow drift on the side of the road. We didn't find anything worth much, but I could always melt their weapons down and make something else. After looking around at the torn-up ground and blood spilled in the snow, I thought maybe it was a good thing that we had been alone for so long.

CHAPTER NINETEEN

Building an Empire

The next morning we left early, eating a cold meal on the road. We kept moving for the next two months without seeing another living soul. According to Kory's map, we should have passed several small villages by now. Instead, all we saw were empty and run-down buildings slowly being reabsorbed by the forest. It gave us plenty of opportunity to train more, and everyone had things to work on.

Our cultivation levels were steadily rising as well. The constant need to power the snow-clearing formation meant that everyone was regularly filling and emptying their cores multiple times a day, providing their cultivation systems with a heavy workout that was beyond any normal training program. We were steadily growing into a team strong enough to fight far above our weight class. I had a feeling we would need every advantage possible when we finally reached the capital.

It was just past the sixth month mark when we finally came across a populated village. They had built the village around the road, with a ten-foot wall surrounding it. There was a thick wooden gate blocking our path, and from the snow piled against it, we could tell it hadn't been opened in a while. We sat for a few minutes waiting for a guard to challenge us, but no one came. Kory jumped down from his place beside me and used a quick fireball construct to clear the snow in his way. He pounded on the gate with his fist, the sound made by the hard thuds echoing through the trees surrounding the village. There was still a long wait before anyone peeked their head over the wall.

A young boy, no older than ten, popped his head up. His face was a comical display of surprise. The perfect 'O' his mouth made as he saw us had Kory chuckling.

"Boy! What say you to finding some people to open this gate for us?" Kory flipped up a copper coin at the boy in an attempt to motivate him. It just bounced off his forehead. Apparently, they hadn't seen someone come down the road for a long time. Fortunately, a helmeted head appeared next to the stunned child.

"Stars above, it's true! Open the gates! A wagon train has come through!" There were shouts of surprise from somewhere behind the wall, but eventually the gates slowly creaked open. We rolled the wagons through the opening to a crowd of villagers waiting on the other side. They were a solid mix of ages, which usually was a sign of a prosperous community. Their worn clothing and dirty faces told a different story, one of a group that had fallen on hard times. Chu, never one to forget his goal of starting a merchant empire, stood on his seat to address the people gawking at us.

"Good people! We have many products for sale, from weapons and armor to food and furs. Let us get settled in your best inn, and then we would be happy to start trading." Chu was smiling ear to ear. I had no doubt he was ecstatic about finally having the chance to make some coin. Looking at the people of the village, I wasn't sure how much coin they might have to spare.

An old woman, hunched by age, stepped forward to speak for the villagers. "It has been over a year since we have seen travelers along the road. The inn will have to be opened, and rooms prepared." She pointed toward a makeshift town square lining a section of road a few dozen yards farther down. "If you park your wagons along the side, we can have some people take your horses to our stables."

We still had plenty of time left in the day for Chu to work, so we moved to line one side of the road and allowed the villagers to look over our wares. The two wagons purchased by Chu had sides that could drop down to show off our goods, and Kory helped me set up a folding table so I could lay out some of the armor and weapons I had made.

The villagers didn't exactly swarm us, but it was close. They weren't kidding when they said there hadn't been many traders in a long time. The majority of our sales were rare foods, spices, and clothing. I sold several knives and a few spears, but there wasn't much of a market for the things I was peddling. I didn't mind. I wasn't out to make coin. Helping Chu make a name for himself as a merchant was much more important.

We spent the night in a dusty and rundown inn. We didn't mind. The chance to sleep on a real bed, no matter how lumpy, was worth every overpriced silver.

And that was how it went for the rest of the winter-year. After that first village, we ran into another small community at least once a week. The memories from my first life sometimes put me in a melancholy mood during our visits. I knew that when Ming became the emperor, he would force all these people to move into the major cities and industrial farms around the province. For the most part, these villagers enjoyed living on the fringes of civilization, living their lives the way they wished. Ming didn't care what his people wanted. He needed workers to till the soil, man his factories, and fill his armies. Most of these people, or their children, would be little more than slaves, struggling to scrape out a living in the slums. I would do my best to make sure that didn't happen this time around.

The frequent interactions allowed Chu to make deals and

set up plans for future merchant trains to travel the forgotten road. They also slowed us down a fair bit, but all of us were happy to see Chu fulfilling his dream of expanding his family's business.

CHAPTER TWENTY

The Capital

It was six months after my twelfth birthday when we finally got to the capital, one month past the halfway point into the spring-year. Our fighting capabilities and cultivation levels steadily increased the whole time, and the occasional battle with bandits and beasts had helped keep us sharp.

I had also begun to make headway with the language I had found in the dark temple. Their writing didn't use letters like ours. It was a mix of hieroglyphs and symbols meant to convey the actual motion of the mouth and tongue to make the sounds you were supposed to speak. I think. Those people had been bug-nuts-crazy anyway, so I wasn't surprised at how weird their language was turning out to be.

At least it had given me the opportunity to work on my light and dark qi manipulation. Keeping the balance of the two energies in my body was a difficult process, but I managed it with some minor trial and error. I had even begun to notice some odd changes in my body the more I used them. The brighter the sun, the more energized I felt. And when it was dark, it seemed as if I could see into the shadows more clearly. Time would tell what other advantages it might bring.

A journey that normally took two years only took us eighteen months to complete, even with the extra time we spent helping Chu build his trading empire. Not having to cross through swamplands, crowded cities, and narrow bridges meant we could keep a consistent pace the entire journey. It also gave the white horse that hated Donny plenty of opportunities to show his dislike for the poor man.

The only repair job on our armor I had to make the entire trip was after the horse kicked Donny in the back of the head hard enough to crack his helmet. That kick also made Donny speak with a lisp for almost a month before Valerie relented and used her healing medallion on him. I still hadn't figured out what Donny had done to make the horse hate him so much, but there was no doubt in my mind that it was only biding its time until the horse found the opportune moment to kill him.

Entering the city required us to wait in a long line of wagons waiting for inspection. There was an entire economy built around the waiting merchants. Throngs of people walked up and down the line, selling food, drinks, trinkets, and maps of the city. We bought plenty of everything, spreading our coin around and asking questions about what was happening in the capital.

I knew from my last time dream walking the Chancellor had mentioned some type of tournament intended to draw in powerful hosts for more *nox*. But from what I was hearing from the locals, the tournament had run into a few snags.

"Yessir, the king's been real mad at his council." An older man dressed in dirty brown robes I had just bought a jug of ale from was happy to tell me the latest gossip. "They musta' done somethin' real bad, since nothin' been done 'cept him sendin' out for th' best crafters this side o' the Imperial City. Th' tournament was put on hold fer the longest, but since all th' folk waitin' to fight been stirrin' up trouble, th' king set it fer next week." I thanked the man for the information and tossed him an extra copper for his troubles. I guessed my 'adjustments' to the weather table had upset the power structure. The thought put a smile on my face. I regrouped with the others around our wagons to see what information they had been able to drum up.

"I heard the king hasn't been seeing any of his supporters recently." Donny was the first to speak up. "Apparently, they have had a falling out. The clans and sects supporting him are all mad about something."

Valerie nodded, swallowing a mouthful of steamed bun before talking. "Mmm, so good! Yeah, I heard they were mad about losing their monopoly on some of the produce markets. Not sure how that is the king's fault, but they blame him for it anyway." She brushed her hands off on her pants. "Anybody else find out anything good?"

"There has been a lot of trouble in the city recently." Kory was fiddling with a blacksmith puzzle as he talked. Probably a trinket from a child he couldn't say no to buying something from. "A bunch of fighting groups, clans, and sects came a few months back to take part in some competition, but it was postponed by the king." He now had a finger stuck in the puzzle. "Gah, cursed thing! Anyway, things have just started to calm down a bit after they announced the competition will start soon."

Chu jumped in with what he had heard before Kory could continue. "Yeah, and I heard the prizes were pretty good too!" He was drinking wine from a crystal goblet, of all things. Where did they find this stuff? And, better question, why hadn't I seen the wine-in-a-crystal-goblet street peddler? "The top three teams even get a private cultivation lesson from the king!"

Jamila stole his glass and took a drink before handing Chu back an empty glass. "It sounds to me like we need to win this competition." Chu was looking at her with a hurt feeling on his face, but she ignored him. "I can't think of a faster way to manage a meeting with the king, and none of us wants to be here longer than necessary." I nodded at Jamila's idea. I was thinking the same, I just hadn't gotten the chance to say it yet.

"Okay guys, I think we need to split up." They all leaned forward a bit, making it easier for them to hear me over the shouting hawkers walking by. "I will find a place where we can sign up for the tournament. Kory, Donny, and Valerie will get us a place to stay. If you can, try to rent a house with a large enough set of stables to hold our wagons and horses. In case you can't, since there are so many groups here for the tournament, get us a few sets of rooms at the Dancing Dame." I pulled out a map of the city I had bought from one of the hawkers. It was an inn I had frequented in my first life nearly every time I stayed in the Southern Provincial Capital. They were very good at keeping their patrons safe at night, and I knew they would exist already. I had known the original proprietor's grandson. It was probably a new establishment right now, but I had faith it was already worth the coin to stay there. "It's here, near the market district."

"And what about us?" Chu was looking over the map, but Jamila was waiting for my answer to her question. Kory had now managed to get a finger from each hand stuck in the puzzle, and wasn't paying any attention to us.

"You two will need to deposit all of the money we made from the trip with The Auction House. I don't think it is a good idea to walk around the city with a storage ring full of coin." I pointed at one of the smaller branch facilities of The Auction House near the gate we were waiting to enter. "This is your best bet. The main building will have long lines, but this one is small enough that your wait time should be short. You can also pay them some gold to send a message back to our families and let them know we made it safely to the city. After you finish, we'll meet back up in the market square closest to the gate." Everyone agreed to the plan, and we mounted back up on our wagons to wait our turn. Except for Kory. He took a good ten minutes to get his fingers free, finally managing it after an impressive full-body shake that might have been misconstrued as a provocative dance if any snakes had been present. I had to explain the plan to him a second time, the whole incident making it difficult for him to keep the details straight.

While we were sitting there, I took some time to shift around my items again. The storage ring that had held the fodder for the horses was practically empty now, so I moved a few spears, a regular bow with a quiver of arrows, two daggers, and a shield into it. I also put in the gallons and gallons of liquid qi I had kept gathering every night, along with the heating rods we no longer needed. Then I took my coin purse off my belt and put it in the ring too. Any major city would be thick with thieves and street urchins trying to steal it, so I decided to just remove any temptation they might have. I only had a few silvers and coppers in the pouch, but better to be safe than sorry.

My three storage studs from my belt that were visible to anyone looking for extra dimensional storage items were almost empty after our trip. I had used up all the wagon-repair kits long ago, and the remaining food and camping supplies could stay. I wanted to make sure there were no outward signs for the guards to notice that we weren't just the simple traders we claimed to be. All of my storage items should easily receive a pass.

Our wagons were much lighter now too, hopefully projecting to everyone that we were *successful* traders. And really, we had been. Even I had sold most of my goods along the trail, and Chu had completely run out of items almost a month ago. He had used the meat, skins, and cores from the animals we had killed along the trail to fill his wagons with something to sell. I didn't ask Chu how much he had made on our little adventure, but it had to be a lot of money. If we could repeat the same success on our trip to the Western Provincial Capital, he could probably become the richest member of the Roh Clan since it was founded.

As we approached, I got a good look at the city by the light of the sunset. The curtain wall was well over fifty feet high, and nearly as thick. It stretched the full length of the city, which took up nearly twenty square miles. It was the third largest city in the entire empire, but by far the most populous. The gates were solid iron, the red streaks of rust giving the thirty-foot doors a menacing look, like blood had already been spilled on their surface. During the summer-year beast waves, they would be. The buildings beyond were all two stories, the bottom floor being stone and the top floor constructed of wood. It gave the city a uniform appearance, but I knew it was really a security measure in the event of an invasion. Something about making sure the ballistae on the interior walls not having to worry about hitting a building when shooting at enemies on the opposite side of the outer wall.

The inner wall in the far distance marked a drastic change in architecture. I thought I could faintly see the tops of palaces, giant pagodas, and the gilded peaks of temples peeking over the top of the eighty-foot walls. No one had ever breached the inner wall of the city since it was founded, and one look would tell you why. While the outer wall was a simple physical barrier, the inner wall was covered in arrow slits, murder holes, and prepared defensive and offensive formations. It was topped by catapults, ballistae, and massive trebuchets that looked brand new and ready to fire. Anyone wanting to take the city by force would have to be prepared to pay for it in blood.

It was just past sundown when we finally made it to the front of the line. The city was busy enough that I knew most places were open for twenty-four hours, but I was still happy we wouldn't have to spend the night looking out for thieves trying to run off with our stuff in the middle of the night while we were outside the wall. Now, we just had to worry about the same thing while inside the wall. The guards approached Kory, as he was the oldest and strongest of our party.

"Name and purpose of visit." The speaker wore sergeant's stripes on the sleeves of his uniform, and a blind man could see he was bored half to death. I looked over the guards and I was more disturbed than impressed. They all wore steel breastplates over chainmail with the blue tabards signifying the city guard, but there was rust in the mail and no signs of calluses on their hands. From my memories of the Southern Provincial Capital in the future, the guards had been a professional, well-trained unit that took pride in their appearance. This was far from that standard. Kory's answer brought me out of my musings.

"We are merchants from the Roh Clan, interested in testing our mettle in the tournament."

The guard raised an eyebrow. "Roh Clan? Never heard of you. Fee for merchants is five gold per wagon. No selling goods in the inner city without a permit. Open markets in the outer city are first-come, first-serve. If you cause problems in the city, your clan or sect will be fined ten gold per person involved. Any questions?" We all shook our heads, and he collected his ridiculously high fee from Chu. As we rolled past, I heard him ask the same question to the next wagon in line.

Kory and I rode in silence as we slowly worked our way through the crowds and deeper into the city. Despite the late hour, the streets were still packed with people. We were looking for a good spot to park the wagons so we could split up, but neither of us were seeing a likely location. After turning down a side street that didn't have as much traffic, we just decided to split up from there.

"Everyone knows where to go?!" Kory had to shout to be heard over the noise filtering in from the main street. All of us nodded, and Donny got off his seat to take the reins of Chu and Jamila's wagon. Chu, Jamila, and I watched them rumble away down the road before we went our different ways. I noticed a few people looking our way as we split up, but I figured it had to be our matching sets of armor. We looked like a small band of mercenaries instead of members of a sect or clan because we lacked a symbol on our armor. It was an oversight I would have to fix later.

I walked toward an area I knew held some municipal offices of the city. It was my best bet to find a place to sign us up for the tournament. I felt eyes on my back as I rounded the corner of a smaller two-wagon street. Now who might this be? More than six centuries of fighting had given me a sharp sense of impending violence, and that inner alarm was ringing with a vengeance.

I picked up my pace, darting around rumbling wagons and zig-zagging around groups of people. The feeling of menace never left. I couldn't shake the feeling that the person following me *had* to know who I was. A random thief wouldn't have this much anger toward a mark.

Not being able to lose my pursuer, I decided it would be best to pick the place I wanted to fight. I took a cross street, deciding to work my way back toward the outer wall of the city. There was probably an abandoned or empty building somewhere that I could use to set up a counter-ambush.

It took longer than I would have liked, but I eventually found a building that looked as if it had recently suffered from a fire. The entire front of the house was charred, and as I ducked inside my nose was assaulted by the smell of woodsmoke. This place had probably burned less than a week ago.

As soon as I went through the empty doorway I went to the right, dropping a formation plate that would slap the next person through the door with an air qi construct. And when I say slap, I mean *slap*. It was a personalized version of the trap plates the Elemental Guard used to train their members on methods of disarming enemy traps, but I didn't go with their boring sphere shape that bludgeoned trainees that made a mistake. The construct was shaped exactly like a giant hand, and it was designed to smack someone hard enough that they wouldn't be getting up quickly after triggering it. I had chosen the trap because I didn't want to kill the person following me right away. There were a few questions I wanted to ask before they had their meeting with the afterlife.

It only took a few minutes for my stalker to peek their head inside, the pitch-black interior of the building making it impossible for them to see inside. The only light that managed to come in was what trickled through the open doorway and soot-covered windows. The bright moonlight and occasional street lamp were just enough to ruin someone's night vision as they came in from outside. My own increasingly sharp vision from using more dark qi would give me an edge. The silhouette of my follower finally stepped into the room far enough to set off the trap, but not far enough for it to work as intended.

Instead of slapping the person across their whole body, it only caught them from the shoulders up. The impact took them off their feet and stuck their entire body into the opposite wall. Do you have any idea how utterly hilarious it is to see a person get turned into a lawn dart? I had to take a moment to collect myself. If this person had been a real threat, the trap I used would have been an inconvenience that gave me enough time to bring more force to bear.

Luckily, that wasn't necessary. I thought at first the impact with the charred interior wall had killed my stalker. The groan of pain they made before trying to extract themselves from the burnt wood dispelled those fears. Well, not fears. More like mild concerns.

"It isn't safe to follow strange people in the dead of night. Bad things might happen to you." They finally popped free of the wall, falling on their back. I was pretty sure their left shoulder was either dislocated or broken. I nudged them hard with my foot. Going by the short scream of pain, I was right. "Who are you, and why are you following me?" It was still too dark to see the stalker clearly, even with my increased night vision, but I was able to detect the sense of anticipation that made them suddenly hold still. Someone was behind me.

I dove over the prone form lying on the ground, rolling to my feet and spinning around to face whoever, or whatever, was trying to sneak up behind me. Looking at where I had stood, the floorboards were steaming as some form of acid ate away at them. The short and portly figure that filled the doorway was familiar, and I finally understood how someone so weak had been able to put out such a powerful sense of malice. We had a blood connection.

"I knew it was you, boy! Xiao said you looked too old to be the useless son of my worthless brother, but I knew it was you. As soon as I saw you riding that wagon past my shop, I realized the gods had given me a chance for vengeance!" It was my

Uncle Hu, and the person rolling around on the ground must have been my cousin Xiao. The two of them had been the bane of my existence through my first life, but in this one they were little more than an annoyance.

Hu and Xiao had taken the losing side of the attempted coup by Councilman Yisi. Instead of facing capture and punishment, they had absconded with a sizable chunk of the Roh Clan treasury and disappeared from the region before anyone had a chance to track them down.

"I can't explain to you how happy I am to see you, Uncle Hu. And you too, Cousin Xiao. We have so much to talk about!" I accentuated my point by pulling out one of the spears from my ring and stabbing it into Xiao's foot, pinning him to the floor. His scream of pain was like music to my ears.

Hu shouted in rage at the wound I gave Xiao, his bulky form rushing toward me at surprisingly high speeds. Despite his corpulent form, he was still a Peak Brain-level cultivator. His level of strength wasn't what truly made him dangerous though. Hu was an alchemist, and they were always dangerous to fight. They had a habit of using nasty and rare potions and powders that poisoned, burned, disoriented, and blinded their opponents. As soon as I had the opportunity, I planned on making several versions of things like that myself.

His first attack came in like a lightning bolt, a simple uppercut aimed at my solar plexus. I didn't have time to activate the shield form of my spirit wood ring, so I took the hit on my crossed arms. The impact lifted me off the ground, my smaller mass putting me at a disadvantage in a brawl like this was shaping up to be.

I was lucky I had chosen to use my arms. The chitin strips on the leather wraps that served as my bracers were shooting out sparks of energy, meaning his fist was empowered with some type of qi attack. Based on the location of his strike, he had been trying to rupture my lower core. My lovely Uncle had gone straight to maiming me, reinforcing the fact that his hatred was not an act. Fine. Two could play at that game.

He was reaching for a pouch with his other hand, so I spun the qi in my brain core hard enough to almost stop my perception of time. It gave me the chance to loop a thin thread of braided qi around his left wrist. Checkmate, asshole.

I knew that my Uncle was taught how to strengthen his body by my grandfather exactly how my father had been, meaning it was comprehensive and efficiently done. A simple, single thread of fire or metal qi wouldn't be enough to cut through his reinforced skin and bones. The thing his body lacked was the secret weapon my reincarnation had given me. He was missing dark and light qi.

My perception of time returned to normal. I tightened the braided thread that included all eight forms of qi as he pulled his hand free of his pouch. He was holding a long, thin vial of some pink fluid I didn't recognize right away. His hand continued to clench tightly around the vial as it was separated from his body. Blood shot out of his newly shortened arm, and he stared at it with a dumbfounded look on his face. His eyes rolled back in his head as he passed out a moment later. Apparently, the shock of losing a limb was too much for his tiny brain to handle.

Ignoring him, I turned back to my dear cousin. He was trying to free his impaled foot, but every time he jostled the spear point piercing his body he whimpered in pain. My dear Uncle Hu had clearly not been teaching his son any proper techniques in strengthening his body. Big surprise, I know. I knelt down in front of him, and he tried to scoot back as far as he could. Which, considering the spear nailing him to the floor, wasn't far.

"Xiao. Before this goes any further, I just want to know something. Why did you always go out of your way to hurt me? I never did anything to you, or to your father. Your hatred for me makes no sense." It was a genuine question. I really had no idea why he and his father hated me so much.

"Because you were weak, and I am strong!" I snorted, but he didn't acknowledge my disbelief. "It is the right of the strong to rule over those weaker than themselves. I have only done what I should have. The fact that you didn't know that already only shows how right I am!"

Wow. I didn't even know where to go with that. This guy was one copper short of a full coin purse. There was just no reasoning with crazy. Or those this willfully stupid. And it reinforced my opinion that an aspect of what was wrong with this world was how people viewed strength over ability. I needed to see about fixing it somehow. Well, after I figured out the *nox* problem, of course.

"I have some questions before you die. Primarily, where did you hide the gold you stole, and what have you been up to since you ran like the coward you truly are?" He flinched as his eyes met mine. He knew I saw his fear, which must have made him mad.

"I won't tell you anything! I don't know how you got this strong, but I'm not afraid of your stupid tricks! I know I am truly the strongest scion of our family!" His comments brought a smile to my face. Based on his reaction, it might have been somewhat sinister. Probably the lighting.

"Xiao, you know I took first place in the Roh Clan ranking tournament held a while back, right?" He didn't answer me. "Well, I did. And one of the things I left the vault with was this neat little ring made of spirit wood." I held up my left hand to show it off. "It has several forms someone set in its qi matrix, some more useful than others." I flashed it through the many shapes it could take, starting with the shield, then the walking stick, spear, stake, knuckle dusters, and finally the spoon. His eyes had gotten wider the more dangerous-looking the forms it took were, but he seemed confused by the spoon. "Until now, I really hadn't seen the point of the spoon. But your refusal to answer has given me a great idea. I should probably thank you for the inspiration." The dozen or so strands of qi that I spun from the meridians in my feet quickly wrapped him up so he couldn't move. I plucked free my spear, putting it back inside the storage ring on my right hand.

"What are you going to do with that thing?" I leaned over him, putting my knee in the center of his chest as he tried to worm away. I brought the spoon close to his face, hovering it over his left eye. "What are you doing? Get away from me. No, not that. No! *Noooo!*" His scream went really high pitched as I used the spoon to pop his eyeball out of his head.

Surprisingly, it was an almost bloodless procedure that the spoon seemed perfectly shaped to perform. Was it actually *meant* for this specific use? What kind of person actually made this ring? After hearing Xiao's shrieks of pain for a few seconds, I realized it was probably a person very similar to *me*.

Xiao eventually calmed down enough to answer all my questions after I started to reach for his other eye. It was pretty amazing how quickly you could get over a serious injury when properly motivated to do so. Which was why I shouldn't have been surprised when I heard the sound of glass crunching behind me.

Uncle Hu had woken up. He must have seen it would be impossible to hit me with some nasty concoction without risking his son, so he had opted for smashing a vial that quickly filled the room with thick smoke. It wasn't poisonous, but it did have something in it that made my eyes water and caused me to cough uncontrollably. Normally something like that wouldn't have kept me from just finishing them both off, but the sound of boots stomping and armor clanking in unison told me the girlish screams of Xiao had finally drawn the city guard to our location.

The coughing and hacking had made me lose concentration enough that Xiao, who was still under my knee, managed to get an arm free. He grabbed at me, but I rolled off of him as I felt a strike from Hu coming in from the side. The mix of smoke and tears killed my ability to see clearly beyond a few feet, but I had still sensed his qi-empowered fist swing for my head.

The guards outside must have sensed it too, because they came storming through the door ready for a fight. I turned and ran, headed for a staircase at the back of the building. I didn't want to deal with being arrested, and it sounded like there were enough of them outside that a fight would be a protracted affair. As I reached the top step of the rickety and charred staircase, I heard them subduing my uncle and cousin. The coughing made communication impossible inside the house, and it gave me enough time to make a clean getaway as I jumped out of a second story window onto a neighboring roof. Stars, but I loved this ring of flight.

While they were trying to find out what was going on, and figure out how to stop the continuously billowing clouds of irritating smoke, I ran as fast as my flight ring and qi threads could help me go.

After a long sprint that took me almost all the way back to the main gate, I started my search. Xiao had told me where his father had opened a small alchemy shop, and I was interested in what was buried under the floorboards. They had managed to run off with a *lot* of wealth, and I felt it necessary for them to compensate me for all the pain and suffering they had put me through over the years. Also, I didn't like them, and stealing all their money made me happy.

It was easy to bypass the lousy wards they had securing the place, and within ten minutes of finding their shop I was once again a man troubled with too much money to comfortably be walking around with. I also stole everything that wasn't nailed down. Well, that was a lie. Anything I couldn't pry loose would be a more accurate description. When they finally got free of the guards, they would return to an empty building.

I didn't *need* to take everything, but the mental image of Xiao finding I had even taken his stars-damned *bed frame* made me actually laugh out loud. Oh, and Hu? I took all his supplies and equipment, which would be difficult to replace. The only thing I didn't get was the cauldron from the Roh Vault I had 'given' him a while back. He must have had it on him somewhere. Oh well. I got something even better. The real thing that would hurt him was the stacks and notebooks filled with his personal recipes, notes, and observations about alchemy. It was probably fifty *years'* worth of work, and I took every last scrap of it. Vicious? Yes. Did I care? Nope. They should both feel lucky that they left our confrontation with their heads still attached to their bodies.

I would need to deposit most of the money and jewels in my account at The Auction House, but for now meeting up with my friends was the priority. They might even be looking for me, considering how late I was for the meeting. And I would have to explain to them that I hadn't even completed my task. We would just have to go as a group tomorrow and sign up for the tournament together. Probably for the best. If we were all there as a team, it should make it less likely for us to get into trouble.

CHAPTER TWENTY-ONE

We Get in Trouble

I made it to the square just as my friends were about to go looking for me. If the marketplace hadn't been almost empty, I might have missed them as they started to walk down a side street. Thankfully, they had just enough patience to avoid a drawn-out search for me across the city.

"What took you so long?" Donny's face showed genuine concern as I ran up to the group. "We were getting worried something had happened to you."

"Sorry guys, but I ran into some old friends that demanded to speak with me." Everyone looked at me with puzzled expressions. "You aren't going to believe this, but I found those traitors, Hu and Xiao." There were mixed shouts of surprise, so I quickly described what had happened.

"Oh, karma can be vicious when she wants to be." Donny, who was the son of my Uncle Don, had also dealt with Hu and Xiao his entire life. "Losing all of their stuff ? Couldn't have happened to better people." His grin stretched from ear to ear. I was glad I could make him smile.

"The bad news is, I wasn't able to get us signed up for the tournament yet. We will have to do it tomorrow." No one seemed bothered by it, which meant they had probably finished their jobs with no problems. "I take it that the rest of you managed everything okay?"

Kory was the first to speak. "We weren't able to find an available house to rent, so we rented rooms at the inn you told us about. Not sure how you knew about it, but it seems like a solid choice." Kory and the others had stopped questioning the things I could do long ago, but occasionally my knowledge still surprised them.

"Jamila and I deposited the majority of our gold, and we made sure to send messages to everybody's families." Chu gave me a questioning look. "What are you going to do with all the stuff you took from Hu?"

"I'll drop off the money at The Auction House and sell what I can from their stuff tomorrow. In fact, I can use my connection with The Auction House to find out where we need to go to sign up for the tournament. It should save us some time." Everyone agreed, so we made our way to the inn.

We all slept late into the morning. Since we hadn't actually made it to bed until well after midnight, it wasn't much of a surprise to anyone. I took my time eating in the common room while waiting for my turn to take a bath. None of us had been able to really get clean in months, and I was the only one without a massive pile of dirty laundry to wash. My self-cleaning clothes were getting close to the end of their lifespan, but I wouldn't have traded them for a dozen high-quality beast cores. I really hoped I could find a replacement set before we left the city.

While everyone else was washing their clothes in a large wooden tub in the yard behind the inn, I went to deposit my newly acquired wealth and find out where the registration location for the tournament was located.

Today I dressed in a simple set of clothing I had picked up somewhere along the way that wasn't quite fancy enough to mark me as wealthy, but the quality fabric would ensure no one confused me with a pauper.

It only took me a little over an hour to find the place, but most of that time had been spent selling the furniture and bric-a-brac I had taken from Hu to some merchants. I had sold it all for coppers on the gold, wanting to make a quick sale. And to give Hu and Xiao one extra mental 'up yours,' just for fun. I kept most of the herbs and ingredients, since I didn't want to waste time trying to track down a shop willing to buy them. As I walked up to the small branch of The Auction House, I was once again stopped by a surprisingly strong door guard.

"Purpose of visit, young sir?" It actually took me a second to answer, because I knew this man. He didn't know it yet, but he would go on to become a General of the North in a couple centuries. The Generals were the first line of defense for the empire, and their job was to discourage the neighboring empire on our northern border from invading. Only the best and brightest were chosen for the position, making it one of the few postings in the army that was based on actual leadership ability, and not political maneuvering. What was a man like that doing as a door guard for The Auction House? He was still staring at me, so I snapped out of it and answered him.

"I am here to make a deposit. I was told to show this when I got here?" I held up my hand so he could see the dots of scar tissue left by the crazy witch. His demeanor instantly changed as soon as he saw the scars.

"Sir, I apologize. I didn't realize, um, what, or, I mean, who you are! Please, go right in." His reaction wasn't quite what I expected, but I just walked past him and went inside.

Before he closed the door behind him, I turned back around. "This isn't going to make any sense right now, but you need to remember what I am about to say. Your life depends on it." He looked confused, as if trying to decide if I was threatening him or not. "Two hundred and thirty years or so from now, there will be an incursion from the north. You will be there to stop it. During the second week of the campaign, their army will make a feint for the fort guarding the road to the Imperial City. The true target will be the town two miles to the west. If you don't engage them early, thousands of innocent people will die. You are the only person who will be in range to stop the massacre." His eyes were as big as saucers, but I could tell he wasn't ready to believe me. "It doesn't matter if you don't believe me. Just don't forget what I said." The future General gave me a faint nod and I let the door close. There. I did my best to right a wrong that had rested heavily on my soul for a long time.

The room I walked into was an exact replica of the one in Roh City. There were rows of items on display, with the 'buy now' prices and auction dates listed. Unlike the one in Roh City, this location had customers and several attendants to serve them. I walked up and down the rows, hoping to get lucky and find another set of clothes with the always clean qi matrix embedded in them. I guess I had used up all my luck when I ran into Hu and Xiao, because I didn't find anything I needed. Most of the items were rare alchemy ingredients, or heavy weapons and armor meant for a full-sized adult. I might look—and be—older than my actual physical age, but I was far too small to use anything they were selling. I would need to reach Saint before I could utilize the alchemy ingredients as well, making it pointless to buy them now. I would want them to be as fresh as possible when the time came to use them.

Eventually, an attendant came up to me. "Is there something I can help you find? Or maybe a specific item you are looking for?" The words were polite, but the tone was not. My snobbish attendant was bookish, with a receding hairline and narrow features. His brown robes didn't do his pale complexion any favors, and his attitude told me he was used to looking down on people that didn't meet with his personal standards. Basically, a run-of-the-mill jerk.

I did my best to push down my irritation and smiled at him. "I need to make a deposit in my account. If you could point me to the bookkeepers, I would greatly appreciate it." I made sure to sound respectful, but I left off any possible honorifics, such as 'sir,' that I could have given him. By the way his frown got deeper, I could tell he picked up on the subtle insult.

"I hope you are aware that this location only deals in denominations of gold, not coppers. If you want to make any *small* deposits into a personal account, I recommend using the main building in the inner city." He sniffed and went to turn away, thinking he had put me in my place.

Instead, I pulled out a cut sapphire gem the size of a shot glass you could find in any tavern. It was the only gem that I had found in Hu's hiding spot, and I knew it was worth several hundred gold coins. I made sure to hold it up using the hand with the scars that signified my friendship with The Auction House, just to tweak the jerk even more.

"Ah, well, ah… I will take you to see the bookkeepers at once, good sir." All of a sudden, he was sweating profusely, as if the room had gotten much warmer. I smirked, silently following him toward the back. I didn't understand why some people loved to be so mean to random strangers, but it was nice to see one of them put in their place. And without violence, this time.

The rest of my visit went smoothly, and I soon had a lot more room for storage in my belt. They also gave me a fair amount of information about the tournament, including where to sign up. After finishing up, I headed back to the inn to collect my friends.

The information they provided me ended up being very useful. As it turned out, it was a good thing I hadn't tried to sign us up last night when I was by myself. If several people wanted to fight as a team, the entire group had to be present when they were signing up. The competition had three different categories. One for individual fighters, one for teams of five to nine, and one for any group ten or larger. I thought about signing up for the individual competition, but I decided against it. These would be in a public arena and I once again would need to hide how powerful I was. Which, as the contestants in the last tournament I was a part of could tell you, I was bad at doing.

The final piece of important information? In this tournament, killing was allowed. No one was scared when I told them, but we all knew this would be a different kind of fight. It certainly made us wary.

We all got dressed in our armor before going. Kory also had us carry some generic weapons out in the open, leaving our best weapons as surprises inside our storage devices. He and I both agreed that the psychological aspects of a fight were important, and he wanted to start trying to lull our opponents from the start. Without giving too much away, of course.

The location to sign up for the competition was at an arena near the main entrance to the inner city, meaning we had a long walk to get there. I looked over our group as we walked toward the large wall looming in the distance. With the exception of Kory, we appeared incredibly young for such a deadly group. Valerie, Jamila, and Chu were all at the Peak stage of Heart cultivation, and Donny was a Middle stage Meridian cultivator. Kory hadn't moved past the Middle stage of Saint yet, but that wasn't much of a surprise. The higher you went, the harder it was to progress. I was now at the High stage of Meridian in qi capacity, but still functionally a Brain cultivator. Basically, we had the same strength as cultivators over three times our age, while Kory was as strong as someone twice his age. Add on to that almost two years of constant training and fighting as a team, and I was feeling bad for anyone that had to come up against us.

The journey through the city to the arena took us until lunch, so we all bought some food from a street vendor and got in line. The waiting area was just an empty plot of land outside the arena, divided up by hanging ropes to show where people were supposed to stand. Fortunately, we didn't have to wait long. The line moved quickly and efficiently, right up until a team of rowdy asshats tried to skip in front of us just as it was our turn to enroll. Chu, being the person that he was, didn't let them pass. He used the butt of his generic spear to block them from getting around him.

This was not in keeping with the wishes of the asshats.

"How dare you try to stop us from entering the tournament! Do you know who we are?" The speaker was a well-built man who looked to be in his late thirties, with short-cropped blond hair, tan skin, and vividly blue eyes. He was wearing heavy steel plate armor that was polished to a silver gleam, with a green serpent etched onto the breastplate. The seven other members of his party looked similar in age, with the normal variations of skin tones, hair, and eye color. My guess was they were a group from one of the more northerly sects, or maybe from one of the more powerful clans to the west.

"I'm not trying to stop you from entering the tournament." Chu lowered the butt of his spear to the ground, but still kept himself in position to keep them from easily getting around. "I'm just trying to keep you from cutting the line like a bunch of horses asses." The man's eyes bulged in disbelief at what Chu was saying. "The end of the line is back there. I suggest you go and find it."

"You insignificant creature! You are speaking to the Green Dragon Sect! We do not stand in line, like this other rabble." Well, that was a quick way to piss off everyone standing in line. In case you were wondering how everyone reacted to his comment, let's just go with the word 'bad.'

I turned to Kory. "Ignore all of this, and go sign us up before what I think is going to happen actually happens. Make sure not to use the name 'Roh' in our team name; we don't want anyone knowing where we came from. There aren't going to be many groups signing up today after the dust settles." Kory nodded and rushed over to the table where a city official was already lifting a communication plate to his lips. Yeah, I had a feeling this was going to go poorly.

"Stand aside, or be moved. It is your decision." His glower at Chu would probably work to intimidate your average individual, but Chu was far from normal now.

"I don't know what your problem is, but where I come from it is impolite to cut in front of someone. If you need me to teach you some manners, I would be happy to do so." Chu didn't do much after he answered, just widened his stance a bit and held his spear in both hands like a fighting staff.

"Teach me a lesson? We'll just have to see about that!" The unreasonably angry asshat punctuated his shout with an impressive blast of fire qi aimed straight at Chu. Which, considering the fact he was wearing a set of armor specifically designed by yours truly to block qi attacks, it simply fell apart as soon as it reached him. To say he was surprised would be an understatement. Which made it even funnier when Chu unleashed his full aura, showing the man that he was a Peak Heart cultivator. Which just so happened to be the same level as most of his group.

"Yep, you definitely need a spanking. That's how you fix unruly children that throw temper tantrums." The parts of Chu's body that weren't covered in armor were quickly covered in a layer of metal qi, and he strode forward into a storm of qi attacks that had zero effect on him.

The rest of us didn't actually do much. As soon as Chu reached the other group, they were beset on all sides by the other people in the line that had also been skipped and insulted. Other groups used the opportunity to strike at people they had a problem with, turning the whole thing into a massive mess of bodies slamming into one another. Cultivators were generally a prideful bunch, and sometimes even the slightest insult could spark a battle. Which was exactly what had just happened, when I thought about it.

Chu did a good job of showing restraint, never using the pointy end of his spear. He just whacked the ever-loving crap out of everyone that went after him with the wooden shaft. It broke after the first three people went down, so he just tossed it aside and started swinging his fists.

I occasionally used a thread of qi here and there to make sure no one was killed, but overall, I was pretty much ignored. Valerie fired a few blunt arrows into the melee for the same purpose, and Donny made sure she and I were left alone. Jamila, though...

Jamila was showing off her skills. Instead of using her customary set of katanas, she just pulled out two solid steel bars of equal length to fight with. It was a good thing she did, because with only those blunt rods, she still managed to lay out over a dozen people in only a few minutes. She flowed like water between combatants, striking out at shins and forearms, breaking limbs with abandon. Everywhere she went, the fighting stopped. No one wanted to face her blurring weapons, and when they did, all they could do was try to withstand the storm.

All of the Green Dragon Sect members were on the ground within the first three minutes, but the fight was far from over. Jamila eventually made her way to Chu, and they both started to work back toward the rest of us waiting on the sidelines. Valerie and I helped clear the way and they were free of the fighting just before a massive group of guards stomped into the area. There were over sixty of them, which put the guards at parity with the people still standing at this point.

The guard captain, a man wearing a silly helmet with a giant blue plume coming out of the top, stepped forward. "You will cease and desist all aggressive activity, and submit yourself for questioning! Do not resist, or you will be immediately arrested!"

The people still standing looked around at each other, and almost in unison stepped back. Weapons were sheathed, or disappeared into storage devices. Nobody wanted to get arrested, but getting beaten and arrested was worse. Several people laying on the ground stood up and limped their way back over to their original groups.

It was a minor miracle, but it looked to me like no one had actually been killed. Some needed immediate medical attention, but there weren't any severed limbs or heads lying around anywhere.

While I was surveying the battle, Kory had walked back up to our group. I turned to look at him and he gave me a slight nod. Good, he had managed to get us into the tournament.

The guards had enough patience to wait for everyone to rejoin their groups before surrounding them and shackling the fighters with irons. They were carved with runes intended to dampen the wearer's ability to use qi. I gave my own set a quick inspection and knew I could easily get out of them if I needed to, but they would certainly slow me down.

The guards brought in medic teams to treat the wounded while the rest of us were lined up and marched into the stadium. It had a basement lined with cells designed to hold beasts for the fights above, which the guards used to separate everyone. I saw a lot of people looking our way with angry faces and ill intent. I had a feeling their version of events wouldn't paint us in the best light.

Yep, we were in trouble.

CHAPTER TWENTY-TWO

Preparing for the First Round

We were the last people questioned by the guards. From the looks on their faces as they approached us, I didn't think this would go very well. They interviewed us each separately, which was smart. And it told me they were actually taking this investigation seriously. The guards finally put us all in one large cell, and the captain walked up to speak with us.

"My job, here in the city, is to keep the peace. You six are responsible for a breach of the peace, no matter the reasons." He was looking specifically at Chu when he said that. "I recognize the restraint that was shown. And I appreciate that." Now he was looking at all of us. "But if I let you back out on the streets, there will be more fighting from people that want revenge. I can't let that happen. So, you will be escorted back to your inn and be placed under guard and not allowed to leave the premises. Since you were registered to fight in the tournament, we will allow you to fight." All of us perked up a bit at that. We still had a chance to finish our mission to warn the king about the *nox* early. Requesting an audience with the king would normally take months to arrange. "However, after the tournament, you will leave the capital and not be allowed to return for a year and a day. And each of you will have to pay the ten-gold fine."

Chu quickly stepped up to the bars of the cage. "Sir, what of the trading and merchant contracts we came to the city to complete?" Chu was still trying to finish his own mission. "It took almost two years for us to travel to the capital from our clan's lands. Surely you don't want the capital to miss out on the revenue stream an entire clan might provide."

The captain thought for a minute before answering. "I will not allow you to leave the inn. I don't want to risk more violence. We have enough of that as it is." Chu went to say something, but the captain held up his hand to stop him. "However, I will allow you to hire a runner, and have meetings in the common room of your inn. That should be enough for any proper merchant to set up some trading contracts."

Chu nodded his head and stepped back from the bars. "I will make it work, sir. Thank you."

The captain didn't reply, he just turned and walked away. Another guard, wearing sergeant stripes on his tabard, opened the cage. "Alright you lot, let's get a move on. The sun went dark hours ago, and I have a mug of ale calling my name."

We followed the guards back to the surface and were led into the back of an enclosed wagon big enough to comfortably hold four people. Obviously, there were six of us, meaning the ride back was *not* comfortable.

The ride back to the inn was blessedly short. Our escort of guards meant we cut through the traffic on the roads with no problem. As we got out of the wagon in the yard behind the inn, I saw there were already a handful of guards stationed around the perimeter. I could probably sneak out, but there wasn't really a reason to do so. With the ultimatum from the guard captain, our mission had turned into an all-or-nothing proposition. Either we placed in the top three of the tournament, or we waited over a year for a second chance to speak to the king. Not to mention the requirement of killing the Chancellor, the second-most important person in the entire province.

Waiting was not an option. After seeing what the Chancellor was up to, I knew I didn't have much time until whatever they were planning came to fruition. We needed to get this right, and soon.

The next few days were spent planning and meeting with merchants. Initially, the innkeeper was angry about his place of business being turned into a makeshift prison, but the big spenders we brought in to talk with us quickly calmed him down. Chu and Jamila handled most of the visits with local traders and tradesmen, but the rest of us helped when necessary. I didn't follow what Chu managed to arrange with the others closely, but he seemed to be happy with the results.

We made our battle plans in the evenings, when the guards' numbers were reduced. None of us wanted to risk one of them being a spy for a competing team, as unlikely as it seemed. I had no doubt that after our little scuffle, plenty of the other groups were interested in what our tactics were going to look like.

There were several plans put in place depending on what the enemy tried to do. A lot of them involved Kory doing the bulk of the work, with the rest of us just running interference. Everyone understood how important it was for me to hide all of my abilities from the wider world, and Kory would be expected to perform the majority of our offense anyway because of his cultivation level. I also wouldn't be able to use my batteries during the fights for anything other than refilling my own cores. If someone were to notice me use them, the emperor himself would be hunting me for them.

I spent most of my free time making alchemy pills, powders, and potions. The fight with Hu had reminded me how useful they could be in a fight. I also loved the irony of using some of the ingredients I had taken from his shop to help my team and I win our fights. I mostly concentrated on things meant to obscure vision or slow down the enemy. I still hadn't started the process of building up immunity to the various poisons and venoms that I knew how to make, and it was too easy for an errant gust of wind to turn 'my' poison attack cloud into 'their' poison attack cloud.

There was one specific type of healing potion I wanted to make before the fights. It was one you didn't drink. Instead, you just poured it directly into the wound. I barely had enough internal qi to make it, so getting it right the first time was important.

I started with some Blue Fire Lotus. It was a pretty common base for several healing recipes, and I set it to boil in my cauldron with some filtered water.

Next, I had to add Red Water Lily, which required me to grind it up into a paste before dropping it in. I had to stir the entire concoction constantly until it reached an even boil. The cauldron was filled almost to the rim, meaning I had to be very careful the entire time. The Red Water Lily overpowered the Blue Fire Lotus—really, the names for this stuff were absolutely ridiculous—which was what I wanted to see.

The next step was to allow some Nineroot shavings to dissolve. This was the hard part. It wouldn't just dissolve on its own, I was required to help it along with a blend of wood, water, and fire qi. The three different threads basically had to both stir and pulverize the mixture until all of it was blended into an even consistency, similar to cake batter. Boiling off that much water with only one strand of fire qi took a *long* time, and maintaining the even flow of heat while still keeping the water and wood qi in balance required intense concentration. By the time it was done, the mixture was dark red and only filled up the bottom quarter of the cauldron.

I laid out a row of thirty small vials covered in etchings meant to help preserve whatever was stored inside them. I filled each of them two-thirds of the way with the liquid qi I had stored away, then topped them off with the concoction I had just made before popping the cork in place. The liquid qi slowly dissolved the thick mixture, eventually making a bright red fluid that had a slight glow to it when I shook them. Success!

By using the liquid qi, it would power the healing without

draining the cores of whoever was injured. These were far from the highest quality I knew how to make, but they were the best I could manage with my current cultivation and the ingredients I had on hand. Hu's ingredients were certainly useful, but the cheap bastard hadn't exactly kept the highest quality possible.

I made sure to make any repairs needed on everyone's armor using my traveling forge in the yard of the inn, and sharpened all the cutting edges of every spear, sword, broad-head arrow, and throwing knife. It took a long time to do all that.

What little time that wasn't taken up by other pursuits was used to carve a few more poppers and some formation plates I thought might come in handy. This tournament allowed contestants to kill each other, so I wasn't expecting our opponents to fight with as much restraint as we would have to show. We would just have to fight smarter.

I made a 'combat kit' for each of my friends that held an assortment of pre-powered formation plate traps and shields, two dozen poppers, five healing potions, three smoke bombs, and one vial of what I liked to call 'stick-um.' When in a sealed glass container, it was a silvery-looking liquid, but when exposed to the air it rapidly expanded into a gray foam that only *looked* harmless. I remember the first time my alchemy instructor had shown it to me. I had to walk around with a chunk of table glued to the back of my hand for a *week*. He thought the whole thing was hilarious, while I had one hell of a time at weapons drill for several days.

Before we knew it, the day of the first fight arrived. I passed around the combat kits to everyone over an early breakfast and went over their uses one last time. Kory made us all repeat our three main strategies, just to make sure they were in the fore-front of our minds. All of them were simple, and all three involved a rather straightforward attack utilizing Kory rushing at the opposite team's strongest person and the rest of us providing support.

The guards used a wagon like last time to transport us to the arena. Considering the crowds filling the streets, I think they did it for themselves more than us. Trying to clear a path on foot would have been nigh impossible.

We arrived at the arena just in time to get our team designation and make our way over to the waiting area nearest our first fight. Donny, ever the opportunist, made a bet with every bookie shouting out odds along the way. He bet on our team to win our first fight every time. Most of the bookies didn't even recognize our team name, meaning no one else was betting on us. I hoped that was a good sign.

Speaking of team names, Kory was as bad at naming things as everyone else in this empire. He had designated us as a mercenary team named 'The Black Marauders,' which sent a spike of pain through my brain every time I heard it.

Eventually, we found our seats and settled in to wait for our turn. Soon enough, it would be time for The Black Marauders to… maraud.

CHAPTER TWENTY-THREE

Marauding

The arena was set up into three pit-like areas, each one a different size. The smallest was for the one-on-one fights, the middle for small team fights, and almost half of the arena was demarcated for the large group combat. Our seats were off to the side of the one-on-one fighting, meaning it would be difficult to gauge the competition we might face. The stands were filled to bursting with people, each of them excited to see others shed blood for their entertainment. What can I say? People get bored.

Of course, before any fighting could start, we had to endure the announcer. When he walked out onto the balcony, I instantly recognized his dark presence. It was the Chancellor to the King of the Southern Province, and the man who willfully joined with a *nox*.

"Attention, good people! It is my greatest honor to thank you for attending the first annual Southern Provincial Tournament of Skill."

You could hear the capital letters in his voice, which was even deeper than the last time I had heard it. I wasn't the only one who noticed it, either. Several people in the audience seemed taken aback by such a deep voice from such a thin man.

"The first rounds will be single elimination, with each person, team, and group fighting twice today. This will continue every day until only ten remain from each category. Then, the true fights will begin!" The crowd roared in approval, and it took a few minutes before the Chancellor could continue. "As you all know, this is a no-holds-barred competition where everything is allowed. Killing, maiming, and general mayhem is encouraged!"

The crowd roared again, this time without the actual competitors joining in. We all looked around at one another, trying to see who might be excited about the prospect of killing their opponents. There were always a few people like that, and I noted more than a few looking our way.

"Those who make it to the final ten in each category will find their pockets filled with riches, and the higher they place, the more wealth they will gain!" That managed to get the contestants cheering again. "Now, without further ado, let the tournament, *begin!*" More roars of approval, and those designated to fight first moved out onto the arena floor.

I knew the true purpose of the tournament was to find suitable hosts for *nox* still out there looking for something to bond with. I had a strong feeling that anyone who showed signs of enjoying killing their opponents would find themselves propositioned shortly after the tournament. That proposition most likely wouldn't be something they had the option to turn down. I was broken out of my thoughts by Donny leaning over to talk to me.

"Did you notice that guy seemed a little off ?" He subtly pointed to the balcony where the Chancellor was seated.

"Yes. He is off. I am almost positive the man is possessed by an extremely powerful *nox,* and we need to kill him." I made sure to keep my voice down, just in case someone was listening.

Donny had a confused look on his face. "I'm not sure if you are joking or serious right now." His eyes widened when he saw the look on my face. "You're serious, aren't you?" I nodded my head. "Jim, you have to know that killing him is next to impossible. He is guarded by dozens of powerful cultivators at all times, and once you get past them, you have to actually fight *him*. He is a Duke-level cultivator, and that makes him the closest thing to invincible someone like you has ever faced!" Well, in this body, maybe, but I had fought and captured or killed hundreds of Duke cultivators in my first life. That gave me a few ideas for taking care of him. Not to mention, even a Duke cultivator hadn't built up a resistance to the light and dark qi that I had access to.

"I am sure we'll think of something when the time comes. Until then, let's just focus on getting through the tournament." I looked back at the fight taking place in front of us, and Donny mumbled in agreement.

The one-on-one battle taking place in front of us was off to a rough start. The fight involved two Peak Body cultivators, so each of them were using mostly physical attacks empowered by qi instead of fighting with qi constructs. They both wore armor marked by some clan or sect I didn't recognize, meaning they were probably affiliated with some minor group headquartered somewhere in the countryside. A lot like the Roh Clan, actually.

It finally ended when the smaller of the two managed to wear out his larger opponent. It took more qi to empower his body, meaning he ran out of energy before the little guy did. It was a mostly bloodless match, disappointing the audience.

If the booing and jeering from our end of the arena was an indicator of what a bloodless fight looked like, then the shouts and cheers from the other two fights meant there were a lot of fighters that would need to be buried tonight.

After a particularly loud exclamation from the audience, a team of nine cultivators jumped out of the central fighting pit. They were drenched in blood, but I could still see the design carved into their lamellar armor. Now *that* sect I recognized.

It was the Flying Sword Sect, the second most powerful sect in the empire. In the future, they would fall all the way into ninth place after a fight with the Golden Valley Sect—a minor sect headquartered in the Eastern Province—which managed to ambush and kill a significant portion of their sect elders in a border skirmish. Until that fall from grace, they would be known as the most ruthless and bloodthirsty of all the sects in the empire.

Even the emperor was forced to send in units of the Elemental Guard, reinforced with his Enforcers, when they got too excessive during their battles. They had a nasty habit of wiping out any towns or villages while marching toward their enemies, even if they had nothing to do with the group they were fighting at the time. I had the honor of wiping out a group that had done just that, right after my promotion to Enforcer in my first life. And I had taken my time with those bastards.

"They look mean. And I think they killed all of their opponents." Jamila was talking to Chu, but I cut in.

"That is the Flying Sword Sect, and they are mean. All of them. If we have to face them, we should kill all of them as quickly as possible. We shouldn't risk them getting close to us, or they might actually manage to hurt someone." Everyone, not just my team, was looking at me. "Their favorite tactic is to take off limbs one at a time before finishing off their opponent. It's a nasty way to fight." Which was why I did it sometimes, but that didn't mean I *liked* causing extreme pain… most of the time.

"I heard that too! That's why no one wants to fight them. After all, the Flying Sword Sect is the number two sect in the whole empire!" I couldn't see the person speaking, but I wasn't about to disagree with them.

"Yeah, if I have to go up against them, I might forfeit!" Several people agreed with whoever that guy was. I didn't blame them.

Jamila leaned in closer to talk to me. "Jim, we said that we wanted to avoid killing anyone. Now you want to change the plan?" I could tell the thought of killing someone for sport, and the amusement of others, was bothering her. I was glad that it did.

"I know what I said before, Jamila, but those people kill women and children for *target practice*. No matter the situation or circumstances, if I can get away with killing people like that, I'm going to remove them from this life. Maybe they can do better in their next one, as a newt or something." She gave me a sharp nod of agreement, the information convincing her.

While we had been talking, the second round of fighters had entered the pits. The two people fighting in front of me now were both High stage Meridian cultivators, and they were throwing qi constructs at one another as fast as they could shout the names of their attacks. Which were ridiculous. I mean, 'Dragon Lightning Fist' sounds like an amazing name and all, but when all it did was give their opponent a little shock, it came off as pretentious.

Both fighters were equally powerful, meaning the fight would be determined by the person with the best training. It ended when one of them missed a small earth qi attack hidden behind a massive wall of water qi they successfully blocked. Classic distraction technique. Use a big, loud, and flashy attack to cover up a small and powerful one. Six out of ten times, it worked every time. The downed contestant was knocked unconscious, but he would survive.

That was how it went for most of the morning. Fighters would battle it out, but only the most bloodthirsty would try to actually kill their opponents. It was close to noon by the time our turn to fight came up. Kory led our group down into the pit, each of us still hiding our weapons inside our storage devices. Our armor gleamed in the sun, the black chitin giving us a sharp and jagged look. We were as ready as we could get.

The people standing across from us were all in green leather armor. I counted four archers and four spearmen with shields. This must be a group from a clan of hunters living in a forest somewhere. The spearmen would keep the enemy at bay, while the archers took them down. A pretty efficient combination when fighting beasts and monsters in the woods, but not that great against a group of cultivators. If they could close with you, it would be over quickly. We all looked at each other, everyone diagnosing which plan would work best against them.

"Contestants, upon my mark, you will fight until your opponent forfeits through spoken agreement, they can no longer fight, or they are killed. If any of you attack before I say, the entire team forfeits the match. Please take your places behind the line."

I had heard the 'agreement' part of the rules. No one had mentioned before that the other side had to *accept* someone surrendering before. That was a pretty underhanded way to do business, in my opinion.

"Ready!" Each of us pulled out a shield in unison. A few of the people facing us jumped at the coordinated movement.

"Set!" Kory pulled out a throwing javelin, while the rest of us grabbed a handful of poppers. The spearmen crouched lower behind their shields, while the bowmen pulled back their bowstrings.

"Fight!" As soon as he said the word, the other team let loose their arrows. We took them on our shields, and retaliated by throwing our poppers underhand at them.

The timing was almost perfect. Kory had leapt toward the other team the moment we tossed the small stones at them, trying to time his arrival for right after the stones impacted. Instead, one of the spearmen actually managed to hit a popper with the very tip of his spear. This set off a roaring chain reaction that blew all four spearmen back into the archers using them for cover. Kory was also thrown back a step, but he was able to stay on his feet.

I saw the other team staring at us wide-eyed, the unorthodox attack managing to unnerve them. At least a few of them were intelligent enough to recognize how effective that attack would have been if it had landed at their feet as intended.

The rest of us sprinted across the pit to support Kory before their archers could scramble back to their feet and get an angle on him. I took a formation plate from my ring, and activated it just as one of the archers got back on one knee and nocked an arrow to his bow. The disk sailed toward where most of their team were still trying to get back to their feet. Remembering what it had felt like to get my own ears assaulted not that long ago, I could understand why it was taking them so long to do so.

The lone archer fired at me as I threw, but I managed to land the small disk exactly where I was planning. As soon as it hit the ground, a massive sinkhole appeared below them. Since none of them were on their feet, none of them managed to get away. The arrow that had been fired at me hit one of the throwing knives sheathed horizontally across my abdomen, bending the knife but protecting my vitals. Kory walked over to the pit, looking down at the groaning pile of fighters laying on the bottom.

"Don't be stupid. Surrender now, and save yourself any more pain! We wouldn't enjoy hurting you further." They shouted something up at him, but I was too far away to hear what they said. I approached the hole myself, peaking over with my shield ready to block any errant arrows.

They had all managed to get back to their feet, but I didn't see what I was expecting to see. I had forgotten that right under the floor of the arena was a basement filled with cages, and the hole my plate had opened up managed to drop them right into one. They seemed more confused about the whole ordeal than anyone. I guess they hadn't been a part of the fight outside the arena, so they hadn't known about the cages. Either way, the series of events had managed to unnerve them enough that surrender must have seemed like a good proposition.

The arena judge called the match, so we collected our things and marched back up to the stands to the cheers of the crowd. From their viewpoint, we had unleashed an almost invisible but incredibly loud attack, I took an arrow to the body without flinching, and the entire opposing team had been sucked into the earth, never to be seen again. The other team had left via the basement entrance, so no one saw them again after they disappeared. I suppose they thought we were as bloodthirsty and ruthless as the Flying Sword Sect.

From the looks of the others when we returned to our seats, the other teams thought so too. Valerie was about to inform them of the other team's survival, but Kory put an arm on her shoulder to stop her. He understood how the psychological impacts of facing a team that had wiped out their last opponents might affect any future bouts.

Donny was the last of our team to return to the seating area. He had made a lap of the arena to collect his winnings from the bookies he had bets with.

"I'm rich! The odds against us were ridiculous, since we were just a mercenary group and our opposites were from a named clan of hunters well-known in the city. I bet they won't make that mistake again!" Donny flashed us a hefty purse of gold before hiding it in his storage ring again. "I tried to make another bet for us to win, but the odds they are giving us now made it pointless." We all shrugged, not worried about it. Everyone who saw us fight would be a fool to bet against our team, so we weren't surprised.

We ate a quick lunch from the food stored in my belt and managed to watch six more one-on-one fights before it was our turn again. As we approached the arena, I couldn't hold in the smile trying to creep across my face. It was the guys who tried to skip the line and landed us in trouble with the guards. We all looked at each other with somewhat sadistic smiles on our faces.

This was going to be fun.

CHAPTER TWENTY-FOUR

The Dark Side of Success

"Ah, look, it's those worthless dogs that barked at us a few days ago! Well boys, I guess the curs need another lesson!" The leader that Chu had given a walloping was actually trying to intimidate us? Well, one thing was for sure, they didn't remember the fight like I did.

"How's the arm? I wasn't sure if I had broken it or not, with all the screaming and crying you were doing about it. I'm sure you remember what it sounded like as it snapped like a twig. You know, when I beat you so bad your ancestors felt it?" Stars. Chu didn't pull any punches when he went to put someone in his place. I was pretty sure a few of them grimaced when they recalled what had happened the last time they had confronted our team.

"You don't have the benefit of outnumbering us this time, peasant! We would have trounced you if there weren't so many of your commoner friends around. This time, things will be different!" Chu just shook his head at them, and I put a hand on his shoulder to pull him back into formation. The same guy as last time recited the rules, and we pulled our shields in unison as he finished talking.

As soon as the judge said fight, we all stood in place. This was plan number three. We would wait for them to pass into our half of the field and allow Kory to pick his targets, while the rest of us stayed on the defensive. It only worked if all of their team were melee fighters. Which, basically, they would be. Since we had already seen these guys fight, we knew what to expect. Their qi attacks were too weak to even scratch our armor, meaning they would have to come and fight us.

Instead of taking a moment to think about why we wouldn't move, they just charged in like the brash idiots we knew them to be. It had always confused me how people of high social standing thought that mattered at all in a fight. Yes, they had probably been tutored since they were very young in the ways of battle, but most never took it seriously. Like these guys, they were usually all talk and no show.

They sent in a wave of fire and metal qi attacks, but all of them broke apart against our chitin armor. As we knew they would, all eight of them drew identical longswords and rushed us after seeing their attacks fail. The only person on our team to draw a weapon was Kory. The rest of us just used a shield on our left arm and an open palm to deflect anything our shield might miss. It was super effective.

Kory had chosen to use the sword I had made for him. It gave him an edge against the leader of their team with the runes making it lighter, allowing him to move it faster. Not that he needed the edge. The fight between those two lasted less than twenty seconds, and most of that was Kory just gauging his opponent. The rest of us were practically playing with the others.

Chu had three people attacking him at the same time, but he just used his shield to force them to get in each other's way. I even saw him lean out and slap one of them in the face with an open palm. It spun the man halfway around and dropped him to one knee, putting him out of the fight for a bit. Ouch. That slap hurt some pride.

The rest of us just had to deal with one person whaling

away with their swords at our shields. Since we were focused almost entirely on defense, they never found an opening to exploit. All they were doing was tiring themselves out. And leaving their backs open for Kory to knock them senseless.

He went from person to person, taking them down one at a time. He was far stronger than anyone on their team, making the whole thing almost unfair. But, with these guys, all of us enjoyed their humiliating defeat. By using Kory to actually take down our enemies, we were all able to better hide just how strong we were. None of us wanted to get scooped up by a recruiter that heard tell of a band of powerful cultivators all under the age of twenty. This method kept that from happening.

The relatively bloodless battle didn't please the audience, but they also saw how easy it was for our team to defeat our opponents. It would have been like murdering a bunch of invalids if we had killed them. Most realized this, which kept the boos to a minimum.

After the last man fell, we tried to go back to our seats. Instead, the guards were already waiting to escort us back to the inn. I guess they didn't see a need to stick around and watch the last few rounds of fighting. Or maybe they were trying to avoid the inevitable crowded streets that would arise from the entire arena emptying at the same time.

It was time for the evening meal by the time we pulled into the yard of the inn. Valerie went to feed our horses in the stables, while I moved to a clear spot so I could set up my traveling forge. The other four went into the common room of the inn to grab us some food before returning to get any nicks and dents in their weapons and armor repaired. Considering the fights we just had, I would probably just need to do some touch ups on everyone's shields.

I looked around the yard as I was setting up, surprised to see there weren't any guards standing around. They usually had at least two or three men stationed back here. Maybe they had decided to reduce the number of guards during the competition?

Just as I was pushing some fire qi into the forge, I heard a shout from the inn. Donny came stumbling out of the back door, an empty crossbow in one hand and his rune-covered dagger in the other. A cultivator in dark clothing and mask was right behind him, a thin rapier making darting stabs at Donny's face.

I ran to help, but another cultivator dressed like the one attacking Donny came bursting through the door as I got close. He oriented on me, and before I could do anything I was being forced back toward my forge. The man fighting me was using two long daggers, so I pulled out my own set of daggers that were sheathed along my ribs, courtesy of my unique armor.

The cultivator fighting me was focused on speed more than skill, which meant I wasn't having a hard time keeping them from injuring me. Unfortunately, they were just fast enough that I couldn't put them down easily. A quick glance over at Donny showed me he was slowly being forced back across the yard toward the stables. He had managed to drop the crossbow and get his axe out of his storage ring, but it wasn't doing him much good.

The glance to Donny forced me to take a quick leap to the side, putting my back against the hot forge. I met the eyes of the person attacking me, and I was surprised to see their pupils were surrounded by a red ring. Ah, stars-damned assassins!

In my first life, there had been several sects known as 'dark' sects. They were focused on a path of cultivation that used pain and death to advance themselves. It was a quick way to advance yourself, but after a while it required the cultivators to commit larger and more heinous acts of treachery and murder to keep progressing. The stains on their souls also tended to manifest physically, from things as simple as their eyes turning red to more esoteric showings like their auras turning into a black miasma, or their fire qi constructs turning into dark red and black flames.

Probably one of the only good things Ming had ever done as emperor was to ensure most of those sects were hunted down and destroyed. I hadn't needed to take part in most of the actual fighting, since I had been his spymaster during most of that time.

I did know that at this point in time, the dark sects were still in their infancy. I also knew that most people considered them to be the closest thing to invincible. Many of the Emperor's Enforcers had died before the key to defeating them had been found. And I knew exactly how to do it.

Donny was already experiencing why most people found them to be invincible. He was more skilled than his opponent, but all of his strikes seemed to slow down right before they could touch the assassin. This was the side effect of the miasma aura they cultivated, and it made it almost impossible to get a clean strike in. The solution was simple once you knew it, but Donny wasn't using the right weapon.

I threw my right-hand dagger at my own assassin, forcing them to take a step back. I reached behind me to grab the blacksmith hammer off of the anvil behind me and spun quickly around in a crouch at knee height. My assassin's daggers swished through the air above my head in a double slash that might have actually hurt to defend against. The low strike with the hammer against the bent knee of my assailant was slowed before impact, but the heavy mass of solid steel would not be denied. The crunch of bone as the joint bent completely side-ways was quickly followed by the high-pitched screams of the assassin. Who, apparently, was a woman?

Their gender didn't matter in the end, as the next swing of my hammer turned their skull into a misshapen lump. One assassin down. On to the next one.

As my kill had shown, the trick to fighting them was heavy, blunt instruments. Their aura was perfect for slowing down edged weapons and qi constructs, but it wasn't nearly as effective against a wide surface area traveling at great speed. I was just about to run to Donny's aid when the stable doors were flung open, the loud slam of them bouncing off the walls causing everyone to pause.

Out rode Valerie, astride her white horse, with an arrow aimed at the assassin fighting Donny. Her horse made a stuttering leap into the yard as she fired, forcing the assassin to roll backwards. In a humorous turn of events, the horse managed to slam into Donny as it skidded to a halt, launching the poor man into the back wall of the inn like a stone thrown from a catapult. I *swear* I saw the horse smile. That horse was going to be the death of him!

The arrow Valerie had fired actually hit the assassin, telling me their aura hadn't fully manifested yet. I used the knowledge to full fruition, whipping my left-handed dagger into the back of the assassin's head while they were facing off against Valerie. Two assassins down.

"What in the stars is going on?!" Valerie jumped off her horse as she nocked another arrow. I collected my two daggers and we both started toward the back door of the inn. Donny was back on his feet, looking around where he had landed for his axe.

"Someone doesn't like how well we did today. They paid for a group of assassins to take us out of the tournament." She took the news in stride, not showing a bit of surprise. "The trick to taking these guys down is blunt attacks. They have a trick that slows down pointed and edged weapons enough that they don't do much damage." Valerie nodded, and swapped out her bow for a shield and her meat-cleaver-like sword. Gods, I loved competent people.

She led the way through the door, her shield held out in front of her. We walked into a mess. The innkeeper was at the top of the staircase, peeking over the edge at the maelstrom going on below. The neat common room was now filled with broken furniture, and I saw that Chu was already down. Jamila was fighting two assassins as she stood over his prone form, her twin katanas a blur that kept both of her opponents on their heels. From the grimace on her face, I could tell it was a good thing we had shown up when we did. There was blood dripping down her leg, meaning they had already made it through her defenses once.

While Jamila might have been having a hard time, Kory was in dire straits. He was facing four of them, and he was bleeding from just about everywhere not covered by his armor. The shield on his left arm was practically in pieces, and his sword was flashing around him, trying to deflect as many attacks as possible.

It looked like the assassins were just toying with them, having some fun before they finished off my friends. I felt a spike of rage, and my cores flexed in response. No one was going to kill my friends, not on my watch. I was done messing around. No more pulling my punches.

Almost subconsciously, hundreds of qi threads sprung from my body. They picked up hunks of broken furniture from around the room and slammed into the assassins as a wave of my anger manifested. It didn't take long until they were little more than puddles of soupy, bloody mess. Eight assassins down. Two were missing, if this was a traditional kill squad.

Everyone still standing stared at me wide-eyed as I dropped the gore-encrusted hunks of wood and reabsorbed the threads. My meridians felt shaky, like an overworked muscle, letting me know that little display had pushed my cultivation system close to its limit. Looking at Chu lying face down on the floor, I realized I didn't really care.

"Sometimes, Jim, you can be downright terrifying." Kory was looking back at the remains of the assassins as he spoke. "I take it some of our competition doesn't want us to keep fighting in the tournament. I wonder where our guards ran off to? I find it suspicious that they disappeared right before this all happened." Valerie, who was still standing next to me, nodded in agreement. Jamila snapped out of it first and rolled Chu over, patting him down and trying to see what she could do.

Kory was already cycling his own qi, using it to stop his bleeding and heal his wounds. Valerie had pulled out her healing necklace and was rushing over to help Jamila with Chu. I heard a thump behind me and turned around with my blacksmith hammer raised to strike. In stumbled Donny, his face bleeding from a gash on his forehead.

"Donny, are you okay? I didn't see you bleeding from the head before we came in here." I walked up to him, already sending out a thread of wood qi to heal him.

"I wasn't bleeding earlier. Just as I found my axe, another one of those masked attackers came out of nowhere! I held him off for just a second, which was long enough for Valerie's horse to kick him straight into my dagger. He's bleeding out next to your forge right now." He pointed behind him as he stepped farther into the room. "What happened in here?"

I didn't bother to answer him, instead moving past him and back out to the yard. If there was one of them still alive, I might be able to get them to answer a few questions.

The assassin wasn't waiting near the forge. Instead, he had crawled halfway over to the stables, leaving a wide blood trail in his wake. His red eyes widened in fear as I approached. I hefted my hammer and smashed it into the back of his calf as he tried to crawl away faster. He shouted in pain before collapsing on the ground fully. I knew how painful it was to get hit in that spot, but I *really* wanted to make sure I had his attention.

"Listen, you have three choices here, buddy." He rolled onto his back to look at me. "One, I slowly crush every bone in your body until you beg me to finish you off. A win for me, not so much for you. Two, you lie to me, and we go back to the results of option one. Once again, only I win. Third, you answer my questions, I heal you just enough for you to return to your employers, and you give them a message from me." The assassin's eyes were cloudy with pain, but I could tell he was following along with what I was saying. "In option three, we both win. I'll let you decide which one you prefer." I saw him try to reach for something in his waistband, so I swung down with my hammer and crushed his elbow. "Ah, you tried to go with option four. That wasn't one of the choices. Let's try this again." I performed a quick search of his body, practically stripping him naked in the process. He had been reaching for a vial filled with some kind of black sludge. Probably a poison intended for ending his own life. I stored it away, along with all of the various weapons he had hidden about his body.

The act of exposing his rather unremarkable face and stripping him to his smallclothes had taken the fight out of him. He was already close enough to death from the stab wound to his guts that I had been forced to use a bandage covered in a healing poultice on his abdomen. It wouldn't be enough to heal him, but I hoped it might keep him alive. The general lack of scars on his body told me he wasn't used to dealing with extreme pain like a more experienced assassin might be.

"Okay. First question. Which dark sect do you originate from?" He just stared at me, refusing to say anything. I swung my blacksmithing hammer straight into his already-broken elbow, smashing the flesh flat into the ground. Since it was practically severed at this point, I finished the job by ripping it the rest of the way off his body. There was something about seeing your limbs getting ripped off that usually unnerved a man. Judging by his screams of pain, it was working on this guy too.

"*Okay*! Okay! I'll tell you, just stop!" He was gasping for breath, the pain really taking it out of him. "We were hired by —" He was cut off by an arrow that suddenly sprouted from his head. I activated the shield form of my spirit wood ring and ducked behind its protection as another arrow thudded into it. I heard the sound of feet running away from the rooftop of the stable. As I went to follow, a bunch of guards came through the gate and into the yard.

"Stop! Drop the… arm? Drop the arm, lay down your shield, and submit yourself to questioning!" Apparently, holding the severed arm of a dead man had them worried. I looked down at myself and noticed that I was covered in bits of flesh and splashes of blood. I dropped the arm and deactivated the shield.

"I will stay, but one of them is getting away! Do your jobs

for once, and catch them before they escape!" My blood was still hot, and my rage hadn't quite cooled off yet. First, my friends were attacked. Next, someone killed the man I was about to get some answers from. Then, these bumbling idiots decided to show up at the absolute worst time? I was not amused.

"Don't tell us how to do our job, criminal! We will do as we please, and I don't want to hear from you unless I—" My knife against his throat shut him up. The man coming up behind me stopped trying to approach when a glittering green glass sword suddenly appeared in my other hand and pushed against his groin, the tip easily piercing through his armor and nicking the flesh beneath.

"I am not a criminal." My voice was crystal clear, and the tone made the guard's face turn white with fear. "I was only defending my life, and the lives of my friends." The man behind me tried to shift his position, but my sword pushing forward a tiny bit made him change his mind with a squeak. The other guards in the yard were frozen in indecision. I was in a position to kill two of their comrades before they could stop me. "If you had been doing your jobs, and guarding us, none of this would have happened. I *suggest* you do your *job* and follow the assassin your *incompetence* is *allowing* to *escape*." I was having a hard time controlling my anger, and it was making me push the knife in far enough to draw forth a bead of blood where it was touching his throat.

"That's enough, Jim. Let them go." I looked over and saw Kory standing next to the captain of the guard we had dealt with before. "We need to talk, and Chu is back on his feet." I nodded and made both of my weapons disappear.

The assassin was probably long gone by this point anyway.

CHAPTER TWENTY-FIVE

Sage Advice

The meeting was a short one. The captain smoothed over my confrontation with the guards, and explained to us that someone had messed with the guard shift schedule to engineer a blank spot in coverage.

We helped the innkeeper clean up the mess caused by the fighting, and the guards even brought in new furniture as an apology to the man for allowing the whole thing to happen. I was still angry, but it was more of a background hum than a storm demanding release.

After getting the inn back in order, we all got baths and worked to get our gear back in order for the next day. Kory's shield took me the longest to repair, and everyone had at least a few things for me to work on. Before I knew it, time had gotten away from me. Donny had to half-drag, half-carry me to my room. The long day had sapped my physical reserves, while the emotional turmoil had drained my mental strength. I didn't even get a chance to cultivate before collapsing into bed.

The next morning we were up, dressed, and ready to go before the wagon even showed up to take us to the arena. The streets were even more crowded than yesterday, and our guard contingent had been doubled after the attempted assassination. I made sure to keep a close eye on the rooftops as we trundled through the crowds. Just because they had failed once didn't mean they wouldn't try again. Whoever 'they' were.

"Yesterday was a sign." We all turned to look at Chu. He had suffered from a stab wound to the chest yesterday, but you couldn't tell anything bad had happened to him today. Valerie's pendant was pretty awesome. "It was a sign that someone is afraid of us. I bet it is one of the top competitors. They see us as a risk, and tried to remove us from the competition to ensure they take first place."

"Who do you think it was?" Jamila was leaning into Chu a bit more than normal. They were only a year away from being old enough to marry, and the thought of losing him yesterday must have reminded her of that fact. Chu was soaking up the extra attention, so it was Donny that answered.

"I think it was the Flying Sword Sect. They clearly don't have a problem with killing someone, and I didn't see anyone else who might want to finish us off outside the arena." Donny was sitting next to Valerie, but they weren't showing the same level of affection as the other couple in the wagon. They were more private in their affections anyway. Both of them were old enough to marry now, but neither of them had made mention of swinging by a temple since we had arrived at the city. I wondered why?

"We can't go forward with an accusation like that until we have proof." Kory leaned forward as he spoke, motioning with his hands for us to keep our voices down. "A sect like that won't be easy to make restitution with anyway. We all just need to be more careful, and none of us can go anywhere alone." Everyone nodded in agreement.

A few minutes later we arrived at the arena and moved to our seats. The drop in contestants meant we could finally sit where we could see the team competitions, although we were far enough up in the stands that it would be hard to make out any details of the competitors. Ironically, one of the first two teams up to fight was the Flying Sword Sect. Today, they only had eight members ready to fight. Interesting. I wonder what had happened last night to their ninth member? Could they have possibly met their end fighting at an inn?

That reminded me, I still had the weapons and equipment from the assassin I had tried to question last night. It was the only person's gear that hadn't been collected by the guards during the cleanup. I would have to check it when there weren't so many people around.

Before the fight started up, the Chancellor appeared in his balcony to say a few words. I had fully intended to listen to his speech, but my concentration was shattered by the girl that stood next to him.

Alya. Her emerald eyes and auburn hair were exactly as I remembered. The face was younger, and more innocent, but it was her.

In my first life, she had been one of Ming's concubines. She and I had been friends from the moment we had first met. As one of Ming's Enforcers, I had served as a guard over the Imperial Harem many times, but Alya had been the only woman I found to be interesting. Her wit, mischievous nature, and undeniable inner strength had made me almost jealous of Ming on more than one occasion. The Jim of the past had never thought of running off with her, because she belonged to Ming. And past Jim loved Ming like an older brother, one he would never betray. Not that he'd felt the same way about me, of course.

The Jim of now was a totally different story. Maybe it was the hormones of youth, but I had the undeniable urge to snatch her from the grasp of the man standing next to her and run off into the sunset. Well, it was still morning, but you get the idea.

Alya hadn't exactly been miserable as a member of Ming's harem, but she certainly wanted more out of life. On many occasions, she had been punished for attempting to sneak into the palace training grounds to practice her fighting and cultivation skills. I didn't want that fate for her. In fact, the way it all ended, I wanted her to—

Wait. How had it ended? What was I talking about? I had known her for decades, ever since her stepfather had managed to land her in Ming's harem. Then it clicked. Her stepfather was the Chancellor! And the blank spot in my memory of what had happened to her must have been one of the memories I lost when I changed the real world from within the dream world. Stupid table that controls the stupid weather! Ugh! What a cruel twist of fate this all turned out to be.

No matter. I knew enough that it had just become very important for me to manage some way to get her out of her circumstances. Looking at Alya, I guessed her to be somewhere between fourteen and sixteen. She wouldn't be headed to Ming's harem for a long time. And I already knew I needed to kill the Chancellor, so this was just another incentive to end his life. Convincing Alya to join our group wouldn't be easy, but I had to find a way.

"Hey, Jim, are you okay?" Donny was trying to see what I was looking at. "Ever since the Chancellor came out to make his speech, you've looked like someone bonked you on the head." I looked back at him, but he did a double-take with the people standing on the balcony. "Wait, were you staring at that girl?" A smile spread across his face. "Ah, man! It's that girl, isn't it? Did you run into her when you were running around by yourself earlier? Or do you just think she's pretty?" I must have blushed, because his grin only got wider. "Guys! You aren't going to believe this, but I might have finally found something that Jim can't defeat!" Everyone looked over at him and he pointed at the balcony. "He likes that girl!"

Luckily, Jamila came to my defense. "Oh, leave poor Jim alone, Donny. It isn't like he is going to chase after some girl he doesn't have a hope of catching anyway." Ouch. Okay, less 'came to my defense' and more 'stabbed me in the chest,' but whatever.

"Enough. The match is about to start." Kory brought us all back to task, pointing down to the arena. I had missed whatever it was the Chancellor said, but it probably didn't matter anyway.

We were too far away to hear what was said, but the judge stepped back and the two teams went at each other. Both sides had eight members, and they paired off to fight one another as individuals. No teamwork was involved whatsoever, but in the end it didn't matter.

The Flying Sword Sect members absolutely demolished their opponents. Limbs and heads went everywhere in a gory explosion spread out all over the fighting pit. I was too far away to see how exactly they defeated everyone so easily, but it looked like pure skill of arms. All eight of them used huge broadswords, their blades flashing in the morning light as they swept through the other team. The whole thing was over in less than a minute.

The audience roared in approval as they exited the pit. I looked over at my teammates, trying to gauge their reactions. The only one that was showing any emotion was Chu, and he just had a smile on his face.

"It looks to me like we are going to have one hell of a fight on our hands when we get paired up with those guys. I can't wait!" His enthusiasm was infectious, and everyone seemed eager to face the bloodthirsty sect.

We didn't wait long until our own team was called forward. The team opposite us was made up entirely of Body cultivators, so when Kory released his aura they immediately surrendered. It was a smart decision. Any one of my friends could have beaten them alone, but Kory could have managed it with just qi attacks. They were lucky that it was our team they got paired with, and not the Flying Sword Sect. Maybe that's what had happened to the first group?

The rest of the day we sat watching teams fight for a chance to move on. No other teams seemed to stand out except the Flying Sword Sect. They had won their second match with similar results. They still didn't use teamwork, just fought each member as an individual. It gave me hope of an easy victory when we finally faced them. None of our strategies would play to their strengths. I would make sure of it.

It was late into the afternoon before we were called forward again, this time to face a team of only five. All of them were Meridian cultivators, meaning we wouldn't get a walk-off win the second time around. As we got in position, one of them yelled across at the girls.

"Ladies! What do you say, after we kill all your men, you surrender to us? We promise to treat you *real* nice!" They all chuckled at the idea of capturing the two girls for themselves.

Hoo boy. That was dumb. I could hear Jamila's knuckles crack as her hands curled up into fists. Valerie just snorted in reply, but I could feel the waves of anger coming off her aura. These geniuses were in for a bad day.

"You remember the rules?" The judge waited until all of us had given him a nod of agreement before continuing. "Good. Then I won't waste time repeating them. Ready! Set! Fight!" The quick start was fine with us. Donny threw a trap plate from the combat kit I had given him on one side, while Chu tossed out a handful of poppers at the other. This wasn't in any of our preset plans, but we had fought with each other long enough to just go with it.

The poppers hit right after the trap activated. The one Donny had chosen was an earth spike design that created six-inch stone spikes in a four-foot radius from the copper disk. The poppers forced the other team straight into them, piercing through their boots and leg armor. One man fell into the spikes, and he found out the hard way that his set of hardened leather armor wasn't of the highest quality. It was a nasty way to die.

The fight was pretty much over after that. Not having functioning feet made it impossible for them to do much of anything, so Valerie killed one with an arrow while Jamila removed the heads of the last three with her katanas. Kory and I hadn't even moved.

"So much for not killing unless we had to, huh?" Kory was

looking around at everyone, not really angry so much as just looking for confirmation.

"Not after that comment. I could see it in their eyes. They might have made it sound like a joke, but those people were serious. Valerie and I just removed them from the breeding population, that's all." Jamila was cleaning her katanas as she answered. It sounded like something I would have said, and it made me wonder just how much of my attitude and mannerisms had worn off on everyone else.

Kory just shrugged. "I wasn't gainsaying your actions. I just wanted to make sure we were all on the same page." Jamila nodded at Kory's words, not wanting to talk about it any further.

I spoke up to break the silence. "Okay team, back to the inn. We can reset and prepare for tomorrow." The rest of them just looked at me.

Donny finally spoke up. "You must not have been paying attention at all when the Chancellor was speaking. All of the team competitions have to keep fighting until only ten remain. They want all of us to keep pace with the one-on-one fighters. This round doesn't stop until the finals."

Well. That sucked. I guess maybe I should have listened to the speech after all.

We all marched back into the stands, this time finding the placards that marked our seats to be much closer to the ring. There were only a few dozen teams left at this point, meaning they could move us down to the level of the fighting. After doing a quick count, I saw that we would need to fight at least two or three more times before we could go back to the inn.

As we took our seats, I saw the Flying Sword Sect team waiting to enter the central pit for their third round of fighting. Now that we were closer to the arena, I could finally gauge their strength. I paid close attention as the judge started the fight, even slowing down my perception of time a little to try to see what style of sword fighting they were using.

At first, I didn't see anything out of the ordinary. After they drew their swords, that all changed. I had been wrong about them the whole time. They absolutely *were* fighting as a team, just in a way that I didn't notice at first. The entire team was using something called 'linked swords.' It was a technique that was completely useless in a large-scale battle due to the tunnel vision it caused, but for something like this, it was perfect.

When they fought, every cultivator was injecting qi into their swords. The longer they fought, the more power there was behind every strike. A pretty common set of runes to enchant a sword with, especially for people that primarily fought duels. What the Flying Sword Sect team had done was to link that flow of qi to each other's swords as well. That meant they weren't fighting with the strength of one fighter, but with the strength of all eight behind every strike. The qi drain to use such a method was sudden and powerful, forcing them to focus only on their own target. Otherwise they risked losing control of all that qi. It could rebound back into their cultivation systems and rupture a meridian. Even worse, it might blow out the walls of a core. Their best hope was for the sword to simply explode, horribly maiming them in the process.

It was a method I would never use, personally, but they had the technique mastered down to an art. I knew of three easy ways to defeat something like this, but all of them required a larger team than what we currently had. If we had Valerie stand back to fight as an archer, we would each have to hold them off two to one long enough for her to disrupt their concentration with an arrow to the face or something. The problem was, they were all Low Saint cultivators. The only one of us who could stand up to two of them at one time was Kory, and even he would be hard-pressed to maintain that standoff for a long time. The other two methods I knew had the same drawbacks.

The only solution I kept coming back to was I just beat them all myself. I knew I could do it. They would be coming straight at me, making it simple to shred them like confetti for a parade. But that would expose my abilities to the entire capital, which was the same thing as whispering into the emperor's ear myself. And maybe even worse, it would show the Chancellor and his *nox* passenger that I was alive, and right in front of them. Fighting a Duke cultivator with little to no preparation was tantamount to suicide. And letting them kill me was definitely not an option. I had to save the entire planet, before it was too late. I refused to let it be destroyed by my actions a second time.

The team fighting the Flying Sword Sect died quickly, the overpowering sword strikes blasting through their defenses with almost no resistance. I was starting to wonder if we should just withdraw from the competition when an old man with a ridiculously long and white beard leaned over from his seat beside me.

"Them nasty sword folks have ya worried some, boy?" I just looked at him, shocked that he was even speaking to me. "Well, if I was ta fight them mean folks, I'd make sure to intimidate 'em real good first." I nodded, waiting patiently for him to finish. "Ya see, when I was a younger man, I got some advice from the best fighter I ever seen." He took a swig from a mug of ale he pulled out of nowhere before continuing. His tone took on a deeper, grander tone, as if imitating someone. "If you aren't sure about winning a fight, you need to try to increase the intimidation factor. Look your opponent straight in the eye, and shit your pants with a look of sheer rage on your face. Toddlers do it all the time, and those little bastards are terrifying. Kids know what's up."

I was literally at a loss for words. What did you say to something like that?

Donny leaned across from me to answer the old man. "Wise words, elder. Wise words." I knew my eyes had to be popping out of my head as he agreed with the old man. "There are few things in this life as terrifying as a toddler."

The old man nodded along with Donny, and thankfully turned back to his ale.

"Wise words?" I whispered, trying to keep the old man from

hearing me. "That was one of the craziest pieces of advice I have ever heard."

Donny chuckled at me before putting a finger to his nose. "There was a fair bit of wisdom in that, if you were paying close attention. Let me explain it another way. If you are about to be eaten by a bear, should you climb a tree and hide? Or would it be better to wave your arms and scream at the bear as loud as you can?"

I thought about it for a second. I mean, I would just kill and eat any bear that threatened me, but I understood what he was talking about.

And, it gave me an idea.

Our next two fights were simple. We kept up a solid defense, while Kory did all the heavy lifting. It wasn't necessary to kill any of our opponents, so we remained unbloodied for the rest of the evening.

It was almost fully dark by the time the final ten teams were decided. We were all ranked on a board hung near the entrance. Our team was number two, behind the Flying Sword Sect. Tomorrow, that would change.

Our carriage ride was uneventful, as was our evening of planning. There weren't any scheduling mishaps this time around. I told everyone what I had come up with for facing the Flying Sword Sect, and they all thought it was a great idea. We refilled our combat kits, made a few repairs, and were finally ready for the next day.

Before going to sleep that night, I made sure to look over the items I had taken off the assassin. Everything was extremely well made, but almost all of it was completely absent of any identifying marks. The only exception was a ring the man had been wearing. It wasn't a storage ring, like I had initially hoped. Instead, it was a signet ring.

The design was unfamiliar, but the initials carved on the surface were not. DS. The Dark Swords. In my timeline, no links were ever drawn between the Flying Sword Sect and the Dark Swords Sect. While the names might imply a connection, there were literally thousands of sects out there with some variation of 'sword' in their name. If you couldn't tell already, just about everyone in this plane of existence was terrible at naming things. A dark sect called The Dark Swords? I mean, come *on*.

After the attack against us, I was beginning to wonder if they were in fact allies in some way. The Flying Sword Sect had always been one small step from becoming a dark sect themselves. It wouldn't surprise me in the least if they counted a dark sect like the Dark Swords as a friend.

That brought about an even worse thought. What if the *nox* found out about the existence of the dark sects? That would be a blending of terrible tendencies and awful talent that the world didn't deserve. All I could do was hope they stayed ignorant of one another for as long as possible. Preferably, forever.

As I laid down to sleep, I couldn't hold in the groan that escaped my lips. It felt like ever since we entered the city, I had been pushing my meridians to their limits. I knew, for the most part, it was no different than the daily use of qi we had expended to power my formation plates while traveling, but there was something about fighting that made it feel different. Tomorrow would continue to push me closer to the edge of High Meridian and into the stage of Peak for my capacity.

Before I finally nodded off, I wondered how long it would be until I broke through to a level that allowed the gods, Pride and Wrath, to speak to me again.

CHAPTER TWENTY-SIX

The Next Phase

I opened my eyes to see the lights of the capital stretching before me. The gods couldn't speak to me yet, but they could show me important things while dream walking, I supposed.

I was standing on the edge of the inner wall, and the Chancellor was only a few feet away from me. He was looking out over the city like I was, but I could hear him mumbling under his breath.

"…already pushed up the time for the tournament. This part was supposed to last several more days, but you turned a two-week-long event into less than one!" A faint murmuring seemed to come with the wind. "It may not seem important to you, but I am the one who must explain to the king why his city lost all of the potential revenue streams those extra days would have brought in." This time, the whispers went on for a good long time. "I understand, but not everything is in place for the next phase. We don't even have all of the guards converted!" More whispers on the wind. "No, it isn't like that. I trust in your power. I just don't want to leave anything to chance!" He flinched, but no blood fell this time. "When they get their rewards, their guard will be down. It will be the best time to pounce. As long as the king stays in his palace, no one will know."

I was contemplating how useful it might be to use some mana to push the Chancellor over the edge—and whether it would actually kill him or not—when the Chancellor's spy approached him out of the darkness.

"My lord, it is done. The hall is fully prepared. All the doors have been reinforced, and extra locks installed. Our people also carved the necessary silence runes all over the outside of the building. When it starts, no one will hear their screams."

The Chancellor's grin looked downright predatory. "Good. Have you found out anything more about the people who made it to the finals?"

The spy nodded, and pulled out a sheaf of papers. "All of them but one. The small team competition has a group of mercenaries we don't have records on, but they appear to be a merchant group that only fights to test themselves. Out of all the possible matches, I would say they are the least compatible."

The Chancellor nodded at the spy's words. "It doesn't matter. They will either assimilate, or die. I don't care which option they choose. We should have more than enough vessels to spare, anyway." While the Chancellor kept smiling, I could sense the disgust the spy was feeling over the entire situation. "Did you arrange the matches to ensure the best would survive their matches?"

"Yes." The spy pulled out a paper with a list of all the competitors. It was almost exactly the same as the rankings I had seen as we left the arena. "I also have the best healers on retainer, to help save any on the edge of death. It would be best if you could incentivize the teams to restrain themselves from outright beheading their opponents tomorrow."

The Chancellor thought about it for a moment. "That is a good idea. I will announce a bonus to the fighters that leave their opponents alive. It won't stop them from culling those who are extremely weak, but it should help leave a few alive." The spy nodded, and moved to step away. "Ensure you have the prizes in place. We want to make sure they are prepared to move into the building. After all, the trinkets they will receive are just the bait for the trap. We can pick them back up off the bodies of any that refuse a contract, like plucking a lure from a fish's mouth once you have it in the boat."

Did this guy just call me a fish? That was it. I was totally pushing him over the wall. As I stepped forward to do so, a bright light flashed over me.

CHAPTER TWENTY-SEVEN

Ambush

I sat straight up in bed, my arms still trying to push the jerk who compared me to a stars-damned carp over the edge of a very high wall. Instead, I pushed Kory hard enough that he fell over backwards in surprise.

"Remind me to be more careful when I try to wake you." He looked up at me from the ground, his grin letting me know that he wasn't actually offended.

"Sorry about that, Kory. I was dreaming about pushing a man who called me a fish off a very high place."

He broke out into laughter. "You dream of the weirdest things, Jim. I wish I had the imagination to make things up the way you do."

I just shook my head at him. If he only knew…

As Kory got back to his feet and left the room, I compiled the facts of the dream in my head. From what I understood— and inferred—the Chancellor had set up this entire competition in order to find a bevy of suitable hosts for several immaterial *nox* that were floating around somewhere. After the winners were identified, they would be given their prizes and led to a room or building where they were supposed to receive private instruction from the king. Instead, they would be ambushed by the unbound *nox*, where they could either join with one or face death.

I might be missing something, but that was everything as I understood it. The supremely annoying thing about all of this wasn't that I would be captured by a bunch of *nox*. That was almost a good thing. They would all be in one place, after all, and any I managed to kill would be one less I was required to track down later.

No, the thing that bothered me the most was that I *still* wouldn't find an opportunity to speak with the king. That was the *entire point* of fighting in the tournament in the first place! How incredibly frustrating this was all turning out to be.

There wasn't much I could do about it now, I supposed. Instead of ruminating about how much this was going to mess up my plans, I got all of my armor in place and tied the chitin-covered wraps over my forearms, calves, and feet. Today I wasn't wearing the boots or cloak that masked my appearance. I wanted them to see me coming.

I walked down the stairs to the common room and saw all my friends laughing and joking as they sat around a table, eating breakfast. They were quickly becoming closer to me than any person or persons had, in both lifetimes. Today I would need to be strong enough, and *smart* enough, to keep them safe.

"Jim!" Chu was the first person to notice me standing by the stairs. "Get over here and put some food in your belly. The innkeeper has outdone himself this morning!" I felt my lips pull back in a genuine smile of happiness as I sat to eat.

"Is everyone good with the plan?" Kory had waited for me to take a few bites of food before he brought business to the fore. "If not, we can go over it one more time." Everyone announced that they were good, and started to get up to leave. I was about to rise from the table myself when inspiration struck. Later, I would wonder if it was a subtle hint from the gods that had kept me from simply getting up and following everyone out the door, or just stupid chance. Either way, many things would have ended up differently if I had ignored my sudden impulse.

When the assassins had fought with us, the well-made and polished furniture of the inn's common room had been destroyed. It had been replaced by the city guard, but they hadn't bought the highest quality table and chairs money could buy. Instead, it was rough-cut pine, with plenty of knots and blemishes marring the surfaces.

Right in front of me, near where my elbow was resting as I ate, were two perfectly oval knots of pine. The exact size and shape needed to make the slow-healing focusing pendants like the one I had hidden in the waistband of my pants. I spun out two threads of wood qi and pulled free the incredibly sharp plain stiletto knife hidden in the rear storage stud of my belt. The threads of wood qi popped free the knots, and I quickly carved the designs needed to attract all types of qi into the thumbnail-sized hunks of pine. I then used my own internal energy, blending all eight forms of qi, into the surface qi matrix of the newly created pendants. Now, the small knots of wood could convert natural qi from the environment to just wood qi, otherwise known as life qi, into the owner. It would allow them to be slowly, but constantly, healed.

There were only two people in my group that could actually use them. Chu, who already had a wood qi affinity, and Kory, who could use all forms of qi as a Saint-level cultivator. Anyone else I gave it to would have their meridians slowly corrupted by the wood qi they had no natural ability to control. Since their bodies weren't used to handling it, they wouldn't subconsciously be using the energy to rejuvenate injured tissue and bone. Once they broke through to the Brain level of cultivation, I would be able to make one for everyone.

As I climbed into the wagon with my impatiently waiting friends, I passed the two items off to Kory and Chu. They seemed confused, so I explained to them how they worked. I also let them know that as soon as they found a *real* focusing stone, they would have to get rid of the pendants. You could only use one at a time, after all. Otherwise they would fight for dominance and pollute your meridians with unusable qi. Since focusing stones were incredibly rare for anyone to have below the Sage level anyway, they were both very happy to have them.

"Why didn't you make anything for the rest of us?" Donny didn't seem to be jealous, just curious.

"There were only two knots of wood, and those two tend to be out in front anyway." I shrugged. "And they can use wood qi. The rest of you can't. When you get to the point where wood qi is as easy for you to use as the other elements you command, I'll make you one too."

Donny nodded in understanding. Valerie and Jamila seemed mollified as well, the tightness around their eyes disappearing. Huh. Had Donny only asked me about it to clarify to the two girls why I hadn't given them something as well? I patted him on the shoulder in thanks, just in case it was what he had intended to do.

The wagon moved through the streets faster than it had the past few times, the crowds seemingly less than they should be. Kory's eyes suddenly opened in realization just as it clicked for me as well. Ambush.

Everyone else in the wagon reacted as soon as they sensed our tension. We were all seated around the edges of the wagon facing inwards, with the walls of the wagon at our backs. I dropped to the floor, trying to use the thin oak boards as cover. Everyone else tried to do the same, with Kory pulling out a tower shield to cover us from any attacks that might come from the rooftops.

The four guards surrounding us on horseback were surprised to see us flopping around in the bed of the wagon, while the two driving the wagon kept looking straight ahead. If they had been doing their jobs, and looking outwards for external threats, they might have survived.

Instead, the arrows that flashed out from the surrounding rooftops found no resistance. The horses screamed in pain as they were hit as well, and there was a lurch as the two pulling our wagon started to sprint down the road. The surprise of their handlers falling to the ground and the sudden pain of the arrows drove them into a frenzy, and the wagon picked up momentum as they rounded the corner we had been approaching. I could hear shouts from our ambushers, the sudden exit of their prey clearly not in the plans they had made.

I tried to stand, but the road I had thought of as relatively smooth when we were rolling over the cobblestones at a sedate speed was now seemingly filled with bumps the size of a fat boar. I was tossed about like a toy doll subjected to a child's temper tantrum. The few pedestrians still walking the streets were screaming in fear, most of them diving out of the way. The few that didn't make it clear just made the road even bumpier. A particularly substantial bump made Kory's tower shield whack me in the face hard enough that I saw stars. I might have even blacked out for a few seconds, because the next thing I knew Jamila was sitting on the wagon seat, yanking on the brake lever.

Things might have been okay at that point if the horse on the right side hadn't collapsed. It faceplanted into the ground, forcing the wagon to skid sideways before flipping onto its side. Jamila was thrown through the window of a nearby tea shop, while the rest of us were thrown into the street.

The wagon basically exploded from the impact with the ground, the forces it was subjected to beyond what it had been built to endure. I watched, still dazed, as a wagon wheel rolled past me. I had been thrown into the middle of the street. Everything seemed to happen in quick jerks, in time with the thumping of my heartbeat in my head.

I saw Kory and Chu rise to their feet first, and they both turned back the direction we had come from instead of rushing to see how the rest of us were faring. Since Chu was our healer, that could only mean one thing. They saw enemies.

I tried to roll over to get back on my feet, but the motion made me throw up my breakfast onto the cobblestones. Somewhere in the back of my mind, I could hear the voice of my trainer from almost six hundred years ago screaming at me, telling me I had a head injury and I needed to focus. Wait. This was now, not before. The future hadn't happened yet. He hadn't told me that I had a head injury. I had a head injury?

An arrow came out of nowhere and pierced me through the hand. It did a wonderful job of clearing up my thoughts. I was on my hands and knees, facing the ten cultivators in black and gray clothing that made up a full kill team, plus one extra holding a bow in the rear. The archer that had gotten away during our first battle had come back to help finish the job. Kory and Chu were fighting them as best they could, but two on eleven was never an easy fight.

Valerie had dragged Donny into a nearby alley, and she was firing arrows from her bow while on one knee. The awkward position of her left leg told me it was broken, but she was still fighting through the pain. Jamila was still out of sight.

It took a massive effort of willpower, but I managed to draw qi through my own wood qi focusing pendant to speed up the healing it offered. The tiny trickle of energy turned into a slightly larger tiny trickle of energy. Apparently, even the massive effort I put forth wasn't very effective. I tried to direct what was coming in toward the damage to my skull and brain.

I focused back on what was going on, and saw that Chu had been knocked down. He was defending himself as best as he could from their many swords swinging down on him from his back, but it was only a matter of time until the four people attacking him managed to kill him.

Then it started happening again. The anger that had been simmering in the back of my mind, in my soul, broke free. It had been building for a long time. Going back to my clan that had betrayed me. Then seeing the innocent lives lost in a road-side inn. A storm sent by those who didn't even know my name, intended to end my life and the lives of my friends. My own uncle and cousin, who, when seeing me again, took the first chance they could to kill me for no other reason than their own bad decisions. A man inside an auction house that judged me only by my appearance. Then, a kill team was sent for my friends, to reap their lives like overripe grain. Not once, but *twice.*

It was all fuel for the fires of the rage that finally allowed me to transcend my injuries. Touching something so expansive and powerful I had only happened upon once before.

The last time, I had destroyed the world.

Time stopped. I was tapping into the hidden mana of the world that empowered all life on this plane of existence. Before, in the dream world, I had created mana. What I made, by layering and structuring qi into a higher form of energy, was like a spring bubbling up from the surface. This was a raging river overflowing its banks. I managed to just brush against the flow of power, barely dipping my proverbial toe into the stream of raw energy. It was enough to connect me to each of my friends, and I could sense how desperately close to death they all were.

Jamila had sliced the inside of her thigh open to the bone when she had been thrown through the glass window. It had severed a major artery in her leg, and she was quickly bleeding to death.

Donny had broken his spine just above his hips, and the nerves there were severed cleanly. He might be able to heal from such an injury, given enough time, but it would take years before he could walk again.

Valerie was suffering from a broken pelvis and a broken leg. A sliver of bone that had broken free from her hip had lodged in her lower abdomen, and from its location, I knew she might never be able to have children.

Kory and Chu were both cut to pieces, their limbs only holding on to their weapons through force of will. They had a subtle poison that had already polluted their blood from the blades of the assassins, one that would ensure they never survived the night.

My own body was in dire straits as well. The brain matter inside my skull had swollen to the point that I was beginning to hemorrhage. I would probably die from a stroke within minutes.

No.

I deny this reality.

I will not let it end like this.

Even through my rage, I knew not to draw upon the power that suffused my body for destruction. Instead of using it to tear down reality, this time I used it to heal.

I painstakingly put each of us back together. It felt like it took months to bring us all back from the brink, but I never broke my concentration for a moment. Jamila's wound was sealed, and her blood loss restored. Donny and Valerie were made whole; they would still be able to bring life into this world. Kory and Chu's blood was swept clean, and their cuts sealed. Finally, my brain reduced in size. As it was healing, my connection to the mana pumping through the world was gradually cut off. Time slowly started back up again.

I sprang to my feet, already whipping my throwing knives at the assassins as hard as I could. I knew there was a good chance their auras would slow or outright stop them, but it gave enough time for Kory and Chu to get some space.

Donny and Valerie rounded the corner of the building they had been hiding behind, him launching a bolt and her firing an arrow, both at the same person.

Jamila, though…

Jamila came out of the tea shop with vengeance on her mind. Instead of her dual katanas, she was using her garrote. The one I had made her as an afterthought. Apparently, she had been practicing with it.

The assassin nearest to her was facing Kory and Chu, making it easy for her to swing the wooden handle around the side of the assassin's head. It looped around in front of him and she caught it in her waiting hand. She pulled straight back, her shorter height guiding it down below his chin. Jamila took a single step backwards and the man's head soon followed.

None of the other assassins noticed the silent death of their comrade, all of them focused on the knives and arrows Valerie and I were sending their way. They did notice, however, when the second man died. Jamila had just walked up behind their only archer, dropped the looped wire over his head, and tried to remove it like she did the first one. This guy must have had a stronger aura, because the tightening wire seemed to slow just enough for him to try to duck out of it. Instead, it caught on his upper lip, and she pulled the garrote hard enough that it sliced through his lips, cheeks, jaw, and finally pulled all the way through the back of his head. It was messy, and he died screaming the entire time.

As the top two-thirds of his head tumbled toward their feet, all of the assassins seemed to freeze. The way that man had died was horrible, and it seemed to make all of them think about their own mortality for a second.

And that was all we needed.

Chu reached them first, his mace whistling through the air as it disintegrated the chest of his target. Kory was right behind, and he had pulled a spiked maul from somewhere that easily overcame the aura of his target. I flung a handful of poppers at the side farthest from my friends, since I was still too far away to engage them directly. The minor explosions threw them around like leaves caught in the wind, which gave Donny and Valerie enough time to hack into the prone forms of the two assassins closest to them.

And just like that, the odds favored us. Five of them, six of us. They were shocked by the loss of their team members and still stunned by the noisy and violent explosions of the poppers. It made them easy prey for me.

I had always been the farthest from the fighting in this battle due to how far the crash had thrown me. It allowed my injured brain the time to tap into the forbidden power of raw mana and heal us all, but it hadn't allowed me to kill the people that tried to take the lives of my friends and I.

I sent fifteen threads of earth qi underground, three for each of them. Their dark auras did nothing for the loops I tied around their legs to keep them from running away. Or for the one I wrapped around each of their throats. I took my time, slowly choking the life out of them. I didn't bother to say anything as they died. I made sure to keep squeezing until I heard the dry snapping sounds of their necks breaking. The smell of voided bowels and blood made the street stink like a slaughterhouse. Which, I supposed, kind of was one now.

We all looked at one another, each of us understanding how close our brush with death had actually been. I wasn't sure how it had felt from their end, but for me the whole thing was a humbling experience. No matter how capable I might be, I was far from invincible. Or unbeatable. The wrong series of events could kill me the same as any other person.

It also revealed to me that there was something about my brain that allowed me to touch the flows of mana when I found myself close to death. As long as I was conscious when it happened, anyway. The few times I had almost died since reincarnating had been a mixed bag of me ending up fully aware or unconscious, and there was no counting on being able to use mana the next time something bad was happening.

"Jim, you can let them go now." Chu put his hand on my shoulder, and looked pointedly at the five assassins I still had suspended from my threads of earth qi.

I dropped them, mentally shaking myself. I needed to keep my head in the game.

"Strip them and collect what you can. Make sure we get all of Jim's throwing knives back, and try to recover whatever arrows Valerie might be able to still use." Kory took control of the situation, and we all fell back on our normal patterns. He approached me as I moved to help the others. "No, Jim, not you. I want you to sit a moment and collect yourself."

I looked at him, confused by what he said. "I'm fine, Kory. I can help. We need to hurry and make our way to the arena anyway. The match is going to start soon." I pointed down the road toward the location of the arena, but Kory just shook his head.

"Jim, your eyes were glowing. They still are, just a little bit. Also, you still have an arrow sticking out of your hand."

I looked down. Huh. I must have missed it when I was healing everything.

Kory leaned in closer and lowered his voice to barely more than a whisper. "I was poisoned, and I felt myself dying. Then, you emitted the strongest force I have ever sensed, and it was gone. I was perfectly healthy. Even the qi in my cores was fully recharged. What did you do?"

I shook my head, not sure how to explain it. Some things were still too much for everyone to understand. To explain mana to him would require me to explain that I didn't just talk to the gods, but I had been reincarnated. I trusted Kory with my life, but some secrets were just too big to share at this point.

"It was the gods. They helped me." Not really a lie. "They also showed me what the Chancellor is going to do next. He and the *nox* inside him have a plan to turn all the cultivators that win the tournament into vessels for possession. We have to stop them." Also not a lie, and this was the first chance I had to tell them about what I knew.

Kory nodded slowly, looking around at the people slowly starting to come back to the street. "We should stick with the plan. There should be some time after we win to figure out how to deal with the rest." He took in a deep breath and let it out slowly. "After all, the gods would not give us this mission if they didn't think we could defeat a Duke level cultivator." If only he knew! Oh well, nothing for it. I let out a hiss of pain as I finally pulled the arrow out of my hand. Kory took it from me. "Good! It is still in good shape. I bet Valerie could use it. The barbed tip might come in handy sometime." I winced as I looked at the torn flesh of my hand.

"Yeah, I definitely should have checked for that before I just yanked it out. Stupid mistake." I watched as the wound closed, and I felt an extra boost of power I didn't realize I still had as it left my body. Apparently, I had held on to just enough mana to get me back to one hundred percent ready. Whether it was the gods, or my own subconscious, I was still thankful.

Kory looked me in the eyes again. "There, the glow is gone. Whatever enlightenment the gods sent your way is over. Let's get out of here. The city guards can catch up with us at the arena. Whenever they finally notice they are missing half a dozen men and a wagon, that is." He seemed angry at how easily the guards had been killed. I was too.

We finished collecting everything and took off at a run. The tournament was starting soon, and we didn't want to be late. While our morning had already been filled with violence, we still had plenty more blood to spill today.

CHAPTER TWENTY-EIGHT

The Flying Sword Sect

The six of us arrived a few minutes late. The speeches had been said and the first matches had already begun. We were still good, as the brackets showed us at the third fight. While we found our seats, Chu asked around to find out if there had been any changes to the rules.

"The Chancellor wasn't here to give the speech this morning." Chu sat down between Donny and I, but he spoke loud enough that everyone could hear him. "Apparently, something happened this morning that drew his immediate attention." We all looked at each other questioningly, wondering if it was our fight that had drawn him away. "One of his underlings announced that there would be a bonus for any fighters that spared their opponents, but there weren't any details on what it might be."

Donny shook his head, looking up at the balcony that held the city officials. "I don't like that the Chancellor was called away at the same time we fought. Do you think he was the one that hired the assassins?"

I thought about it for a minute before answering. "No. It wasn't him. The Chancellor didn't care about us in the least.

The assassins had to come from the Flying Sword Sect." I had an idea as to why the Chancellor suddenly had cause to look into matters going on in the capital, but I didn't like it. "Do you remember how I said the Chancellor was possessed by a *nox*?" Both Donny and Chu nodded. "I think it sensed when I tapped into the power of the gods to heal everyone." They all thought about that for a good long while. I was worried. It wouldn't take long for him to put two and two together and figure out that I had survived the weather attacks last year. And to know that the 'seal breaker' was at least in the city, maybe even on the team of mercenaries fighting in the tournament.

Chu broke the silence. "Just because you used the power of the gods, doesn't mean he knows it was one of us. It could have been a passerby that stepped in to fight the assassins. Stars, it could have even been one of the assassins! It will take him some time to figure it all out."

I sighed. Maybe he was right.

While we had been talking, the fighting in front of us had continued. Both teams were pretty evenly matched, and I figured the win would go to the team that could outlast the other. They actually seemed to be taking care not to kill each other, so maybe the vague incentive had actually worked.

After the match finished, a team of healers rushed out to try to save the losing team. It looked like most of them would make it. Such was the life of a cultivator. You either continued up the steep path of advancement, or you tumbled off to your death.

The next fight was between the Flying Sword Sect and another team of eight cultivators that looked to be from a fairly prosperous clan. Their group seemed to be an even mix of Meridian and Saint cultivators, which meant they could have a chance against the murderous sect members. They wore high-quality steel breastplates over enchanted leather armor that projected a thin shield of air qi. It might add enough defense to block a blow or two from a Heart cultivator, but not much more. Still, it was an expensive set of gear.

The shouts of the crowd let us know that the other fights

were progressing as well, and at least a few combatants wouldn't be leaving here on their own two feet. I pushed out my senses, trying to detect anything new about the Flying Sword Sect that might give us more of an edge. Today they seemed to be more jittery than normal. Their qi churned inside their cores, and I saw more than a few of the team shaking their head as if to clear it. Had they taken some type of drug, or potion, to give them a bigger edge in the fight?

"They seem off. I don't know if our plan will work. It depends on them being aware enough to understand what is going on around them." Kory was speaking to Jamila, but I could hear what he said easily, since my senses were already pushed to their maximum. I looked closer, and saw that it was only their two lower cores that were out of balance. Their upper cores were all perfectly calm, leading me to believe that they had taken some form of stimulant that affected how much qi they could hold, and how fast their bodies could move. Their minds should be clear enough for our strategy to work.

"Do you think they are going to actually let their opponents survive this time? I mean, it isn't like they *have* to kill everyone." Donny was about to answer Chu's question when the fight started.

I will say this for the Flying Sword Sect. They didn't make them suffer. The sect members tore through the other team like they were made of wet parchment. As they left the fighting pit, more than a few of their members were staring at us. Jamila returned their stares with a bored look on her face, idly rolling a shuriken across the knuckles of her right hand, while her left hand made a rude gesture in their direction. Valerie pretended to be asleep, while the rest of us simply smiled. Well, I might have been playing with a dagger that had belonged to an assassin not long ago, but I wasn't sure if they noticed.

Next up, it was our turn. We were facing a team of seven cultivators that specialized in attacking with qi constructs. Since our armor was specifically designed to stop such things, it was an easy fight. Actually, Chu was the star of the battle. His blowgun darts tipped in chitin were able to easily punch through their qi shields, making it easy to finish them off. The crowd wasn't sure whether or not to be excited or angry about the unorthodox win. Since none of us really cared, we just quietly returned to our seats. The six other teams seemed to think the win was as odd as everyone else, but Chu seemed to have elevated in their estimations.

There were two more matches before the judge announced an hour break for lunch. We didn't bother getting up from our seats, and all six of us refused the food and drink offered by the wandering concessions people. After two assassination attempts, we weren't willing to risk poisoned food or a knife in the back while traversing the crowds. We simply ate whatever food we had stored away and paid close attention to anyone walking past our area of the stands.

Once everyone returned from the break, it was finally time. Our team was called on to fight the Flying Sword Sect. We waited for them to march down the stairs first.

As they passed us, one of them turned to face Kory. "I'm surprised to see you here. After the *messages* we sent you, I figured that your little mercenary band would be halfway to the nearest hiding place you could find."

Kory just looked at the man, but Jamila couldn't stop from saying something. "Wait until you see what we prepared for your sadistic little team of killers. You are all going to die here. And you will die ugly."

The apparent leader of their group just laughed and walked down the stairs. We followed them down into the pit, and lined up as we had planned.

Kory was a few paces in front, while the rest of us were standing in a half-circle behind him. Instead of waiting for the judge to speak for us to pull out our shields like we had done every time before, we pulled them early.

These shields were different. Instead of our finely-wrought circular shields, these were thick tower shields that interlocked with one another. Little more than giant iron rectangles, they were tall enough that I had to stretch to my full height to see over the top. They were too heavy to fight with, but they were great for blocking things like massive qi attacks, or helping to direct the blast wave of an explosion a certain direction. Which was exactly what we were going for.

Kory pulled out a stone disk the size of a wagon wheel and dropped it on the floor. He then poured out a large flask of liquid qi onto it, powering the runes carved on its surface. Kory stood in the center of the stone, creating a massive swirl of qi from one of his upraised hands. In the other, he held a ridiculous sword almost as heavy as the shields we were using, last owned by a certain foolish recruiter.

The judge still hadn't started the match yet, but the Flying Sword Sect was already charging toward Kory. The massive formation plate, combined with the flashy qi display and our giant shields had clearly worried them. Anyone could see the shields were meant to defend the weaker members of our team from an explosion, and Kory sure did look like he was about to ignite a massive explosion. All those flashy lights from his qi tornado and glowing runes from the shield would make anyone think the fighting pit was about to go up in a massive conflagration.

It wasn't. You see, we were like a toddler screaming in rage as we crapped our pants. That toddler couldn't really hurt you, but it sure could intimidate you. The lights and glowing formation plate were only a bigger, flashier version of the shield I had used in the market square of the Roh Clan when I created a diversion. There wasn't going to be an explosion. But there was going to be a shield they couldn't break through for several minutes, no matter how hard or how often their 'linked swords' attack hit it.

Technically, we had already won the match the moment their team crossed the centerline. The judge had never started the match, meaning they broke the rules. We were winners by default. However, after all of the things these absolute *bastards* had done to us, no one was willing to let them walk away from this.

They pounded on the shield around Kory, all eight of them completely ignoring the rest of us. Their swords skidded and bounced less than a foot from Kory's stationary form as they completely encircled him. He waited for a few heartbeats, letting them expend their qi uselessly. Then, the Flying Sword Sect found out the shield only blocked things from coming *in*.

The ridiculously huge sword I had given him was pretty much useless in most situations. The incredible mass of the thing made using it in a real fight against a trained opponent a hindrance instead of an asset. But when an incensed enemy was kind enough to stand in a neat little circle all around you, it was a different story.

Kory infused the swirling qi tornado into the slab of metal pretending to be a weapon. Since it was mostly air qi, it helped speed up the swing of the sword. Which, with its heavier mass, made it perfect for shattering the enemy swords within reach.

The explosion was intense. Those swords had the majority of the qi from *eight* different Saint cultivators passing through them. And with that much power, literally four times what the batteries in my belt could hold, the results were absolutely incredible. Not exactly 'destroying a dark temple' kind of explosion, but impressive nonetheless.

Only three of the eight swords were actually shattered, but it had been enough. The five of us huddling behind the massive shields popped them back inside our rings to survey the damage.

Kory was fine behind the shield, but the pit was in rough shape around him. The end of the giant sword that had been sticking out of the shield had been melted and was dripping molten metal onto the stone disk. Our tower shields might have been for our protection, but they actually had done a pretty good job of funneling the blast wave back into the people standing around the shield. Two of the enemy cultivators had been killed outright. It was the two that had been standing between the dome qi shield over Kory and our own iron shields. There wasn't much left of them.

The other six weren't as bad, with the man standing opposite our physical shields faring the best of the lot. Their toughened Saint-level bodies were weakened because the majority of their qi had been in their swords, making them more susceptible to physical damage. It had all turned out even better than we could have planned.

Kory and I had suspected that we would still need to fight at least half of them, but we couldn't have known that the swords would actually blow up. We had just hoped to break their concentration and cause some qi backlash, diminishing the power of their link. For so many to actually explode, I suspected there was some type of safety feature built into the swords that didn't allow them to hurt their wielders from qi backlash. I guess, in their eyes, the physical damage was easier to heal. Well, not today it wasn't.

Since there were now six of them and six of us, we each stood over one of the surviving members of the Flying Sword Sect. Everyone pulled out a dagger taken from the bodies of the assassins we had killed and held them up, ready to stab down into the people responsible for so much needless pain and death.

Just as we were about to stab downwards, over twenty guards jumped down into the fighting pit.

A familiar-looking captain of the guard stepped forward to speak. "Hold! Do not kill these people!"

I thought about just stabbing downwards anyway, but this place had too many witnesses for what I would have to do afterward.

"Give us one good reason as to why we should let these cultivators live, Captain. They all but admitted that they are the people responsible for the assassins that killed your very own men!" Kory was progressively getting louder, his own desire for revenge making it difficult to stay his hand.

"That is precisely why you can't kill them." The captain was looking around at all of us, trying to gauge his chances if we outright disobeyed him. "They are to face a tribunal, and they will pass judgement on their actions."

"A tribunal!" Donny was pissed, his arms waving about as he shouted. "You mean a chance for their sect to bribe and politic their cultivators out of the hangman's noose? No thank you, Captain! I say they face their rightful punishment here, with the citizens as witness! They killed your men; don't you want to see them pay for their crimes?"

The captain shook his head. "The people who killed my men are already dead. You left them on the street. Along with those same men whose deaths you try to flaunt in my face!" He was getting upset now. He pointed up at where the judge normally stood on the ledge above the pit. Apparently, the man had not hung around during all of the explosions. "This fight was never officially started, so the arena rules do not apply. You have no right to kill these men. Now, stand down, before you find yourselves facing the same tribunal as these murderers!"

Damn. He had us there. The fight hadn't actually started. We could get away with defending ourselves, but killing the survivors would certainly not end well. Everyone was subtly looking in my direction, waiting for my decision. I slowly lifted my hands and made the dagger I was holding disappear. The rest followed my example.

"Good decision. Now, go back to your seats and let us get this mess cleaned up." He did seem genuinely thankful that he wasn't going to have to fight us.

"You got lucky." Jamila was standing over the leader she had threatened earlier, the least injured and most aware of their group. "But this changes nothing. You will still die, and it will still be an ugly death." She spit in his face, and kicked him in the ribs hard enough to make him curl into the fetal position.

Valerie led our team out of the pit, the guards moving out of the way to let us leave. The crowd didn't like the interference from the guards any more than we did, their boos and the occasional rotten vegetable thrown down into the pit letting the interlopers know they weren't appreciated for their actions. As we reached our seats, Chu wrapped his muscular arm around Jamila's shoulders.

"Don't worry. If they weasel their way out of the courts, we will be waiting for them." While the words were meant to console Jamila, the rest of us gave a sharp nod of agreement along with her. I knew what they almost cost my friends. They would pay for their unprovoked attacks, one way or another.

We would make sure of it.

CHAPTER TWENTY-NINE

Awards and Rewards

Since our match didn't really count, we were forced to fight again almost immediately. We had enough of a break to refill what little qi we used while they repaired the fighting pit, and the match was almost over before it began.

The other team, another well-prepared sect, seemed to think we were all a bunch of crazy killers. Which, I mean, I could see where they got that…

So, that match was an easy win. It did have the positive side effect of allowing us to work out some of our frustrations over what had happened. Everyone made sure not to hurt them too bad when we won.

As we got back to our seats, I overheard Donny and Chu talking.

"Did you ever imagine something like this?" Chu waved his hand around. "That one day, we would be taking on cultivators from sects all over the empire, and beating them?"

Donny shook his head with a sigh. "No, not at first. I mean, I grew up with Jim. I helped care for him when his parents were gone on missions. There was no warning about what he would become." Donny looked at each of us. "What we all would become."

"I know what you mean." Valerie leaned in, trying to keep her voice down. "That fight wasn't even hard, and they are supposed to represent one of the strongest sects in the empire? Just how strong are we?"

Kory butted in before they could say anything else. "Don't get cocky. This tournament didn't allow any fighters above Sage, and most sects have dozens, sometimes hundreds, of powerful fighters. We have only been fighting their students. The masters would be a completely different proposition."

They all nodded at his words. As the next fight between two other teams started, I took the opportunity to draw in qi from the meridians in my feet. No one would be able to tell, but I was trying to be fully prepared for what came after the tournament.

We were expecting to have to fight one more round, but instead the Chancellor finally made an appearance once the current round of fights finished up. I sensed as he pushed out a massive qi construct that was invisible to the naked eye, designed to increase the volume of his voice so that the entire arena could hear him speak.

"Congratulations, good people! The cultivators before you have shown themselves to be the best of the new generation of warriors, and we have decided to give them their *proper* rewards. Please, give these champions a round of applause!"

Everyone seemed confused. None of the three types of competition had finished their brackets. In fact, the large group competition still had six teams vying for first place, the one-on-one had four, and we had two. This would completely ruin all the bets everyone had placed. It didn't take long for the crowd to figure that out either.

It started on the opposite side of the arena from where I was sitting, but pretty soon the entire audience was shouting and hollering in rage at the Chancellor. His decision to end the tournament before even a single individual or team could take first place was incredibly unpopular. In fact, I was expecting a riot to start in the next few minutes.

Instead, the Chancellor, a Duke-level cultivator, released the full might of his aura. The pressure exerted on the entire arena was like gravity had instantly tripled. A few people even fell unconscious, their bodies unable to cope with the sudden change. The Chancellor was much more powerful than a normal Duke cultivator, almost to the level of a King. It had to be the *nox*, their connection artificially boosting his power. He smiled out at the crowd.

"I am sure you can all understand, the empire cannot afford to lose any more of these inspiring warriors to possible mishaps in these fights. Instead, they will all proceed to the place where we have prepared the items they will be awarded with. Thank you for your support."

What? If that was the case, he could have just changed the rules to ensure no cultivators were killed.

I understood the real reason for him ending the matches early. He was scared. The *nox* must have sensed when I used mana to heal everyone. He didn't know what I had done with it though. All he saw was a bunch of dead elite assassins, and his *nox* was telling him a true threat to him was running around in the city. My guess was the Chancellor wanted to get as many people as possible to bond with all the untethered *nox* he had hiding in the capital as fast as he could.

The crowd quickly dispersed under the pressure being emitted by the Chancellor. Soon, the only people left in the arena were the judges, the guards, and the surviving competitors. I watched as the Chancellor worked his way down the stairs to where we all waited for him. This might be our only chance to talk before we were corralled inside a sealed building filled with untethered *nox*, so I needed to make the best of it. I pulled everyone into a huddle so we could design a basic plan.

"Okay. This is going to get messy. I can't tell you how I know, but just listen." Everyone nodded and leaned in close. They were used to this kind of stuff by now. "We are going to be taken to a building where a bunch of immaterial dark mana demons are going to try to possess everyone. I'm not really sure how it works, but I think they try to come up with some type of agreement with their hosts."

The shocked looks on everyone's faces only lasted for a second, their professionalism keeping them focused.

"That being said, they might try to just force a bond on someone that says no if their soul is black enough to allow them a connection. I haven't seen how it works, but we need to be ready for anything." Nods all around. Good. "As soon as it kicks off, we need to try to take the high ground, if there is any. We each have a shield formation plate in our combat kits, so don't be afraid to use them if you start to get swarmed. Once we take the high ground, we hold it for as long as it takes. As long as we stick together, we should be fine."

We all looked at one another, confident in our ability to work together as a team.

"Oh, and one last thing. If we actually get some type of prize, don't touch it with your bare hands. It might have contact poison or something on it. Just put it in storage, and we can inspect everything when we leave." Everyone agreed, and we all took a moment to pull on some leather gloves. We would shred them if we used the meridians in our hands, but they would work for something like this.

Chu leaned forward a bit to talk. "Don't forget, if you get isolated, just wait for us to come and get you." We all nodded in agreement.

Before we could say anything else, the Chancellor finally made it downstairs. That was the best plan I could think of, considering the situation. It would have to work.

"The first part of the Trials is complete! Congratulations, everyone. Now, to your next Trial. You need to choose your prize!" The other contestants laughed. We didn't. I hadn't missed how he placed emphasis on the word 'trials.' To him, this had been the set of trials he set up to determine the most likely and powerful hosts for the *nox*. To me, this had all been a trial of my patience. I really, *really*, just wanted to kill this guy and move on. Stupid emperor and his stupid need to control everything! If it weren't for his recruiters that would inevitably track me down, I wouldn't have anything holding me back.

"Please, follow me." A few competitors were brave enough to shout questions about the order in which we would be selecting from the prizes, but he waved them away. "Don't worry! We have everything arranged. Let's just move to the necessary location and get things underway."

We all trailed behind the group keeping close on his heels. I didn't have an exact count, but there were more than seventy contestants that walked down an empty side street to a nondescript building a few blocks over. That was a whole lot of potential pairings of *nox* and cultivators. Or a whole lot of victims.

We held back as everyone started to file through the entrance to the building. It was a single narrow door, so we all had to wait to get in. The place looked like an abandoned warehouse. Looking at the walls, I even saw where the former loading docks had been filled in with large blocks of stone. Standing outside, I could already feel the menace of the creatures hidden inside. This was bad. There were either a few extremely powerful *nox* inside, or a seriously *huge* number of them. I knew only around two hundred *nox* had slipped through into this dimension, so I was guessing it was the former.

I wasn't the only person that felt the dark energy. Some of the cultivators were slow to enter, their instincts telling them to run away. The thought of the treasure held within saw their greed win out, driving them to enter.

Since we were at the rear of the group, I soon realized there weren't any guards standing behind us. I nudged Kory, and he looked around as well. I took a step back from the others and double-checked that we weren't being watched, sending out a few invisible threads of air qi onto the rooftops. After confirming that we were alone, I motioned for everyone to get closer.

"New plan. Kory and I will go inside, while the rest of you

wait outside." They raised sounds of protest, but I talked over them. "I know you want to join us, but you have a more important job. Hidden around the building are silencing runes, meant to keep any sounds of fighting from being heard. I want you to go over the whole thing, even the roof, and remove them all." They still didn't seem happy. "Look, we could end up fighting inside for hours before anyone noticed that something was wrong. This way, you can make sure that doesn't happen. As soon as people start to notice, bust inside and kick the stars out of whoever gets in the way."

Everyone was quiet for a bit, but they eventually agreed. They might not like it, but they understood the difference this could make. As they split off and went around the building, it was time for Kory and I to enter.

The door led into what was once a small office, probably meant for the manager when it was still an operating warehouse. There were two very large guards that were hulking by the entrance. Once we entered, they looked around outside for anyone else before sealing the door behind us. The other one activated a ward rune that ensured anyone trying to enter would have to make a lot of noise to do so. And by that, I meant break the thing down.

They didn't say anything, just pointed toward the only other door in the room. Kory led the way, the tension in his shoulders letting me know he was feeling the strong emanations of the dark mana demons like I was. It was so thick, I felt like a disgusting film was coating my exposed skin. I was also pretty sure the two guards following behind us were possessed by *nox*, but I wasn't sure. I hadn't gotten much experience with them yet. Although, what I had dealt with so far was definitely memorable.

Kory and I walked into a giant room filled with rows of rectangular tables. Each of them had identical sets of items, and it looked as if there were enough tables for twice the amount of people that had survived to see the end of the tournament. This meant they didn't have an accurate count of how many people were supposed to be here, and I couldn't hold in a sigh of relief. They had no idea that my four team members were missing. Kory and I each approached a table, looking everything over but making sure not to touch anything. Other people were already going through their items, not worrying about what was going on around them.

There were two hefty pouches, one of gold coins and one of cut gems. An open box lined in velvet held six Earth-grade beast cores, one of each known element. Not the Sky-grade cores I needed to operate the mirror from the Roh Clan, but definitely good enough to let me make a few items I needed. It also had a set of simple linen and canvas enchanted clothing— thank the gods—and an almost plain double-edged longsword. The sword had a row of runes running down the center that I was having trouble deciphering. I recognized them as mostly communication runes, but a few of the carved designs seemed off.

I leaned over the sword to get a better look, but the Chancellor finally chose that moment to speak. "I want to congratulate you all once again on your victory. Each of you has earned the opportunity of a lifetime." He was standing on top of a table in the middle of the room so we could all see him. "After you take your prizes, those willing to push the limits of power will receive an offer they will find difficult to refuse." Wow. Little on the nose there, Chancellor. "I encourage everyone that receives this offer to think long and hard about the benefits it will provide them, far into the future. Please, gather your items and wait for those with the proper qualifications to decide if they will accept their final gift."

There was a round of quiet applause, as several people felt the need to acknowledge the speech. It actually wasn't too far outside the norm, as far as post-tournament speeches went. Cities, clans, or sects that held tournaments like this were well known for trying to recruit the winners into their guard forces or armies. Which was probably what most people were expecting. Some general or guard captain to come out and give a spiel about the benefits of joining their organization. That didn't happen.

As people were grabbing their items, some of them seemed to freeze as they touched the swords. I saw one man, a cultivator that had fought in the large group fights, seize up and fall over. I turned back around, throwing everything but the sword inside my belt. No way I was going to just leave the good stuff lying around.

I finally gave the sword a good once-over, and I realized what was happening. The runes had been twisted in a way I had never seen before. Instead of allowing for two-way communication between cultivators, it looked like this sword allowed whatever it was connected with to send a one-way message straight into the brain. Something like this could allow someone with a strong will to literally destroy the mind of the person holding the sword. This was, obviously, very bad. Mind control was one of the nastiest things a powerful cultivator could ever do to another person, and these bastards had found a way to mass produce and weaponize a way to manage it.

"Don't touch the swords! They're a trap!" I shouted as loud as I could, trying to save those who hadn't picked up their weapons yet. This, of course, made the Chancellor look directly at me. I ducked under my table, making sure to pop the sword into my storage ring without touching it as I did so.

There were enough people and tables between the Chancellor and I that it was easy to shuffle around a few rows and pop back up farther into the room. Since I just so happened to be in an area of tables loaded down with goods, I did my civic duty and cleaned off all the items stored on top of them.

Some people might say I stole everything but the actual tables, but that would be a lie. I totally took those too. Before anyone could stop me, I had cleared off at least a dozen tables worth of items, and three or four tables that seemed particularly stable. What could I say? I liked a good table. I was moving to take the bag of gems off of table number thirteen when the Chancellor finally found me.

By this point, the room was in quite a fracas. About thirty people had picked up the swords and were frozen completely still. The other forty or so had either heard my warning, or figured out for themselves that touching the swords would do something bad to them. The look on the Chancellor's face was pure fury. He wasn't happy that his neat little plan had so easily been messed up. The people that weren't frozen were all shouting for an explanation, while those with friends that had been affected were trying to snap them out of it.

The Chancellor jumped on top of a table and released his aura again, dropping several people to their knees. I was one of them. Being in the same room with him when he uncovered the power of the qi in his cores was entirely different than standing a few hundred feet away in the open air. He also was directing most of the pressure right at me, so that didn't help either.

"I was trying to do this the nice way." He looked around at all the people struggling to rise. Interestingly enough, the people who were frozen seemed to be unaffected by his aura. "Instead, we can do this the *easy* way." I had to admit, that was a great line. I was a little jealous that I hadn't said it. "Guards! You know what to do." The two exceedingly large men walked over to a cultivator that had just managed to get back to his feet. One of them wrapped his meaty arm around the man's neck, while the other guard shoved a trap sword into his hand. The effect was immediate. The first guard let him go, and the cultivator stayed in the same awkward position without being held there. They then moved on to the next nearest cultivator and repeated the process. I tried my best to move, to spin out some qi threads, do anything to help them, but it was no use.

Stars. This was bad.

CHAPTER THIRTY

Kory's Sacrifice

As I mentioned before, the room had clearly served as a warehouse at some point in its past. Whatever activity or storage function it was used for had required a walkway installed near the ceiling, which ran the circumference of the big room, as well as two narrow sections that ran perpendicular through the center of the room. They basically split the room into four squares, if you were to look down from above.

Kory, always the perfectionist, had managed to follow the plan and make his way to the high ground. Which, in this case, was the aforementioned walkway. If I had actually followed the plan instead of running around and grabbing all the stuff I could, I would probably be up there with him right now. Instead, he had to figure out how to fix this by himself, with no backup from me. There was definitely a lesson in there somewhere, but now wasn't the time to ponder it.

The guards had moved to their third victim when I finally noticed him moving around up on the walkway. I saw him fiddling with something as he positioned himself above the Chancellor. The guards were moving on to a fourth cultivator to force into the frozen state when the Chancellor pointed at me.

"No. Do that one next. I don't like the look of him." The two burly men started weaving through tables and kneeling cultivators on their way over to me. I only had seconds to figure something out. Which was when Kory worked some magic.

Remember that big stone formation plate the size of a wagon wheel we had used against the Flying Sword Sect? The one that makes a big shield? Well, one thing about a piece of rock that big was that it was really heavy. So, when Kory dropped it over twenty feet onto the Chancellor's head, it certainly had an impact. Get it? *Impact?* I don't care what you say, that's hilarious.

The Chancellor was suddenly on the floor with his face buried in the floorboards, and a big stone disk laying on top of his head and shoulders. For some reason, Kory had activated the qi formation on it, so it formed a shield around the Chancellor. I know something like that certainly wouldn't kill the Duke-level cultivator, but I sure hoped it gave him a headache.

It also did something that changed the way the one-sided fight was going. It made the Chancellor lose control over his aura. While it didn't go away entirely, it was no longer being directed to suppress everyone in the room. Which was enough to let everyone get back in the fight.

Everyone not frozen immediately jumped to their feet. The two guards had almost reached me by that point, but the three cultivators between the guards and I instantly went on the attack. I wasn't sure how long it would take the guards to win, but I could use every second I could get.

I gave a wave of thanks to Kory, who nodded before going back to whatever else he was working on. Then, I ran over to the nearest frozen person and tried to get the sword out of their hands. The only safe place to grab was the cross guard, so I put one hand on either side and tried to pull it free. It was useless. Their grip on the sword was immovable. So, I tried my other idea.

I grabbed the green glass sword I had acquired from the Roh Vaults a few years ago out of the storage buckle on my belt. It had two properties that made it a treasure worth keeping. The sword was supposed to have some ability that allowed a cultivator to tame animals, or at least helped them tame animals. I had tried it out a bunch back when I was hiding for almost a year in the woods by myself, but to no avail. The other property it had was the ability to cut through just about any material, as long as it wasn't being actively reinforced by qi. Time to find out if any of those communication runes were also powering the swords with qi meant to strengthen the actual blade.

The green sword wasn't *really* made of glass. It was created from a material called malachite, which is a mineral based in copper ore. The trick to shaping it as if it were metal was a closely guarded secret held by only the most elite blacksmiths across the empire. What made it truly valuable was its ability to hold incredibly complex qi matrixes without straining the material. So, if a blacksmith were skilled enough, they could create amazing weapons and armor. And in a world filled with amazing and magical creations, this sword still stood out as pretty amazing.

It managed to slash through the steel sword as if it were made of butter. The cultivator still holding the sword instantly collapsed, but I could see he was breathing. A quick scan with my qi told me he was just exhausted, and he should be able to wake up soon. Now that I had a way to free everyone, I got to work.

I ran as fast as my legs would move, leaving a trail of collapsed cultivators behind me. I was swinging the green sword through steel blades as if my life depended on it. Which, let's be honest, it probably did. If all these people ended up possessed by *nox*, I wasn't sure if I could survive the fight that would ensue. The Duke that was groaning as he got back to his feet was going to be enough of a challenge as it was.

There were several people trying to escape, but I saw thirteen or fourteen cultivators still fighting the two guards, who had revealed themselves to *definitely* be possessed by *nox*. They had swollen to the size of Greater Iron Bears, which, you know, was pretty big. They even had elongated mouths like a bear, but with the blunt teeth of humans. It was very disturbing to see. Their hands were thankfully clawless, but that just meant they could still use them to manipulate weapons. Since not many weapons could actually be useful to something that big, they had just picked up some tables. Which, note to self, were excellent at swatting cultivators like they were just annoying flies. The people fighting them were not particularly amused, but I could still see the funny side of the whole thing. In a scary, oh-crap-I'm-gonna-die kind of way.

As terrifying as that duo was, I was far more concerned about the Duke-level cultivator that was still shaking his head to clear it. Once he got back into the fight, this would all be over. The shield Kory dropped on the Chancellor meant I couldn't attack him while he was down, which was why I was still confused that he had activated it. I even threw one of my throwing knives at it to test how strong the qi shield was, and I knew there was no way that thing was coming down anytime soon. I was convinced Kory had made a mistake by activating the shield at all. That was, until the Chancellor tried to take a step out of the shield and bumped into an invisible wall.

Kory was an absolute genius. Somehow, he had messed with the carvings to turn the shield completely solid. Nothing could go in, but nothing could go *out*, either. He had bought me some time.

The Chancellor started slamming his fists into the shield, slowly and deliberately draining the liquid qi that was powering the plate. I needed to hurry.

I ran around the room, finishing up freeing the cultivators that were still frozen. I also might have scooped up some more treasures on the way, but who's counting? The first few I had freed were slowly getting to their feet, confused looks on their faces and internal energy mostly depleted. I needed to get these people out of here. The cracks starting to show on the shield over the Chancellor only drove the need to hurry up even further.

Finally, I made it to the last person holding a sword. This had been the big guy that fell over, one of the first to touch a sword. I swung the glass blade down to shatter his sword, but this time it didn't work. It bounced off, doing that stupid vibrating thing that made my teeth hurt. I looked down at the man, only to see his eyes open as he sat up, still holding the mind-control sword.

And, since my life was *still* an ever-evolving shitshow, the whites of his eyes were solid black. It was a weird look, since I was pretty sure the cultivator had originally had blue eyes. The iris was still blue, it was just surrounded by black. Creepy. And to make it worse, he smiled so wide his lips split, dripping blood down his chin.

Total. Shitshow.

"*Ssseal-breaker!*" His voice was more of a hiss, with an odd echo to it. Like multiple voices were using the same mouth. It was fleetingly familiar, but I didn't have time to dwell on it as his sword stabbed at my face. "*We thank you for bringing usss to this world. It will be deliciousss…*" The possessed cultivator kept talking as it was swinging the sword at me in choppy motions. It felt like I was facing a puppet, I just couldn't see the strings making it move. I guess the *nox* inside the cultivator wasn't used to controlling its new body yet. I could work with that.

I put my sword away, swapping it for a small round buckler shield. I then spun out a strand of metal qi into a flexible metal whip for my right hand. As soon as the demon wearing a man suit attacked, I deflected the sword out wide with the buckler. It gave me an opening to snap the whip around his neck, which pretty much ended the fight. I ripped his head off, making the guards and Chancellor scream like they were in pain. I felt bad for killing the cultivator that had been possessed, but now wasn't the time to dwell on such things.

The sound of the qi shield around the only Duke cultivator

in the room shattering was much more of an immediate concern. Especially when he went straight for me.

I grabbed a handful of poppers and threw them in his direction, which was probably the only thing that saved me. I wasn't slowing down my perception of time yet, which was definitely a mistake. I couldn't even see the blur of the Chancellor sprinting at me. When he hit the poppers I had thrown, they were less than two feet away from my outstretched hand. His speed was so great that he didn't have time to dodge them—or he didn't think they were a threat and just ignored them—which meant they all hit him at once.

I was still in range of the blast, so I went flying back in a heap of jumbled limbs and broken table pieces. The Chancellor was thrown upwards somehow, but his forward momentum was so great that he ended up sailing over me and slamming into the wall all the way across the room. I would guess it was at least sixty or seventy feet of flight. Pretty impressive, really. He also managed to shatter a hole straight through the wall and out into a side alley. The wards sealing the place must have been attuned to his energy signature. Otherwise, they would have kept him from going through the wall.

The Chancellor was back on his feet quickly, but so was I. I had lost my buckler shield, so I pulled out the Dagger of Boom before changing my metal whip into a thin braid of all eight forms of qi. The dark and light qi seemed to pulse in the presence of the *nox*, making the whip strobe with power. It made the Chancellor pause, and I could see it worried him. Instead of closing within range of my whip, he formed a thick lance of red flames out of his qi and hurled it at me. Fast.

I barely had time to shift the dagger into position to absorb the attack, but I managed it. The heat it was putting off scorched the skin on my face, and made me thankful that I was still wearing leather gloves. It might have burnt them to the bone instead of just making them *feel* like they had been burnt to the bone. Ouch.

"That isn't going to work, demon. You will have to get close to beat me." I snapped the whip at him, causing him to flinch backwards.

"I thought I had killed you a long time ago. Like a cockroach, you just don't know how to die!" He punctuated his words with another blast of fire, this time using several smaller darts of qi that I had to scramble to absorb. The heat wasn't as bad this time, but the glove covering the hand holding the dagger was definitely smoldering.

"I can do this all day. Like I said, you are going to have to get close if you want to win." His eyes flicked to the side. Crap.

"Very well. That's what we will do." I tried to dive away, but the guard that had snuck up behind me was too fast.

His arm wrapped around my waist, so I stabbed it with the dagger and made it go Boom. I was mildly injured in the shockwave of released energy, since it was pointed toward me, but I definitely came out the better of the two of us.

I looked up from where I had been blasted to the ground. He was missing his right arm, and the major portion of his right side. The thick flesh of his bear form had directed the majority of the energy back into the squishy parts of his body, turning it into a really big mess. I could see most of his ribs, and his head was only attached by the flesh on the left side of his neck bones. I didn't have to look around for all his missing parts, because I was wearing most of them. Which was disgusting, in case you were wondering.

As the first guard toppled, the second guard picked me up by my legs, one in each hand. He wasn't nice about it. Killing his friend must have made him mad at me. I still had the dagger in my hand, but without any absorbed qi attacks, it was just a plain dagger. I popped it back in my belt and grabbed a spear instead. I tried to stab the guard in the face, but he pulled my legs apart hard enough that I felt my left hip get pulled out of its socket. Which hurt enough that I forgot all about stabbing him in the face and just screamed for a bit. If I had been in my six-hundred and fifty-year-old body, I would have been able to ignore the pain and keep fighting. Unfortunately, this body didn't have the same training to keep fighting, no matter the pain or discomfort. I was vaguely aware of the Chancellor approaching me.

"I severely underestimated you. That is five of my brethren you have killed. I was going to take you for a vessel, but you are far too dangerous to continue to exist. Goodbye, seal-breaker." I could see him form another lance of red flames, this time compacting it until it was as thin as an arrow shaft. I was trying to get my brain core to spin up fast enough to slow time, but he wasn't going to give me enough time. That was when Kory jumped off the walkway and landed on top of him. Getting squished twice in one day had to be incredibly frustrating, I imagined.

Kory hadn't been idle while he was hiding up there. The instant he landed, six formation plates flashed out of his hands and stuck to the guard holding me. I felt them activate upon contact, and the guard dropped me as he roared in agony. I hit the ground, the impact knocking the breath out of me. Then, to add insult to injury, the stupid guard's limp form fell on me. Double ouch.

Somehow, the guard falling actually helped me a little bit. His weight popped my hip back in place, which also hurt, but in a good way. Kory was suddenly there, trying to lift the dead weight off of me. Behind him, I could see the cultivators that were still ambulatory running out of the hole in the wall that the Chancellor had made.

"Sorry that took so long. I am not as good at making changes to formation runes as you are."

I looked at the dead guard. "At least you have good timing. What did you do to him?"

He grinned, proud of his actions. "I just modified your spike attacks to work on bone instead of stone. He was just ripped apart on the inside by his own skeleton. I thought of it aft—"

Kory cut off suddenly. I heard a scream come from the direction of the hole in the wall. I looked over, confused at who would be screaming.

It was Valerie, and she was looking at Kory. I looked back at him, and he smiled down at me before coughing up a mouthful of blood. I looked at his chest, and I could see the Chancellor smiling from the other side. Through his chest. Because there was a hole the size of a fist going all the way through the middle of it. I could literally see Kory's heart beating inside his chest, the hole just missing it. Kory dropped to his knees in front of me. I tried to tap into the network of mana flowing through the world like the last time one of us was hurt, but I couldn't do anything. My lack of a brain injury, or maybe because I wasn't about to die, kept me from touching it.

"It's okay." His voice was barely even a whisper, but I could hear it even through the sounds of my friends fighting with the Chancellor. "I'm okay." I was still stuck under the dead body, not able to get free. He smiled again, laying his hand on my shoulder. "If I would have ever had a son, I hope he would have been like you." His hand dropped, and I watched as his eyes glazed over.

"Kory, stay with me! *Stay with me, gods damn it!*"

He fell.

CHAPTER THIRTY-ONE

Fate

As he dropped, I could see everyone else on their knees in front of the Chancellor. Their fight hadn't gone well. A Duke was just too much power for them to handle.

"Your friends will make excellent vessels. I think it is ironic that you have brought enough to replace what I have lost. Well, you did have enough, until I tired of the other one dropping things on my head." He smirked at me. I looked around and saw that the only witnesses remaining were my friends and the *nox*. Finally.

"You know, I think it's funny." I tapped into the batteries on my belt, and the heavy body of the guard still on top of me was hit so hard it turned into mist. None of the blood and bits touched Kory's body. I made sure of it. "You people are all the same." I floated to my feet, and eight whips of qi, one of each element, formed around me. "You started this. Remember that. I didn't even know you existed until you attacked me. You *took from me*." I paused, regaining my cool. "You took from me someone that means more to me than you can probably understand."

The Chancellor had stopped smiling, but he still had an

arrogant tone when he spoke to me. "You would have come for me eventually. I was just—"

"Shut up. The dead don't speak. That is what you are. Dead. You just don't know it yet." He was stunned, not sure what to say to that. I didn't care. I wasn't lying. He was a dead man that hadn't stopped breathing yet. I turned to look at my remaining friends. They were battered, but none of them had any sign of defeat in their eyes. "While I finish this, you take Kory out of here. We can't risk any more damage to his body." Chu and Donny both nodded solemnly, while Jamila and Valerie growled. None of their eyes were dry. Neither were mine.

"I don't think—"

"I am aware you don't think, demon. Now stop talking. No one cares what the dead have to say."

He roared in anger and frustration. Apparently, he preferred it when those he saw as victims listened to his stupid monologues. "If you don't—"

He had to stop talking when I smacked him with a table. There weren't any whole tables left, but I made do with one that was just missing its legs. It didn't send him flying like the guards had sent the other cultivators flying, but it got my point across.

"You don't listen well, do you? Well, I guess that makes sense. I can't expect a dead man to hear the living speak." I attacked, every whip flying independently for his most vulnerable places. I had to make this fast. One battery was already halfway drained.

They struck hard, but the only two that he seemed to be concerned with were the light and dark qi whips. The wood qi whip wrapped around his left arm when he raised it, redirecting the blast of fire he had aimed at my friends. His left hand was aimed my direction, so I wrapped the metal qi whip around his index finger and the earth qi whip around his pinky and ring finger. Just as he started to project a dart of fire out of his hand meridian, I pulled. His hand was ripped in half, splitting his palm and tearing all the way up to his elbow.

Using the opening, I wrapped the fire whip around his neck and started to squeeze. I balled up the end of the air whip and rocked him in the groin. Then, I used the water whip to spear him in the abdomen.

I was only able to do all of this because all of his focus was on keeping the light and dark qi whips held away from him with his own strands of fire qi that came from one of the meridians on his back. I kept beating him bloody with the other six, and he just stood there and took it. Finally, the first battery was drained. The whips dissipated, leaving the Chancellor a wreck. While all that energy hadn't been projected through my meridians, it was still mentally exhausting to control that many constructs at the same time without slowing time. I was still waiting to use that, and I didn't want the *nox* to know I could do it yet.

As I dropped to one knee, the Chancellor's body started to repair itself. He was a Duke, after all. I had been a Duke for a long time in my first life, and I knew exactly how much damage it would take to bring him down. Let's just say, it was a lot more than two Saint batteries could produce. He finished healing, the only sign that he had been in a fight was his torn, burnt, and bloody clothing.

"Is that all you have, seal-breaker? I'm disappointed. After all that talk about me being a dead man, I expected more." Behind him, my friends finally made it out of the building with Kory's limp form thrown over Jamila's shoulders. They had even managed to drag all the other injured or unconscious cultivators out. And I could have sworn I saw Chu stuffing a bag of gems I must have missed down his pants, but surely, he wouldn't do that. As they left, I saw Donny look back into the hole in the wall.

He didn't make any sounds, but I read his lips. 'For Kory.'

Yes. This was for Kory. Time to end it.

"This is over." The Chancellor seemed confused by my comment. "I'm tired of playing with you." His eyes widened as he sensed what was coming, but it was too late.

As I said, I knew exactly what was necessary to kill a Duke. One of the hardest parts as a lower-level cultivator was being able to survive long enough to drain at least half of the qi from their cores. Once they were below half, they could no longer cultivate fast enough to refill their cores if they were also using qi to fight or defend themselves. Meaning, you could wear them down to the point that they couldn't heal themselves as fast as you could damage them. And eventually, they would die.

The only way to convert other types of qi from how they were stored in a battery was to pull the energy inside you first, spin it through your cores, and then use your affinity for the type of qi you want to use on that energy before projecting it from your own meridians. Which was what I started to do.

I spun up my cores as hard as they could handle, pulling in the qi from the remaining battery as fast as it would flow through the meridian in my left hand that was wrapped around the stud on my belt. I lifted my right arm and started blasting him with bolts of alternating light and dark qi, trying to keep the damage they were causing to my meridian even.

Now he was scared. He tried to run, but I had finally slowed my perception of time. This was the end game, no sense in holding back now. I pushed him back to the corner with the bolts, where he tried to just bust through the wall. No sir, I think not. I had plenty of time to throw up a net of light qi from the meridians in my feet, then returned time to normal so I could make two sweeping kicks of dark qi to keep my meridians balanced. He dodged both of them, but it forced him to bounce off the light qi net.

His grunt of pain told me it hurt. He tried fighting back, using huge qi constructs that tried to envelop me with their ridiculous amounts of power. I used just enough qi strands from my back meridians to shift them around me, conserving my power while his was draining from his body like a leaky bucket. The darts I kept sending his way were tiny but dense enough that when they impacted, it caused him real damage. The light qi, especially, seemed to burn him worse than the dark qi.

I still hadn't mastered the two elements, not like I had the other six. I was using the simplest forms possible to wear him down, trying to minimize the risk of making a mistake. Which happened when I underestimated how powerful his next set of attacks were.

The Chancellor was looking rough. I had burned him badly with the net when he tried to run, and while he was dodging more darts than not, I had still managed to burn several holes straight through his body in different places. It was enough that he committed almost all of his remaining power into an extremely condensed set of fire and wind blades into a tornado that almost completely filled the room. I didn't have room to run. All I could do was endure.

I dropped to one knee, pulling out two of the massively thick iron shields we had used on the Flying Sword Sect. I had just enough time to lock them together and reinforce them with metal and earth qi when the construct hit. The clang of wind blade against the iron shields was deafening, and the stone floor cracked beneath me as we were driven down into the ground. As the construct started to overtake the edges of the shields, I pulled the Dagger of Boom back out and absorbed everything I could.

There were still blades that got through. They bounced off my armor, the wind qi dissipating against the chitin strips. It wasn't enough to stop the heat of the fire qi from reaching me. I felt like I was a Thunder Chicken getting roasted over a fire. Plucking hot. The shields were even starting to turn red hot, softening the metal and allowing the wind blades to slice sections off of the edges and score deep cuts into the center. I cycled as much wood qi as I could through my makeshift healing focusing pendant to keep me alive. I gauged how much power the construct had left. It was going to be close. As the last of the tornado was running out of energy, the Chancellor decided it was time to monologue. I didn't mind. I needed time to finish building my own large construct.

"It was not my fate to die by your hands, seal-breaker! I am a Knight of the Dark! Do you truly think someone like you could ever have defeated me? Ha! I have seen entire planes of existence destroyed. An insignificant nothing like you was never meant to face something like me! Just know, before your soul is condemned to reside in eternal darkness and pain, that your entire world will be soon to follow!" He was panting, the exertion and subsequent shouting making him short of breath.

I stood up slowly from behind the remnants of the iron shields, my burnt and crisped skin splitting open and dribbling blood onto the ground. "I thought I told you to shut up. Don't you get it, you stupid knight of nothingness? You killed my friend. That was the end of your life. I don't care who you are. I don't care where you are from. I don't care what fate wants. Fate is stupid. Your fate is to die by my hand, because I said so." I released the power I had been building, draining the second battery completely.

My construct was a solid wave of dark qi that boiled over the ground, dissolving everything it touched. I heard him scream something at me, but I wasn't paying any attention. I was preparing the next part.

He raised a wall of fire, his go-to element, to protect himself. I could also sense him trying to cycle wood qi through his body to heal himself. He didn't have much left for anything else.

As the wave passed over him, hiding me from his sight, I held up both hands and cupped them into a ball in front of me. I had used all the qi in my batteries, so this I would have to power myself.

I slowly formed a ball of light qi, layering it as densely as I could. It slowly grew from the size of a child's marble into something about the same size and shape as the Chancellor's head. I waited a heartbeat, slowing time again to make sure I had perfect aim before I launched it at his face.

The ball of light qi was moving slowly to my enhanced perception of time, but it was plenty fast for the Chancellor. He barely had time for his eyes to widen before impact.

It took his head off.

Classic trick. Hide a small attack behind a big one. Six times out of ten, it worked every time.

He fell forward, his body making almost no sound as it impacted on the shattered ground. I sat down before my knees could give out and collapse. It was done. And I was right. This *nox* had been from some kind of leadership caste, and I definitely remembered how they all reacted in pain when I killed that first one. I was beginning to suspect they all had some kind of connection with each other. Or maybe they were able to share information and sensation when they were physically nearby. At least we had managed to kill all four *nox* that had shown up. But the cost to do so had been incredibly high. No. I wasn't going to think about that right now. I would grieve later.

First, I needed to check the bodies that were still in one piece after the fight. They might have information on more *nox*, or clues to their future plans. Second, I would regroup with my remaining friends, and we would get out of this accursed town. I needed to find some way to get a message to Alya about what to avoid in the future, but now wasn't the time.

I leveraged myself to my feet, putting the Dagger of Boom and the remaining scraps of shield in my belt. The wind blade fire tornado had destroyed pretty much everything else, so I moved over to the Chancellor's headless body to search it. Just as I rolled him over, I felt an overpowering presence, even stronger than the Duke cultivator had been, unveiling itself outside the hole in the wall.

"What in all the gods is going on in here?!" I swear. My fate must be to have problems with authority figures. "Guards, arrest that man! Or, boy. Young man. Arrest that young man! Charge him with the murder of the Chancellor to the Southern Provincial King!" He looked at me before growling under his breath. "That was *my* Chancellor you killed, and I will have your head!"

Oh, good, I finally ran into the king.

CHAPTER THIRTY-TWO

Prison Food

I was waiting for my trial in a six-foot-by-six-foot underground cell. It looked a lot like a stone cage, but it was more than that. There were flecks of orichalcum ore in the stone, making it pretty much impossible for most people to escape. I wasn't most people. I knew the trick to working around it, but I hadn't bothered to do so. As long as I wasn't up for execution, I would keep that little trick to myself.

It was in my best interests to stay in the cage, as I still needed to speak with the king. And there was another, more personal reason. She would be down here in a few minutes, like she had every day over the past fifteen days. Well, what I thought was fifteen days.

That was how long I had been here. I hadn't seen or heard anything from anyone since I had been slapped in orichalcum irons and marched down here. They had taken everything off of me, stripping me down completely naked before dumping a few dozen buckets of frigid water on my head and tossing me into the cage. The cold water had actually been a relief.

Since they had even taken my pants, I didn't have my wood qi healing focus to help me with my burns. I had still managed to repair my body, it was just much slower than normal while naked inside the qi-dampening cage. I wondered if she had noticed my injuries slowly disappearing, day by day.

I finally heard her approaching, the quiet footfalls seemingly loud in the silent darkness. I eventually saw the light from her single candle lantern she brought with her, allowing her to see in the pitch-black darkness.

The only person down this deep underground was me, so she knew exactly which cage to approach. She was carrying a small plate of food, mostly mashed potatoes, and a large water-skin. As she approached, I caught the pause in her footsteps, her hesitation to come closer clear to me.

"Good evening, Alya. Or morning. I'm not entirely sure which one it is anymore." Like every other visit, she placed the food and water just outside my reach and sat down on the floor facing me.

Alya was wearing a hooded cloak to hide her face, but it didn't matter. I had known it was her the moment she had walked down here to stare at my burnt and naked form the very first night. I stayed against the far wall of the cell, doing my best to convey how harmless I was to her.

She hadn't said much, but for some reason she kept coming back to visit me. And she brought food, which I appreciated. As always, she started with the same question.

"Why did you kill him?" It had been the first thing she had said to me when she came down here. And like always, I gave the same answer.

"Because he tried to kill me first. He killed my friend right in front of me, along with dozens of other innocent cultivators. And he did all of that because he was an evil man." She stayed silent. Sometimes she would do this. Wait for more of an explanation. Other times we skipped this part and she asked me something else. I guess today it was the first option. "You have to know he was an evil man. Every major criminal organization in the city was controlled by him for decades. He did everything he could to gain more power, and he didn't care who he hurt to get it." I took a breath. "If it hadn't been me, in a few more years it would have been someone else. He made too many enemies for it to end any other way."

She leaned forward a bit. "No talk of evil demons possessing him today? No talk of fanciful tables that control the weather? Or maybe you were thinking of warning me again, about how *awful* my life was going to turn out, pampered and living in a gilded palace as a member of Prince Ming's harem?" Her voice was angry, her tone sarcastic.

I sighed. "Everything I have ever told you is the truth. I would swear it on any truth stone or blood diviner you bring me. But you don't want to hear the truth, so you refuse to believe me." It was her turn to sigh. Before she could say anything, I did something new. I asked her questions this time. "What, exactly, do you think happened? How do you explain all the evidence I know must have been collected by this point? What about all of the witnesses? There have to be close to fifty people that survived that terrible place. Are all of them lying to the king's questioners?"

She seemed taken aback by the sudden turn. I didn't want to run her off, but I was getting tired of answering the same stupid questions. And I was even more tired of being called a liar. After a long, uncomfortable silence, she finally answered me.

"I don't know." Her voice was small, like a little girl's. "I tried to get a truth stone, but no one will give me one. The king has ordered any available stones to be brought to the palace so he can confirm that the stories he has heard are true. I am not the only person who is having a hard time accepting these fanciful tales." Well, that was good news at least. In the future, truth stones were almost impossible to find. In this time, there were enough to ensure my head would stay attached during the trial. Probably. Hopefully.

"Then you will see at the trial. I will tell the truth, again, and you will know that everything I have said has not been a fanciful tale."

She stared at me a few moments longer. "We will see." Her voice went back to normal. "But if you have been lying, I will kill you myself. Count on it." She stood up quickly and stormed off, leaving the food and water out of reach. Again. Gods, she could be annoying.

I had worked out a way to get the plate of food on the second day. I could have used my little trick and just grabbed it with a qi thread, but I was afraid it might set off a hidden alarm system somewhere. Instead, I dislocated my thumb and pulled it out of the shackles they had left on me. Which hurt. I managed to get the loose shackle to drag the water skin over, and then I used the water skin to drag the plate closer. I had just managed to get the food back between the bars when something new happened.

Ever since I had started to use dark and light qi more often, it had become easier to see in the dark. Even in the complete lightlessness of the underground, I could still see as if it was a moonless night, with only a few stars for illumination. Which was how I saw a person silently sliding through a door in the wall opposite the only normal entrance to the room. I must be slipping. I had been here for all this time and I hadn't noticed the secret entrance. My mentors in the Elemental Guard would be ashamed of me. I should have noticed the difference in qi the faint airflow would have made.

The figure must have had a charm or device that let them see in the dark, because they came straight to me without stumbling once. As they approached, I realized they were familiar. It was the spy that worked for the Chancellor. I waited until he was halfway across the room before I said anything.

"I am curious." He froze at the sound of my voice. "How does a former employee of the deceased Chancellor still have access to a hidden route to the lowest level of the dungeon?"

After I didn't make any threatening moves, he came closer. Instead of sitting on the ground, he pulled out a stool from some hidden storage item and sat down almost exactly where Alya had been.

"I have to admit, Jim Roh, I'm impressed. You can clearly see me without the aid of qi, you know a little of who I am, and you even know this is the lowest level of the dungeon. You don't even show the slightest signs of fear, when we both know I could easily kill you right now."

I snorted. Easily kill me? What did this guy think, I killed his old boss on a fluke? I mean, a Duke doesn't get taken out by a Meridian every day, you know. To show him how much I didn't fear him, I threw one of the wooden dinner plates Alya had been leaving behind through the bars of the cage. He bent over and picked it up after it didn't do anything. "Wait. Is this a trap plate? How did you get this? I know for a fact they stripped you of everything before you got thrown in here."

I smiled, holding up a second plate of similar design. I had thirteen more, after all. It also didn't escape my sense of humor that I was using actual dinner plates as formation plates. I was pretty sure some god somewhere was laughing at me. In this case, maybe it was with me.

"It is designed to force your bones to extrude spikes upon impact. Your own skeleton would have ripped you apart from the inside if I had activated it before throwing it at you." His eyes widened in surprise. "A friend showed it to me. I just carved it myself from the dinner plates my reluctant benefactor keeps leaving behind." He visibly swallowed. I smiled. "So no, I wasn't afraid when you came through the door. But maybe you should have been." He let out a slow breath, but I didn't miss it when he made the plate disappear.

"I apologize. It appears I severely underestimated you." While he was talking, I popped my thumb back into place. He noticed it, and flinched. "I have to ask, why are you still here? After meeting you, I have no doubt you could escape somehow."

I dislocated my other thumb, which hurt even more than the first one. It wasn't used to that type of abuse yet. I pulled the other half of the shackles off and tossed them in the corner before fixing my thumb. Being the tough guy I was, I held in the whimper of pain that tried to escape. I couldn't show weakness in front of this guy.

"I have a few reasons why I haven't escaped yet, but the most important one is my need to speak to the king." He seemed confused by my reply, so I kept going. "The entire purpose for my team and I joining the tournament was to meet with the king. We would never have exposed ourselves to scrutiny otherwise."

He nodded. "Very well. But I have come here to give you a warning." He paused, waiting for me to say something. I just motioned for him to continue. "Tomorrow morning is your trial. They intend to use a truth stone." I smiled, but he shook his head. "It isn't a real truth stone. No matter what the truth is, the king could not allow someone to kill his Chancellor and then walk away unscathed. They will put you to death, and wash their hands of the matter." Well, crap. That wasn't good. "I recommend that you leave tonight, and do not return. They will send their best to hunt you down."

"Their best? Is that you?"

He waved his hand, as if dismissing the notion. "I would not accept such a mission. Someone that can defeat a Duke-level cultivator is not someone I want to willingly fight."

I extended my senses at him, trying to gauge his level. He was doing a good job of masking it, but I was pretty sure he was either a Peak Saint or Low Sage. Definitely someone powerful enough to hold their own in a fight.

"What of the information they have uncovered? Has the king said anything about the dark mana demons?"

The spy shook his head. "No. The king is a stubborn man. He does not want to see, so he will not see. It is hard for anyone to believe. I worked directly for one of these demons for who knows how long, and I still didn't realize until near the end. By then, it was too late for me to do anything."

"Then I will need to see him. I can't leave. The fate of this entire continent, possibly the world, hinges on the support of the empire's leaders. I have sacrificed too much, *lost* too much, to fail now."

He slowly shook his head. "If you don't escape tonight, you will die. There won't be any other opportunities for you to get away. They will take your head immediately after the end of the trial to ensure your story doesn't spread."

Stars-damn it all. Why couldn't it ever be easy?

"Fine. I will go. But first, tell me, do you have news of my friends?"

He nodded and pointed above me. "The females are being held on the ground floor, while two of the males are just above you. The other one is still in the infirmary near the entrance to the palace, inside the gate house."

What? He must be confused. I said as much. "I only have four friends. The fifth did not survive the fight."

He pulled his hood back, finally letting me get a good look at his face. It was very forgettable, mid-forties looking, with plain features, brown eyes, and dark brown hair. The only thing of note was a small scar near his left eye. He gave me a genuine smile.

"You didn't hear. Of course you didn't hear, you have been stuck down here!" My face must have given away my confusion. "Your friend was gravely wounded, but he had some kind of wood qi device that kept him alive long enough for the healers to get to him." Kory was still alive? If I hadn't already been sitting, I would have collapsed. The healing focus I had made from the table in the inn. I had forgotten all about it. "It isn't all good news, though. He survived, but his heart core was almost completely destroyed. He may never cultivate again. Unless he receives a fortune in alchemy pills to heal, and only *if* they work, will he be okay. Otherwise, your friend is now a mortal." I didn't care. Kory was *alive*. Death was the only final defeat. Well, for most people. Like I said, I wasn't most people.

"I don't care what it takes, or how much it costs, I will make sure Kory is healed." I said that more for my benefit than his, but he nodded anyway. A weight lifted off my shoulders, and it felt like I could breathe again. Okay. Time to make a plan and get out of here. Before I did that, I needed to know one more thing. "Why did you come down here? Why tell me this?"

"I was already pretty sure, but after what you just said, I am positive. I want to work for you. I am unemployed, after all, and I am tired of working for people that see me as a tool."

I thought about it for a second. I definitely didn't trust him yet, but the fact that he was here, warning me, put him in a positive light.

"Why not just go your own way? You are strong enough to walk into any sect and become a pampered elder with almost no effort on your part. Why work for anyone at all?"

His eyes got a faraway look in them. "I tried that once. My cultivation stalled, and I found myself embroiled in a game of politics that had no winner. I wouldn't be welcome in a sect now, and working toward something larger gives me purpose. Helping you stop those demons is probably the best purpose I could hope to find."

That seemed like a fair and honest answer. I would need to extend a bit of faith to accomplish everything I needed in a short amount of time, anyway. For now. Stars be damned, and especially him, if he was deceiving me in any way. There's a saying about giving someone enough rope to hang themself. Well, let's see if he swings, or if he can start to be trusted.

"What is your name?"

It was his turn to think about what to say. "You can call me Wisp. It's as good a name as any."

I could handle that. "Okay Wisp. I have a job for you. Find out where the king is right now, and meet me at the infirmary when you do. We will go from there."

He gave me a sharp nod and pulled a key from his belt. "You didn't ask what my rates are. I'll take that as a good sign. Now let me get you out of here, and you can follow me through the tunnels. You will have to come back around through the surface to free your friends, but it should be okay. They don't have many guards in place during the night." I stepped out of the cage, stretching as I came to my full height. I was still naked, but I was already feeling better. The influx of qi loosened up my muscles, knots I didn't even know I had disappearing.

"Go on ahead. I have something in the next room I need to get." I could clearly feel the connection to my blood-bonded gear through the thick iron-banded wooden door. It was time to get my stuff back. My stomach rumbled. And it was *well* past time to get some decent food.

CHAPTER THIRTY-THREE

Making Plans

The door creaked open, the sound echoing down the corridor. They hadn't even bothered to lock it, secure in the strength of their cages. I took a step inside, the orichalcum shackles held in my hand ready to throw at any guards. It was empty. These people really must have thought it was a fluke that I killed a Duke-level cultivator. Otherwise, this room would have been packed with guards.

Instead, it had rows of wooden crates lining the walls. I let my senses bring me to one at the bottom of a stack near the door opposite the one I had come through. It took a minute or two to shift the crates around, but I eventually pried mine open with the edge of a shackle.

My stuff wasn't in good shape. The clothes that stayed magically clean were ruined, burnt to a crisp. The flying ring was misshapen, and my spirit wood ring was a few shades darker than it should have been. I didn't remember them getting damaged, but I had been burnt pretty bad. The flying ring wasn't a huge loss, but I would definitely spend the time to repair the spirit wood. It was too versatile to lose. My strips of leather and chitin were now more like scraps of leather and chitin, but I had enough left to work with. The leather armor vest lined with throwing knives wasn't in terrible shape, but I wanted to make sure it held together before using it.

The most important item was still in good shape. My belt looked the exact same as it had the day I had picked it up. Tarnished copper studs, beat-up leather, and a plain copper buckle. I let out a sigh of relief. I also found my spare storage ring, which was soot-covered but still usable. Surprisingly, they hadn't taken anything from either the ring or the studs on the belt they could have accessed. They must have thought a Meridian cultivator didn't have anything they would be interested in.

I checked the other boxes around mine, trying to see if I could find my friend's gear. It didn't take long, since most of the crates were much older. Some of them were barely holding together at all. Considering no one would miss them, I just took all of the crates and put them in the belt. There might have been something I could use in all that junk. I made sure to put my friend's stuff in a separate stud, so I didn't get it mixed in with everyone else's.

The belt held plenty of replacement options for clothes and armor, so I picked a set that resembled the equipment the guards wore. It wouldn't fool anyone up close, but it would keep any archers from firing at me for trespassing. Adding a plain spear completed the look.

I cracked the door open to the next room, checking for guards. Instead of guards, it was a set of stairs. They were going up, the direction I needed to go, so I took them. At the top there was only an arched opening, with no door. I stepped out like I belonged, walking into a room where two guards sat playing some type of card game. They didn't even look up as I walked past them, instead more interested in their own conversation. Which was weird.

"I don't know, it just doesn't make sense to me." The older of the two put down a card, causing the younger one to grunt.

"Stop thinking about it then. If you don't, you will only

drive yourself crazy." He laid down his own card, but it didn't take the frown off his face.

"There has to be an answer. Somebody came up with it, so somebody knows why." His friend just looked at him. "Why is it that feet smell, but noses run? It just doesn't make sense!"

"Okay, okay, I get it. Can we just focus on the game now?"

I hurried out of the room, not wanting to hear any more of that madness.

The next room was lined with cells, these much nicer than the one I had enjoyed spending some time in. The last one held both Donny and Chu. They were asleep, practically sleeping on top of one another. I was going to give them the benefit of the doubt and say it was to share body heat so they could stay warm.

I pulled out my glass sword and slowly cut through the lock holding their door closed, trying to stay quiet. I pushed the door open and woke them with a light shake.

"Whaaa?" Chu, always quick on the uptake, couldn't have said it better.

Donny helped him out. "Jim!" He did a shout-whisper, trying to control his excitement. "You're okay! Thank the gods. We hadn't heard anything. The only thing we knew was that the Chancellor was dead."

Chu finally came around enough to realize what was going on. "I *knew* you were alive. They kept asking us about you, which meant they were either looking for you, or they had you hidden away somewhere. So, what's the plan?"

I handed them their crates and they got geared up while I talked. I didn't even have to tell them to wear something like what I had on instead of our normal matching armor. Competence really was a blessing from the gods.

"The girls are in cells on the ground floor. Once we free them, we need to get to the infirmary."

They nodded, but Donny raised the obvious question. "Why the infirmary? Shouldn't we try to get out of here as soon as the girls are free?"

I smiled. "No. I have some good news." I took a breath, settling my own nerves. "Kory is alive, and we need to get him. Or, at least, I was told he was alive."

Chu let out a very loud whoop, completely ruining the keeping quiet aspect of our escape. I didn't mind. Donny openly wept. Some dust must have gotten in my eye, because I was holding back some tears as well.

Chu's outburst luckily didn't alert the two guards deep in philosophical discussions, so we pushed on. There were two more rooms of empty cells before we found the doorway to the next set of stairs, and we moved up another floor. None of us were sure how deep underground we were, but I knew it couldn't be too far. I was pretty sure the foundations of a palace this size wouldn't be stable if it had a large underground network.

We passed two more floors, each holding only a few people. There was only one guard who paid us any attention, but all he did was stare at us for a moment before returning to his meal. Finally, the presence of windows let us know we had made it to the ground floor.

It only took us a few minutes to find the girls. They were in two cells on opposite sides of a long hallway, so we ended up freeing Jamila first. Both her and Valerie were ecstatic to hear about Kory, and they led the way out of the prison complex after gearing up like the rest of us. It was still nighttime outside, but the sky was beginning to lighten to the east.

None of the guards tried to stop us as we left. Most of them appeared to be fighting sleep, and our close approximation to their uniform in the sparse lighting was good enough for them. This was definitely one of the worst guard forces I had ever seen.

We quickly found the infirmary near the main gates to the palace and slipped inside. None of us wanted to watch the door, so I just dropped an alarm plate and we moved deeper inside.

Wisp was waiting for us near a room toward the back. Well, well. Looked as if he'd come through, *so far*. A guard was lying on the floor, still breathing but unconscious. I nodded at him in thanks and he pulled open the door for us.

"He still hasn't woken up from the last round of healing they performed on him. I don't know where they put his things, otherwise I would have grabbed them for you." Everyone seemed to relax slightly as he spoke, his words assuring them for now that he was on our side. We moved past him to look in on our friend, still aware that this could all be a trap. Stars, did I have a well-oiled group that used their heads.

Kory looked a decade older, and twenty pounds lighter. I scanned him with a strand of wood qi, checking over the damage done to his heart core. It wasn't good. If you imagined a core as a glass orb, his would be filled with cracks, and missing a chunk from the area near where the Chancellor's fist had punched through his chest. I honestly didn't even know how it was still holding together. I sent a wave of wood qi into his body to help where I could, but it didn't affect the condition of his core. That would take special care from a dedicated healer and alchemist working together to make him whole.

"Is it safe to move him?" Jamila was leaning over my shoulder to look at him. "He doesn't look too good."

I shook my head. "It isn't good. He needs special healing to get back to his regular self." I looked at Wisp. "How many expert alchemists and master healers are there in the city?"

He thought for a moment. "There were only three alchemists in the whole city, but last month it was down to just two. Something happened to make one of them leave." Whoops. That might have been me… "As for healers, the only one at the Master-level works for the king. Everyone else would be a Journeyman at the most, not even close to Expert, and especially not Master." We stood there quietly. "I'm sorry. There might be a few at some of the nearby sect towns and enclaves, but I never tracked information like that for the Chancellor."

Damn. Well. Time for a change to my first idea.

"Okay. This is how it is going to work." I laid out my plan to everyone. They didn't like it, and there were a few raised voices about us splitting up again so quickly after we just reunited, but they eventually came around. "Wisp. Your job is to make sure Kory is taken care of. If he isn't, you know what to do. Once he is back on his feet, travel with him back to Roh City with our wagons. They should be loaded up with goods by then, and Chu's family will be expecting their return. After that, try to meet up with us in the Northern Province. You might get there before us, so try to do what you can to set up a way for us to meet with the Marshall General. We will be traveling to the Western Province first, then work our way up to you." He nodded, not fazed by the large gaps of time my instructions were covering. After all, this would take him years to complete. "And Wisp, know this." He met my eyes. "If you betray me in any way, I will rip you apart, piece by piece, as slowly and painfully as possible. I'm sure by now that you understand there isn't anything you can do, anywhere you can go, that would stop me."

He swallowed before answering. "Don't worry, Jim Roh. I will not betray you. I am firmly in your camp. I will make sure your friend is safe. And the North will be ready for your arrival." He looked at me. "While your cause is more noble than most, I still will need funds to do everything you asked."

"Take these. If you need more, contact an Auction House branch and tell them who you are. I will make an expense account for you. Within limits." I handed him four heaping bags of gems I had taken from the tables during the fight with the Chancellor. It was a lot to him, but I had plenty more. A lot more.

"They have been looking everywhere for these. My former employer didn't exactly have permission to take these from the treasury."

I smirked. "Maybe after this, the king will do a better job of guarding his valuables. And his Province." I gave a quick glance toward the guard still unconscious on the floor. "I haven't seen such sorry excuses for guards in all my life." Wisp looked at me with a raised eyebrow. Crap. He wasn't as used to my eccentricities as the others. What teenager says that kind of thing?

Donny spoke up and saved me from having to explain myself. "We need to hurry. The sunrise is soon, and we all have places to be." Everyone agreed, and we shuffled out the door. Before I walked away, I turned back to Wisp.

"Tell Kory… Tell him I'm sorry. And let him know we will return to Roh City once we visit the other provincial leaders."

Wisp waved me away. "Go. He already knows. Now do what you must to save your friend." He bent down and untied the guard.

I didn't ask what he was going to do with him.

CHAPTER THIRTY-FOUR

Blackmail

The king's bedroom was on the top floor of the central tower of the palace. Why? Because the gods think it is hilarious to make me climb stairs. I didn't used to hate stairs this much, but my reincarnation had changed all of that. The climb up the stairs took enough time that the sun was already peeking over the horizon as I finally reached the door to the king's chambers.

There weren't any guards, which isn't much of a surprise. King wasn't just a title for this man, but also his cultivation rank. Only the emperor himself was a true threat in his eyes. It was stupid, and exceedingly short-sighted, but I would expect nothing less from this man.

In my first life I had seen him as a competent and decent leader, if a little dense. After finding out about the weather-control table and the way he was going to handle my trial, I realized how wrong I had been. This guy was worthless.

I cracked the door open, finding him asleep on a canopy bed that had more square footage than the compound I had lived in for almost a year in the woods. There were several other people in the bed with him, their tangle of limbs making it difficult to figure out just how many there were. To be honest, I didn't really care. I had never gone for the hedonistic lifestyle myself. It was entirely too sticky. Let's not go over how I knew that.

I took a few minutes to set up some formation plates around the bed, and even more around the room. Finally, I pulled out a spare giant stone shield disk I had made a while back, since the one I gave Kory had been lost when he dropped it on the Chancellor. Like the original version, this one would allow me to still send qi out, just not allow anything *in*. I poured out a fair amount of liquid qi, most of what I had left, and then waited for it to seep into the runes. Right before they activated, I pulled out the still incredibly-charged Dagger of Boom and tucked it into my belt. Just in case.

The crackling sound of the shield activating woke most of the people sleeping. Not the king, of course, but pretty much everyone else. I motioned for them to leave, holding a finger to my lips and smiling. They smiled back and left, as if this was all one big joke. That's right, goat-for-brains. All just a big joke. No need to alert any guards…

I was honestly surprised something so simple had just worked. Maybe it was the gods balancing the scales for making me climb up all those stairs. Once everyone was gone, I spun out a whip of metal qi from each hand. Time to wake him up.

The canopy portion dropped on top of him a split second before the mattress exploded. I might have gone a little over-board, but I had a few frustrations to work through. And this guy had planned to kill me because the truth was inconvenient for him. The only reason I didn't kill him in his sleep was because I didn't have the time to wait for his replacement to show up and then explain everything to whoever was next in line. And there was nothing saying they would be any better.

He jolted awake, but it took him a bit to fight free of the sheets, canopy, and mattress remnants that ended up on top of him. It was hard not to laugh at him, but I only wanted to make him a certain level of angry.

"Wakey-wakey, you gigantic walking cesspit of human filth!" Okay. Maybe I didn't care how angry he was.

"Grawragrfriga!" He wasn't the most eloquent individual when waking up, apparently. That's okay. I could help him. I activated the formation plates I had spread around the room first, then ordered the plates around the bed to go to work.

The whip design used a mix of two-parts water qi and one-part air qi, making them flexible strands of ice. If you have never been brought fully awake by being beaten with ice cubes, I wouldn't put it on any of your to-do lists.

If it weren't for the sound-dampening plates spread around the room, I was positive his screams would have woken up half the city. He managed to eventually stomp all of the formation plates around the bed to pieces, after getting pummeled for a few minutes. He stood there, on the edge of going full rage-monster, his shoulders heaving as he took giant breaths in and out.

"Now that I have your attention, I think it is time we talked. And maybe you could put some pants on. I mean, you were just beat up by a bunch of ice, so I can give you the benefit of the doubt, but still. No one wants to see that."

His face went from red to purple. The next few seconds were filled with a series of qi attacks in a downright impressive display of absolutely zero ingenuity. He just kept pounding on the shield with a giant fist construct of metal qi the size of a large cow. I was actually disappointed. Don't get me wrong. It was strong enough to flatten most people into a sheet of bloody parchment, but he didn't vary the attack at all. His eyes were still a little wild, but the fist paused its attacks while he caught his breath.

"Are you done yet? Or is that potato you call a brain still too hot to let words in?"

Nope. Not done. He went right back to smashing on the shield with the fist construct. I pulled out the rest of the liquid qi I had with me and poured it on the formation plate powering the shield. It was draining faster than I had anticipated, but I still had time.

"I'm getting bored. Can we skip to the part when you realize you can't do anything and finally listen to me? Or would you rather I jump further? You know, to the part where you lose your province to revolt, and the emperor executes you for negligence." He still kept pounding away. "Fine. But in one hour, your entire capital finds out about how you have been controlling the weather for the past few decades. How do you think they will react when they learn you have been keeping the best rain for those who support you, and starving those who don't? All those innocent people caught on the fringes of your personal vendettas might not appreciate everything you have been up to." The giant fist finally stopped pounding. "Good. Now, do you recognize me?"

"No." His voice somehow managed to be gruff and petulant at the same time.

"I'm the innocent kid you were going to kill after a pretend trial because you don't want to deal with the consequences of what I say being the truth." He grunted, finally looking at me with eyes not clouded with rage or sleep. "Don't worry, your people will hear about that too. I bet I'm not the first person you have killed for convenience. I bet some families will be happy to learn their loved ones were innocent before they died. I sure hope none of them were influential enough that their complaints might reach the ears of the emperor. Otherwise, that would be pretty bad for you." The size and scope of what I was saying seemed to finally click. His eyes widened for just a flicker of a second, but I saw it. I had his attention.

"What do you want? Money?" I shook my head. "Power?" I shook my head again. "Land? Treasure? A pardon? What? What will it take to get you to go away?" Interesting that a pardon was last on that list, but I just shook my head one last time before answering.

"I don't think you understand how bad you fornicated the

goat on this one. You see, this kind of stuff doesn't *go away*. This is the kind of blackmail that sticks around the entire time you remain in power. There isn't a way you get to sweep this away like it doesn't matter. There are no bargains to free you from my grip. Either you do exactly as I say, the way I say, without double-crossing me in any way, or you die. Not by my hand, but by the very people your selfishness has hurt, marginalized, and destroyed. Or by the emperor, when he hears about it. The end result is the same. You. Die." He seemed to finally understand what I was saying, but he still had a shifty look in his eyes. "And if you kill me, or fail to follow my instructions in any way, over ten thousand people across your city will open a letter delivered by one of hundreds of my people. The only way to stop it is if I keep them from sending those messages. Every day, for as long as you remain in power. Even if it isn't your fault, the day I die is the day you die."

"Fine." His features were calm, but I could sense his qi inside his cores fluctuating like crazy. He was freaking out. "Just tell me what I have to do." At least he was smart enough to process the turn of events he was facing. Now that I gave him the stick, it was time for the carrot.

"What I want isn't onerous. I just want you to do your job, and protect the people." He seemed confused. "And make sure my friend with the shattered heart core is healed. Don't try to use him for blackmail against me, or the same thing happens. You might kill him, but you would die in the end as well."

"I already protect the people. I at least manage that part of my position well. All of my best men are spread out across the countryside, putting down a swelling tide of vicious monsters unlike anything we have seen. And bands of bandits as organized as they were during the forming of the empire. No one knows what is going on, but I am doing my best to save my people!" Well, that explained the lack of quality guards.

"You are an absolute dunderhead, you know that?" His face started to go purple again, but I raised my hand to stop him from going all smashy-smash again. "The rise of dark creatures and evil people—get this—is from the arrival of *dark and evil demons!*"

He looked like a man struck by lightning. "You mean, all of this, all of the problems—"

"Yes, you idiot! The thing I was warning you about, the *nox*, are real! You need to mobilize your forces and put together a plan of action to hunt them down. They will be able to bond with any person who is genuinely evil, or has a sufficiently dark soul. It works the same way with animals, beasts, even the occasional sentient plant that has absorbed enough qi. They might seem invincible at first, but every *nox* has a weakness to at least one form of qi. Well, almost all of them." He didn't know about dark and light qi, so if that was their weakness, they would seem basically impervious to qi attacks from his perspective. "All of them can eventually be worn down and ripped apart, it just takes planning and the right information."

"Okay. I get it. You can stop with the dumb comments. I made a big mistake." I went to say something, but it was his turn to talk over me. "*Okay*, I made several mistakes. But I will make sure my people know what to do."

"So, you will fight the *nox*, fix my friend, and let me go without a problem? We don't need to do all the blackmail stuff?"

He smiled, but it didn't reach his eyes. "Of course! Just tell your people to stop, and I will make sure everything is okay."

I smiled in return and bent down to turn off the shield. As I stood up, his fist crashed into my face. I flew backwards off the shield plate, already pumping wood qi into my cheek and nose bones to repair the damage he had done. I rolled as I hit the ground, stopping when I hit the wall next to the door. When would I ever learn? Trusting those who thought they were more powerful than others always ended in disaster. The king plodded over to me, cycling qi to deliver another blow while I was down. I stood up and faced him, spitting the blood from my mouth in his face.

It blinded him, so I pulled out the dagger and activated it.

All that energy went to the very tip, a tiny surface area, and detonated against the fist that was flying toward me hard enough to obliterate my entire body.

The huge amount of qi stored in the dagger pushed into such a small space made even a King's powerfully reinforced body susceptible to damage. Instead of obliterating my body, it vaporized his arm all the way up to his elbow.

It was clear to me that the king had forgotten what pain felt like. That was a common problem with high-level cultivators that didn't train at their peak consistently enough. He dropped to his knees, mouth open in a silent scream.

"You know, if you hadn't lied to me, you wouldn't be in so much pain right now. Oh, man, regrowing that limb is going to hurt even worse than losing the arm, isn't it? That must really suck. To be you. I mean, to have the intellect of a goat during the late stages of a syphilis infection must be bad every day, but now your life is even worse." I collected the shield plate and turned back to him. "Don't forget what I said. Fight the *nox*. Fix my friend. Leave me and mine alone. Break the deal, and you die. If you piss me off enough, I will come back here and do it myself. And just like what happened to your friend, I will make sure it hurts for a long time before it's finally over." I finally saw what I was looking for in his eyes. Fear. He didn't want me coming back. "You better hope you never see me again, asshole."

I turned my back on him. I knew he wouldn't be able to resist a free shot at me like that. He was too stupid to know when he was beat, and I needed to put a little more fear in him before I left. The gravity trap plate I dropped behind me activated as he tried to jump over it. It was the same one that I had used on the treasurer outside Roh City, and it worked just as well this time as it did then. His head bounced off the plate, shattering it and embedding shards of stone in his face. I had to raise my voice to be heard over his now not-so-silent cries of pain.

"Last chance. You clearly have the intelligence of a brain-damaged rodent, so I will say this slowly. You. Can't. Beat. Me. I win. Get over it. Now get to work."

Either he did as he was told, or I would make good on all my promises. He understood that now. I was feeling pretty good about everything, until I remembered I still had to go down all those flights of stairs.

CHAPTER THIRTY-FIVE

Campfire

"We'll see you soon, Wisp. Make sure you keep an eye on the king, and don't be afraid to leave a message with the Auction House. I will check them every chance I get."

He waved away my concerns. "Don't worry so much, Jim. I can handle things here. You just get a move on."

I nodded and shook his hand, looking him straight in the eye before turning around and walking down the trail toward where my friends waited.

They were in the back of a carriage I had purchased and then modified to handle the higher speeds the two white horses pulling it would produce. We needed to make one quick stop, and then we would be on our way to the peninsula known as 'The Claw' at the southern tip of the province. It was named 'The Claw' because its shape looked like a crab claw on a map, not because it was made of actual claws. The way people named things here, sometimes it was hard to tell.

Our plan was to catch passage on a ship headed to the capital of the Western Province. It would be taking the long way around, but the actual time spent would be much shorter.

It had been several days since my 'meeting' with the king,

and I hadn't slept for most of that time. There were people to hire so my threat to the king wasn't an empty one—although it was just a few people told to check once a month at the Auction House for a message from me, not hundreds of folks—and supplies to arrange. I had set up the account for Wisp to use— with another warning about not abusing my trust—bought this carriage, prepared and repaired weapons and armor, and waited by Kory's bedside to see if he would wake up. No such luck.

I had also tried to track down Alya, but to no avail. I was technically still an escaped prisoner since the king hadn't dropped the charges against me, but no guards had tried to come after me. And I hadn't been hiding, either.

I figured Alya would make good on her threat to track me down at some point, but until then there wasn't much I could do. I didn't have time to look for her and I was pretty sure she hated me anyway. That dream was dead. No point in pursuing it further.

"Donny, would you make sure the harness isn't rubbing too much on the horses?" Valerie was on top of the carriage, trying to strap down the bags and boxes we hadn't deemed worthy of keeping inside our storage items. Donny gave her a thumbs up as he walked up front to check on everything.

While he was doing that, Chu opened the carriage door to talk to me. "We just need to follow the second trail to the left for a few miles. Afterwards, we can just circle back to the main road and keep moving until we need to rest the horses. I imagine we will reach The Claw before the middle of summer-year at the latest. If all goes well, we can reach the Western Province before fall-year starts to cause the beast-wave migrations."

I nodded, pleased that things were finally working out. The carriage and fast horses on the main road would cut down our travel time considerably, especially since we didn't need to hide from anyone this time around.

I looked up at Valerie to ask her if she was ready to go when I felt a whoosh of air pass behind me. I turned in time to see

Donny skip off the ground a few times before he rolled to a stop. A horseshoe-shaped dent in his breastplate told me exactly what had happened. Have you ever heard a horse laugh? Let's just say it's pretty infectious. I swear, that thing was going to be the death of the poor man one day.

It took a little longer than I would have liked, but eventually we got on the trail. We followed Chu's directions, making good time. It was just past sundown when we finally saw a campfire off to the side of the trail. It was my turn behind the reins, so I steered us to the opposite side of the trail almost a mile past where we had spotted the small camp. Jamila hopped out of the wagon and took off back down the trail. The rest of us unhitched the horses and set up our own camp. I made sure to set up a mix of trap and alarm plates to protect it, and we waited for Jamila to return.

"It's them. Let's go." We silently rose to our feet and started a leisurely stroll back toward the campfire in the distance. Jamila kept fingering the sheathed katanas at her waist, but the rest of us didn't show any outward nerves or excitement. It was no different than any late-night stroll among friends.

We spread out as we approached the camp, the six figures all sitting quietly around the fire while they ate something from a skewer. I waited for the signal, and it came when an arrow thudded into the chest of the cultivator closest to the fire. It all happened quickly from there.

They reacted fast, jumping up and fighting back without hesitation. Chu got slammed with a particularly powerful blast of air qi, but his armor took the brunt of it. Donny had gotten creative and attached a vial of stick-um to a crossbow bolt. When his target tried to deflect the bolt with his sword, the glass broke and coated him and the person next to them with the sticky foam substance. The more they fought against it, the more tangled they became.

Jamila and I took care of the rest of them. I was slashing at knees and elbows with my glass sword, while Jamila danced between them all, her katanas never stopping their spinning dance.

In almost no time, the six cultivators were all lying on their stomachs, their hands tied together behind their backs. Jamila was standing next to the one wearing the fanciest set of robes. He was the one to speak first.

"Do you know who it is you have just attacked?" Can we just take a moment to all agree, if you ever feel the need to ask that question, you should *never*, under any circumstances, *actually* ask that question? "We are the—"

"The Flying Sword Sect, we know. The real question is, how you could have forgotten us?" Jamila crouched in front of the leader, making sure to look him in the eye. "After all, I told you all of you were going to die. And you were going to die *ugly*." It finally registered to him who he was dealing with. "Out here, all your connections, all the secret politics of your bloody sect, they can't protect you." He tried to say something, so Jamila stabbed him in the meaty portion of his thigh. She just raised her voice and kept talking over his screams. "You sent assassins after us. Killed innocent people. Risked the lives of dozens of innocent bystanders. All for a chance to avoid a fight with us in the pit. And none of us, not one, had ever done *anything* to *any* of you." He finally stopped screaming, so her voice returned to conversational levels. "So, I made you a promise. And I keep my promises. Especially to scum like *you*." The look on her face told me she wasn't happy. It was more like she had an unpleasant job to do, but she wasn't afraid to do it.

And keep her promise she did. They all died. And they died ugly.

We left everything but their coin and returned to our own camp, where all of us slept like newborns. The next day we were back on the road, off to continue our mission to save this continent from destruction.

And maybe take care of a few other problems as well.

AUTHOR'S NOTE

Well folks, that's book two. Be sure to let me know if you liked it. This one took a few darker turns than the first one, but real life has a tendency to do that. I hope you and your loved ones are safe during these trying times, and I will do my best to produce as much content as possible to help give your imagination a different world to inhabit. The next book will reflect real life as well, especially if your life involves being a pirate. It is going to be a lot of fun, and I hope you enjoy the ride.

Once again, I have to thank my wife and three daughters for being the reason why I keep getting out of bed in the morning.

To my brother, mom, dad, and grandparents, I love you guys. Thanks for reading my books, even if it isn't what you would normally pick up off the shelf.

Eric Peterson, my genius editor, thanks for sticking with me through this series. I'm glad you like Jim and friends as much as I do. And my beta readers, thanks again for helping to polish these books until they shine.

Dakota Krout and his team made all of this happen, so once again, thank you.

Last, but not least, my readers. Thank you for spending your hard-earned cash on my stories. I promise to keep writing for as long as you will let me. Stick around for book three, you won't regret it.

- Michael Head

ABOUT MICHAEL HEAD

Michael Head is the author of the Threads of Fate series. He was severely injured while serving in the military, and used his time recovering to rediscover his love for books. After medically retiring, Michael went back to college to finish his degree and become a professor. When the coronavirus shut down his school, his wife encouraged him to finally take the leap and try writing his own books. He found his experience in combat allowed him to write detailed and realistic fight scenes. Those battles, combined with his attention to detail and ability to plan vast, elaborate, and comprehensive worlds, make for fast-paced and thrilling books. With, of course, the occasional touches of humor and sarcasm thrown in the mix.

He currently lives in Texas where his wife, who is still currently serving in the military, is stationed. His days are filled with hiding from their three daughters, two dogs, and three cats. He is also losing an ongoing war with the neighborhood squirrels, but he will continue to fight until the bitter end.

Connect with Michael:
Facebook.com/Author.Michael.Head
Patreon.com/Michael_Head
Sendfox.com/Author-Michael-Head